Destino

Destino

SIENNA MYNX

Battaglia Mafia Series Book I

Destino © Copyright 2012 Sienna Mynx. ALL RIGHTS RESERVED
ISBN-13: 978-0615729664
ISBN-10: 0615729665
Cover art by Reese Dante
Cover Artist: Jimmy Thomas
Interior Design: A'ndrea J. Wilson
Electronic book publication November 2012

Destino is dedicated in loving memory to
Cammie Byrd (1968-2011)
The friendship and love you showed for this story has inspired
me in more ways than you can ever know.
May your sweet generous soul rest in peace.

Chapter One

"**P**APA, IT'S TOO FAR," Giovanni said. The longer he stared down into the rolling waves the worse his plight became. His head grew heavier on his small shoulders, and his vision blurred with the threat of tears. There could be danger below. The mere thought of his tipping over paralyzed him with fear. A long tide rushed in and broke across the stranded rocks near the shoreline. From his angle, twenty-feet above according to Uncle Rocco, he could see the depths of the water where it went from turquoise to midnight blue. The lunch in his tummy bubbled up into his throat and his tiny hands shook as he suppressed his terror. Another cool wind combed through his tightly wound locks, crowning the top of his head. It pushed against his bare chest. He was only six years old. Why would his father command this of him? Would the leap prove him to be courageous, or just worthy of the title son?

"Tomosino, he's just a baby, don't do this," Eve pulled on the Don's arm and tried to reason with him. Don Battaglia glared at Giovanni's mother, and her pleas softly fell away. He returned his cool dark gaze to his son, and Giovanni resisted the urge to cry.

"You are old enough boy." The Don answered in his thick Sicilian brogue that made most men obey without question. "You can swim. Now, show Papa and everyone."

No one dared question his father once his desired wish was explicitly stated. Not his mother, uncles, or the men that vowed to serve and respect his authority. Don Battaglia's word was law. Giovanni's blinking gaze shifted to Lorenzo. His cousin stood near his mother with a towel draped over his shoulders, visibly shivering. He nearly drowned from his failed attempt. The men had to go in and rescue him. The women were crying hysterically. Now the humiliation of defeat left Lorenzo hanging his head in shame. Young Lorenzo was only a year older than Giovanni. Tomosino had announced that his son was braver and smarter than his nephew, smarter than any other six year old within Sicily. The Don boasted that Giovanni would need no saving. And it was time to prove his father right.

"Do it."

"Si," Giovanni said. He stepped to the edge and stared down into the glistening water. He could swim, better than Lorenzo, and better than his uncles. Still the leap would be the highest and longest dive of his young life.

"No please! No! I beg you, don't make him!" His mother wept. He glanced to her and forced a brave smile. Her scarlet red hair blew from her face, and her clear blue eyes held such sadness. He had eyes like his mother, but the bravery of his father. He'd prove it. Show them all. Indeed he was strong enough. And though his beloved mother may not be the chosen wife, she had given birth to the Don's only son. Even in his tender years, Giovanni knew how he could ease his mother's suffering from her tormentors if the Don proclaimed him as so. It made her special, too. He nodded in the direction of his mother and stepped back several paces. *Taking in deep breaths like his uncle Rocco had taught him, he counted to three and ran for it.*

The wind lifted him. Giovanni kicked his legs and crossed his arms over his chest because his heart beat so hard and fast he thought it would explode. He sailed downward. The invisible pull of gravity roped around his ankles, drawing him closer and faster toward the sea. And he crashed into its icy depths. He felt as if rocks were strapped to his shoulders driving him to the sea floor. He puffed his cheeks and held his breath. The pressure closed in around him. It was as if the water strangled him by the throat and squeezed around his midriff making him want to take a breath. He knew better than to do so while submerged. His eyes opened under the current, and he swam toward the light above. But salvation was too far. He'd gone really deep. He swam harder though his arms tired with heaviness, as did his legs, which he kicked feebly. He wanted to cry, but there was no time to, he had to swim or else Papa would be displeased. When he believed there would be no end to the struggle, freedom overwhelmed him as he broke clear of the waves. His mother and uncle had already run down the side of the cliffs to the shore. But his father and his men stood atop the clearing watching his success. A few cheered and several threw their hats up in celebration. Don Tomosino had indeed proven his only son was worthy to take on the Battaglia name.

Giovanni treaded the water smiling up to his father. Tomosino stuffed a fat cigar in his mouth, turned, without a word, and walked away.

Napoli (Naples) Italy – 1989

The day had been balmy in the middle and crisp around

the edges with the night carrying in the steamy sea air from the not so distant Amalfi coast. A single tear of perspiration dropped from his brow to the tip of his nose, which he swiped away. Under the cover of darkness Giovanni Battaglia stalked up the narrow cobblestone alley, passing tightly squeezed in shop owners and restaurants. A man of his stature never travelled alone. *Isabella's* was at the end of the narrow street. Fine dining was offered through its doors to the front and top levels. The steps that led to the lower floors were locked behind doors that only opened upon invite. Giovanni Battaglia needed none. In his black on black attire, only his tall form could be seen as he and the men accompanying him blended with the night.

Giovanni slipped his hands deeper in his pockets, parting the front folds of his sports coat. A half smoked cigar was tucked tight between his tongue and his left jaw. Danny-boy, his gun, was situated in the back of his pants, well hidden. The street symphony of honking horns and laughing diners or passing tourists blared as a nice cover to the business conducted in the belly of *Isabella's*. The doorman glanced his way. When their eyes met, acknowledgement was immediate. Those who knew his true name didn't dare evoke it casually. He received a few respectful nods and curious stares, but no one approached him. Carlo stepped ahead to the door and opened it. Giovanni and the others continued on, they descended a spiral stairwell with tiled walls and hard marble steps.

Tonight he was out for blood. He'd spill it in his own organization before he tolerated disobedience. There were rules in this life. From birth he'd heard the vows of secrecy recited by the men in his family. His cousin, Lorenzo, heard them too. Yet, he found ways to continue to walk the line of disobedience within their brotherhood. At the end of the stairs the lighting dimmed, and the faint sounds of music pulsed through the walls and doors. Nico waited. He was so tall and broad shouldered he crowded the space. Nico bowed his large head and reached behind him to throw the door open.

Giovanni's glare sliced through the smoke-thickened air, scanning the scene. Of course, the sparse seating circled the dance floor. Under spinning lights bodies gyrated in synchronization with dance music. Women in short dresses with ruby red lips and dark flowing hair danced with men twice their age. Whores, they were instructed to empty the pockets of local businessmen and lucky tourists who were granted entrance.

Above the dance floor, on raised platform pillars facing each other from either side of the club were two Sicilian born beauties seated on their knees in claw-foot black porcelain tubs. With arms raised, fingers entwined, under a light spray from an overhead sprinkler designed to look like rain, they moved. Iridescent droplets, thanks to the red spotlighting, rained down their golden tanned bodies. Their breasts bounced and glistened as the sudsy streams drained down their curves, and they rolled their hips giving seductive moves to the music while simulating a bath. One locked eyes with him. She gripped the edge of the tub and slung her dark hair trying to entice him to maintain her stare. He continued to scan the scene.

Carlo moved in closer to his left. "He's in the back, Boss."

Giovanni nodded. They stepped directly through the crowd with Carlo and Nico shoving dancing bodies out of his way. Soon many caught on to his presence and parted without any resistance. The gambling tables were packed tight. Dice were thrown, cards dealt, and to the back of the scene his cousin sat amongst others laughing under a heavy cloud of smoke. Giovanni removed his cigar from his mouth and dropped it on a smoking tray. Their eyes met.

Lorenzo stood and so did the men at the table. His cousin spoke a few words and those gathered discreetly withdrew as a young woman, with a leather mini so short her butt cheeks dropped from the hem with each step she made, sidled up to his cousin. Lorenzo patted her on the ass and dismissed her as well. She walked on shiny spiked heels, giving Giovanni a longing look. He stepped to the table, and Lorenzo greeted him with a kiss to both of his cheeks. Before a question was asked, before he was able to warm his seat, his cousin began to run off at the mouth.

"Excuses. I'm done entertaining them."

Lorenzo wiped his hand along his jaw.

"Flavio called. The doors will close. Permanently." Dominic stood behind him. He spoke in a clear but lowered voice. "Consider tonight the last for business."

Lorenzo slammed his hand down on the table silencing Dominic. He leaned forward under the lamp, and his scowl deepened into a snarl. With his voice lowered, he directed his words to Giovanni only. "The Albanians brought the girls here. I would never drag our family into trafficking of any children. If you will just listen to me, Gio..."

"Doesn't matter how you lost control. What matters to me is *you* did. And that failure is a reflection on this family and me. Must I remind you of this each and every time you fuck up?"

A few of his men snickered. Lorenzo clenched his fist resting on the table. "We can't close the doors. It solves nothing. Francesco's entire fortune is invested in this place, as is mine. You only gave us ten percent. We put everything we had into the remodeling. How do we recoup the loss?"

"Burn the place to the ground." Giovanni shrugged. "I don't give a shit about your loss." His order resonated with the men gathered. "I want my fucking investment back and the family name out of the papers. Ten percent equals thirty now that you have disgraced yourself. Tomorrow it will be forty. Every day the doors remain open, the more indebted to the family you will be." Giovanni's gaze swung left. Carlo nodded that the order would be enforced. Lorenzo struggled with the inevitable, which was evident by the tension tightening his jaw.

"*Appunto. Ti seguo.* I get it. I follow you." Lorenzo nodded in respect. "Dinner? Have you eaten? *Prego!* Why don't you join me upstairs for dinner?" Lorenzo ground out between his clenched teeth. "Francesco should be part of this discussion. No? Let's go above and talk reasonably."

He hadn't eaten all day. He had slept even less.

"*Andiamo.* It's time I see Francesco." Giovanni declared.

"Fabiana? Where are we?"

Mira held tight to her clutch purse and resisted the hand that reached inside the back of the box shaped taxi to help her exit. She was hungry and felt a bit overdressed for the occasion. Napoli was a noisy city during the day and an interesting mix of people in the evening. Young Italians mixed in with tourists from all over the world in clusters along the streets. Most smoked, chatted, and dined outside of restaurants.

"I have a friend who owns this place."

"You do?"

"I do. He invited us to dinner and a night tour on his private yacht. You look fine. Trust me. Relax and forget our troubles okay?"

"How? The police put a padlock on the doors to my boutique today. My designs are there Fabiana! We only have two days before Milan. I need—."

"To eat. To laugh. To dance under the moon." Fabiana laughed, forcing a smile to Mira's lips. "I have a plan. Trust me. This friend of mine might be able to help."

A gentle shove to her shoulder pushed her closer to the door. Mira accepted the hand for assistance and eased out of the car. A hot wind lifted her curls up from her shoulders. Naples was pleasant but not as nice as some of the other towns she'd seen since her arrival in Italy. Fabiana wanted them to open a business in the coastal city due to the affordable cost, and initially the idea made sense. It was less expensive to live there than in Rome or Florence. Mira sensed the city had a seedy feel to it at night. She couldn't shake it. And the trash issue, it littered the street corners and peppered the air with a bitter stench.

"Ready?" Fabiana asked, slipping her arm around hers.

"There's a line."

"Don't worry, we get VIP treatment."

Giovanni sensed rebellion before the words escaped his cousins lying lips, and he was ready to deal with it in the most unpleasant way if necessary. Whores. They were everywhere. In *Italia* prostitution was legal, but organized prostitution, as in brothels or by third parties, had been outlawed since 1958. Very few places like *Isabella's* remained open. And the whores under his employ were of a high dollar and quality. It disgusted him to see women publicly debase themselves. Pussy was thrown at his feet regularly, and he almost always declined. The messy business in dealing with this side of his operations was a part of his father's legacy he couldn't wash his hands clean of. Lorenzo didn't share his sentiment. He clung to the back door business like a bitch who had received her first diamond. Now Giovanni had learned that his family name had been sullied with the association of trafficking. He itched to draw Danny-boy and empty it into the bastard that thought he could move young girls through his business.

"To your left." Dominic whispered close enough for him to hear.

Giovanni glanced toward the entrance of the restaurant. Two women entered. The first had skin so polished she looked as if she'd been dipped in buttercream, and scarlet red hair that reminded him of his mother's. Though he suspected the striking color of her mane wasn't natural, it was a lovely contrast to her beauty. She wore a magenta dress that snuggly fit her hourglass figure. When she turned, the revealing low backline plunged to the rise of her shapely hips and ass. Nice. His gaze switched to the other person in the woman's company. He could barely see the woman. His attention readied to drift as it often did when he observed beauty from a distance and his interest waned. However, Francesco's burly voice rose and Giovanni's gaze held. An un-obstructed view of the other woman took him by surprise. Not often did he see one like her enter his establishment. All others around her fell away. The track lights to the front of the restaurant defined her feminine curves. His attention centered on the low-cut V of her dress, which parted her breasts. The dress drew snug around her hips with a rhinestone pin. She had thick hair the color of sable that fell about her face in dark waves, and skin dusted in ginger, flawlessly covering every inch of her that was revealed.

Again his interest peeked over the shapely swell of her breasts, slender waist, and flat tummy, long enough to linger a moment on the nice heart shape of her hips. She wore black. The fabric of her dress appeared smooth, like velvet, though the hem of her dress moved as light as silk.

The trio was on the move. Giovanni's dark beauty stepped forward and the split to the front of the dress revealed her shapely legs as the long fabric pooled around her feet, elevated in silver spiked heels. Riveted, his gaze tracked her until she disappeared.

"She's the one. The lady in black." Dominic cleared his throat. "She's American."

"Her answer?" Giovanni turned his gaze to his young *capu*. Dominic ran his hand back through the thick dark crown of locks to the top of his head. He shifted his gaze to Lorenzo and hesitated over the response before uttering it under his breath. "She said to go to hell."

Carlo choked on his malt. The other men gathered, and looked out into the restaurant to get a glimpse of the woman who would dare insult the most powerful man in the *Cammora*.

A sly smile crossed the lips of Lorenzo. "Of course, she doesn't know how to respond, Gio. She's American." Suddenly Lorenzo's sour mood had lifted. He sat upright and tossed down the last of his drink before glancing back over his shoulder to where the ladies entered. "I'd say it's because you have a boy doing a man's job. When does Flavio return again?" He gave a pointed look at Dominic.

"She was only granted a temporary lease. It's happened before." Dominic clarified. "Flavio made a call on your behalf and the doors to her storefront were chained by an officer of the court. We intend to make sure you gain sole proprietorship. In the past we've dealt with foreigners who needed to be taught lessons of humility. She's no different."

"Interesting," Giovanni said. Now that he'd seen her, his desires had changed altogether. He was a bit pleased by her refusal. Too many people in his life said yes before the request was asked. Dominic was correct. She'd soon learn what a costly mistake her rejection of him would prove to be. One word from him and the fucking place could be burned to the ground. He drummed his fingers on the smooth wood surface of the table.

"I stepped in." Lorenzo announced. Giovanni glanced up. "They're here to meet me. With Flavio in Sicily I know there are matters that need a more skilled approach. I can assist, cousin, no disrespect, Domi."

"I thought you preferred to deal in the business of whores." Giovanni sneered.

Lorenzo chuckled, dismissing the sting of the comment. "The Irish hold more interest to me. Would you not agree that it's best we transact business without attention? The canals have to be open to us." Lorenzo leaned forward. "Those two designers can serve us well, by running the store above. The *Polizia di Stato* would never suspect."

The *Polizia Di Stato* was the Italian Republic's response to organized crime and the Mafia. Staying a step ahead of them was critical to men such as them. Lorenzo unfolded from inside of the booth and ran his hand down his black silk tie, smoothing it across his equally dark shirt. He gave Giovanni a respectful nod then turned and left.

A refreshed glass of Giovanni's favorite malt was delivered to the table. The brunette leaned in extra close to give him a full view of her supple cleavage before she withdrew. The young woman was then snatched by the hips and drawn to the lap of Carlo. Laughter exploded from some of the men as the woman fought Carlo to be set free, and he buried his face in the pair of ample breasts she thought would entice Giovanni. The scene was typical of his men. He ignored them both. How could he concentrate on anything other than the warmth in his chest from the mere sight of the dark beauty who passed him by? He'd been told her name was Mira Ellison, a high profile designer out of America. Twice he'd invited her to meet with him to discuss the boutique she opened in his territory, prime real estate that his father had extended to that Sicilian bastard Mancini. The only reason Mancini wasn't forced to turn it over after Don Tomosino's death was because it served Giovanni's purpose as a discreet cover for his business dealings. Mancini thought himself above the *Cammora* because of his reign and prominence within the Sicilian Mafioso. But even Giovanni was surprised when Mancini turned the keys over to the Americans without his permission. He would not tolerate the insult. The last invitation extended to Mira Ellison had been a dinner invite. He picked up the glass and drank the contents down. *Maybe he should handle introductions personally?*

"*Grazie.*" Mira smiled up at the server and accepted the menu.

"*Prego.*" The tall Italian with dark olive skin and eyes the color of honey smiled down at her. He looked to be her age, and god he was handsome, but his keen stare made her bravery slip and her gaze flickered away. Thankfully he moved on.

"He's cute, huh?"

"I guess." Mira shrugged. "I want to strengthen my Italian. So continue to practice with me, okay?"

Fabiana winked. In every occasion she tried to use a word

or two in conversation. The problem was she found herself stuck on the basics. Living in Italy would surely expand her vocabulary; just as dating Kei had taught her some of the most beautiful words in Mandarin. She glanced to Fabiana. "This is a nice place. Really nice. You said Teddy came here?"

"Oh yes, girl. He and I tried every restaurant along *via Posillipo*. This house vino is so good. Up here and below is a lot of nice dining. However, there's a bit more than meets the eye."

Mira glanced up from her menu. "What do you mean?"

Fabiana lowered her menu and leaned across her plate to smirk. Her red lips glistened by the candlelight on the table. "Teddy said that the basement is where people gamble, among other things. Some real freak nasty stuff if you're into it."

Mira laughed. "Bullshit."

Theodore Tate was their financial advisor and attorney. Mira trusted him and Fabiana on all business affairs. However, Mira knew Teddy, as they called him, had an affinity for fast living; women and gambling were a constant in his life. Kei would constantly question her over his abilities, and though she may not have agreed with Teddy's methods, he found loopholes and opened doors no other man under her employ could. If Teddy said there was something more to this place, she was inclined to believe him.

"It's true. Isn't it just decadent! Gosh I love Italy!"

"You being Italian have something to do with it?" Mira joked.

Fabiana shrugged. "It's like coming to the home you never knew. Being around family you always dreamed you had. Bet you'd feel that way if you went to Africa."

Mira considered the comparison. She wondered if a trip to the mother continent would do for her what being in Italy for three weeks had done for Fabiana. She'd never seen her friend so excited and happy.

A hot breeze blew in causing the string of lights above their heads to sway. The balcony setting was very serene with large leafy plants and candle lit lanterns. The tables were covered in white linen, and the plush chairs with white cushions. All tension drained from her bones. She relaxed in front of a spectacular view of the Amalfi coast with luxury yachts resting upon the dark calm waters.

The manager of *Isabella's*, who Fabiana introduced as Francesco, brought his chair inappropriately close to hers. She offered a curt, yet universal smile of decline to no avail. He stretched his arm around the back of her chair, and she could have sworn he let a few fingers brush her shoulder.

"*Benevenuti a Napoli*," Francesco said, his raspy voice only inches from her ear. His breath, hot and garlicky, became a pungent wash across the side of her face, and her stomach muscles clenched in response. Francesco was a short man with wide nostrils, thick pink lips, and brown stained teeth, but he wore a nice suit and had taken the time to curl the tips of his mustache upward.

"*Grazie*," she answered to his welcome.

"The place looks wonderful! You've done so much with it since I last visited." Fabiana gushed. "We've been here three weeks and do you know this is the first time either of us have ventured out at night?"

"It is lovely." Mira tried to force a light jovial tone to her voice. His close proximity didn't help. She swore she'd leap from her chair and throw herself over the balcony if he touched her again.

Francesco whispered in Italian. From the hard look of lust

in his eyes she had to wonder if it was indecent. Fabiana laughed. Mira frowned.

"*Mi scusi,* can you move your arm *per favore,*" Mira said through clenched teeth. Francesco obliged and Fabiana ignored her discomfort and sipped her wine. The *antipasti* was delivered to their table first. A mouthwatering mix of cured meats, olives, fresh ricotta and a crostini with vine ripened tomatoes. Mira reached with her fork, and Francesco stayed her hand. He leaned in speaking directly into her face a mix of garbled words that made no sense. Before she could politely ask her suitor to allow her the liberty to breathe clean air, another man approached. He was vastly different than the guy seated to her left.

Darkly tanned, his handsomeness was strengthened by the serious glint in his eye. He fixed his piercing stare on Fabiana first. He was tall. Very tall. She guessed his height to be just over six-foot five or six. And though she admittedly loved to tailor suits for men of his stature she was quite impressed with how nice and trim his attire fit his large frame. When he lifted his hand to smooth his tight dark locks his expensive watch gleamed on his wrist then slipped back under his sleeve. He exuded masculinity certain to stir desire in any woman. She bet he smelled good, too. This meant trouble for her friend. Mira volleyed her gaze between the man and Fabiana. Her suspicions were right. Fabiana's face flushed and she stared up at the guy with open adoration.

"*Ciao,* Lorenzo," Fabiana breathed in her sex kitten voice.

"*Signora Girelli,* I've been looking forward to seeing you all evening." Lorenzo's accent wrapped warmly around his words, and Mira thought her friend would drift up from her seat into his arms. He lifted Fabiana's hand to his lips, pressed a kiss to her knuckles, and then leaned forward to kiss both of her cheeks. His gaze then shifted over to Mira. "And who is this?"

"This is Mira Ellison." Fabiana extended her hand to her friend with a radiant grin.

"Ah, the renowned designer. There has been much talk of the fashion events in Milan this year, and I've heard your name mentioned more than once. Congratulations."

Mira nodded her thanks.

"May I join you?"

"Of course, you and Francesco invited us." Fabiana gushed.

What did she mean Francesco invited them? She glanced to her left and noticed Francesco's wicked grin. *Dammit, this is a double date. A setup. She should have known better than to trust Fabiana's girls night out invitation.* She had half a mind to get up and walk out. Before she could question her friend a conversation began at the table in mostly Italian between the three and she felt angrier.

More wine was poured.

Mira took a sip and smiled at the garbage breath man. He ogled her breasts as if they were a pair of pork chop sandwiches. It felt degradingly icky and was the final straw. She'd give it maybe ten minutes, and then she'd announce a headache and make a break for the door. Surely she knew enough Italian to get a taxi back to the hotel.

To her relief a reprieve came. A member of Francesco's staff approached. He offered apologies with an unsolicited kiss to her cheek and promised to return. All of which he said in Italian. Unfortunately, this Mira understood. Fabiana seized on his departure, and she did so in English. "Lorenzo what's with your friend? I thought you said he was one of the most sought after bachelors in Napoli?" She slipped Mira an apologetic wink. "He's not what she expected."

"Please don't speak like I'm not at the table." Mira said. "Besides, I never told you I wanted to double date."

"I know. But you *need* to double date."

"Fabiana!"

"Ladies." Lorenzo chuckled. "Francesco isn't just the manager here. He's part owner of *Isabella's* along with me. Here in Napoli he's the most sought after bachelor. Women are constantly climbing over each other to gain his affection."

"Then someone should give him a toothbrush." Mira mumbled.

Fabiana laughed. The humor drained from Lorenzo's sly smile and gleamed in his unwavering stare. Mira felt a bit uncomfortable with the depths of the baby blues fixed on her. She sipped her wine and tried to ignore it. The conversation became less strained when Lorenzo asked her about Naples and how she enjoyed his city.

"Unfortunately, we haven't seen much of it, have we?"

"No." Mira conceded. Naples was an interesting city. Certain areas reminded her of the slums of certain boroughs in New York, and others were so pretty it had to be plucked right out of her dreams.

Fabiana continued. "I would have preferred to purchase property in Milan to start Mirabella's Design House, but The Republic would not grant it."

"You mentioned a sponsor?" Lorenzo slipped Fabiana a look. "It's unfortunate your building was closed, and he couldn't aid you."

Fabiana flashed Mira a smile, and she gave one in return. Her girl could always find a way where there was none, now she was stumped. The politics of this country had them caught in the middle and even Fabiana couldn't undo it. Kei, Mira's former lover, said he would no longer fund her company and pulled out a large investment. It hurt deeply, both financially and emotionally.

"My family may be able to help. I've already discussed it with my cousin."

Mira cleared her throat, noticing the uncomfortable tension rising over the conversation. Their benefactor wanted to remain anonymous. Fabiana refused to drag him into the matter further. Instead she wanted the help of this man? Why?

"Can I offer a toast?" Mira asked. The two looked up at Mira's request. After a pause they reached for their glasses. "To Napoli, and all the wonderful friendships to come."

Glasses clinked and the tension eased.

Lorenzo set his glass back on the table. "Where have you been since your arrival in Italy? Have you visited Capri yet?" Lorenzo pressed.

"Mira hasn't ventured out of our place in the evening since the incident." Fabiana said.

Lorenzo's eyes stretched. "Incident?"

"It's nothing. I'm over it."

"No, you aren't." Fabiana frowned.

"May I ask? What happened?" Lorenzo pressed.

Mira really didn't want to share her embarrassment, but she saw no way out of the conversation. With a burdened sigh she relented. "We were walking down *via Toledo* in the evening doing some light shopping. There was a scuffle or argument between two people in the street."

"It started from nowhere," Fabiana interjected. "Pushing and shoving, loud voices. Kind of startled us both."

"Yes." Mira nodded. "And then it happened. A man on a

motorbike sped by and snatched my purse from my arm. So forceful the strap broke." She snapped her fingers. "In a flash. Gone."

"It was awful," Fabiana added. "Scared the hell out of both of us."

"I lost my passport. The embassy is helping me obtain a new one. Doesn't matter. I lost something irreplaceable in that purse."

"*Che*?" Lorenzo asked.

She ignored the ache in her heart and stole a deep breath before she could speak. "It's personal and it's gone. I can't believe I was stupid enough to keep it in my purse."

"You didn't lose it. Someone stole it from you." Lorenzo corrected.

"She's been on edge since it happened. Damn bastards." Fabiana grumbled.

"Safety is important ladies. You need to rethink my offer; I can ensure you'll have the protection you need." Lorenzo said.

"Excuse me?" Mira lowered her glass. "What kind of protection?"

"You plan to make Napoli, *Campania* your home? Open a business in the heart of the city, and crime can be an unfortunate consequence. Sometimes it's best to have allies. Though I can't guarantee a gypsy won't go after your purse again." Lorenzo kept his gaze leveled on her. "I can however, promise he'll wish he didn't."

Mira grappled with understanding what he was suggesting, and her best friend looked incensed. She spoke hurriedly to Lorenzo in a cool exact manner. She did so in Italian. Lorenzo sipped his wine and listened. He didn't seem fazed or impressed by Fabiana's short rant. His steely gaze slipped over to Fabiana who held firm in her position. "*Beh*...have it your way."

"What's going on? Stop speaking in Italian to keep me out of the conversation, it's rude!"

"We'll talk about it later." Fabiana waved off her concern.

"No. We'll talk about it now." Mira demanded. She returned her focus to Lorenzo. "What are your terms?"

An easy smile crossed Lorenzo's lips. "Things are done differently here. I'll let *Signora Girelli* explain. *Mi scusi belle*." He eased his chair back and rose. Fabiana forced a wan smile before she drank down the contents of her wineglass and reached for the bottle to pour more. Mira shook her head at her friend's attempt to shield her from the dirty details of their business. Of course, she couldn't blame her. Both had been stressed since they decided to relocate to Italy.

"What is it now? First the store closes and my designs are locked up in there and now there is more?"

"Mafia." Fabiana blurted.

Mira sat back. "Huh?"

Fabiana chuckled. "We're in Italy girl. Don't be surprised."

"What the hell does the Mafia have to do with you?" Mira asked concerned.

"Not me. Us. We've had a few encounters."

"We? From who?" she glanced around the empty balcony for Lorenzo. "Did he threaten you? Is he part of the Mafia?"

"Lorenzo? No. Well, I don't think so. He's from a very powerful family in Napoli. The Battaglias. They're well respected throughout the southern region. He's been trying to advise me. I just don't like his advice. Those terms he's speaking of involve weekly payments to men you don't want to know, men in the *Cammora*."

"Okay I'm afraid to ask. What is the *Cammora*?"

"It's what the Mafia is called here. Several families make up the *Cammora*, and they run things inside and out of the Republic. Very corrupt. There's nothing to worry about. We don't need that kind of help. Those leeches pray on naïve Americans. Trust me you're a celebrity, and our being American protects us."

"You're leaving something out." Mira felt like an idiot for not knowing more of this end of her business. "I want to hear about these encounters. Details."

"Actually you don't. Besides it's not a big deal. We have friends on our side, remember the Sicilian investor, our sponsor? Name's Mancini, he's a good ally."

"But you didn't want to involve him I thought?"

"Our boutique being closed has nothing to do with *Cammora*, just some red tape that we can cut through with the local authorities. That's where the Battaglias are useful. If I drag Mancini into the matter it will just become more complicated, since he's not a favorite with these men. That's the only help we need from Lorenzo's family and that's what I told him before he left."

"I don't like this." Mira could feel her skin goose pimple and rubbed her arm against the night breeze. "Feels off to me."

"We are to refuse all contact with the *Cammora*. We start paying these men their little taxes and before you know it you'll have investors you don't want."

They'd been together since Parsons and were closer than sisters. It was Fabiana who introduced her to Kei, a Chinese Wall Street businessman who would keep her naked and in bed all day in the beginning of their relationship because he couldn't let her out of his sight. He later became the first investor in Mirabella Couture and secured her a spot at New York Fashion Week. Now they were over. Their love affair had been strangely fulfilling and different compared to the limited love life she'd had in Virginia. She'd never dated outside of her race or been around so many people from different cultures. New York was an explosion of new experiences. Several years later Fabiana was her best friend, and she had found the courage to start a new life in Italy.

"I'm sorry. I'm not accusing you of anything." Mira softened.

"You're right. I should have told you. We'll talk more on it, just not here. I swear. Let's enjoy the evening. Okay? I really like him, girl."

"You barely know him."

Fabiana's eyes sparkled. "So? Does that matter? Tell me your honest opinion of him so far. And forget the Mafia stuff because he's nothing more than a businessman. A sexy, tall, handsome, Sicilian businessman that would make my mom smile if I brought him home."

"I don't know. Something about him is off. I can't pinpoint. He's a little intense."

"Ha!" Fabiana laughed. "And Kei wasn't intense? The man treated you like you were his chocolate covered love toy."

Mira chuckled at the comparison. Kei had never been as controlling as Fabiana thought. Mira was very old fashioned when it came to relationships. She believed in catering to her man as long as it was a shared experience. Kei was the type of man who'd paint her toenails while she read her favorite book or rise from bed in the middle of the night to get her pain pills because she had menstrual cramps. When they were alone he always proved to be very loving and tender with her. "Kei and I had an understanding. But we grew apart, and it makes me sad. I've changed. I'm not the nineteen year-old girl who needed a father figure, lover, and friend. I'm a woman now. Kei said he didn't want me to change, and I couldn't stay the same for him no matter how much I tried."

"He wanted to marry you."

She nodded. "Yes. And I have my regrets. Things ended badly. I hurt him. But it's over now, and I'm ready to move on. I think."

Francesco returned to the table with the arrival of a meal she hadn't had a chance to order.

"He says it's prepared just for us from the chefs." Fabiana translated Francesco's announcement. Mira found herself a bit disappointed that the evening would be shared with the man who was all hands and bad breath. Francesco sat next to her again, embarrassingly close. She could stand it no more.

"Oh, good grief! I don't feel like putting up with this tonight." Mira knocked Francesco's hand from her knee and shot him a murderous warning. He began to apologize in Italian, and she rolled her eyes when his hand returned to her thigh.

"Lorenzo should be back soon," Fabiana said.

"Well this one here is giving me the creeps. Would you keep your damn hands off me?" Mira snapped. Francesco threw his napkin down on the table and rose saying something heatedly in Italian before storming off. They looked at him and then each other before exploding in laughter.

Fabiana picked up her wine in a mock toast to his departure. "Yeah, sorry about Mr. Gigolo. Apparently, he thinks you're a stuck up American bitch."

Mira frowned. "Is that what that pip-squeak said?"

Fabiana nodded. Mira sighed, resigned to the fact that she'd never escape the place until Fabiana had at least one more conversation with her heartthrob. She rose from her seat. The bathroom had to be close. "I'll be back."

"The monk fish is good, hurry." Fabiana grinned.

Mira searched for the way to the bathroom and found herself in a dead end. She stopped a drink waiter with her hand to his arm. The young man blinked at her. *"Bagno?"* she said, asking for the bathroom in her limited Italian. He pointed to the far left, in the direction of the private dining area. She nodded and made her way.

A man dining with what looked to be a young group of friends actually yelled something to her from across his table, startling her for a moment. The men weren't shy in Italy. She did however notice that most things in Italy were small. The plates were small, the men were short, the rooms were tiny, the closets, even the cars. That was until she saw Lorenzo. He was quite tall and imposing. A giant among the men she'd met thus far.

And she'd met quite a few men. The flattery over the attention her dark skin drew had become a bit overwhelming. Older men in particular took notice of her when she entered or left a room. She flashed the guy a sweet smile and kept moving. When she drew closer to the hall, which led to the bathroom, she caught the shadow of a man's tall form from the corner of her eye. Her gaze flickered left.

It was Lorenzo. He walked up three purple velvet steps where four men were seated in a private meeting. The walls circling behind them held shelves of wine bottles, and the large round table spaciously sat ten to twelve easily. Mira's attention was immediately drawn to the man seated before the center of the table. Who wouldn't be? Even in the dim lighting it was clear he had a strikingly handsome face compared to the others. She found him a bit similar to Fabiana's heartthrob Lorenzo. His hair was dark, thick, it brushed his collar and was tucked behind his ears combed back from his face. And his dark brows were drawn together over piercing light eyes. She guessed them to be blue, but wasn't sure.

The man in all black tilted his gaze up to Lorenzo upon his arrival. He appeared remote, cool, and a bit disinterested. An air of authority clung to his persona and reminded her of how at times Chinese store owners in Chinatown would behave when Kei took her to dinner. They always regarded him with respect and humility. Kei dismissed it, but she knew there was more to him than the investment banker he claimed to be. And this one here was Kei magnified by ten.

Deep within her core her body warmed with mounting curiosity. She watched him lift a glass and take a sip, causing a ring on his pinky to catch the light. The center was a black stone, possibly onyx, but there was something engraved in gold on top of it. She had an eye for detail, and the ring thankfully wasn't on his wedding finger. The stranger possessed broad shoulders. She guessed his height equaled Lorenzo's. Without thought or reason she moved closer, drawn like a penny to a magnet, desperate for a better look.

Despite her best efforts, her clear view of the stranger had become obstructed. Lorenzo's towering form before the table forced her to step forward and to the right to get another glimpse. He clasped his hands behind his back as he spoke to the group. For a moment everyone at the table seemed to tense and go still over whatever news Lorenzo delivered. The man in the center studied Lorenzo. An impatient scowl had hardened his handsome features and stopped Mira cold. The stranger spoke. She wished she could hear his voice; a man's voice was always telling for her. The group exploded into a chorus of laughter, including Lorenzo. Whatever tension occupied the gathered men had subsided. Without warning, his gaze shifted and locked on her.

Surprised, she froze.

Dammit! What are you doing Mira?

He was undeniably focused on her solely and the raw intensity made him still as well. An eternity passed before she could even muster the courage to take a breath. *Run! Girl, turn and run to the bathroom. You look like a fool watching this man. Go! Go! Go!* The corner of his mouth curled up sly and easy, half shaping a smile. She felt her cheek twitch with the making of her own smile. *Oh good grief, are you flirting with this man?* He winked at her. It was as if he telepathically transmitted into her thoughts an invitation through his wink. Lorenzo noticed. He glanced back over his shoulder, and he too soon wore a darkly suggestive smirk.

She lost her nerve.

The attention from them both forced her legs to move. She quickened her steps and beat a path to the bathroom. Once inside, air returned to her lungs. "Goodness!" she laughed. "What the hell was I thinking?"

It took several minutes for her heart to calm to a manageable beat. Mira walked over to a chaise in the suite outside of the stalls and dropped on it. She needed to get her emotions under control. First, she couldn't stop the memories of the life she'd abandoned with Kei in New York. Then a wink from a stranger had her conjuring up rebellious naughty thoughts. Even now she felt a bit giddy remembering the cool calm leveled at her in his gaze.

"Fabiana is right, I really do need to get out more," she sighed. Three long years of hard work and sweat had garnered her the acclaim to show off her designs along one of the most sought after catwalks in the world.

The success, however, had come with a heavy burden. It was a hard business to be in. Many marginalized her work by labeling her a 'black' designer. It was a fickle business, too. Financial backing could be extremely lacking if she failed to stun critics with original and trend setting material. This was why her focus had been singular, and she remained so committed. It's also why her relationship began to suffer. No matter how sexy the man in black appeared, she had no time for flirting or God forbid a new romance. She shuddered at the thought of it.

Determined, she collected herself and used the facilities. In Italy, they referred to the bathroom as the *toilette* and she always had to flush by pressing a button above the commode. She washed her hands with perfumed soap, and refreshing her makeup, she felt a bit more at ease. There were times when the death of her grandparents would drill her purpose in her hard. She was alone in the world. Her mother died when she was a baby, and she never knew her father. She would often wonder about who he was. Maybe she could convince Fabiana to abandon the romantic notions of the city and just do some fun girl things. Neither of them had the time nor energy for much relaxation. A spa trip and some snorkeling along the beaches of Capri might do them some good after the show. Mira escaped the bathroom and stopped. Francesco paced angrily outside of the door.

He followed me?

When she emerged, he paused, and his puffy lips spread into a hideous yellowish brown, toothy smile. Mira frowned. She tried to sidestep him, and he matched her movement, blocking her in.

"You were rude earlier, *Signora*," he spat, his English almost perfect.

"So were you," she countered.

He advanced on her.

"I don't appreciate your tone. Show me respect!"

"Get out of my way." Mira refused to take another step back.

Francesco sneered. Even for his pint-size he bulked in the chest and arms. He definitely had the ability to deliver on the malevolent threat she read in the depths of his black-layered irises. The grip she had on her clutch bag tightened, and she readied to use it as a weapon. The deep baritone of a man's voice broke above them. He said three words in Italian that drained the color from Francesco's face. Mira dared to break eye contact with Francesco to glance beyond him into the face of her hero. This time the stranger didn't focus on her solely. He kept his eyes trained on the back of Francesco's head. She could see him much clearer now. He towered over them both. The rich outlines of his broad shoulders and muscular form filled his dark suit nicely. His hands were shoved down in his pockets and his posture relaxed, but his stare remained fiery hot. Francesco began to apologize profusely to Mira. He tried to reach her hand to kiss it, but she stepped back and away. Francesco turned and nodded his head in respect to the stranger and almost scurried out of the tight hall they shared.

"*Grazie*." Mira said.

The stranger tracked Francesco until he was gone and then

returned his focus to her. His smile was quite charming. He extended his hand. "Giovanni Battaglia."

Mira accepted his hand and he immediately drew hers to his lips. He spoke with less of an accent than the rest of the men she'd met that evening. His voice was smooth and commanding.

"I'm Mira."

"*Ciao, Bella*," he continued to hold her hand. "Are you okay? Did he touch you?"

"Him? No. No, he was just a jerk. He did nothing." She swallowed another bout of nervousness that made her want to giggle. His hand naturally fell away from hers, and her body registered the neglect. His appreciative stare travelled from her toes, up the front part of her dress, over her tummy and the swell of her breasts to her face. He did so unapologetically. The heat banked in those dreamy sapphires captured her breath.

"Thank you, uh, again," she stammered and walked around him. The heady scent of his aftershave nearly convinced her to return. She dared to glance back and was glad she did. He stared. She felt alive, sexy, and desired under his gaze. It had been a long time since Kei stared at her that way. Mira hurried through the tables back to her safety zone.

"What took you so long?" Fabiana asked irritated. "Your food is cold."

"I...I got lost."

Fabiana kept eating. "Lorenzo came back while you were gone. He apologized. I think I was a bitch to him. So I apologized too."

Mira unfolded her napkin and laid it on her lap trying to appear normal. "You weren't a bitch to him."

Fabiana smiled, nodding in agreement. "Tonight's a bust.

He can't take us on a tour of the coast on his boat, business matters or something. So he wants to make the whole thing up to us. He's invited us out to his vacation home when the show is over. It's not far from Milan. He says that Francesco won't be there."

Mira glanced down at her pasta and felt famished. Her adrenaline spiked and her stomach churned with such raw hunger. "Sure sounds like fun," she said forking some of the fresh rolled rigatoni and savoring the rich spicy garlic tang to the sauce.

Fabiana blinked at her confused. "You feeling okay?"

"Oh yes! Girl, I feel great."

****

"*Per favore!!* No! No! I'm an innocent man!" Francesco squealed as he was thrown into the kitchen. The cooks and wait staff immediately fled from the stoves, leaving all food unattended. Lorenzo cringed inwardly over the sniveling ball of apologies Francesco curled into. Did the man have no pride? Nico grabbed Francesco by the collar and forced him to his knees. The man slumped over with his palms tightly pressed together and his head bowed. *Was he praying?* Lorenzo cut his eyes in disgust. What would be next? Pissing his pants? Could he not hold it together long enough for Lorenzo to think of a way out of the mess? Francesco would be useless. Stupid fucker.

"*Un figlio di puttana!*" Carlo chuckled, the toothpick in his mouth switched to the other side. He and the others got a thrill over the sight of the man whimpering before them. Lorenzo had to agree. Francesco was a bastard, the dumbest of them all.

Yes, he was innocent, but the begging and crying only made him appear all the more guilty.

The raid on the club wasn't their fault. They never dealt in human trafficking. Someone had set them up, and he half suspected who. The truth of the matter was he and Francesco had committed another crime against his Don and their family, and Lorenzo had to quickly think of a way to keep his true sins from being revealed. Lorenzo feared the truth would spill from Francesco's quivering lips and blow his world to smithereens. If Francesco even hinted at their business dealings Lorenzo silently vowed to put a bullet in the coward himself.

The praying stopped. Francesco openly wept. His head hung low and his shoulders shook through his sobbing. The doors to the kitchen opened. Lorenzo didn't bother to look up. Tension rippled through the men like a cold wave, and he knew Giovanni had entered. Lorenzo's gaze lifted from Francesco to confirm. His cousin locked eyes with him and then swept the room of those gathered. Francesco's head lifted, and his eyes stretched to the point of nearly escaping their sockets at the sight of Giovanni. Even Lorenzo felt a twinge of dread over what was to come next. Violence was in their blood. They were all their fathers' sons. Giovanni ignored Francesco, whose attempt to crawl over for mercy was halted by the hand of Nico. Instead he approached the stove and a large boiling pot of tomato based gravy for some pasta dish. No one spoke as Giovanni removed a spoon and sampled it. Lorenzo glanced to Carlo. His best friend was focused on Francesco, a bloodlust in his hateful stare.

"*Bennisimo!*" Giovanni exclaimed after one taste. He turned his gaze to Lorenzo. "I always say the food is much better here than the pussy you try to sell out of the back door."

The men laughed in agreement.

"We didn't have anything to do with those girls cousin." Lorenzo grunted.

"I'm no fool. I know where there are lies, underneath there is some truth." Giovanni tossed the spoon to the stove.

"Don Battaglia! I can assure you, I have done nothing. I swear it."

Giovanni set his focus on the pleading man. He studied him for a moment. Francesco crawled, scuttled over to him and grabbed his pant leg. He reached up and snatched Giovanni's hand to kiss his family's ring. Francesco vowed to prove his innocence if he was shown mercy. Lorenzo looked away incensed. Even though he loved his cousin, the jealousy over Giovanni's role in the family ate away at his pride. He didn't know how much more of this scene he could stomach.

"Bring her in." Giovanni said to Dominic. He stroked the top of Francesco's head like one would do a pet. Lorenzo tracked Domi's movements a bit curious. Who was *her*?

In less than three minutes Dominic returned with a very frail, very pale, young girl. Lorenzo guessed her to be no more than thirteen, and by the way she was dressed he could tell she'd been abused quite often. Draped over her thin shoulders she wore Dominic's suit jacket. Underneath it a tattered sequined green mini with a thin grey halter-top. Her feet bare, her thighs and knees were covered in bruises, scrapes, and welts. Shock registered through him. Yes. He dealt with whores, but they were over the legal age, and willing. The raid on his place, he assumed, was a set up. Possibly by the runt Calderone out of Genoa, and he intended to deal with it. Now this child before him revealed he had no idea what Francesco had sunk their business into.

The man he thought he knew stopped his sniveling and stared at the girl. His gaze glazed over with something indecipherable for Lorenzo. The stupid fucker actually looked at the child with lust.

Giovanni walked over to the girl. He lifted her chin with his index finger so she could lift her gaze upward to his face. He spoke softly to her in Spanish; his cousin spoke six different languages. Lorenzo only knew Italian, English and Spanish. Giovanni told her she had no reason to be afraid. She was to do as he asked and then she would be returned to her family. He cast his gaze behind him to Francesco who now managed to stand. "Who is this man to you?"

"My master." The child answered.

Francesco shook his head fiercely. "I found the poor thing. Saved her. I gave her a place to stay. Protected her. Tell them. I protect you don't I?"

Lorenzo's rage gripped his gut turning it sour. He itched to draw his gun and unload. He was wrong. *Again he was wrong!* This motherfucker was trafficking young girls. Doing it under his nose. He took a step forward and Giovanni stopped him with a look. He cleared his throat and spoke to the room. "I knew nothing of this. Francesco never brought that girl here, any girls this young here."

"Take her away, Domi," Giovanni ordered.

The girl rushed Giovanni and hugged him. Lorenzo noticed the discomfort in his cousin's face but saw that he tolerated the child's gratitude. She glared at Francesco. Spat at him and cursed him in Spanish as Dominic led her away. Francesco put his face in his hands. Lorenzo could do nothing but be a spectator in silence. To say anything more would damn him for sure. For his family, he was now guilty by association. There was no explaining it away. There was lowlife scum in the *Cammora* that dealt in the prostitution of kids, trafficking, drugs. But it was not something the Battaglias did. There was pride to be taken in their family. Pride Don Tomosino died protecting, and Giovanni swore to uphold. Yes, Lorenzo wanted them to move into the future, but after witnessing Francesco's actions first hand he had to wonder if again he was wrong.

Giovanni approached Francesco, never taking his gaze off him. His hands eased into his pockets. Carlo and Nico both stepped on either side of Francesco. "You like *bambinas*?" Giovanni asked.

"No. She looks older than..."

Giovanni slapped him.

Francesco whimpered.

"You like babies?" he repeated.

Francesco looked to him again. He didn't know how to answer Lorenzo supposed. Giovanni's gaze hardened. "You are a sick man. Aren't you?"

Francesco nodded.

Giovanni patted the cheek that he struck. "I'll cure you of this sickness. Carlo!" Giovanni commanded.

"*Madonna santa!* Wait! Wait! No!" Francesco squealed. Carlo grabbed one arm and Nico the other. The two of them lifted Francesco up from the ground. Renaldo swiped all pots and dishes off the steal table and Francesco was slammed on top. "I swear to you on all that is holy and sacred, I only wanted to help her. Lorenzo! Speak for me!"

Lorenzo raised his chin slowly and shrugged his shoulders. "*Che me ne frego?* What the fuck do I care?"

Giovanni plucked a knife from the butcher's block. Lorenzo

silently cursed the fool and the mother who birthed him for his despicable crimes and denounced their alliance. He wasn't sure if Giovanni believed his innocence, but he *was* innocent. His cousin set the knife aside and folded the sleeves of his shirt up to the bend in his arms. He selected two large oven mittens from the stove and Lorenzo stepped back. He could act. Say something to spare Francesco his fate. But after seeing the abuse heaped upon that child he agreed with Giovanni that this punishment was just.

"No! No! Noooo!" Francesco begged. Giovanni lifted the pot and carried it before him. The sauce continued to bubble within its self-contained heat. Francesco kicked and bucked against the strong arms holding him down. Giovanni dumped the bubbling hot sauce over the man's head and face. The screams were ungodly. Francesco thrashed as his skin and hair boiled away from his skull. The men released him and the death screams filled the room. He bucked so hard he flipped over the table and landed with a thud to the floor. His feet kicking, his hands and arms twitching, nothing but horrific gurgling sounds escaped him.

Lorenzo glanced around as others stood there watching his death throws curiously.

"I had nothing to do with what he has done. NOTHING!"

After a pause and once Francesco went still and silent, possibly dead, Giovanni tossed the empty pot, and removed his oven mittens. Lorenzo braced for whatever was to come next. To his relief his cousin turned and walked out of the kitchen. Lorenzo glanced to Carlo and silently pled for understanding. His best friend nodded that he believed him. Somehow he'd convince Giovanni. He had to.

****

After three carafes of the best wine she'd ever drank in her life, they barely made it through the door. "I'm going to bed." Fabiana announced with an exaggerated yawn. Her friend spun on her heel and started toward her room.

"Freeze." Mira said. She stepped out of her high-heels and staggered across the plush carpeting down into the sunken living room area that separated their en-suites. Mira began to gingerly remove the diamond studs from her ear. She swayed right and left as if she'd topple over. The urge to explode in a fit of giggles kept forcing smiles to her lips even though she meant business. "Out with it, Fabiana."

"With what?"

"This Mafia business, that's what." Mira placed the earrings in the side zipper of her clutch bag then flopped down on the sofa. Fabiana threw her hands up in defeat and marched in to join her a bit more steady on her feet.

"Oh, girl, we already talked about this." Fabiana patted her mouth, suppressing a genuine yawn this time.

"I don't think you told me everything."

Fabiana put on a serious face when she sat folding her legs under her. Mira had to admit that her friend was far better at managing the treacherous highs and lows of running a fashion house than she ever was at designing actual clothes. She trusted her. But the idea that they were in trouble with people in another country sobered her.

"I was approached three days after we arrived in Naples. Wait. No. You received a message from the *Camorra* three days after we arrived. I declined the request for a face-to-face meeting. I also told them to go to hell when they threatened us with a fine to operate our own business. They demanded monthly payments that were not only ridiculous but also damn right insulting. We already have to pay them for the trash disposal that is littering the streets.

"Why would we have to pay them for our trash disposal?"

"Things are different here, Mira. They control sanitation and other things in the city. These bastards think they're entitled to full access to our building. If we didn't comply, they'd have us removed. Bullshit! All of it is bullshit scare tactics. Our solicitor and attorneys here in Italy met with Teddy and me. We were to ignore them. Things like this happen all the time to foreigners. What I didn't know was that they could have our building seized."

"So it's the Mafia that's locked me out of my business?"

Fabiana rolled her eyes. "I told you no at first. After what Lorenzo said, I have to wonder. He's a good ally. Let me work with him."

"We can't wait long enough for you to seduce some thug to give me my designs. This is a disaster! Christ!"

"Calm down. I'm handling it. He'll help us."

"No! We have to get my designs out of the building and be in Milan in days, not weeks."

"Lorenzo says his cousin would be willing to make a call, except he now wants to invest in your company. I'm negotiating. They are offering protection from future harassment."

"Extortion?"

"See this is why I didn't want you to know. You've been under so much stress—"

"You don't keep something like that from me!" Mira said. Fabiana looked away. They sat in silence for several minutes before their anger subsided enough for either of them to speak without voices rising. Fabiana went first.

"Things are done differently in southern Italy. Not many Americans leasing along the *Spaccanapoli*. It's expected."

"I don't like the sound of this. We're in another country. Things are done differently here like you said. Did you or Teddy notify the Embassy?" Mira pressed.

Fabiana let go a gust of laughter. "No. They won't do anything."

"This isn't some game, Fabiana. Extortion is serious. Everyone wants a piece of my business. This can't be legal. They can't get away with this."

"The Battaglias are legit. What they are offering means the doors to the building open, and you won't have to be harassed any more. I told Lorenzo we will consider his offer if they help us first. I'm sorry, but I know what I'm doing."

Mira shook her head. There was no getting through Fabiana's stubbornness. "How do you know Lorenzo? Is he the guy you told me about a couple of months ago? The one you met when you came here to finalize things."

"Yes. He approached me when I visited his restaurant with Teddy, and we shared a bottle of wine. We kept missing each other and could never hook up after that night. I've been trying to get my schedule clear to see him. He's a good guy."

Mira drifted on the memory of her tall dark stranger. His name was Giovanni. She liked that name.

"Mira?"

Mira sat upright. "Giovanni."

"Who?"

"Giovanni Battaglia. I met him. Tonight."

"You did? When?"

"At the bathroom, I forgot to tell you. Francesco cornered me."

"Wait... slow down."

"He's Lorenzo's cousin. He's the one who Lorenzo was speaking to."

"Dial it back to Francesco. What happened?"

"He cornered me. It got all heated, and Giovanni came. The man went running. I just put it together."

"Did you talk to him?"

"No. Not really. He introduced himself, and that was it. Really nice looking guy, tall, with crystal blue eyes."

"Sounds like Lorenzo's cousin." Fabiana nodded. "Why are you grinning like that?"

"Nothing," Mira chuckled. Her insides felt warm and her head fuzzy from the wine. All she could do was smile. It had been a weird night. Her debut was in less than seventy-two hours. If the Battaglias could get her back into her building then so be it. However, she would not take on investors. No way in hell. She wanted nothing to do with the Mafia mess. Mira rose, bone weary tired. "I've had enough of this intrigue over the Battaglia men. I'm done. Going to bed."

Fabiana shot to her feet. She grabbed Mira by her hand and dragged her toward the doors to their outside balcony. "What are you doing?"

Mira was forced outside into the warm night. "Look out there!" she exclaimed. "We did it! You and I together. We're finally here."

She held Fabiana's hand and stood at her side on the balcony. They always vowed to celebrate their successes. Tonight was the first night she truly believed in her talent without reservation. Maybe it was the wine.

"What's that over there?" Mira pointed.

"Egg Castle. Isn't it pretty?" Fabiana said in a wistful tone.

"Yes. All of it is. The cathedrals, monuments, bridges and mountains. All of it is like some dream."

"It is a dream. Our Dream." Fabiana squeezed her hand. "And it's just begun. So is your new life, social or whatever. From this day forward you are going to live it. We both are. Deal?"

"Deal."

****

Giovanni reclined in his smoking chair. He didn't sleep often. The dreams overwhelmed him when he let his defenses down. He had it within his power to do away with the prostitution houses they owned under his father's reign. He allowed Lorenzo to operate to send a message to his enemies, to give the appearance of not being soft. The thought of it turned his stomach. They were not good men; he had no illusions that they would ever be. But women were not to be abused and used in this way. He thought of his mother's suffering, and his adoration for Catalina. He could not face her or Zia with his family sullied this way.

He closed his eyes.

After a bullet was put in the head of the dying scoundrel Francesco, who dared bring dishonor to his family, he gave the order. There would be no more prostitution brothels, period. The men didn't seem shocked. Even Lorenzo held his tongue against any protest. He was done with the shit.

A nightmare lingered in his memory, and he forced the hot ache in his chest to subside. Tonight he thought he might have awakened with the sounds of his own screams still lodged in his throat. He wasn't sure. No matter how hard he tried to understand his failure as a son, he found no peace. The first life he actually took with his own hand was the life of the bastard he believed shot his father. Even now he took no satisfaction in revenge.

It was my fault.

He rose from his chair, his shirt hung open and his feet were bare. The clock declared the time to be close to three in the morning. He had the bitter taste of tobacco and whiskey in his mouth. The room to his suite opened to a balcony and he decided to spend the rest of the evening smoking his cigars waiting for the sun to rise on the Amalfi. Soon he'd return home. Catalina would be expecting him. He needed his family strong. He could forgive or try to forgive this one time to gain his cousin's faith and trust.

They were brothers. In blood.

Chapter Two

FOR TWENTY-EIGHT HOURS she and her team worked. Nothing would be missed. Determined, committed, she fretted over her final choices for her collection. Her line had been inspired by autumn's seasonal colors she'd often watch bloom out of her bedroom window over the rolling hills of Virginia. It had better translate well for her showing.

Fabiana's voice rose above the chorus of staff members buzzing around half-clothed models and cosmetologists. Each one marched to an explicit directive from Mira on how they were to serve the needs of her big event. Through it all she remained frazzled and over sensitive when mistakes or accidental mishaps occurred. The last thing she needed or desired was Fabiana 'her bossy best friend' Girelli inserting herself in the midst of pandemonium.

"Where is she?" she heard Fabiana's voice crack like a whip over the apologies of an assistant. Mira cut her gaze away. On her knees with pins in her mouth, she hand stitched a ruffled hem that unraveled along the train of the evening gown.

"Mira! What are you doing? Let Eduardo or Angelique

handle the retouches. We don't have time for this. You're supposed to be in hair and makeup." Mira glanced up. Her vision blurred a bit, and her stomach rumbled. She'd survived on 3 to 4 hours of sleep at a minimum. The day of a show often became this melodrama between them. Fabiana would harp on how she needed to be cared for, and Mira would escape her tyranny to tend to the necessities often forgotten before her clothes graced the runway. Food, even grooming herself, all came in second to last on her list of priorities.

"Drink this. You look like death!" Fabiana held out a cup of coffee.

Mira ignored the order. After she added the ruffle, she wanted to revisit the straps and loosen them a bit to ensure the fabric fell low around Zenobia's breasts.

"You're going to make me hold you down and pour it down your throat." Fabiana half-teased. Mira knew that her friend wasn't opposed to trying. "If you don't eat or drink something, you won't be standing by the time Zenobia hits the catwalk. Now do it."

Mira glanced up. She was pleased Fabiana had worn the dress she made for her. It was a tangerine linen summer dress with a low back line, which crisscrossed with a multitude of tiny straps in a web-like design. The front of the dress had a scoop neckline and plainly slimmed out her curves with the hem rising two inches above her knees. She liked the understated look that turned sexy when her friend walked off and a person caught a glimpse of her backside. It complimented the multifaceted layers of her friend's personality to a tee. Fabiana's hair flowed in scarlet waterfall curls and bounced on her shoulders.

"Enough!" Fabiana stomped her foot in protest. She tossed

her locks and scanned the crowd for someone to seize. Mira continued to sew the inseam of the train.

"Angelique!" Fabiana barked to one of the better seamstress. "Finish this hem, please." Fabiana reached for Mira. Spitting the pins out of her mouth into Fabiana's hand, she sulked as her friend passed them off to Angelique. With no other choice available, she allowed Fabiana to help her rise.

"Look at you!"

Mira lowered her gaze down to her khaki pants and all white cotton shirt with the sleeves rolled up to the bend of her elbow. Her hair had undergone a hot press and curl earlier but she had smoothed her tresses into a ponytail.

"Once again my designing diva looks more like an apprentice instead of the brilliant starlet she is." Fabiana frowned at her disapprovingly. "The show starts in less than an hour, and you aren't dressed!"

"Stop talking so loudly. I have a headache." Mira accepted the cup of cappuccino. The roasted bean aroma awakened her senses. She inhaled deep before taking a swallow of the scorching bitter liquid. A shot of espresso is really what she needed.

"Let's go, and I mean now, Mira." Fabiana gave her a gentle push. They passed models lined up in studio chairs getting their makeup and hair done. She walked through the heavy black curtain heading to her trailer with Fabiana on her heels. Behind her she could hear her friend speaking through the headset clamped down on her head like a pair of iron earmuffs. Mira flung open the door and suddenly her frustration had a name. It was her bossy friend coming between her and what could be the critical minutes of work to be done before the show. She had to bite down hard on her tongue to keep from voicing her anger. Besides, the fatigue had depleted her of energy. She craved sleep, though it wasn't an option. She had more work to do, though her runway event would last no more than twenty minutes. And when it was all said and done, her fate as the new international sensation would be decided.

She wanted to throw up.

"Don't ever talk to me like that in front of my staff again," she grumbled.

Fabiana nodded, "Okay, sweetie, whatever you say. Are you hungry?"

"Don't patronize me!"

"Mira," Fabiana removed her headset. "I don't have time for this shit. I know you're stressed, but it's my job to get your ass in line, to keep this operation from falling apart. So drop the attitude okay?"

She groaned an apology, which Fabiana waved off. "You've been wound so tight since we got to Milan you're going to make yourself sick. I've checked and triple checked everything. You and I both know there isn't a garment out there that you couldn't find a flaw with. Trust in what you've created."

Mira pulled her shirt over her head, turning she walked toward the back of the trailer intent on washing up and appeasing her friend. "You know what they said about my fall collection last year Fabiana." She called out from the bathroom running the water. "That bitch Gale Greene and Henry Sutherland had the nerve to call me stale, unoriginal. One of them said my collection had no harmony."

"Two critics hated your line while the other sixteen loved it. True to form you would only focus on those two hacks. You need tougher skin. Not everyone is going to love what you do. If enough people in the industry respect your talent, it validates your work."

"It's not just that they didn't love it." Mira stuck her head out of the bathroom door. "They said Kei was the only reason I had a place in New York. Well, his money was the only reason. Now, we're flying solo and that bitch in Variety put it on the front page. Everyone is going to be critical. If we fail, they will say it's because Kei and I are done, and—."

"Oh who gives a shit what the supposed 'they' think? Sweetie, the bottom line is Kei could write you a million dollar check, and if your designs suck, they suck. You and I both know what you do is fresh. It's innovative and so is that killer ass runway show we got planned. Did we get this far doubting ourselves? Hell no. This time you will knock them on their collective asses! And I promise to make sure that bitch at Variety does a retraction!"

Mira appeared from the back in her bra and bikini panties brushing her teeth. "Did you make sure Zenobia tried on the apricot chiffon dress again? This morning I touched up the waist, she's lost more weight."

Fabiana nodded. "Yes. Zenobia's got all three dresses fitted."

Mira headed back to the cramped bathroom to finish brushing her teeth. The phone rang inside the trailer.

"I'll get it. You hurry up and finish dressing so I can work on your makeup and get you in the chair to do something with that pretty hair of yours."

"Fabiana Girelli speaking," she said.

"*Ho bisogno di te,*" A deep yet smooth voice whispered through the receiver. The underlying sensuality of the words spoken to her made her heart flutter. It was Lorenzo. He said he *needed* her. *How did he get the number inside of Mira's trailer?* She was certain the man on the other line was him. The call couldn't have come at a more perfect time. Being needed is what she thrived on. After they parted she was a bit disappointed over the brief time they spent together. Now he was calling? It had been several days since she last saw him and she hadn't even had the chance to thank him for helping them.

"Hello?" Lorenzo said.

"Hi. How'd you know it was me?" she asked, feeling her cheeks flame hot with a blush.

"I'd know your voice anywhere," he answered.

Fabiana sat in the small booth seat. She couldn't help but smile. "You say that to all the girls."

"You look amazing in that dress. *Bellissima!*"

Immediately her gaze flashed upward. "What?"

"*Bellissima*? It means very pretty..."

"I know what it means." She exhaled a nervous chuckle. She hustled out of the booth seat and pulled the phone cord over to the window. She drew it back and scanned the people bustling about. "Mira and I wanted to thank you and your family for having the doors to our boutique reopened. You saved us a lot of grief. I called and... well you didn't call me back."

"Forgive me. There's been a lot of business to tend to recently. It couldn't be helped."

"You're here?"

"Yes, I'm here. You've been working, so I decided to wait."

How was that possible? Security was gridiron tight. She should know, she paid a fortune to keep Mira's designs under lock and key. No one was allowed in or out without her approval. And he was there, watching her? "Where are you?"

"The phones outside your tent. I want to take you to dinner tonight, afterwards."

Fabiana looked over to where she could hear Mira dressing. "I can't. I have this press-op to oversee and the after party. Why don't you come?"

"An invitation, to another man's club?"

"It's a party I'm throwing. Surely you can make an exception this time?"

"I think I can."

"You'll need VIP passes to get in. I can get them to you."

Lorenzo chuckled. "That won't be necessary, *a presto*."

"Bye," she said, and the phone clicked off.

"Who was that?"

Mira held out for the small chance Kei would call to wish her good luck. She peeked out at Fabiana. Her friend's face was red as a tomato. Fabiana looked like she'd explode into a rainbow of happiness. She jumped up and stomped her feet shaking her head in triumph. "What the hell is going on with you?"

"He called. That's what! Wait a second, what are you wearing?" Fabiana frowned.

"Who called?" Mira tucked the blouse into her slacks. She'd chosen a neutral color of bone for her business suit.

"Never mind that. I left a dress in there for you to put on."

Mira looked down. "What's wrong with this?"

"Stop with the games, and put the dress on."

"For Christ's sake, Fabiana, I can't walk around in that thing!"

"You designed it!"

"It's a party dress! I can't –"

"You can't work in it? Exactly my point." Fabiana dropped her hands to her hips. "The work is done. Now I need you to shine like the designing superstar you are. Please with sugar on top. Put it on."

Mira threw her hands up in defeat. She marched to the back of the trailer to change. "Who was that on the phone?" she called out.

"Lorenzo. He's coming to the after party."

"Oh? Did you tell him thank you for helping us with our store?"

"Yep, and he wants to celebrate!"

"Oh goodie!" Mira sassed. She found the dress Fabiana had chosen and froze. A Spanish style emerald-green glamour dress she had decided not to include in the collection. The top fit like a corset and would push her breasts tastefully upward. This corset however had ties to either side instead of the back, which was done to accentuate a trim waistline. The hem of the dress was raised higher in the front above the knee, with ruffled slips of chiffon underneath to give it a whimsical flow when the person wearing the garment made a step forward or backward. It hung silkily low to the back in a train of fabric that swept across the floor. She could object and fight with Fabiana until they were both hoarse and stressed to the limit. Or she could concede and get the hell out of the trailer and back out into her operation before her line was called to grace the catwalk.

She gave in.

Mira slipped the dress on and did her best to tie the corset strings on either side. She eased her feet into three-inch high heels and stomped out.

"Brava!" Fabiana clapped.

"It's too much and you know it."

"This line is going to take Milan by storm, and you will be an even bigger success! You need to dress like one. When Kei picks up the morning paper in New York and sees you on the cover dressed like this, he'll finally call you and beg you to reconsider. Isn't that what you want?"

The question hit her hard in the throat. Her stomach clenched over the mere thought of Kei trying to force another proposal on her again. No. She didn't want him back. She just wanted to know he didn't hate her, and he didn't think she used him for her success and abandoned him. Maybe someday they could be friends.

"Now, about this make up."

"I can let one of the makeup guys do it." Mira groaned.

"Nonsense, no one can do your makeup like me. Sit down."
****

The techno swing beat thundered around the audience and nervous designers backstage. Statuesque models over six feet tall climbed up a set of small stairs to the runway. Mira checked the girls lined up for the final display of eveningwear. Each model sported the very best of her creative expression with their hair styled in a 1920's motif with deep finger waves. Some over accessorized with long waist length pearls and orchids behind their ears.

Zenobia, a six-foot two model from Ethiopia would be crowned the darling of *Italia*. Mira dressed her in an apricot and golden yellow, flat shift dress with a wide circular neckline that stretched past her collarbone circling her shoulder blades. A wide belted trim gathered the material tightly just below her hips, allowing three chiffon ruffled layers to flow just above her knees and drift to the back of her calves. She flipped the rest of the style by making the top so sheer you could see the dark points of Zenobia's nipples and adding iridescent golden stones in the fabric to give a sparkle from every angle.

Proud of Zenobia's beauty, she stepped back nodding. The model winked and took to the runway. The roar of applause from the spectators let her know that the audience loved it. Mira glanced over her shoulder for Fabiana who appeared magically at her side. Her friend put a protective arm around her, and they embraced.

"You did wonderful, sweetie."

"We did it, Fabiana. Without you at my side, I could never pull this off. I love you."

"I love you too. And I got the easy job. You my dear are the visionary!" She kissed her cheek. The models from her line began to circle to do a final runway walk, and Mira wiped at the tears she held back. Her dreams had become a reality. Each time she successfully launched a collection felt like the first time. This was her passion.

Fabiana patted her on the back. She gave her a gentle push, and Mira grabbed Zenobia's hand to step out on the runway with her after the last piece of her collection returned. The crowd seated on both sides stood, clapping once she headed down the shiny catwalk with Zenobia at her side smiling.

Camera bulbs flashed and clicked at every side of the runway causing her to blink, and her heart pounded. This part of the show was hard to do when all the focus narrowed in on her. Zenobia let go of Mira's hand allowing her to strut down the runway alone. Mira sashayed the rest of the way, the train of her dress moving fluidly behind her, catching the breeze with each step. Tossing her long curls she smiled and blew a few kisses at the press and some fellow designers she recognized.

Once she neared the end her eyes locked with the bluest pair in the room. He sat front and center watching her. He wore all black, even his tie. It had to be close to eighty degrees, but he looked untouched by the humidity. His dark hair was tapered low to his ears and a wave of thickness was combed back from his face. And his eyes. Jesus, the man's eyes were as blue as rain. Even from the elevated point of the catwalk she couldn't get past his eyes. Mira's steps slowed, and then she stopped. In this crowd of celebrities, dignitaries, the richest of the rich, he claimed an air of authority. Those around him, and it had to be at least seven men seated, all wore tailored black suits like his. Mira swallowed down a breath and felt her heart hammer hard and fast in her chest. She tore her gaze away from his beautiful stare and shifted it to the stunningly gorgeous raven-haired brunette at his side. *What is she nineteen, twenty?* This woman should be on the runway not her. She had the same devastatingly blue eyes, and golden olive skin. A burn of envy for how she sat next to Giovanni broke the spell he cast over her and severed the glimmer of attraction they shared. Was she a girlfriend, or worse, his wife?

Lorenzo leaned in and whispered something in Giovanni Battaglia's ear. Neither man looked away. They were definitely discussing her. As if she were in a display window and Giovanni was deciding whether to make the purchase. A man seated behind him touched his shoulder and Giovanni nodded. He stood. Her breath hitched in her throat. He extended his hand to the brunette and the woman accepted it graciously. Together they turned and walked out. He never glanced back. Lorenzo followed with his hands in his pockets. Suddenly the clapping and camera flashes returned her to reality.

Realizing she lingered far too long at the end of the runway, she gave a slight bow, and blew a few kisses to her audience, before turning and heading back. Hurrying down the steps behind the curtain, she nearly collided with Fabiana who was making a beeline to her. "What happened at the end of the runway?" her friend whispered, concerned. Everyone behind the curtain applauded her for a job well done.

"Huh?" Mira asked confused.

"At the end of the runway you froze. Something wrong?"

Mira blushed, "I did? It must have been the lights." She walked off to thank her models and staff.

****

The circus behind the curtain came to a close. Several head designers gathered in a conference room to do a Q&A with the press. Once it concluded, they filed out exhausted. Fabiana saw to the business of securing their equipment and garments to be shipped back to Naples. Mira wandered through the thinning crowd headed for her trailer. She daydreamed throughout the interviews of how wonderful it would feel to release the ties to her corset and shed her dress. The sun had set and the after parties in Milan were in full swing. She needed to put her feet up before making her appearance then retire for her much anticipated vacation.

"*Signora*?"

Mira turned and was greeted by a dozen long stem, blood red roses held together by a black silk ribbon in his hand.

"Yes?"

"*Signore* Battaglia wishes you congratulations." A very handsome young man said.

She accepted the flowers. The man gave her a single nod then turned and strolled off. Mira inhaled the flowers and the strong aroma filled her with a slight buzz. Reaching in between she pulled out the tiny card. She struggled to open it retrieving the card.

Bella,

I am sorry for the unfortunate way we met. I wish to reintroduce myself properly.

You are as talented as you are beautiful. Congratulations on your success.

I look forward to getting to know you better as we conclude our business.

Giovanni

"Wow, they're gorgeous!" Fabiana gushed walking up behind her.

Mira spun around holding the card, confused. "Business?"

Fabiana took the card from her and read it. "Giovanni? Lorenzo's cousin? What business do you two have?"

"I guess he wants a thank you for helping us?"

Fabiana smirked. "Uh oh, how do you plan to show your gratitude?"

Mira laughed. "Please. Not that way," she rolled her eyes, shoved the flowers on Fabiana and walked off.

****

Nephenta

The in-town nightlife buzzed with the excitement of a thousand honeybees. Each side of the narrow cobblestone street was congested with models and other beautiful wealthy people enjoying Milan in springtime. The private after party thrown by *Mirabella Couture* was an all-white affair and the ladies had dressed accordingly. Her best friend chose to wear a white halter, jersey material dress that clung tightly to her curves. Oh, how Mira tired of dresses; she'd been on her knees for weeks working on one design or another. This evening she wore slimming white jeans that molded her backside, thighs, calves and complemented how athletic and shapely they were. A wide white rhinestone leather belt looped around her low-waist jeans with a slant at the rise of her hip as if she was a futuristic gunslinger. Her sleeveless white top slimmed down snug to the waist to give her breasts an appealing lift.

They were late. Fabiana had to help her press out her hair. She needed to look fresh and revived for the fashion critics awaiting her arrival. Her hair was silky straight, parted down the middle. Her smoky earth tone eye-makeup and lip-gloss enhanced her natural beauty tastefully. She accessorized with oversized rhinestone hoops and matching bangles.

"So did I mention that Lorenzo was coming?" Fabiana asked. The driver navigated his way along the single lane road to deliver them to their event.

Mira smiled. "Yes, you did." She stiffened remembering the woman she saw Giovanni with, and sobered the spark of interest burning in her chest. And to think she flirted with the two-timing jerk. What did his brunette wife think of him kissing her hand?

The car stopped. "You want me to ask about his cousin? The man did send flowers."

"Oh good grief. Please don't. Our business with the Battaglias is done."

"Hey? You sure you're okay? You seem tired. I promise we won't make it an all-nighter."

"Thanks. I really am wiped out." Mira sighed. A slender long fingered hand eased inside the car to assist her with exiting.

"Wait." Fabiana grabbed her arm. "We keep our deal."

"Which deal?" Mira yawned.

"Two weeks' vacation starts tomorrow. Everything is set. The team has assembled in Napoli, and Angelique is going to deal with the American offices to handle all of the orders. Let's do Tuscany; really get the feel of Italy. We'll get you rested and ready for business, and after today it's just us having a bit of fun. You need it sweetie, and to be honest, I do too."

"Yeah, yeah." Mira nodded. After the past four weeks she craved a break. Solace and solitude sounded so yummy to her now. The wine villages in Tuscany would be great. She and Fabiana talked about taking a few cooking classes, too. The possibilities of waking up and sketching her designs under the Italian sun made her giddy with excitement. Oh yes, she wanted this vacation most of all.

Careful in her four-inch heels, Mira eased out of the car like a lady and shed her fatigue. They entered the club both wearing warm smiles. The place looked fabulous! Illuminated by the large blue lanterns hanging from the drop ceiling, the décor mainly consisted of white walls and white floors with electric blue tables and chairs. The dance floor had a checkered white and blue pattern and a bluish colored, mirrored disco ball spinning above it.

Music blared from a wall to floor speaker system. "Wow, you did a great job." She yelled back at Fabiana who followed her closely.

"Thanks, sweetie. Just promise me to have some fun. You do remember how?" Fabiana yelled in her ear over the music.

Mira smirked. Carole Montague, a rival, and fellow designer, rushed to her and kissed both sides of her face. The haughty Susie Chu, a fashion critic from China who used to date Kei and who wrote an unfavorable review of the event before it started, trailed her. Susie glanced her way but didn't smile. Carole gushed over Mira's show. They chatted up the event and the fantastic designs that graced the runway before promising to do lunch in New York if she returned this year.

"C'mon, I think Armani's here. Let's go say hello."

"No. I can't. I want a drink and to unwind first. I'm going to the VIP for a bit and sit down. Where is it?" She glanced around.

"No, Mira. Business first."

"Please greet everyone for me. I'm just not in the mood for the crowds."

Fabiana studied her for a moment. She relented. "Go ahead, I'll bring him to you. The top level has several sections roped off. Security will take you to ours. Over there."

Mira glanced to the left of the club. She squeezed Fabiana's hand before pushing her way back through the crowd. Several people stopped her as she passed, congratulating her. The head designer of Deveraux kissed her on both cheeks. She smiled graciously and made small talk. Finding an opening she escaped with the promise to meet him on the dance floor. Nothing was marked off or designated for her section. There would be no escape this evening so she might as well make the most of it. She headed toward the bar.

"A martini, three olives, extra dry," she said while nodding to someone who went on and on in Italian about her show. Mira blushed over the flattery and waited patiently for her drink. Accepting it, she moved away from the crowded bar, sipping, careful not to spill a drop. The music tempo changed to American rap and she grew even more tired of the atmosphere.

"Can you? *Per favore*? Follow *Signora*?"

The deep commanding voice spoke clearly above the music behind her. He spoke directly in her ear so he could be heard over the music. Her head turned and tilted back at his towering presence. She was reminded of the popular series she watched a couple of years back, The Incredible Hulk. Except this man wasn't green. He was darkly tanned and gorgeous, with the body of a giant. The alcohol lingered on her tongue and she swallowed. Her voice came out weak and unsure. "Excuse me? Follow?"

"*Venire...* this way."

He gave a nod to the roped off destination she intended to make her way to. She frowned at the giant's attire. His dark suit was a striking contrast to everyone around her who wore white. Then it dawned on her. He must be the security Fabiana hired. "Oh, yes, I was looking for our section. Fabiana sent you to find me?"

The man blinked at her. He didn't appear to speak English that well. A woman passed by them really close, taking the time to run her hand over the giant's arm. She referred to him as Nico. He ignored her. His hand swiped left and forced three to four people to stumble back with a squeal of protest. He had cleared the path for her. No one dared challenge the blatant rudeness. She noticed the stairs he wanted her to climb. She nodded and headed in that direction.

Careful of her martini, she ascended the velvet blue staircase.

Fabiana kissed Armani on the cheek and said goodbye. The crowd had thickened to the point of claustrophobia and she had to turn sideways to escape those clamoring for ten seconds of the designer's time. Just as she emerged she felt a large calloused palm capture her hand. Her head turned to offer a polite refusal of the unwanted touch, only to find Lorenzo staring down at her. She had to blink to be sure it was him in the dim lighting of the club. But how could she miss those eyes, and that strong, determined, handsome face of his? He wore all black to her all white party. Fabiana shook her head smiling. Gently he pulled her through the gyrating bodies on the dance floor to an open space.

"I found you."

"Yes, you did. I had hoped you would."

She made sure to leave his name at the door. But when she glanced down he wasn't wearing the card that would grant him access to all the private levels. She glanced around at the security and wondered how again he had made it in without being stopped.

"Really?" His dark brow arched.

"Of course. I've been in your country for four weeks now and only seen you once."

Lorenzo smiled. "Let's change that. Tonight you and your friend should come to my villa, Lake Como."

"Tonight? I don't think we can."

The strong arms circling her waist drew her in closer and his palm slid down the curve of her backside. It was a bit forward for him to touch her so intimately so soon, but pressed against his hard frame with his jeweled eyes shining down on her, she couldn't summon an objection. "I want to know you better," he said softly before brushing her lips with his, then licking her gloss from his mouth as if it were honey. Fabiana raised her arms around his neck. *Fuck it, why not?* She rose on her toes because he was indeed that tall and brought her mouth up to his. Parting her lips she intended to entice his tongue to slip inside. He tasted of mint, and the feel of his hand easing slowly down her hip sent shivers of excitement up her spine.

"Mmm, okay. I have to convince Mira," she grinned.

Lorenzo brought his mouth to her ear and kissed it before he spoke. "Trust me. I think she'll agree."

Mira scanned those gathered. She didn't recognize the faces staring back. None of the familiar people who frequented her circle of friends were present. Most of the ladies were in white, but the men weren't dressed appropriately. Their dark suits separated them from all the others.

"This way." Her escort said in an exact firm manner, which drew her attention to the opposite side of the roped off room. Two menacing looking men stood on either side of the table where Giovanni Battaglia waited. His gaze travelled over her face and searched her eyes to see if she would join him. Her curiosity as well as her vanity was aroused, silencing the warning voice in her head. The men seated at the table with him rose as if it were expected. Two of them silently walked away. The third stepped to the back of his section and stood silent. Mira forced her legs to move. When she reached the table, he stood to greet her.

"*Ciao, Bella,*" he smiled. The pronunciation of the word was near perfect. The man had definitely lived abroad. She was grateful that she didn't have to struggle with an interpreter for this conversation, but even more nervous that despite her strong willed personality she saw no way to avoid a sit down with him. Giovanni extended his hand. She extended hers. He again kissed her knuckles tenderly. He lifted his eyes to hers, and the firepower made her cheeks warm. "Please," he said gesturing for her to sit.

The wait had been far too long. He'd sat in the noisy club for nearly two hours before his men told him that she arrived. He sent for her over twenty minutes ago. *It was ridiculous!* Then she appeared. He'd never seen a woman make white look so damn sexy. Those pants of hers were painted to her curves and the rhinestone belt made her hips sparkle as she approached. Her smoky brown eyes fell upon him, and he was captive again. This he liked. It was a bit more subdued than the flash and glamour he saw walking down the catwalk. Don't get him wrong, he liked her sexy dress, but preferred a woman of her caliber not reveal so much cleavage and legs to an undeserving audience. If she were *his* woman, he'd never let her flaunt for others what was his only.

There appeared to be a problem with his greeting. She didn't look pleased to see him. In fact her smile was thin, and she hesitated with her martini before she even accepted his hand. It made him a bit nervous, and Battaglia men were never nervous. Had she not received his flowers?

Nico pulled out her chair and she sat, placing her martini gingerly on the table, causing the olives to stir in the cloudy drink.

"You sent me the flowers?" she asked.

"I did."

"Why?"

A soft chuckle escaped him. "This is different. I'm rarely questioned by a woman as to why I would send her flowers."

She cleared her throat. "What I meant to say is I owe you

gratitude."

His brow arched.

"I know you helped us gain access to our building. I appreciate your assistance."

He gave her a gracious nod. She swallowed and her gaze darted everywhere but his face. In a moment she would rise and end their meeting. He felt the decision brewing inside her. "I make you uncomfortable?"

"Your note did."

"How so?" he asked.

"You said we had unfinished business? Other than the favor asked, I don't know you."

"But you do. We met."

"Briefly."

He tried to understand the reason for her open hostility. "Why are you so distrustful? Have I done something to offend you?"

She looked a bit thrown, then recovered. Her pretty eyes lowered to her martini when she spoke. "No."

"And the flowers?" he asked. "Were they upsetting?"

"No." She said in a flat tone. Her gaze returned to his and lingered before she spoke. "The flowers were beautiful."

"Like you."

A hint of a smile touched the corner of her glossed lips. "Let me guess, you summoned me because you'd like for me to design something for you and your wife, *Signora* Battaglia?"

Giovanni chuckled as he lifted his wine glass. Her gaze fell upon his ring and lingered. It was his father's ring. At its center an onyx stone with a gold letter B in the middle. "What makes you think I have a wife?"

"I saw her. She was quite lovely, *and* young."

"I'm not married. I have tailors if I want a suit, and she doesn't need me to negotiate a dress."

A waiter returned and offered to refresh her drink. She declined. He ordered his brand of malt, and the man slipped away. There was laughter from a neighboring table. Carlo and his boys were a bit loud. She glanced over causing her sparkling earrings to sway lightly. It gave him the opportunity to study her. She was different than most women. She possessed a gentle calm that mixed in with her beauty. Every man in the room had to lift their gaze when she passed by. He should have had this meeting with her much earlier. After all, she occupied a building that was rightfully his. Mancini was at the bottom of the little coup. He was certain of it. If the old Sicilian Don weren't a needed ally in Sicily he'd send him a message for interfering with his affairs. But Giovanni was painfully aware of how men looked upon him and his leadership because of the mixed blood in his veins.

Her curious round brown eyes returned to him. "You don't have an accent. Not as heavy as everyone else, are you—"

"My father is Sicilian and my mother is Irish."

"Oh."

She sipped her drink but again she averted her gaze. He'd prefer she look him in the eye the rest of the evening. There were moments when she came across bold and assertive and others when she was shy and uncomfortable.

"Why did you ask to see me?" she asked.

"I enjoyed the show and wanted to know more."

She smiled. "Oh. I see. You want to know more? Sorry, I don't entertain strange men."

Giovanni smiled. "Good. I'm not like those other men," he said softly.

"That's right your entourage is quite intimidating. Makes you important doesn't it?" She asked the question with a sexy smirk. He couldn't hide his approval in his smile. He studied her lovely face a moment before he answered.

"Am I?"

"Care to explain how you open doors closed to me in Italy and why?"

"No."

"Oh, c'mon, give a girl a hint. Who are you? Why did Francesco scurry away when you found us in the hall?" she chuckled.

"I'm not sure what kind of explanation you need."

"I'm new here," she began. "I've heard things about the men of southern Italy. Good and bad. I'm just trying to understand why you look at me the way you do. Why you sent me flowers and summoned me? What is it you expect, *Signore* Battaglia?"

"I'm a simple business man. I'm also a man." He leaned forward keeping her within his gaze. "A man who knows what he likes, and I have to say, *Bella*, I like you."

The tense frozen smile on her face and shock in her stare pleased him. She was delicate, but there was fire there. He sensed it. He caught a hint of a smile form over her luscious lips. And suddenly the spell was broken. She collected herself and spoke to him in a direct challenging fashion. "I missed the Italian gangster movie genre, exactly how does this work? Am I supposed to fall to your feet and be flattered that you're interested? Do I even have a say or will I be tossed in the Amalfi with bricks strapped to my feet if I reject whatever offer I'm sure you plan to make for helping me regain access to my building?"

"Gangster? You Americans and your imaginations. Just because I'm different than you doesn't make me nefarious."

She blushed. She glanced to Renaldo who stood behind him and then lowered her gaze. "I'm sorry if I offended you."

Giovanni chuckled. "Hardly. I do find it interesting that you feel the building is yours. It's a lease no?"

"Yes, but our solicitor—"

"It's only a lease." Giovanni said firmly.

Mira sat back. "What are you saying?"

"Protection, security, these are things you will need, *Bella*, so nothing unfortunate prevents you from conducting business in our lovely city. An investor like myself can prove to be quite useful."

She paused at the sweet endearment, and he knew she understood what *bella* meant.

"So your help comes at a price? You want in on my company. No. Absolutely not! This ends here. Do you understand? I want you to stop harassing me."

"It was you who noticed me if I recall."

"I didn't."

"As much as I would like to make this personal between you and I, we do have business. If you won't accept my offer to invest, then here is the final deal. You can continue to lease the property with a modest fee for my inconvenience, and I will have full access to the canals beneath your building that run out to the Amalfi coastline. The doors to the cellars in your building will remain under lock and key at all times. Are we clear?"

She blinked at him, a bit thrown by his frankness.

Satisfied, he relaxed his posture. She however, didn't. This one wasn't prone to hysterics. Her silence was as much of a warning as the sharp tongue she used when she sat down. He really did find her appetizing.

"How long does this celebration of yours last? I'd like you to join me for a late dinner," he said.

"No, thank you."

"You enjoy rejecting me?" he asked amused.

"That surprises you? I think you just threatened me."

"It's a first." He dismissed the comment of his threatening her. If he'd threatened her, she'd know it. She picked up her martini, took a long swallow, and placed the glass back on the table slowly. After a deep inhale of a steady breath, she spoke in that soft voice of hers. "Mr. ah, *Signore* Battaglia, I understand things are done differently here. I owe you nothing including access to whatever you think is beneath my building. I want you to stay away from my business and me, or I will... I'll contact the authorities."

Giovanni's brows lowered.

"I'm serious."

"I wish you would reconsider. I'm really harmless, until I'm disappointed."

"It was nice meeting you. *Buona sera*," she said rising from her seat.

"*Prego.* We'll meet again, *Bella*, and soon," he said raising his glass and toasting her.

The harsh uneven rhythm of her breathing made her exit less graceful. Still she straightened her spine and walked from his table without looking back. He didn't try to conceal who or what he was, and she'd known a few dangerous men. Maybe he wasn't a mobster but she knew a shady person when she met one. Kei had a checkered past before he became the King of

Wall Street. And the men he dealt with in business were more ruthless than any Mafia kingpin. Every now and then she'd meet some former clients of his at a party or social event she accompanied him to, and he'd dismiss the dark sinister leers she'd get from these men. Giovanni Battaglia didn't leer at her. His stare held more warmth than she knew what to do with. But he had made his wishes clear, and that did piss her off. *Who the hell did he think he was to try to intimidate her?*

In spite of her vow not to look back, when she reached the stairs, she gave a parting glance over her shoulder. He was lighting a cigar and exhaled a stream of smoke when his gaze lifted and connected with her. Two men who stared her way as well had joined him at the table. He spoke to one of them, and the man nodded with his eyes locked on her. Mira passed her empty martini glass off to a passing waiter and quickly went down the velvet steps. Fabiana was off to the side of the dance floor with a deep blush to her pale cheeks, and her large green eyes blinking up at Lorenzo. She marched directly to her friend.

"I must borrow my friend for a moment." She pulled her away gently. Lorenzo nodded.

"Having a good time?" Fabiana grinned.

"Looks like you are."

"I have some great news—"

"I don't. We need to get out of here and talk. I just met—"

Fabiana grabbed her by both hands and shook her head hard. "Listen to me first. We're going to start our vacation by the lake. Lake Como."

"What?"

"Tonight. We'll leave tonight and have so much fun. Ready to go? We need to pack."

"Well... I..."

"C'mon." Fabiana blew a kiss to Lorenzo and pulled Mira toward the door.

"Wait, I haven't said a thing to the guests. Shouldn't I?" Mira asked.

"The party can go on without us. They barely know what they're celebrating. Let's get out of here and pack. We have a car to pick us up in an hour." She could barely object as her friend dragged her out of the club. She tried to explain about Giovanni Battaglia's demands. Fabiana laughed. Said he's a businessman trying to cut a deal. She'd handle it. Mira sighed inside of the chauffeured car and figured she'd reserve the sobering questions for when they were sunning at the lake. She'd also give Teddy a call to look into the lease agreement. Gangster or not, Giovanni Battaglia's request didn't seem like one she could ignore.

Chapter Three

1970 Virginia

"ME-MA, CAN I HAVE IT? Huh? Can I?"

"What is it baby? Bring it closer so that Gran can see."

Mira hurried, though she'd been told countless times not to run in her grandmother's sewing room. She dodged a few boxes of clothes out of practice, and chairs stacked with books on different sewing techniques. She would be six in two days and her Me-ma had sewn a new dress for the party. Mira couldn't hide her excitement. She'd drawn three pictures and prayed really hard for a puppy. God would bring her one. Mira was sure of it. Bouncing on her feet she opened her palm and showed her grandmother the shiny thing she found in a soft black box in the back of the closet.

Her grandmother's smile dimmed. She didn't look happy.

"Me-ma?"

"This is yours baby." Her grandmother nodded. She plucked the gold link bracelet and fastened the clasp around her wrist. It fit. "See here..." Her grandmother turned the gold pate in its center around so she could read it. "It says Mirabella."

"That's not my name."

"It's what your father called you. You can wear it today, and then we'll take it off and put it back in the box."

"My father?" Mira's eyes stretched. She touched the engraving on the gold plate and blinked in wonder. All of her cousins had a father, and a mother. She knew her mother. They had her picture in the living room. She prayed to heaven for her and often visited her grave with her grandparents. But no one told her she had a father. "It's prrreeeetty."

Her grandmother pinched her chin and lifted her face. "You are a special little girl. Very special. Never forget that."

"I won't Me-ma... I promise. I'm Mirabella!"

The crescent moon against the starless sky cast such a lovely romantic glow across the mountains and sloping hills they drove through. The misty atmosphere rolled across the valley. Mira slouched against the backseat of their chauffeured luxury vehicle with her lids sagging to the point of closing. Every bone in her body had succumbed to exhaustion. The driver said it would be a little over an hour drive into the mountains to reach the lake. She prayed for speed.

"Where are we going again?" Mira yawned.

"To Lake Como," Fabiana mumbled. She used the tiny light pad on her day planner to cast enough of a glow to review something Mira couldn't see.

"What about Tuscany?"

"We'll do that in a few days."

Mira closed her eyes. "You've been rushing me since we left the club. What's up?"

"Oh stop. I wanted to get you out of Milan before you switched up on me and found an excuse to return to Naples. I called Angelique before we left, and New York is hammered with orders already. The press is climbing the walls to get an exclusive with you. Neiman Marcus wants to get your daywear line in their stores by August. Even the Prime Minister is inquiring. See here?" She turned the planner to show a calendar with the meetings and events planned for next month. "He's invited you to a charity dinner. Now be honest. If you found out any of this, you would have called off our vacation."

Once again her friend had her nailed to the wall. Mira smiled and relaxed. "It was a success, wasn't it?"

"Of course. It's time to celebrate. Reap what we've sown, pun intended," Fabiana smoothed her hand out across the plush peanut butter leather interior. "It's like we're floating instead of driving down the street, to paradise. I love this car. Hell I love our life. Don't get me wrong I'm a New Yorker, but I can really see *Italia* as home. You know?"

"You like him, huh?" Mira asked.

A sheepish smirk crossed Fabiana's glossed lips. "Whatever do you mean?"

"I saw you with him. When we got back to the hotel you were on the phone. Don't think because you're speaking Italian I can't tell. I saw you. My guess is he's coming to meet you in Como isn't he?"

"Close."

"Close?"

"We're going to his place."

"You have got to be kidding me!"

"What? I told you the other day he had extended an invitation for us to visit his vacation home. You seemed fine with it."

"Driver! Stop the car!"

Fabiana let go a gust of laughter. Mira had to suppress the

urge to join her. She was half-serious.

"All joking aside, if you will stop and listen to me I have something to tell you. Giovanni Battaglia propositioned me. I think he threatened me too."

"When did this happen?"

"At the club."

"How? How did he threaten you?"

"He didn't exactly, he implied I had to give him access to our building and pay him for his inconvenience. He was rude about it."

"Oh, Mira. They aren't in the Mafia. Damn I wish I had never mentioned the *Cammora* to you. The villa Lorenzo owns is in Bellagio. It's a beautiful lake city in Como. They call it the 'Pearl of the Lake'. I want us to really start again here. Enjoy everything *Italia* has to offer. Giovanni Battaglia helped us cut through some red tape. He knows how successful you are. He's working through the political landscape of Napoli to clean up the city's reputation and draw more foreign investors, I think. I'm sure I read it in the papers. He's trying to align with us, and that's to be expected. But he's not a threat."

Mira couldn't shake the uneasy dread filling her. "Fine. I sound like a broken record."

Sighing deeply Fabiana looked away to conceal her smile. "No. You sound like my best friend. The cautious, wise one. I'm the impulsive wild one. We balance each other out."

Mira burst into disbelieving laughter. "Please, Fabiana. When it comes to business you're a shark with lipstick. No one takes advantage of you. I want you to be the same way about your heart." Mira reached over and took her hand. "We're a team. We're sisters. We look out for each other."

Fabiana nodded. "Thank you for being the sister I always

wished I had."

"Promise we'll keep it light, and you won't be too impulsive this weekend," Mira said under a raised brow.

She smiled in defeat. "I promise that Lorenzo Álvaro Battaglia will have to part the red sea before he parts my legs."

Mira laughed leaning over to hug her friend. "Good enough."

On the lower level of his cousin's villa there were few doors and many open walkways that led to the outside veranda with a stunning view of the lake. The lonely rustle of the night breeze echoed softly. Giovanni stared out across the lake at the villas and hotels. When darkness covered the small city of Bellagio, the golden amber lights from residential windows and street lamps almost made the city and the lake appear mystical. Under a crescent moon the water shone like polished glass. He clasped his hands behind his back. Violence was the least of his worries. The fact that a man like Francesco could disrespect him under his cousin's watch unsettled him.

"Shall we discuss it now or later?" Lorenzo asked.

Giovanni cast his gaze back over his shoulder. "My decision is final. Arranging all of this won't change my mind. The club closes. Carlo will see to it. The insurance on the place should more than compensate you, after all debts are repaid to me of course."

"You think I invited the ladies here to appease you? I invited them and you here so we can get past our differences and understand each other again. I know *Isabella's* was my idea. I had no idea Francesco was the monster he turned out to be. It doesn't convict me. Ignorance is my only sin here."

Weary of the argument Giovanni turned and faced his

cousin. Lorenzo understood him better than any of those in the family, next to Catalina. They were raised together, blood. However, his cousin wouldn't be above arranging a romantic interlude to soften him for manipulation. What irritated him more after all these years was his cousin's continued struggle for recognition. They were supposed to be stronger than this petty jealousy bullshit.

"You failed."

Lorenzo threw up both his hands in defeat. "The family cannot survive like this. It's bigger than the grudge we hold with the Russians for Papa's death. Or the Albanians! You control *la Cammora*. Which means the girls, the business; all of it should belong to us. You can't have part of it; you have to own it all."

"We are not this bullshit!" Giovanni shouted. "Not anymore. Two hundred years ago we changed our fucking name to decide the family destiny. Baldamenti and the blood legacy that's washed through our family for two centuries is over. We are Battaglia men." Giovanni stepped closer. "Why do you think this was done? So we never evolve? Continue to wallow in scum? Become the men not fit to sit at the table with our ancestors? Can you only find glory in the slums with those gypsies you let in and out of our business? Or are you planning something else cousin? With Calderone?"

"Never."

"I know you aren't totally blameless. If I could prove your motives, well you should be grateful I haven't proven what motivates you lately, cousin."

"*La Cammora* is fracturing. The Calderone family plans to make deals with the Albanians that you won't, and they are growing in numbers. In Sicily, we're tied to tradition within *mafioso,* but here we can do things differently. That's why Papa Tomosino loved it best here. I know you have another vision for us, and I respect it, but I would fail you if I didn't advise you. The time to strike is now. Now." Giovanni shook his head in disappointment. Lorenzo continued. "You desire to legitimize us, and it's a lofty dream. No one would dare speak to you like this but me. Flavio is *consigliere,* and where is he? Listen to me, Giovanni, gambling, extortion, weapons, it's who we are no matter what deals you and Flavio make in the Republic. Nothing changes that fact. Why not go after the real money?"

"*Stai zitto!* Shut up." Giovanni walked away. "The Calderones and other families are laughing at you. At you cousin! And you expect me to lower myself for your glory?" Giovanni silenced. "I will tell you about lofty goals. Before the week is out, I plan to own the triangle."

The announcement landed hard between them. Lorenzo blinked in astonishment. Giovanni nodded to be sure he understood his words.

The *triangle* consisted of Milan, Turin and Genoa. The Battaglia family had run the *Cammora* out of Naples for close to eighty years. But Tomosino always wanted to expand into legitimate business. Real estate was prime in the triangle now, and Giovanni intended to fulfill every one of his father's dreams.

If he hadn't returned six years ago and accepted his birthright, the Battaglia family would belong to his cousin. He knew Lorenzo denounced the old traditions of the Sicilian Mafia publicly, but at his cousin's core, Lorenzo believed in the restrictive values that clearly said a non-Sicilian should never run the Mafia. Giovanni's mixed blood made some snicker behind his back. He had hoped by now that prejudice wouldn't be between him and his cousin. He had to wonder if that too was a lofty dream.

"While you were off in your fancy schools, I was here. I should be your *consigliere* at the very least. Flavio is out of practice and you seem to rely more and more on Dominic. He's a fucking kid that we both raised. What of me?"

"I can't trust you. I know this disappoints you, but it's the truth."

"I have earned my place at your side!" Lorenzo's voice boomed.

Giovanni shrugged. "Drugs will never be part of this family and neither will prostitution, not going forward. Let's be clear, though part of you thinks we are equals because we're blood, we are not. We took an oath. I run this family. You never will. If I hear of you meeting with Giuseppe Calderone again on my behalf, I will be forced to make an example of you cousin. And I'll enjoy it."

Lorenzo drew his lips in, and his jaw quivered with restraint. They were the same height, the same physical build; they even had the same blue eyes. At first glance, a person could mistake them for brothers. But they were as different as night and day.

He watched his cousin approach. Lorenzo kissed Giovanni on both of his cheeks and grabbed his shoulders to be heard. "*Ti amo, cugino.* I love you, cousin. Of course, of course, you are the boss of all bosses. Now let's stop fighting and enjoy the ladies. They will arrive soon." He stepped back with acceptance.

As an act of forgiveness, Giovanni pulled Lorenzo into a fraternal hug. He hated to fight with him as well, but the divided loyalties were becoming a real problem. He'd heard from Dominic that Giuseppe frequented Lorenzo's restaurant, and the men were becoming allies. The Calderone serpent only intended to feed Lorenzo's greed. Giovanni and the elder Don Calderone had bartered an agreement, which would allow the Calderones to conduct business within the *Campania*. In return, Calderone would help him with his bid to acquire more land in the northern territories. Giuseppe didn't want to see this deal through, and he needed Lorenzo at his side if he were to present a strong family front.

"Now, do you like this friend of Fabiana's, this designer Mira?"

Giovanni blushed. He'd been unable to stop thinking of her since he saw her long legs sashay down the runway. Even now his blood surged to his groin when he recalled her full lips and dark brown eyes. "She pleases me." He cleared his throat to rid it of the wavering confidence he heard in his voice. Together they walked inside.

"I don't ever recall you making a request for me to set you up cousin. I would say she does more than please you."

"Let's just say I'm intrigued. She's different."

Dominic, an enforcer and adopted little brother to them both, stepped in. Giovanni's father had taken him into the family at the age of three, and both men loved him like blood.

"I need to speak with Giovanni." He switched his gaze over to Lorenzo. "Alone."

Lorenzo nodded. "You can use my office. When the ladies arrive, I will send word to meet us upstairs in the parlor."

Giovanni turned and followed Dominic out. He glanced back over his shoulder. Lorenzo watched him. His cousin looked to be accepting of his decision. Only time would tell.

The narrow road paved in cobblestones jostled them in their seats. The car climbed upward at a reduced speed. Their destination appeared to be a villa carved into the mountainside. Mira gripped the inside door jam. "I feel like we'll roll back down the road. Jeesh, how far does he have to drive?"

Fabiana leaned forward with a hard squint. "The gates, look."

Double wrought iron gates were pushed open by the aid of men who blended with the night. Their suit jackets parted under their outstretched arms to reveal guns tucked in their pants. Mira careened her neck to be sure she saw the weapons. But the car moved on.

"I've been trying to convince you to buy a vacation place in Italy for years. Maybe now you'll consider one for Como after we finalize our real-estate issues in Napoli."

"Not sure if I can afford the army to guard it. Did you see that? Those men had guns."

"Guns?" Fabiana's gaze swiveled to the back window. "No they didn't. It's illegal."

Mira frowned. "I know what I saw."

The car came to a complete stop, and the ladies collected their purses. Mira emerged inhaling the sweet fragrant air. Wind whipped through the large palms circling the drive, and their leafy skirts rustled, as did the other lush cypress that was groomed immaculately. Her hair was blown away from her face. She smiled, fixated on the three-story block shaped mansion that was painted a soft melon orange with a flat rust-colored, shingled roof.

Fabiana walked around the back of the car. "Nice right?"

The villa appeared spacious enough to really make this mini vacation worthy of the effort. Mira glanced over at the driver who removed their luggage. Her most treasured piece being her leather portfolio case. "While you and Romeo do Lake Como, I'll sketch some new designs that have been keeping me up at night. Oh and sleeping. I can't wait to sleep in late for a change."

As they climbed the stone steps, Lorenzo filled the open doorway. The warm yellow light behind him cast shadows over his face, making him even more handsome. Mira watched Fabiana quicken her steps. Maybe Mira had been too judgmental of him. He did seem to be taken with Fabiana, and she knew how much her friend wanted to find love again.

"Fabiana, Mira, *benvenuta all'Bellagio*." He withdrew, allowing them to enter.

"*Ciao, Lorenzo.*" Fabiana blushed.

They were led inside between two regal Corinthian pillars. Mira entered a home of vast dimensions, as if someone with claustrophobia designed it. And what a beautiful villa it was. Vivid cool colors reminiscent of a spring garden covered the walls. Crystal, silver, and gold antiquities perched on marble pedestals all punctuated the cultural flavor. The high ceiling hall they were led down opened into an oval shaped entranceway with two elegant stairwells that connected up to the second level. The floors were polished marble under a massive pewter chandelier that absolutely sparkled. Tucked to the corners of the wide stairwell were two eight-foot tall statues of goddesses that looked authentic. Mira's eyes swept over the artwork. When her gaze returned to her host, he was staring at her intensely. A shiver went through her from the dark hard stare he gave her. In a blink, his gaze moved on, but she was sure she'd noticed something in the exchange.

"This way, ladies." He continued toward the large semi-circular staircase to the second level. Fabiana followed without thought, and Mira forced her legs to move. Pondering where they might lead, she slowly and cautiously climbed the stairs, all the while running her fingers across the smooth polished banister. What was there not to love about Italy? Who knows what the future held. The country had already inspired her work. As they strolled into an open parlor, she noticed how her friend's suitor slipped his arm around Fabiana's waist, keeping her close.

Again Mira checked the time on her watch. Maybe she would join them for a drink and retire to give them some privacy. Lorenzo stopped in the middle of the room and swept Fabiana up in his arms for a long kiss. Mira watched and waited, a bit uncomfortable. Her friend swayed when he released her. "If you don't mind waiting here, I have someone coming to take you to your room. I'm sure you're exhausted from your eventful day."

Neither girl objected, but they exchanged looks after his announcement. Mira half expected Fabiana to speak up. Instead, her friend held his hand and winked at her before she was swept out of the room. The pair passed another tall man, again with a gun tucked to the front of his pants. He positioned himself at the entrance of the parlor. His dark eyes, encased in long lashes, fixed on her.

Alone, she glanced around. It was a well-furnished parlor with bright lamplight. The cozy seating arrangement softened an elegant room divided into two distinct conversational areas. The L-shaped white sofa and a few large peach upholstered back sofa chairs were to the left. A mirrored bar with wine racks and a few large conversational chairs were to the right. How long did he intend to have her waiting here? Her gaze lingered on the bar. She loved Italian wine, and she was sure Lorenzo would have the best. She'd already had enough to drink for the evening, so she decided against the temptation. Mira passed the sofa and dropped her rectangular clutch purse. She ran her hands over her hips in her tight white pants, rubbing out the exhaustion in her fingers. Instead of a nightcap she decided on some air. She approached the outside balcony that overlooked the lake and smiled at the breathtaking sight before her. The moon had receded behind the clouds, but the lights of the city twinkled against the mountainous landscape.

"Amazing isn't it?"

She whirled on the voice behind her.

"I was below you staring out at the same moon. One of the loveliest moons this season." Giovanni entered with his hands shoved deep into his pockets. "Like you, I couldn't stop thinking of its beauty."

Stunned, she managed a reply. "You don't know what I was thinking."

"You'd be surprised all the things I know."

For a short moment, he enjoyed watching her. When he entered the parlor, he watched her stroll around the empty room, then out the French doors. She wore what she had on earlier and looked even more beautiful under the moonlight. The long layers of her hair blew slightly around her shoulders. His gaze lowered to her apple shaped bottom and slender legs. Lorenzo was right. He wasn't prone to pursuing women who didn't return his desires. However, from the moment he met her in the hall of his cousin's restaurant, she'd been quite unforgettable. She intrigued him. Was his keen interest because of her stubborn refusal of his charm or the suffocating loneliness he'd endured? He wasn't sure.

"What are you doing here?" she asked.

"I could ask you the same. As I recall, you had too much to do to entertain my dinner proposal."

Swiping her hair from her face, she expelled a frustrated laugh. "Did you know I was coming? Is this some kind of setup?"

"It's a response to your invitation."

"I didn't invite you here." She frowned.

Giovanni walked in closer to her so she could read the determined look in his eye. "Here, in *Italia*, if a woman takes notice and makes direct eye contact with a man like myself, it's considered an invitation."

"Oh please. So I can't look at an attractive man without him thinking I want something more?"

"You find me attractive?"

After a flirty laugh she turned back to the banister and faced the lake. She cast her gaze over to the left revealing her profile. He studied the delicate perfection of her slender nose, high cheekbones and full lips. "You find yourself attractive. Guess I was just agreeing with you."

Her head turned, and she continued to stare out into the night. Unable to resist, he stepped directly behind her. He was sure she could feel the heat of his desire radiating from his chest; his heart beat so fast and hard inside of it. But she didn't acknowledge his closeness, and it disappointed him. Flowers hadn't softened her, and his charm had no effect. What excited this rare beauty in his midst?

"I owe you an apology, *Bella*."

"Do you?"

"*Si.* I should have never insisted on you granting me access to your building."

"So now it's my building? Thought I only had a lease."

"It was impolite. I'm a little rusty on negotiating with someone... as beautiful as you."

At any moment, she'd know what it felt like to receive his touch; he stood so close. The smell of him caused her stomach to flutter. A spicy mix of cologne with a hint of something smoky and potent like the dark whiskey she watched him drink earlier. It was the most masculine appealing smell she had the pleasure of knowing in quite some time.

"You find me arrogant?"

"Extremely," she admitted.

"Pushy?"

"Definitely."

"Presumptuous?" he said, not hiding his amusement in his tone. Mira was grateful he couldn't read the smile lifting the corners of her mouth.

"When it comes to the way you've approached me, I'd say that word is key."

"And you still have to turn away from me so I can't see how much you enjoy this, us."

"I was here first. I'm not turning away from you *Signore* Battaglia. I'm just enjoying the night."

"Then why did you give me the same sexy look you gave me the first night we met? Forced me to rise from my chair and follow?"

"So you admit to following me?"

"I'll admit to much more if you turn around and face me."

If she honored his request, they'd inevitably be closer than she needed at the moment. The man was right. He did excite her a bit. But he was wrong to presume closeness would grant him any access to her past the sparring they've indulged in so far. He stepped back. She felt his body heat withdraw and exhaled, tightness forming in her chest. She turned and stretched her arms out with her hands gliding over the smooth surface of the railing she leaned against.

"That's much better, *Bella*. Tell me how do you like *Italia* so far?"

"I've had a very interesting time," she began. "After a few days here, someone stole my purse. I lost some precious items including my passport. Then I learn that the Mafia isn't a myth and wants to force me to pay them to operate my new business in Napoli. To make matters worse the Italian Republic puts a padlock on the doors and forces me to shut down my operations three days before the biggest show in my life. And wait. There is more. A handsome business man who seems to command a small army of men that follow him around with concealed weapons comes to my rescue, only to ask that I now pay him for the courtesy. And, of course, now I'm here with that same man, who thinks he can charm me with a few smiles and sexy winks."

"Someone stole your purse?" he frowned.

"My point is, I'm tired *Signore* Battaglia. I only have two weeks of vacation, then I return to a life that requires all of my energy. I'd like to spend the next few days relaxing, not fighting off the advances of men like yourself."

"Forgive me. I understand." He nodded.

"*Grazie*." She tried to step around him, but he slipped his arm around her waist so smoothly she stumbled forward and landed up against him bodily. Out of instinct her hand rose and pressed against the hard planes of his chest. He was tall. She stood in heels and had to tilt her head back to meet his intense gaze. "We're not done. What of my request?"

"For?"

"Redemption."

She swallowed. "How?"

"It's really simple, *Bella*, I'm here in Bellagio for a few days. You and your friend are guests of my cousin. Let me show you some of the beauty of the city. No strings attached."

The firm way he held her didn't lessen. She felt drugged by his clean-cut manliness and the firepower in his heavenly blue eyes. How did she go from escaping awkwardness to standing within his embrace and loving every inch of him?

"If I say no, will you leave without further argument?"

"Leave?" He seemed surprised by her request. "No I won't leave. I like the idea of arguing with you. We'll discuss it further until you see things my way. I'm a good negotiator." His gaze traveled from hers to the opening of her shirt, which she knew revealed the swell of her breasts pressed into the hard ridges of his chest.

"I think you should let me go now." Mira said under her breath, making no effort to pull away.

"If you insist. I wish you wouldn't."

"I insist."

He released her.

Mira adjusted her blouse. "If you want to stay here, it's your family's villa. I can't object. Do it. Just don't touch me again until I give you my permission." She walked around him and fast.

"There you go extending invitations again. Sounds to me

like you're considering it." He called out after her. Mira stopped and looked back. He stepped to the balcony when he spoke. Not bothering to address her directly. "I'm a man of words so be careful of the ones you choose with me, *Bella*. I may just take you up on your offer and do exactly what I want."

Her mouth opened to say something more, but she was out of words. He finally cast his gaze back over his shoulder.

"Lorenzo said you would be able to show me to my room. Do you mind? I surely can't find it on my own."

Giovanni nodded. He walked out to join her. "That's easy, your room is next to mine," he smirked

"Of course, where else would it be?"

Together they walked side by side with his long strides matching hers. Again she admired the artwork on the walls. It was a welcome distraction from the glances he kept slipping her. And when he spoke, her heart beat so fast she nearly jumped out of her skin. The man had her on edge.

"Care to tell me more about this purse incident?"

"Huh?"

"You said your purse was stolen."

"Oh, that. Yes. I keep trying to put it out of my mind. Fabiana and I were on *via Toledo* shopping. It happened so fast. A commotion in the streets then the next thing I know some madman on a motor scooter snatched it off my shoulder. My wallet was in it with my grandparents' picture. I also lost something irreplaceable."

"May I ask what?"

"A bracelet. My father gave it to me when I was a baby. It's gold with the name Mirabella engraved on it. I keep it with me always. Stupid to have it in my purse I know. But we moved here, and I've not really unpacked everything, so I kept it on me. I can't replace it or the pictures of my grandparents, which are all I have of them."

"Mirabella? Sounds like Mariabella." Giovanni said.

"And what does Mariabella mean?"

"My beautiful Mary, a Sicilian name given to precious little girls by their fathers. Your father Sicilian?"

Mira laughed. "Do I look like my father was Sicilian?"

"You look beautiful," he responded. "And your father thought so. He named you my beautiful Mira. You were precious to him."

"Thank you for saying that." Mira smiled. She felt precious every time she looked upon that tiny bracelet. Now its loss burned a hot ache into her heart. Giovanni's hand went to her lower back, and he gently held it there. To her surprise it was a comfort. She glanced at him, and he smirked down at her. They fell again into a comfortable silence. She stopped at a painting and smiled. "This is lovely. Who was the artist?"

"Morandi."

"It's bright. Lights the entire hall with the oranges and purples."

"I have a few of his originals at our family home in Chianti."

"Really?"

"Maybe I'll show you sometime."

Mira smiled and started walking again. "Maybe."

Stopping, he pointed. "Here we are. Your room. Should I come in and turn down your sheets? Wash your back, make you comfortable?"

The laughter felt free of tension and genuine when it escaped her. Despite her inner voice warning her to keep things light, she was beginning to like her charming suitor. She glanced over to the man positioned at the end of the hall with his hands clasped in front of him, standing stoic. The tall gentleman wore a gun tucked in the front of his pants. He looked at her and then moved his eyes away quickly.

"What's with the men all over the place with guns? What kind of business do you do?"

He looked over at the man then returned his gaze to her. "Occupational requirement," he said softly.

"So you are some kind of thug?" she asked frowning.

Giovanni only smiled. "No, Mira. I'm not a thug, just a business man with a gun."

She turned up her nose. "Good night," she said turning to leave. He grabbed her hand before she could escape him.

"Will you give me an opportunity to show you who I am without prejudice of who and what you think I am?"

"I didn't mean to be rude."

"It's okay, I'm a big boy. I can handle it. I only ask that you let me show you a nice time for a few days. You might enjoy yourself."

"Okay," she said letting go of his hand, going inside of her bedroom door.

Giovanni watched her close it in his face and wiped at his jaw, wishing she'd chosen to invite him in.

"Boss?"

Looking back over his shoulder, he saw Dominic appear from the top of the stairs, coming toward him, and he stared irritated "What is it?"

"Just wanted to let you know that all is handled. Don Calderone would like to meet."

Giovanni nodded. "I don't want Lorenzo involved in this meeting."

"Understood."

"And where is Catalina?"

"I've sent her back to *Melanzana*," he said referencing the house that Giovanni owned in Sorrento, which was south of Napoli.

"Send word to Calderone that we will meet tomorrow." He entered his room and closed the door. He needed a cold shower.

****

The sun waking her was a welcomed event. She would've overslept if not for the warmth that covered her face and burned away the remnants of sleep from her eyes. Normally, she preferred that all curtains and blinds were drawn shut. But after her goodbye with Giovanni Battaglia, she lay in her bed and stared out at the lake thinking of her heart's failing choices in the past. She didn't need a man. What she needed was a new life full of independence and adventure. She wanted to make her grandparents proud.

Mira squinted and slowly opened her eyes to the serenity beyond her large oval shaped window facing Lake Como. She lifted on her elbows to stare out across the calm waters. The serene beauty of it all made her a believer in paradise. In the morning the blue waters, green mountains and hills, and ice cream colored buildings looked vibrant and wonderful. She'd get out today and explore.

Rested, she dropped back against her pillow. The time check of her watch revealed it to be just after nine. Mira rarely slept this late. Most mornings she was awake at five, consumed with thoughts of her next big project. She'd work off what fatigue she had left on her treadmill and then begin her day.

Vacationing meant a complete change in plans. Sinking in to the soft cushion of the pillows she stared at the ceiling with thoughts of Giovanni Battaglia returning to her. The intensity in his stare and his self-confidence sent a rush of desire through her veins. He was unlike any other man she'd met. Feeling inspired, she rose from the bed in her revealing black lace camisole, and retrieved her portfolio folder. Her large sketchpad and sharpened pencils slipped out.

Maybe she knew how to vacation after all. Walking over to the vanity barefoot she dragged the chair to the window. Propping the sketchpad against her bent knee she began to sketch the scenery. Paying attention to details, she smiled as she felt herself relax under the flow of her pencil.

A soft click echoed from the door and her gaze lifted from her sketch. At first she smiled, waiting for Fabiana to enter. She had one pencil in her mouth and the other in her hand. The sketchpad rested on her lap with her knees raised and the heels of her feet pressed at the edge of the chair. Before she could lower her feet, the door opened, and Giovanni's head appeared. He walked in staring at her empty bed. Mira scrambled to cover herself. She rose abruptly with the pad clutched to her chest. "What are you doing in my room?" The pencil dropped from her mouth.

His gaze swiveled to the left. He dropped his stare to her exposed thighs, hips and the barely shielded dark V of her sex. She hadn't worn panties to bed. The camisole didn't pull down smoothly over the rise of her backside. So she discreetly pushed the pad down lower to keep that intimate part of her body shielded, which only revealed the tops of her breasts. It would be the best she could do. The blood began to pound in her temples and her breath quickened. He stood silent, staring, and her embarrassment soon turned into outrage. Mira wanted to scream at him. For some reason she didn't. The tension building between them forced her to reserve her energy for breathing. She glanced at her robe on the bed and knew it was too far of a walk to retrieve it. He'd see more of her. To her relief he understood her dilemma. Instead of leaving, he entered the room and picked up her robe then walked over to hand it off to her. She accepted the robe, and he turned his back.

"Why are you in my room?" she asked again, tying her sash into a double knot.

Instead of answering, he ran his hand over her sketchpad. "This is beautiful." He lifted it, held it in front of him, and compared it to the scenery beyond the window.

"Excuse me, I asked you a question?" Mira took the pad from his hand. She tossed it on the bed and faced off with him.

The new gentle persona he'd adapted to gain her attention had become exhausting. He wasn't used to overcoming suspicion over his motives when vying for the affection of a woman. Even his time spent abroad in college hadn't been strained when he had pursued young coeds of all races. This one here appeared to wake with a sourpuss. Yes, he found her attractive, and he enjoyed her coyness, but he wanted to be done with her refusal to trust him. "I came to wake you, but looks like you're an early riser like me," he forced civility in his tone.

"Will you leave, please, so I can get dressed?" She nervously ran her hand through her hair to smooth down the puffiness. Last night her dark tresses had a silky flow. Now it was thicker, untamed.

"Forgive me. We will be leaving for breakfast in an hour."

It would prove best if he honored her request for privacy, so he turned for the door. He paused. When he cast his gaze back to her, he saw the irritation in her face. She wore little to nothing under that robe. He'd seen enough of her curves to know any man who ever touched her had to be a lucky bastard. Fuck it all to hell, he wanted to be added to the list.

"Is there something else?" she asked.

"You're a designer, so you might care to know today is pretty casual."

"In *Italia*, no one dresses casual." She sassed him.

He suppressed his smile. "True. Maybe you can wear something you've made, anything but green. I think you'd look really nice in yellow today."

"I'm supposed to believe that you don't like green, and then put on green to spite you? You really must think I'm stupid."

"No, *Bella*. I think you're quite beautiful. That's the point. I'll be waiting."

She rolled her eyes at his remark, hearing the door close behind him. "Jerk!"

Mixed feelings surged through her. She tried to force her confused emotions into order. At this point she wasn't sure if she wanted to smile or frown. Who barges into a room uninvited? The man had nerve. At her foot was one of her many bags. She heaved it up to the bed, unzipped it and rummaged through the many pieces she had created.

"Dammit I didn't hang any of this up last night."

The crumpled silks and linens would require ironing, and

she hated ironing. Snatching one colored delicate garment after another, her hand landed on a pale yellow sundress. Holding it up, inspecting it closely, she smiled. "Green huh?" She turned to find an iron and stopped. Mira sighed. She glanced back to her luggage. "What is it about that man?"

The angry voices echoed from the parlor to the hall. Fabiana wavered, trying to comprehend what she was hearing. The loudest voice of all was Lorenzo's, and it appeared he had reason to be upset. His business investment in *Isabella's*, the restaurant, went up in smoke. He shouted in Italian over the injustice. She turned the corner and peered inside. Lorenzo leaned forward on the mantle above the fireplace, his head bowed, his hands gripping both ends. Without warning, he exploded and swiped his arm across, knocking over the small alabaster figurines. Several went crashing to the floor and shattered. He whirled on the two men watching, and his eyes flashed up to her. That glare held her frozen in limbo where all her decisions and actions hinged on what would come next.

The men took notice of her as well.

From somewhere deep in her core she summoned her voice. "I'm sorry, I thought we were um, leaving. I didn't mean to interrupt." Fabiana took a few hurried steps back and collided with a wall of a chest. The man steadied her on her feet and stepped aside. She became acutely aware of his tall presence. It felt as cool as the shadow of a passing giant. Like her he observed Lorenzo and the destruction around his feet with interest. She sensed the stranger's gaze shift to her, and she dared to look him in the face. He had dark black hair, and a dimple that dug into the crease of his cheek when he smirked down at her. It perfectly matched the notch in his chin. It was his eyes that threw her. Lorenzo's eyes were a dark shade of blue, almost like sapphires. For a moment this man's eyes shifted in color from clear blue like rain to a seductive shade of violet. She blinked. Was he for real? The guy smelled rich, stood taller than most, had broad shoulders and arms, and an edge that was razor sharp. Who was he?

The moment passed. He returned his gaze to Lorenzo.

He spoke in Italian and addressed the one he called Carlo. The man answered. He said he just arrived to deliver the news to Lorenzo that the club was gone and the whores were gone too. They spilt little blood in the entire ordeal. Apparently none of these men, except for Lorenzo, knew that she spoke Italian too. Fabiana's stomach turned sour.

Lorenzo cleared his throat and silence fell over the room. Again the eyes of the men returned to her.

He approached. "You look beautiful."

She rose in her heels and gave him her cheek to kiss. He ran his hand down her back and around to her hip, and Fabiana tried to remain unfazed by the brazen act. The truth was she had been rocked to her core. She suspected they had dealings outside of the law, but she couldn't deny it now. These men were dangerous.

"Is Mira joining us?"

"She's dressing." The man said in a tight controlled voice. Now he was staring at her again. As were all the men.

"Giovanni, allow me to introduce Fabiana Antonia Girelli. She is Mira Ellison's manager and business partner. Fabiana this is my cousin Giovanni Battaglia."

Fabiana felt momentary panic as her mind jumped on the name. This was the man Mira had told her about. "He's your cousin?"

"Yes," Lorenzo chuckled. "My mother was Giovanni's father's sister."

"Oh." A renewed wave of apprehension swept through her.

The tall handsome stranger nodded. "Nice to meet you, Fabiana."

"Thank you for your help. We both are appreciative. I think you men have business to conduct, maybe me and my friend should go, um, we were thinking of continuing down to Tuscany and um, I mean to Firenze or no, maybe Venice. Yes. We had plans to go to Venice to visit friends, so, we, um, we will leave."

Giovanni's brow arched.

"Silence woman." Lorenzo dismissed her ramble. "You and Mira are my guests for the next few days." He then addressed his cousin. "We'll rejoin you and Mira out front."

He tugged her by the hand and walked her out of the sitting room away from the glaring eyes of the other men. Fabiana stepped briskly in her heels trying to keep up with his long strides. They headed in the direction of the dining room area. She yanked hard on her hand, freeing it from his grasp. "Stop pulling on me!" She backed away from him. "You lied to me. Who is your cousin really? Is he connected to the *Cammora*?"

"No."

"And back there. Telling me to be quiet? How dare you!"

"You talk too much! Ask too many questions that are none of your concern. Don't speak on things you don't know. There is no alliance with the *Cammora*. My cousin is a businessman. That's it."

Fabiana narrowed her eyes on him. "Are you kidding me? I heard what they said. Whores, blood? What was that about?"

"None of your affair." Lorenzo dismissed.

"Then why were you so enraged?"

"It is none of your affair!"

"Mira said he asked for access to our building and payment for his friendship. Now I know why. You set us up, all the while you're telling me how good things can be between us. Go to hell. Mira and I are leaving." She turned to march away, but he grabbed her and brought her back to him.

"We are not done, Fabiana."

"Release me.

His hold tightened and his face came in close. "Relax, there is nothing to fear with me. Shhh..."

She stopped struggling, and he released one of her arms to stroke the side of her face. "Ah, *Cara*, so lovely. Forgive my rudeness. I reacted impulsively and frightened you." His voice was smooth in ways that thrilled and frightened her. His mouth brushed hers, and she felt currents of desire ripple through the tease of a kiss and warmly course down her neck to her breasts and quivering belly. She was brought up against his tall imposing frame, and his tongue escaped his mouth entering hers slow and easy. "Yes, relax," he breathed between the kiss until her arms lifted and circled his neck. He kissed her wildly, seizing her breath and draining all of her resistance. Fabiana's head rolled back, and she fought to remember why she should be cautious. All of her ached to be explored by him.

The kiss ended naturally. His forehead pressed to hers, his nostrils flaring, he held her tight to him. She blinked at his closed eyes and the long lashes that rested upon his high cheekbones. He was the most complicated, sexy man she'd ever known.

"I didn't mean to upset you." He confessed in a soft

unsteady voice. "I had hoped that if Giovanni and your friend met, this entire mess with your lease could be settled. What happened wasn't how she perceives it, how you perceive it. It's business. How things are done."

"Bullshit." Fabiana touched his cheek. "That's bullshit, Lorenzo."

He kissed her again. She circled his neck with her raised arms, returning his passion. The taste of him intoxicating, she felt weightless. He sucked on her tongue before his kisses trailed the slender length of her neck. He lifted her in his arms, feeding on her as her feet left the ground. She tried to say more, but her voice melted into soft moans.

Grabbing a fistful of his hair, she brought his face back to her mouth, devouring him with her own desperate kisses. Lorenzo walked her backward, pushing her up against the wall, causing her to lose one of her shoes as his massive frame pinned her to the wall. Fighting for control, she turned her head, breaking the kiss. "Wait," she said putting her hands up to his chest. Kissing her forehead, he lifted up from her, allowing her to ease to the floor.

"Too fast?" he panted, his face desperately close.

"Don't confuse me," she said trying to escape him. His arm flew up and kept her before him. Their eyes met. She struggled to catch her breath, staring into his eyes.

"Slow and easy. I can do that. Don't punish me for this misunderstanding. Trust me. I'm not the bad guy here. You know that, don't you?"

"Yes," she smiled up at him shyly.

"*Sono spiacente, Bella.* I'm sorry, beautiful. You keep me wanting more."

Timing could seal a man's fate. The perfect example would be the first time Giovanni watched the woman, who would soon own his heart, descend a flight of stairs. In a single moment, he was changed. It began innocently. After a brief update from his men on why Lorenzo threw his temper tantrum, he strolled out *il soggiorno* headed for the front foyer.

And then he saw her.

She wore a classy, yet sexy sundress. It was simple, strapless; the skirt did flare a bit at the hem and swirl around her knees. And she'd chosen the loveliest shade of mint green to flatter her medium brown skin, which stirred the loneliness in him. How long had it been since he felt anything outside of raw lust for a woman? What was this fresh, new desire that calmed his inner beast when she smiled his way? She hadn't fallen for his trick, or maybe she knew what would please him and for once decided to give in a little. Whatever her reason for the dress choice, he was grateful. Her hair was a riot of curls, picked out lovely and bouncing on her shoulders behind a matching headband.

Their eyes met.

"*Ciao*," she said.

He admired her legs as they came into view with each measured step she took. Smooth, hairless, and flawless as he imagined the rest of her body to be.

"*Bennisma*," he said more to himself than to her.

"*Grazie*."

Giovanni touched his chest. "I knew you were beautiful, but even I didn't know how much more lovely you could become."

She stepped down and walked directly toward him. "Is Fabiana around? I'd like to talk to her before we leave."

"Yes. She, uh, she is," he said, held captive in the deep brown swirls of her irises. They remained silent for a moment staring into each other's eyes. Fabiana and Lorenzo reappeared. Mira noticed first. Giovanni, however, could not look away from her.

"There you are!" She smiled in a way he wished she had for him. He blinked out of his longing trance and watched her go to the redhead and embrace her. He felt like a lovesick schoolboy. It had become ridiculous. He could see the smirk of humor on Lorenzo's face, and it made his chest tight with frustration.

"Excuse us." Fabiana said, taking Mira's hand and pulling her toward the hall out of earshot of the men. Her friend began to pace, wringing her hands. "I had no idea Lorenzo would bring him here. He's the one, isn't he? The one with the flowers, the man you said threatened you?" She spoke in a hushed hurried manner that alarmed Mira.

"He didn't threaten me." Mira touched Fabiana's arm. "What's wrong? Did he say something to you?"

Fabiana put a hand to her forehead and closed her eyes. "Here's the thing. I think I might be wrong about these men. The two of them could be connected to some dangerous people. Wait. No. The two of them are dangerous people. Lorenzo denies it, but I'm not stupid. I'm sorry, Mira. I screwed up. Again. I can think of something to get us out of here. You don't have to go anywhere with him. We can leave today. Let me think of something." Fabiana began to pace again.

Mira's heart sank a bit. She couldn't hide her disappointment. The more she felt herself drawn to this man, the more she tried to ignore that he might not be who he appeared to be. But this was just breakfast, and her time for fun was short. She glanced back out to the hall. The voices of the men speaking in Italian drifted along the hall, indicating they remained close. A small voice in her head warned her that she should tread carefully.

"I got it. I'll have Angelique call. You stall the men, and I'll have her call here. Say we have some trouble in Napoli, that we need to come back."

"No. No. That's silly. Do you think they will do us harm?"

Fabiana sighed. "No of course not. But I sure as hell don't think we know enough about them to stay here."

"Well, we are here." Mira shook her head. "And we accepted their help. Look. I spoke with Giovanni. We'll have breakfast and do some sightseeing. That's all. I don't want to antagonize them. And be honest, you aren't done with Lorenzo. Are you?"

"You don't have to stay here for me. I like Lorenzo, but you and Giovanni are not part of that."

"I know this. Fabiana stop. It's okay. Let's go." Mira turned and walked back out to the men. She could hear Fabiana on her heels.

"Shall we?" Giovanni extended his arm. Mira exchanged a look with her friend. For a minute he thought she'd further humiliate him by not responding. But she graciously walked over and hooked her arm in his. He walked them out, a bit more encouraged by her willingness to comply. Four armed men climbed inside cars and she was led to his Ferrari. The doors were raised and she eased inside covering her thighs with her skirt like a lady.

"Nice car," she said when he climbed in and the doors

lowered.

"Would you like to drive it?"

"No thanks. These roads are kind of narrow and scary."

"Hold on."

The car spit a cloud of dust and gravel as he wheeled it around and zoomed toward the open gates. Mira's heart lodged in her throat. "Could you slow down please?"

He nodded and eased them into a manageable speed. "We'll dine at *Villa Melzi*. I've had it arranged. I believe your friend and Lorenzo will take the yacht out."

"Wait? We're splitting up?"

"Is that a problem?" he asked.

She chewed on the inside of her jaw. "I suppose not."

"I was hoping to take you on a tour of the eastern hamlets, especially after seeing your sketch this morning. It's what you see from your window."

"Oh. Okay." She tried to force the nervous quiver from her voice. She needed to be confident. The man made her anxiety spike. Again she wondered about his interest in her. It couldn't possibly be her lease. And she did see him with a drop dead beautiful Italian girl, so he couldn't be lonely. *Stop it, Mira. It's just breakfast and a tour not a proposal.* She closed her eyes and forced herself to relax.

"Do you design men's clothes?" he asked.

"I do."

"Maybe you can design something for me?"

"I'm expensive."

Giovanni chuckled. "A lady of your talents should be."

Mira blushed and looked away, back out the window. They glided along until they entered the city. The cobblestone roadway made him more careful of his speed. From her peripheral view, she could see him shifting gears. Looking down at his strong powerful hand, she noticed the ring with the B on it, and she wondered about him.

"Is that a family heirloom?" she asked pointing to the ring.

He looked to his hand then at her. "It belonged to my father."

"It's beautiful, you two close?"

"I loved him very much," he answered.

His car phone began to chime, and she saw his hand leave the gearshift and him navigate the car with one hand while he picked it up with the other. She wondered more about his life and the kind of man he was. Deciding before she went any further with him that she would ask. He spoke in Italian, and Mira stared at his profile. When his gaze slipped to her instead of the road, she glanced away. She didn't need an interpreter to know that the call wasn't good news. Hanging up the phone, he down shifted.

"Is everything okay?"

"It will be," he said, and a hint of a smile tugged the corner of his mouth. She smiled back and relaxed in the soft leather of the bucket seat that seemed to be molded to her body perfectly. The day had promise.

Chapter Four

Mira admired the leafy groves of cypress until palms disappeared behind the looming architecture of the city. Every block shaped building in an array of colors from rose pink to mango stood at least four-stories tall with flat rust shingled roofs. Tourists and locals mixed along the sidewalks or zipped by on motor scooters. To her right, Lake Como glistened with still waters. She could see a few yachts with open sails resting lazily upon the deep blue under the morning sun. A ferry blew its horn as it approached the pier to unload anxious travelers. The car coasted into a reduced speed.

"You arranged breakfast for us here?" she asked, the question nearly stalled in her throat and nervous energy swelled into a tight ball in the center of her tummy. Of course, she didn't want to sound undeserving. However, the small lakefront town of Bellagio nestled between volcanic shaped mountains, two distinct lakes, and covered in bright colorful flowers, evoked such romance it was hard not to notice. Had he seriously gone this far to get her alone in a setting such as this? They really didn't know each other, and she hadn't been gracious about his advances so far.

"I wanted to be alone with you." The words slipped from his mouth in a husky voice that caused her to glance over, intrigued. Mira stifled a smile over the intense way he focused on the road. Did he always take himself so seriously?

"It's a beautiful day, isn't it?"

He didn't respond.

"Why do they call Bellagio the Pearl of the Lake?"

"Not sure. The temperature here is always nice," he began. They drove slowly along the stone roads. She peered out at the little quaint shops. "The island town is a peninsula. It sits in the heart of the *Lario*."

Intrigued, she glanced back. It was then she noticed the cars behind her. She was certain they were the same ones from Lorenzo's villa. Mira parted her lips to say so when her gaze fell upon his profile once more. He had such strikingly handsome features. His hair was dark as coal and thick. It reached just behind his nape and smoothed back from his face. His brows were silkily black and his strong jawline fit his cool serious demeanor. A man of his height with such broad shoulders and chest should have appeared stuffed in the expensive sports car. Instead his reclined posture looked relaxed. He covered his eyes with dark shades, the lenses reflective. But from the profile she could see his gaze slip over to her. She returned her focus to the road to avoid the awkwardness over being caught once again staring.

"I'm sure whatever you've planned will be nice, but I do want to see the city a bit. Before we go back to the villa, that is."

When he didn't respond, she admired the scenery outside of the passenger window. His sleek sports car parked a distance from the stone white villa, he turned to her, removing his sunglasses and tucking them in his front shirt pocket. The Ferrari doors lifted. His steady gaze bore into her with silent expectation, and she felt compelled to look at him directly. "We'll have to walk the rest of the way," he said. "I've requested a private tour of the villa. This too isn't allowed. I did it for you, *Bella*."

There was a tingling in the pit of her stomach. Her mouth went dry, and she swallowed trying to remain unaffected by his nearness. "For me? You sure about that?"

"Meaning?" A sly smile eased across his lips causing a dimple to rise in his left cheek. The man sure was confident. He stared directly at her as if he were to be rewarded. So she gave him a polite smile and single shoulder shrug.

"I think you have your own private motives."

"You do inspire me. Yes, I have my motives. Does that make you uncomfortable?"

Mira laughed. "Thanks for being so honest. I guess not."

"Good."

Once out of the car, he strode around to her side to offer assistance. She accepted his hand and stepped into damp grass. The four-inch spiked heel to her strappy sandal sank deep in the moist earth. "Oh crap!"

"Something wrong?" His gaze dropped to her feet.

"I wore the wrong shoes obviously." She lifted a foot and felt the other sink deeper. Before her hand slipped from his, a strong arm circled her waist. In a flash she was lifted, weightless. "Giovanni!" she gasped.

Effortlessly, he carried her around to the front of the car and placed her gingerly on her feet onto the stone pavement. "Better?"

She chuckled fixing her dress that gathered higher up her waist making the hem reveal too much of her thighs. "Yes, I guess so."

Mira discreetly stomped her feet and dropped clumps of dirt from her heels. The wind blew her hair forward. She was glad she chose to wear a headband to keep her thick locks from her face. The connection she felt with him returned when his gaze lifted and latched to hers.

"I'm fine. Really."

To prove her point she sashayed away. His long strides had him walking at her side in a flash. She glanced back and noticed they had a shadow.

"Is that man following us?"

"He and others." Giovanni answered, not bothering to look behind him.

It was then that she noticed two other men. One across the street and another a few paces ahead of them. They were covered on all sides. Mira held back from questioning him. Together they walked along the path and passed a very distinctive hostel. His stroll was slow and easy. The view of the lake and the gentle serenity of the city had her head swimming with ideas. Maybe her fall line could have some photos with Zenobia shot here in Bellagio. The scene was perfect. She'd have to remember to run it past Fabiana.

"Have I told you how beautiful you are today?" Giovanni asked when he gently placed his hand on her lower back to steer her toward the open entrance of the gardens.

"Oh stop." She rolled her eyes. His smile dimmed. *Had she insulted him?* He was trying so hard to impress her, and she wished he wouldn't. Maybe she could glean just what type of man he really was if he said something more genuine. After they continued their stroll in silence for a while, she eased her hand into his, and it was a perfect fit. "How old is this place?"

The villa could be seen just beyond the trees erected between the foot of green sloping hills and the lake. Whoever designed it had a real appreciation for where the beauty of Bellagio could be best seen. Mira cast her gaze out toward the lake and again felt a warm breeze soothe her.

"This was built in 1808 for Duke Francesco *Melzi d'Eril* as a summer home."

"How do you know the date?" she asked. "You sound like a tour guide when you say it that way."

"School. The Duke was assistant general to Napoleon and Vice President to the royal Italian Republic. Every school boy knows about the *Melzi d'Eril*."

"Oh."

"The gardens are open to the public, but the villa often isn't." Exotic trees with long leafy branches trimmed into an umbrella arch shaded the walk along the slender road. Mira noticed their destination would end at a bleached white paved terrace before the villa. The landscape was bright and colorful with exotic blooms. She kept glancing over trying to think of how to continue a conversation with him, but when he looked her way she lost her nerve. It wasn't just her. She noticed how he fumbled over his words or kept his jaw tight and his posture tense during their frequent uncomfortable pauses. Neither trusted the other to be themselves. That made her sad. It was such a romantic place.

"Do I make you uncomfortable?" Mira asked.

Giovanni chuckled.

"Is something funny?"

His stare was bold, and he assessed her frankly. "It's been

quite a while since I've felt less confident."

"Why? Because we're different?"

"Maybe, or maybe it's just because you don't *know* me."

As strange as she found his statement, something within the message remained clear. The man was the biggest mystery to her and that was by design. She doubted few people knew who Giovanni Battaglia really was.

"Those are gorgeous." She pointed to the wild blooms of red, lilac, and pink flowers. "What are they?"

"Rhododendrons and a few azaleas. They aren't my favorite. I will introduce you to my favorite flower."

A man, tall and pale with a flat unreadable expression, waited for them at the center of the lower level steps. A divided picturesque stairway circled him and ended at the doors of the villa. On either side, four austere, large lions carved of stone stood guard. Mira's mind conjured images of the days of Napoleon's men bounding up the steps with their swords holstered in their royal uniforms. An elderly couple stopped to gawk along a trail to the east. She'd gotten a few stares once she ventured out of Naples. At first in Milan they were because of her celebrity, but here she knew the stares were quite different. She figured not many people of color vacationed in Bellagio. There was a distinct feeling of privilege that went through her. She wasn't sure if she liked it.

The gentleman dressed in a dark navy blue suit stepped forward to greet them. His gaze volleyed from her face to Giovanni's before their eyes could connect. He greeted Giovanni with a kiss to both of his cheeks. Strange. Men greeted each other in Italy this way often. At home, she'd never seen it done so freely.

"What did he just say?" Mira whispered.

"They're ready for you." Giovanni extended his arm for her to lead. She climbed the steps and went left up another spacious flight before walking through the villa doors. They entered a cool unnaturally quiet entranceway. Portraits hung above busts carved out of marble. Each bust depicted nobility and was centered on an elegant pedestal. They passed a few baby cannons that were aligned symmetrically and pointed north.

"This place looks like a museum." She observed. Giovanni wasn't at her side but a few steps behind. Mira tried not to walk with too much of a sway to her hips. She didn't dare check to see how he watched her. Each time their eyes met, the pull on her insides made her courage falter. Even now her stomach fluttered with excitement from his unwavering interest. Kei was once passionate for her. Always attentive and romantic, their cultural differences in New York didn't matter. Being different transformed her life.

The light sway of her hips made his blood hot in his veins. The hem of her dress only reached two inches above her knees. She had lovely toned legs, and with her feet perched in her high heel shoes, the calf muscles to the back of her legs bunched and her thighs became tight, shapely with each step. All of which excited him. Giovanni rubbed his jaw and shook it off. The lady wasn't one he'd likely pursue. She challenged him too much, had too many opinions, and questioned everything she saw. He liked his women more accepting of things they didn't know or understand.

A quick glance at his watch and he knew the business with Calderone required a few discreet meetings with the other families in this region. Word had spread of the raid of

Lorenzo's restaurant, and he intended to silence all wagging tongues. His cousin's recent tantrum had not been forgotten. However, she compelled him to delay the matter, and this intrigued him. Dominic had made the arrangements for their day. A woman like her would expect to be romanced rather than seduced. He could aim to do both.

The villa didn't often open its doors to the public. They would dine in the glass house with the panoramic view of the gardens. The staff had set the table over white linen with navy plates and gold utensils. The centerpiece had an elegant arrangement of blue roses; his mother's favorite flower was among them. Dominic had an odd sense of humor. The sight of the flower made his heart skip a beat and his mood lighten. Should he share the reason?

"Oh how lovely! I've never seen a blue rose before," she exclaimed. It was the reaction most women had when they saw the flower. He assumed it was also how his father seduced his mother away from her family.

"It is my mother's flower. Our family grows them; we even have blooms here in the gardens."

"Really? That's the first time you mentioned your family interests."

A sly smile lifted the corner of her rose-colored lips, and he felt his temperature rise. She liked to tease him. "Someday soon I'll show you more about my interests."

He eased out her chair, preferring to be the only man in the room to do so. Gracefully, she lowered into it and removed the dark blue napkin to spread across her lap. "This is sweet... all of this. I didn't expect it."

Giovanni held his tongue. He had no intention of apologizing further. In fact he found it surprising that she kept mentioning his prior behavior, especially since she had moved her business into property that was rightfully his. She was one of the few people living he'd ever apologized to. His father had probably sat up in his grave when the words fell from his lips.

"You American women like to lead." He stated, his tone purposefully flat with little accusation.

The smile she offered in return was radiant. Her chocolate brown irises sparkled with curiosity. "Lead?"

"Yes, you and your friend are quite independent. Did you two build your company alone?"

"If you are implying that I didn't need a man for my success, that's correct. I have investors, but I own Mirabella's. Fabiana and I have built our business from the ground up."

"I'm not implying anything. I stated it." Giovanni relaxed in his seat keeping his attention trained on her. She met his stare dead on. This, too, he appreciated. Her full bow shaped lips glistened with the loveliest rose-colored gloss, and her long lashes made even a blink from her a seductive invitation. "How is it? Being the boss?" he asked. The drink waiter came forward with a carafe of his selected wine.

"You tell me. Looks like you're more of a boss than I."

"A bit lonely at times. Unfulfilled?"

"No, not really. I stay busy."

He nodded. "Which is probably why you're so... uptight?" he mused.

"How dare you suggest that I'm cold?"

Giovanni released a gust of laughter. How did she make that leap? Cold? The heat radiating from her would warm any man's bed, or heart. The last thing to cross his mind was her being cold. She missed his point. The woman reminded him of an overstressed spring ready to snap at the slightest prodding.

Though she had her moments, such as holding his hand and the polite smiles during conversation, he could not really break through the force field around her. If he touched her without permission, she'd flee. He was certain of it.

"I would never presume you were cold. In fact, I find you quite remarkable. I'm only suggesting that like most people you have a lot to learn about what it will take to make you happy."

"And you're an expert on happiness?" she smirked. "Looks like your talents aren't used for making people happy but evoking fear."

"Fear? An interesting choice of words." Giovanni glanced toward the private chef and drink waiter. He spoke directly to them in Italian and asked if they were afraid of him. The men glanced at each other then back to him not sure how to respond.

"What did you ask them?"

"If they were afraid."

"Why ask them? They won't answer you directly." She glanced toward Renaldo who stood off to the corner of the room. "I'm sure even your hired escort tells you what you want to hear."

Giovanni looked to Renaldo and smiled. "I guess you make a valid point, *Bella*."

"I wasn't trying to insult you."

"Don't apologize to me for speaking your mind. I will admit that I'm not used to it, but I don't want you to ever feel that you can't be yourself around me."

"Are you a drug trafficker?" she blurted her next question.

The humor in the moment faded. In a flash, she went for his balls. Taken aback, he didn't know quite how to respond, but the intensity in her stare suggested he say something.

"What did you ask me?"

Clearing her throat, she spoke in a direct manner. "I realize the question is incredibly rude. I've wanted to ask it since I saw the men with guns. First the demands you made on me disguised as a favor for helping me with my business—"

"I've already explained that—"

"And now all of this. They treat you like you're the Prime Minister. You aren't the Prime Minister. Are you a drug dealer?" she asked again.

"No, we detest drugs. No one in my family or business deals in that poison." He let the answer settle with her until he felt she relaxed a bit before he continued. "If you get to know me, you'll find me as harmless as a lamb."

It was her turn to laugh. "I doubt it." Her plate was placed before her, then his before him. He had no appetite. But he did want to watch her eat. Everything she did aroused the sleeping giant in him. Maybe Lorenzo was right, and it had been too long since he had the pleasure of a woman's company? It could explain the burning interest he had in this one.

She studied her breakfast. The chef poached some eggs and sautéed fish, scallops and sea urchin in olive oil and basil. This he explained to her. He'd been to America and knew that eggs were expected for breakfast. Everything else was his own special request.

"Sea urchin?" she frowned.

"It's love on the palate. Give it a try."

"I guess I'm not used to this." Her gaze flickered back up to him and then swept the glass house.

"Used to what? A man taking a sincere interest in you?"

"A man as arrogant as you, who's obviously dangerous, so intent on pursuing me. It's a little hard to take at once."

"How can I relax you?"

She sighed. "It's not necessary, I'm relaxing."

"No you aren't, but thanks for pretending. Tell me what it will take to make you comfortable around me."

Mira picked up her wine and sipped it. "Okay, how about a friendly game of Q and A?"

"Q and A?" he repeated not understanding her.

"Question and answer...I ask you answer."

Giovanni stared at her for a moment deciding on the interrogation. "I'm willing to try," he said not touching his food, preferring her and the new game between them. She smiled and put her glass back on the table.

"First question, where were you born?"

"Mondello Beach. It's in Sicily."

"Did you go to college?" she asked.

"I did."

She stopped chewing. If she weren't such a lady her mouth would probably be agape. Did she really think him a thug?

"You did?" She used her napkin to cover her mouth while she spoke.

"Shocked?"

"Oh, no. I mean... I'm sorry what school?"

"Harvard."

She stared into his handsome face, realizing her impressions of him were unfounded, and she'd been extremely prejudiced. He went to college in America? She hadn't expected to hear that. "What did you study?"

"International law. I left my last year of school."

"Why?" She swallowed, her voice soft with concern.

"My father summoned me. Two days after my return he was shot. He died of those wounds later. The family needed me."

"That's awful." Her hand reached across the table and covered his. Giovanni smiled, turning over his hand so his palm could grace her soft smaller one. He imagined all of her was as soft.

No, he didn't find her cold. He wanted more of the warmth he felt like this. "*Grazie, Bella.* I'm okay now with my choices."

"And his death?" she asked. "Did they catch the people who did it?"

Giovanni hesitated. He never picked at that wound. "No." He half-lied. The *Polizia di Stato* didn't catch his father's murderer, but he had. Thanks to his cousin. The lovely woman before him wouldn't appreciate his brand of justice, so he kept that information to himself. The softness of her touch drew away and he clasped her hand tightly to prevent her escape. He brought her palm to his mouth and pressed a soft kiss to the center. "My turn."

"Okay."

"Where were you born?"

"Small town in Virginia. The United States."

"Do you have a husband?"

A shadow of regret passed over her pretty features. It was so fleeting he couldn't be sure. She flashed a sweet smile and shook her head slowly. "No."

"Boyfriend?"

"No."

"Lover?"

Her gaze lifted and rested on his. They stared into each other's eyes for another uncomfortable pause before she spoke. "No."

"Why Italy? I've read in the papers that you are

permanently relocating your business to Napoli."

"It's true, I plan to make Napoli my home. I chose Italy because, well, it's a good balance between tradition and fashion. I love all that I've seen."

"Sounds like a statement you'd make for the press."

She blinked, shocked. Then she laughed. "You're right. It's the statement I gave to the press."

"Okay. I'll ask a more personal question. Why did you choose to design women's clothes?"

"What woman doesn't like fashion? It's all I've ever wanted to do."

"Surely there's more, another reason?"

Mira eased her hand from his. She sliced into her fish. "You've seen my work. That's my passion. End of story."

A more patient man would have moved to another discussion. He was never a patient man. There was more to this woman than the fancy dress he saw her grace along her runway. She looked stunning, but out of place around the flashing bulbs and applause. Dominic told him that the Milan show was the first she'd been invited to in *Italia*. Lorenzo shared that Fabiana was intent on a vacation for them both. An escape. Why would she need an escape from her passion?

"You're doing it again."

"Doing what?" He smiled.

"Staring."

He nodded. "I guess I am."

"Something else you want to say?"

Giovanni fingered the stem on his wine glass. He watched her lips part to accept a small portion of fish from her fork and the way she chewed lightly, the tip of her tongue peeking out to swipe at the corner of her mouth. What man wouldn't stare?

"Who are you? Really?" she asked.

"Now we're back to me? Is that your final question?"

"Depends on your answer." She winked.

"I'm a man who makes it his business to understand the motivations of people. What they want, what they need, what their weaknesses are."

"Why would you become that kind of man?" She frowned.

"A birthright."

"Interesting." She ate a bit more.

"When I was a boy my father decided to test me. He made me stand on the edge of a cliff and jump into the sea."

Her gaze shot back to him. "What? How old were you?"

"Five or Six." Giovanni said. "Do you know why he did that?"

"That's awful. Your father forced a six year-old to jump off a cliff?"

"I survived." His lips twisted and settled into a smile. "Do you know why he did this?"

"No. I don't know why any sane parent would do that to their child."

Her bitter reply was followed by a deep frown. Giovanni conceded that Tomosino had ways that kept his mother in fear most of her life. But as a man he understood his father much better now. "Shall I explain?"

"Please."

"A father wants a son in his own image. Mine did. The events in our childhood strengthen character, shape our lives, and decide the steps we will take to be the people we are born to be. I'm his son. Many still question this fact, and I suppose he did too at one point. Not because of the blood in my veins but my heart and what it was made of." Giovanni's voice became hoarse with emotion. He never spoke of his father so openly, not even with Catalina. To show weakness in his life would be a deadly mistake. Mira listened intently. She soothed him, even seduced him with her patient understanding. So he continued. "We are who our parents raise us to be. My accomplishments and failures are because of what I learned the day I jumped off the cliff. I'm Tomosino Battaglia's son and someday I'll be made to prove it. Now I'll ask you again. Who are you, Mira? And why do you design women's clothes?"

Mira recoiled a bit inside to hear the hard truths of his childhood. He seemed so jaded by it all. A father who would force his young boy off a cliff sounded like a madman. To hear Giovanni speak of him, it was an act of love. She lowered her fork. Her heart softened for the man in front of her. Though handsome and obviously wealthy, he sounded empty She stared into the misty blue swirls of his eyes. All too quickly, she ran out of diversions. Her chest swelled with remembrance and emotions of her empty childhood. The choices she made were shaped from it. He was right.

"Who are you?" he asked again.

"I'm Mary Ellison's granddaughter."

"And what does that mean?" He pried at her in a voice both comforting and compelling.

The sadness surfaced as it always did when she thought of her long dead grandparents. She opened her mouth to explain her doubts and couldn't find the words. To talk of them in the past tense only made the present bleak, void.

"She's gone? Mary?" he pried.

Mira glanced away. The invisible hold he had on her lessened when she looked away from his eyes. How the hell did the conversation take this turn? His hand eased across the table. The tips of their fingers touched. He didn't take hold of her hand. She forced herself to return her gaze to his. The man preferred it. She could tell. Swallowing a dose of courage she spoke but her voice sounded shaky and small. "I lost my mother when I was a baby, and I never knew my father. My grandparents raised me. I had no other siblings. My extended family wasn't around me as a child, so I didn't get to know my cousins or aunts. I spent a lot of time with her. I called her Me-ma."

"I wish I could see you as a girl. I'm sure you were quite excitable."

"I could be. My grandmother said I was inquisitive. She taught me to sew. Together we created so many pretty things for us and the women in our church. She never had her own store, but she had the talent. She taught me so much with a sewing needle. Designing women's clothes comes naturally to me, and it's who I am." The admission was dredged from a place of pride and strength and suddenly the truth of her past didn't hurt as much. However, he had no right to those memories. No one did. She pushed back from her table and rose. "I need some air." She mumbled and walked off. Her steps became a bit hurried once she left the glass house and entered the villa. Sometimes being alone in her life suited her. She had her work, and she had her friendship with Fabiana. To not have a family to share her success with was a price she had grown to accept, until she met Kei. He helped her believe they could achieve more, but when he tried to offer it she realized that even with him she felt alone. What did that make her? Cold? Lost? Incapable of happiness?

"Mira?"

She wiped at the corners of her eyes and turned to find him in the hall with her. Lost in her thoughts she hadn't considered where she was walking to, just that she needed to get out and into some fresh air so she could breathe again. "Give me a minute."

She faced away and wiped at the tears brimming in her eyes. He walked up behind her so suddenly she whirled to fend off his closeness. But he kept his pursuit until she was flush against the wall.

"I said give me a minute."

"I upset you. I seem to have a habit of doing this. What makes you cry now?" He brushed his thumb under her eyelid and her breath caught.

"Now? I wasn't crying in there."

"You know what I mean."

"All I know is I need a minute. It's personal, okay?" She tried to shift aside and away from him but he crowded her. Her cheeks burned hot with shame but the dominant reaction was regret. She regretted exposing this wound to him; he seemed like the kind of man that could turn her inside out if she allowed it.

"What can I do?"

Mira wanted to laugh in his face. Instead she closed her eyes and shook her head slowly. There was little left of her grandparents now. Just memories. She had her damn purse snatched and lost the picture she had of them and the bracelet she's carried all of her life. Dumb. Stupid. How could she be so careless with her treasures? A sob wedged in her throat and she neared tears again. The sensual rub of his palm against her cheek was shockingly comforting and she found herself turning her head toward his touch instead of away. Despite the warning of her inner voice not to do so she lifted her gaze to him. Mira couldn't break the instant connection between them. It felt like her life depended on maintaining his stare.

His chest rose and fell a little more deeply and her nipples extended from contact. Each brushed hard ridges that sent sweet quivers through her abdomen. She drew a deep breath to ask him to step aside, and he obliged by stepping closer to kiss her.

The brush of his lips over hers was more persuasive than she dared to admit. His moist firm mouth demanded a response, and she gave it willingly. Her arms slowly lifted and his hands smoothly traced down her sides to grip her hips and bring her up against him once their tongues united. The smoldering passion she found in his kiss was hotter than a thousand suns. She held to him by his nape, her head went back, her eyes lowered in submission. A deep intake of breath filled her lungs with his strong aftershave and clean male scent. Giovanni covered her with his broad chest and powerful arms. She felt her knees weaken as his mouth descended with a series of slow shivery kisses along her neck.

How could she abandon everything for a kiss? Easy. One kiss from this man and all her long suppressed feminine desires surfaced. A fresh, uncharted arousal stirred and made her moist between the thighs and achy at her core. Mira sighed. His mouth returned to hers. He crushed her up against the wall. Taking one of her hands by the wrist he pinned it above her head while he pressed what felt like steel against her lower abdomen. She wasn't prone to giving into a man so easily. He'd seized on her weakness and became her conqueror. As his firm demanding lips caressed hers, and his tongue darted in and out of her mouth, he whispered in Italian, words of desire so decadent they melted her insides.

"I don't understand all of what you're saying," she groaned.

Once more her head began to spin. Raw lust and frustration clashed within her. She could barely move, but her legs parted under his instruction allowing him greater access. She bent her knee to place her foot on the wall and steady herself. Otherwise she'd slip in a puddle of emotions to the floor. There would be no escape. The hold on her wrist tightened, and she tugged on his grip to no avail. So she pushed at his arm with her free hand and then his shoulder, all the while deepening their kiss.

For air and some sense of control, she turned her mouth from his, but his lips across her neck were just as lovely. She groaned deep in her throat and summoned a single word.

"Stop!"

He did.

Giovanni's head lifted, and he blinked, a bit confused, trying to look into her face to understand her command. It was then his grip lessened enough for her to pull her wrist free and press hard against him. "I said stop. Don't kiss me again!"

"Why?" he demanded, keeping her pinned to the wall.

"Because it's making me uncomfortable."

"Never pegged you for a liar, *Bella*."

She glared. "I'm serious. Let me go."

The humor in the moment drained from his face.

"I just need some air. Now, please!"

Giovanni stepped back, keeping his hands raised to show her he would oblige. She hurried away from him. The doors to the villa and terrace were open, and she marched out into the sunshine. Finally, she could breathe. She'd lost her head. Flirting with the man was one thing, but kissing him was something far more scandalous. The press was hot on her heels after the breakup with Kei and his divestment of their business. She could see the headlines now. No one believed her talent unless a man's name was in the byline. Mira shook her head and hugged herself against a balmy breeze coming in through the thin leafy branches of the surrounding large trees. "Excuses, excuses, you know the real reason girl," she mumbled. The truth was she enjoyed the lapse in control too much.

Soft footfalls drew her attention back over her shoulder. Giovanni hurried down the steps to join her. His hands shoved down in his pockets he looked unfazed by her rejection. That stung too. He probably thought she was some flake or maybe just a quick conquest not worthy of the trouble.

Ugh! Weak and needy is not attractive, Mira.

"Don't move. Wait right there." He called out to her.

Mira rolled her eyes. "I asked for a minute please. I just want to be alone." She turned left and started toward the tiny bridge that crossed into the gardens. She thought his request was a command and not a warning. Before her was a bed of lilies covering a shallow pond. Too bad she realized it too late. One step and her foot sank. Mira's arms flapped out from either side and her eyes stretched so wide all the muscles in her brows went tight. She turned to escape the fall and went backward screaming. Water splashed upward from all sides drenching her. She landed on her butt. Giovanni stopped. He blinked at the scene. At first shock registered on his face, then laughter exploded from him further wounding her pride.

"Don't laugh at me!" She pouted.

The shallow water of the pond reached her waist. White lilies floated around her on the rippling waves and a spray of tiny bugs flew out of their petals. She squinted and swatted them away. "Oh my God! I'm so embarrassed."

"I'll help you!" Giovanni surveyed the scene. He gauged his step but still his expensive loafer sank in the murky pond, drenching the hem of his pants leg. Mira smirked once his palm extended out to her. The smugness in his eyes and smile could not go unnoticed. She reached for his hand. When Giovanni aimed to pull her up, she summoned all her strength to pull him down. He anticipated her move, and with one quick jerk of her palm he lifted her and caught her up against him. His powerful free arm scooped up her soggy dress and legs, and he held her in his embrace as if she were a child. His men stood off in the distance, observing. She glanced over to see them frowning at their boss. He not only carried her but the water and lilies she had been submerged in. They were a sight.

Giovanni snarled a few curse words under his breath stomping out toward the paved walkway. She stuttered out hard laughs. "Guess the tour is over. I have to change." She told him once he set her on her feet.

"Let's go this way. It's a shorter walk and you can see more of the gardens. Breakfast is ruined." He took her by the hand, and they began to walk.

"Breakfast was fine. I enjoyed it."

He sucked down an impatient breath and kept walking. Mira couldn't think of anything to say in response. The smile on her face didn't fade. Seeing him trying to remain rigid and in control with muddy pants and ruined shoes was far too cute to ignore. This time he took her hand, a bit more possessively. Of course his men remained as their shadow. When she glanced back she could swear they were suppressing the urge not to laugh.

"I embarrassed you?" she teased.

"I said never mind it."

"You're cute when you're embarrassed. Your eyes stretch and your nostrils flare like a bull."

He lost his step. He glanced down at her. She winked. He shook his head and smiled. Together they walked along a short path at a moderate pace. She blinked at the most exquisite of sculptures in the center of a stone fountain. An enchanting likeness of a woman from ancient times stood at least seven feet tall. It looked Egyptian, definitely Egyptian from the headdress and features.

"Napoleon kept the treasures he'd stolen from Egypt and brought some here. That is one of them. She's a goddess of some sort. Not sure which."

"She's stunning. I wonder what her name was? Probably a Queen or—."

"We should go." He pulled her past the sculpture. Mira frowned. She removed her hand from his and he finally took notice of her disapproval. He stopped and stared at her.

"What's your hurry?"

"I'm done here. I want to leave."

"You are angry."

"I can take a joke." He dismissed the incident in the pond with the wave of his hand. Of course he would since she failed to pull him in.

"No. You're angry because I kissed you and then pushed you away. Right?"

Exasperated his hand flew up in defeat. "I kissed you. You have every right to turn me away. It's your choice."

"That's not an answer."

"I'm not angry. Disappointed? Yes. Angry? No."

"Well sorry to disappoint you, but I don't take to kissing

men I don't know." She crossed her arms and tossed her chin upward.

His face was hard, cheeks stark red, and his gaze intense, focused solely on her. "Are you toying with me, *Bella*?"

The question was valid. She wanted to argue with him, play with him, and make him chase her a bit. She realized if he took her back to the villa then it could very well mean the end of their mating dance. And she kind of didn't want it to end on a sour note. "I'm not a tease, Giovanni, I just expect things. A girl has a right to, you know. Not every man is entitled to a kiss. At least not a kiss from me."

"Which makes me want to kiss you even more." He stepped closer, her attention riveted. She lifted her chin higher to maintain the connection they shared. "Boils my blood to think any man has tasted you before me."

The gravel in his voice made her toes curl. Mira drew in a quick, harsh breath. "You can't be serious?" Her entire body quivered with heat after his proclamation. His left brow quirked upward and a sly knowing look of her inner weakness covered his features. Damp and sticky between her thighs her wet panties clung to her like another skin. Nothing alleviated the heat gathering in her core and warming her inner channel. She forced her gaze downward to her ruined designer original. Muddy stains had the fabric shriveling and looking worn. How anybody could find her attractive now was a mystery. Yet she felt like the most desired woman under his stare.

His eyelids fell to her lips, darkening his crystal violet stare to the deepest shade of sapphire blue. She held her breath and braced for his lips to reunite with hers. Oh yes, she wanted another kiss. Did he know? Instead he shifted his gaze to one of his men who had wandered too close, and the spell was broken.

"Let's get you changed. Maybe we can see more of the city and salvage the day."

Giovanni again extended his hand. Mira felt as if even the insects held their breaths waiting to see if she would accept. She did. He walked her out of the garden toward his car. Mira felt drained and empty by the end of the short tour. She sat in his car quiet. Would it have been so terrible for her to loosen up and just enjoy the man? Fabiana would have. Kei told her she was cold inside at times, and she believed him. She didn't trust happiness. She knew how badly it hurt when one lost it.

"Can I ask you a question?"

"Yes."

"When we kissed."

Again he wore dark sunglasses but she felt his stare shift in her direction. "Yes?"

"You said something in Italian, what were you saying?"

The sly smirk on his mouth made her heart flutter. "Why? You didn't enjoy the kiss?"

"I never said I didn't enjoy it." She gripped the inside of the door as he accelerated around a very narrow curve along the mountain. "Slow down, please."

He eased off the gas, and she relaxed. Still the cramped roadways made cars and the ride uncomfortably close.

"Thank you. I want to know what you said. I know a little Italian, and I could understand some, but not all."

"I cursed where we were when you gave me our first kiss. I said if we had a bed I'd spread you out on it and taste every inch of you. Shall I continue?"

The kiss had been wildly erotic, but lord what he said had her nipples tingling and extending. She averted her gaze to the passenger window. Silence lengthened between them. He shifted gears again, and they accelerated toward the gates of Lorenzo's villa. Giovanni parked. A man approached the car but remained at a distance.

"Thank you for breakfast. The tour was nice. Sorry about the pond."

He nodded. *I guess there's no more to say.* She left the car and hurried for the steps to the villa and then the stairs to her room. She could barely close the door before she was reaching under her wet dress skirt and removing her panties. She dropped them on the floor. Taking in deep breaths she aimed her attention toward the doors of her shower, while trying to reach the zipper at the back of her dress. She really needed the temperature turned to frost to cool herself off. The man made her feel like her skin was on fire. In her dreams, she would remember the tender roll of his tongue and the groans as he whispered to her in Italian. God, if she had known he was saying those things she would have dropped.

"Fabiana, girl, I can't wait to tell you this—." Her voice hitched in her throat when she heard voices. They sounded close enough to be in the room. Slowly Mira lowered her hands from her zipper. Men entered the hall behind her. Giovanni's voice rose above the others. He said he'd take the call in his room. Then a door closed. He was in the room across from her. Mira suffered a twinge of disappointment that they didn't spend the rest of the day together. Maybe she should change and hurry to remind him of the promised tour of the hamlets. Or maybe she'd blown it. Seriously what did she have in common with a Mafia gangster who once wanted to be a lawyer?

From the corner of her eye, she glimpsed something. The closer she stepped to the bed, the deeper the realization. It was her purse, the one stolen in Napoli with the cut strap. Mira marched over and opened it. To her surprise everything, including her passport was accounted for. With shaky fingers she drew aside the inside zipper. A three-inch square shaped velvet pouch was tucked right where she found it. Hard and fast relief filled her and her mind stilled long enough for a deeper realization. She'd misjudged his arrogance. The man obviously had skills and power that reached further than her imagination. For him to do this, he couldn't be all hardness and brawn. What lie in her hand was more valuable than the hope diamond. Did he know what this meant to her? Maybe he didn't. She removed her grandparents' picture and the tiny bracelet. She pressed it to her heart and exhaled deeply.

Giovanni grunted, shed his shirt and tossed it to the chair in his room. He wasn't the heroic type, didn't believe in denying himself anything. Most women spoiled him, saw to his emotional needs without asking. This was true of Zia and Catalina, and of every girlfriend he'd ever had, and he'd had plenty. Now he felt like an idiot. He glared down at the muddy streaks to the front of his trousers. His men had seen him wade in a shallow pond for her. Saw her laugh in his face, and still he couldn't get enough of her.

These were troubling times with his family. The other families and outsiders were all slitting each other's throats with the introduction of drugs. He wanted no part of it. But to take this stand put him and his people in danger. He had to show strength. Even Lorenzo warned so.

Why should he spend the next few days chasing an American fashion designer who had snubbed him? They were different, in every way imaginable, and still the unfamiliar was as tempting as the apple in the Garden of Eden to Eve. He knew he wouldn't be able to turn away from her. Convincing her would be another problem. He picked up the phone and dialed Don Calderone.

Mira marched out into the hall. She ignored the man standing off to the other end and his curious stare. She knocked twice before the door opened. He appeared with his shirt off but still wore the same mud stained trousers. Stunned at the sight of his chest and the tattoos on his arms, she stepped back instead of forward. He looked as if he expected her and turned to go back into his room. The tattoo that spread across his shoulder blades was more intricate. And though she wasn't into that kind of thing, it just added to his raw handsomeness. She entered and closed the door.

"*Un momento, Bella,*" he said.

Silenced, she waited. Giovanni returned to the phone and spoke in his native language to the person on the other end. The room he had was twice the size of hers but absent of the magnificent view. The bed nearly seized half the space.

He ended the call.

She kept safe to the door. "I'm sorry to interrupt."

"It's no interruption. I thought you were going to change?" He looked her over.

She managed a smile. "I found this."

Giovanni's gaze lowered to the tiny bracelet in the center of her palm and then lifted back up to her eyes.

"Did you do this?"

"Do what?" he asked.

"Have my purse and things brought back to me. Did you find my bracelet?"

"Find it?" He smiled. "No, Mira. I had my men go and collect your purse. Do you understand the difference?"

"That's impossible. I just told you about it last night. It's been gone for several weeks."

"You'll learn with me *Bella*, most things are possible." The distance between them closed, and again she felt herself backing away toward no escape. His arm lifted, and his hand rested on the wall. She sank back on it, staring into his eyes.

"Thank you. You have no idea what this means to me."

"Did you come into my room to thank me?" he peered down at her. Tendrils of black hair clung to his forehead.

"Yes." She breathed, focused on his lips. *Maybe I should kiss him this time as a reward. Just a quick sexy kiss to show him I'm grateful?* His mouth loomed close to hers just a kiss away, and his free arm circled her waist dragging her up from the wall to bring her against his chest. The bottoms of her bare feet left the ground, and she rose to her toes. She wasn't a short woman, but his height could not be matched by her gender. To avoid their mouths crashing together, she tilted her head back and braced herself by grabbing his arm and side. In a flash she felt desperate, breathless, on the verge of collapsing if he didn't hold tight to her.

"Should I ask for permission this time?" There was a faint tremor in his voice, revealing how hard he fought for control. He too must have felt the electric current of excitement charging the air. "I don't want to scare you. You've been teasing me all day with this sweet mouth of yours."

"No," she answered, with deceptive calm. Quivers worked their way up her thighs to her belly, and she softened just before accepting his kiss. His tongue swept inside of her mouth. Her hand slid to the top of his shoulder and cupped the back of his neck and the sexy tenor of the kiss shifted. The tension between them was depleted.

He released her and lowered his face to suck and nibble an undiscovered sweet spot on her neck. Mira's lids fluttered, then shut. She ran her hand over his broad shoulders, giving into the passion swirling through her being. His free hand gathered the wet hem of her dress then disappeared underneath. Mira's eyes flashed open as soon as he uncovered her secret.

Dammit I don't have on any panties!

Giovanni's left brow arched and his eyes shone with interest. Five strong fingers caressed her bare buttocks. Her lips parted to explain but nothing escaped. Silence enveloped them for what seemed like an eternity. Should she force him back, run, or discover what lie behind the beauty of his eyes? Giovanni answered with a kiss. He seized her mouth, his tongue plunging deep and fast, turning over hers. He eased his hand around her hip then between her thighs to cup her mound. Excitement cramped her chest and wound tighter and tighter around her lungs. It left her desperate, breathless, on the verge of self-implosion. He eased two fingers into her at the same time using the pad of his thumb to massage her clitoris. She reached and grabbed his wrist. Her mind stilled long enough for her to realize she could be making a huge mistake. Air returned to her lungs and she found the ability to speak.

"Okay. That's enough," she exhaled a nervous laugh.

"*Sei molto bella.* Don't pull away." Giovanni brought her up against the wall while he fondled her sex. His forehead bumped hers, and his nostrils flared.

"English please."

"I said you are very beautiful."

She took a deep breath and adjusted her smile.

"*Ti adoro*, it means—"

"You adore me." She finished his sentence.

His expression was hungry, and lustful. His gaze softened, and his smile eased the corner of his mouth up smoothly. He continued to rapidly thrust his two middle fingers in and out of her, and ran the tip of his tongue over her tightly sealed lips. The pleasure took her under and she released a soft sigh of joy.

"You're mine now."

His other hand gripped the corner of her hip to hold her still as he fucked her in a controlled fashion with his fingers. She was pressed hard against the cool door as if she could escape through the wood. There would be no escape. Her thighs parted a fraction in response, and she felt her pelvis tilt accordingly.

"I can't take anymore," she cried out.

"You can, let me give you more."

Mira pushed hard against the pleasure consuming her and grabbed his hand once more. "No. No please..."

"I need to touch you. Like this." Two fingers slipped out and slowly rubbed up and down her slit before he gave her clitoris a gentle pinch.

"Move your hand, *please*."

"I don't know if I can, *Bella*. I'm not a man who retreats. Maybe we should find a compromise?"

She swallowed her nervous chuckle and tried to give him a serious face. But with him touching her the way he was, a shy smile kept forming over her lips. "Compromise?" her voice croaked, and she found it hard to not move her hips in response when a finger slipped in again, knuckle deep. He nipped her bottom lip and lowered his face to rub his strong jaw across her cheek.

"What is it... the compromise?" she nearly gasped.

"I'll replace my fingers with my tongue," he said against her ear. Mira's heart pounded out of control. The prospects of his lips and tongue down below sent such a thrill through her she couldn't help but smile her consent.

Giovanni forced her feet apart with his. He rubbed her long and slow before withdrawing his hand from her sex. He gathered both sides of her skirt into his hands slowly drawing the wet fabric up. She felt the coolness brush up her thighs then her center.

"Hold it for me," he ordered.

She blinked. "Huh?"

Giovanni smirked. "The skirt."

He forced the fabric into her clenched palms and she was unable to resist his command. Like a good girl she hiked her skirt even higher to her hips. Their eyes never left each other as he lowered to his knees. The man was so tall she still felt as if he were standing. Of course the promise in his wink made her heart flutter.

The exchange was broken when Giovanni's focus returned to what she so brazenly exposed to him. His gaze lowered to the neatly trimmed hairs over her shaven mound. She wasn't vain, but even she admired how evenly brown and hairless her legs were. She worked out often, and ran daily to alleviate stress. Today, in this moment, she felt appreciated for her efforts.

With careful but firm hands he stroked both palms up over the curves of her thighs to her hips and reached around to cup both halves of her ass. A gentle squeeze made her exhale with anticipation. Without consciously agreeing she widened her legs for him and dropped her head back to the door. Mira squeezed her lids tightly shut. Of course, sensibility had left the room. She felt no need to follow her golden rules. Thou shalt never let a man give her oral or other pleasures with his tongue on a first date. Thou shalt never secretly wish he then bend her over and give her even more.

God help me...

A man of his word, he did what he intended. Fingers gently parted her sex and his tongue teased the engorged knot from its hiding place. He began with long sensual swirls from below her folds, piercing her opening with his tongue then sweeping up across her clit. Tender kisses came next, followed by a slick and slow lick. Quivers worked their way up her thighs and belly. The tip of his tongue flicked the rigid knot, feathering it with soft lashes and her hips gyrated. Mira bit down on the inside of her jaw to keep from crying out. When his face pressed in to devour her she lost all strength in her legs. He explored, licked, and tasted her. His firm moist lips tugged on her clit with a sharp pinch that was soon soothed by the way he flattened his tongue and ran it up and down between her folds. As if understanding or sensing her weakness his hand went up to press against her abdomen and keep her pinned to the door. She aided by lifting her left leg and throwing it over his shoulder.

Mercy...

Her legs trembled and she neared climax. Soon Giovanni's tongue play became her waking fantasy. From the way his tongue plunged deep into her pussy, to the sexy swirls of her hips that aided and gave further access, the flood of pleasure quickly hurled her toward an orgasm. God help her but his tongue sought pleasure points no man had discovered. Ever so slowly he began the delicious torture again, and she sank deeper into madness. Her head dropped back and she smiled the biggest grin she'd ever worn. Her body shook all over with glorious tremors. It left her wet with a fiery hot ache in her core.

As she reached the peak of her climax, her mouth gaped in a silent cry of submission. He allowed her release, taking every drop of her essence before he kissed her below once more and rose to capture her lips with his. The strong hardness of his lips and the salty taste of their forbidden passion felt as if her brain spun in her skull like a spinning top. Delicious. She held to him, nearly ready for anything, begging with her racing heart that he do her. Demanding lips caressed hers with a promise for more and then stopped. Giovanni pressed his forehead to hers while they both struggled for a breath. He groaned deep in his throat and squeezed his eyes tightly shut, before he released her, but not before his middle finger slid between her folds and tickled her clitoris to remind her of how perilously close they'd come to exploring the depths of passion now stirring between them.

Stunned, Mira searched his face for an explanation. He stepped back and kept his hands raised as if she had drawn a gun on him. Confused and a bit embarrassed she fled the room. Fast. She headed to hers and closed the door locking it. Mira heaved down several quick breaths. Second time was a charm, third time and she'd strike out for sure. Here she was lecturing on quick and easy sex with Fabiana, and she had gone to the man's room.

"My bracelet!" She realized she dropped it sometime during the kiss. "No! No! No!"

The knock to the door startled her. Exhaling she composed herself and opened the door. He filled the space before her with his arm raised, his hand braced on the top of the doorframe. He leaned forward and looked into her eyes.

"You dropped something." He opened his palm. The bracelet was in the center of it. She accepted her treasured item. "The next time you come to me, I won't let you go so easily."

She smiled. He winked and turned and went back to his room. Mira closed the door shaking her head. "Next time, huh?"

****

Giovanni showered. Not that it was necessary, but the woman had left him with such an unyielding hard-on he needed the cool jets for relief. He shouldn't have seized her when she came into his room. Like a frightened bunny she leapt from his arms and hurried away when all he wanted to hear was that she felt his passion for her. Hell, what did she expect? Showing up in his room barefoot, bottomless, eyes wide and lovely, with a mouth like hers, the moment he discovered she was weak for him he lost all control. He was only a man after all. And the taste of her? Never tasted anything sweeter.

His day had been filled with a few surprises. The first kiss she gave him took his breath away, but the second set his blood to boiling. A sly smile split his face at the thought of her rebellion. He hadn't expected it to end with her falling into the pond. And the joy in her pretty brown eyes when she told him that her precious items were returned to her made him the hero. He missed the soft vulnerability that could be found in the arms of a headstrong woman.

Of course she had the perfect body for a man like him, supple in all the right spots. The kind of curves that would be a comfort to him when chaos returned to his life, and he knew it was coming soon. Territory wars were brewing with the expansion of tourism in southern Italy. He needed the alliance with Calderone to stay ahead of his enemies.

He joined Dominic and Carlo on the open terrace that wrapped around the side of the villa and caught the cool breeze from the *Lario*, which was the lake. The men finished lunch and awaited his arrival. Most in his family preferred to dine in the sun. Dominic and Carlo pummeled him at once with business matters, while his mind kept flashing to thoughts of his and Mira's brief time together. Every time he heard movement his heart thundered in his chest. He could feel the ache return to his groin and extend through his semi-erection. She did not reappear, and after an hour of hoping, he shifted his attention to the men who needed him.

"Did you hear me? Catalina has called. She wants to talk to you."

"Handle her." Giovanni ordered Dominic as he swirled the cubes in his glass. "Who found the purse?"

Dominic frowned but Carlo answered. "Renaldo made a few calls. It was with Maximo's men. He had it brought in this morning."

"Well done." Giovanni downed a shot of his malt and swallowed an ice cube. He needed something to cool him off. The doors to the villa opened and in drifted the soft giggles of a woman. He glanced up as Lorenzo strolled inside with his arm draped over the redhead. Both of them had wet hair and deep flushed looks. It appeared that his cousin had done much better in his pursuits.

"This looks serious," Fabiana smiled at the men. "Is Mira upstairs?"

Giovanni nodded.

She rose on her toes and kissed Lorenzo. "I'll go find her. See you for a late lunch. Okay?"

Lorenzo nodded and let her go. Giovanni noticed how his cousin kept his eyes trained on her hips. "Woman is a firecracker. You have no idea." Lorenzo whistled. Carlo snickered but Dominic cut his eyes away in disgust.

"How are things?" Lorenzo asked.

Dominic rose. "I'm heading back home, to see to Catalina."

Lorenzo nodded. "You do that little one. I'll handle business with Giovanni. That is until Flavio returns."

Dominic glared. Lorenzo never missed a moment to point out that Flavio was consigliere and their young surrogate cousin was just a stand in. Giovanni waited for the tension to pass. He didn't need to speak. The men gave each other a nod of reprieve and parted. Carlo rose next. He walked over and slapped Lorenzo on the back. Grabbing his neck, he whispered in his ear. Lorenzo roared with laughter. Carlo sauntered out.

"You don't look to be pleased." Lorenzo tossed Giovanni's way.

"I have a lot on my mind."

"And the designer? She was supposed to give you some relief. How was she?"

"Watch your fucking mouth. Don't speak of her in that way."

Lorenzo's brows shot up. "*Scusi.* Guess she's made an impression on you."

Giovanni headed to the bar to refresh his drink.

"Are you falling for that designer?" Lorenzo pressed.

"What?"

"This is a first. You usually don't visit Bellagio for long. On my way in, I saw the boys. Looks like you might be here for a few more days."

"I have business in Bellagio thanks to you. The *carabineri* have dispatched two inspectors. They've asked to see me directly."

"Of course." Lorenzo grumbled with forced restraint. "What are your plans for afterward?"

"Afterward?"

"Our guests?" Lorenzo's gaze switched to the ceiling to emphasize his meaning.

"Aww, Mira. She and I have unfinished business. A private matter."

"The favor she owes for the building you want in Napoli? Still negotiating?"

"I don't negotiate, you know that." He'd forgotten her rebuke of his offer. Fuck he'd buy her four buildings if she'd let him run his hand up under her skirt just once more. "She's unlike any other woman I've met since my return to *Italia*. I find her interesting." He turned from the bar and sipped his drink, locking gazes with Lorenzo from over the top of the glass.

"You do know she could never fit in your world. A fling is the best you could hope for."

"What about her friend? You two look pretty cozy." He returned to his seat and plopped down.

"Fabiana? Don't let the red hair fool you. She's Italian. A hot little sex kitten. I can't get enough of the pussy, now that she's finally given me a taste. But I'm not a man to settle down. She understands this. You, however, cousin, well let's just say we see things differently when it comes to women."

Giovanni chuckled. "No shit."

"That friend of hers, I'm not too sure about. She's a bit jumpy. A bit of a *donna*. Imagine molding her into a Battaglia wife?"

"I don't want a woman to be molded into anything. And I don't want a wife."

"You have Catalina back in Sorrento being molded into the perfect bride."

"Different. And you know it." Giovanni said, his throat dry and his patience short. Lorenzo looked poised to counter and the phone rang. Both of their eyes switched to it. Giovanni observed him while he took the call. There was a short exchange and then he asked the caller to allow him to ring him back.

"Something I should know?" Giovanni asked.

"No. It's my gift for Fabiana. An artist I've commissioned to do her portrait."

"Thought she wasn't worth the effort?"

Lorenzo gave a thin-lipped smile. Giovanni narrowed his gaze on his cousin. He could tell when he wasn't truthful. In that moment he knew he was lying.

"You said the *carabineri* have come. Is it one of our friends?"

Giovanni didn't bother to answer.

"Should I attend the meeting? It was my restaurant, and Francesco *was* my partner."

"I owned the damn place, and they know it. I'll handle it." After another long swig of his whiskey he slammed the glass on the bar. "I'll leave now. Send *Bella* my regrets. Maybe I can join you all for dinner."

"Giovanni?"

He paused at the door.

"My request, to be part of the meeting with Don Calderone? Domi is headed back to Napoli. Will you allow it?"

"No. I'd rather you focus on returning my investment."

He waited for Lorenzo to challenge him. The flash fire of rebellion sparked in his cousin's eyes. Instead he nodded his obedience and held his tongue. Giovanni shook his head and walked out.

Once alone Lorenzo picked up the phone and dialed. *"Che cosa?"*

"We need to meet." A deep voice rasped on the line.

"Where and when?" Lorenzo asked, checking his timepiece.

"Now. The Denelli place."

Lorenzo ended the call. He walked over to the closet behind the bar and located his gun. Giovanni would be occupied, and with Carlo and Dominic gone he could manage the meeting with little consequence. So he hoped. Things were getting further out of his control, and Giovanni was too close to the truth.

****

"Where are you?" Fabiana threw her door open. Mira had chosen another green dress. This one had a long skirt that covered her knees, and thin spaghetti straps. She was working on her tangles when her best friend charged in.

"There you are. I saw Giovanni downstairs. He said you were up here."

"Did he?" Mira tried to sound unimpressed. She could still

feel herself tingle between her thighs at the mere mention of the man. How on earth could she face him after what transpired between them?

"I had the most fantastic of times. We took Lorenzo's yacht out. I met with an artist who took pictures of me. He's going to do my portrait. Can you believe it? And after breakfast I gave Lorenzo a little dessert. Let's just say it was everything I thought it would be." Fabiana plopped down on the bed. "Wait, why are you changing clothes?"

"Long story." Mira turned on her heel and smiled. "So what's up now?"

"Nothing. The men have business. Lorenzo got a call, and we had to come back. Is that why your date ended too?"

"Wasn't a date," Mira mumbled.

"Oh. Didn't go well?"

She pondered the question for a moment. Things between them went beyond well. However, it was far too soon to define what the passion they shared meant. "Let me show you something." Mira went to the dresser and picked up her purse. She turned and showed it to Fabiana.

"Is that—?"

"Yes. And guess who gave it to me."

Fabiana inspected the purse. "Are you serious?"

"He had it delivered to my room. Now how do you explain something like this?"

"I can't."

"Exactly."

Fabiana scanned the contents. "What about your bracelet?"

"Everything was returned, including my passport. You know that purse has been missing for over three weeks and now it shows up as if it was never taken?"

"You think he set you up to be robbed? Why would he?"

Mira shook her head. "No. I don't think so. It's not his style. I have no clue what he wants. Surely a man like him can have any woman he wants. But he seems fixated on me. Or maybe that's the wrong word choice. He's so mysterious and opinionated I can't tell what his motivations are. And I feel so overwhelmed when I'm alone with him. I don't think I will make that mistake again."

Fabiana laughed.

"What?"

"You kissed him didn't you?"

"What!"

"Oh I can tell. Something is up."

"Shut up."

"Good grief. So what? A little kissy-poo between consenting adults isn't a sin. The man is hot, and we're vacationing. What harm could it do?"

"Have you forgotten the conversation we had this morning? Mafia men. Plenty harm can be done. Access to our building with locked cellar doors we can't enter?" Mira kept her gaze averted so Fabiana didn't read more. The man's kiss was the least of her worries. What he did with his tongue still had her knees wobbling.

"I think that purse over there is a peace offering. So what, he's a bad boy? Not telling you to marry the guy. His friendship could be a benefit to us. I had a long talk with Lorenzo. Not saying I'm totally sold on us becoming involved with the Battaglias, but what they are asking of us isn't illegal."

"Fabiana, you know I'm in no need of a new relationship, casual or otherwise. Have you forgotten about Kei?"

"The asshole who broke up with you because you said no to

his marriage proposal? No. You don't have to remind me. I just want you to have some fun the next few days. It's a different country, a different time for us both." Fabiana almost beamed with happiness. She studied her for a moment. Her wet hair was suspect.

"You really did sleep with Lorenzo?"

"We're not talking about me."

Mira shook her head. "I hope you know what you're doing."

"Of course I do. I'm falling in love. Now get dressed. We still have the city to see. Screw the boys. I think we should do it together. Be right back while I tell Lorenzo and get us a driver."

"Wait. I... Giovanni and I had planned to do some sightseeing." Mira said.

"Really? Oh. Okay."

"Go find Lorenzo. I'll talk to Giovanni. Maybe we can do it as a foursome."

Chapter Five

THE DAY HAD BURNED AWAY faster than either of them anticipated. It was near dusk when they returned, exhausted. Fabiana could always out shop, out drink, and out eat her, but on this day she managed to do all three. They laughed as they strolled side by side through large double doors drawn open as if in anticipation of their arrival. With shopping bags swinging in their hands, the two of them finished each other's sentences.

The villa in the evening had a spacious airy feel to it. Every window and door on the lower level was open. It allowed a sweetly fragrant tropical breeze to flow through the long halls. Soft yellow lamp fixtures on the walls and posted in the corners of the rooms chased away the shadows. Even the chandelier, twinkling from the high vaulted ceiling, cast beams of light over the hanging portraits and marble statues. Together they bounded up the winding stairs. Her friend chatted her up over something funny they'd seen in a storekeeper's window, and she pretended to agree. Her mind was elsewhere.

All day her thoughts were filled with him. The man had left

one hell of an impression. From his larger than life imposing stature to his handsome tan gold face and dreamy eyes, it had become hard to shake thoughts of him. Even the strong spice of his cologne lingered in the back of her mind and caused her blood to rush to her face with shame. He'd used his tongue masterfully, gave her the first climax she'd had in months, and she was sure he had done it all on purpose.

At first she intended to decline Fabiana's invite for a day in town without the men but found that Giovanni had left on business when she returned to the parlor in search of him. Mira half expected to hear he'd left Bellagio for his life in southern Italy. And that had been disappointing.

"Are you even listening to me?" Fabiana walked in her room ahead of her.

"Yes. I think." Mira answered.

Fabiana slipped her a look under dark lashes. Mira pretended not to notice. She placed her bags on the chaise, and nervously rubbed her hands together.

"You've been weird all day." Fabiana began, circling her. Mira rolled her eyes upward. Her friend went to the window in the room and leaned against the sill. "You've been a bit spacy. Is it work? Do you want to call Angelique and check in?"

"No. Don't be silly. I'm trying to unwind, and you keep taking out the measuring tape to see how much. I'm relaxed. We had a good time, didn't we?" She dropped on the bed and crossed her legs. Fabiana observed her with a scrutiny she had grown to loathe. If she weren't careful she'd confess it all before she had time to decide on how she truly felt over her and Giovanni's passionate moment.

"Wonder where the men are?" Mira said through a forced smile. "We haven't seen Lorenzo. Shouldn't you let him know we're back?" Fabiana rose. She glanced out the window and paused. Her brows furrowed together with concern.

"What is it?"

"Come here! Quick!" Fabiana stepped closer to the window. Mira pushed up from the bed and hurried to her friend's side. Together they watched Lorenzo speed up the sloping driveway on a motorbike. He climbed off with a flushed hard look to his face. The front of his shirt, and his trouser legs were caked in dirt, as were his shoes.

"What in the hell happened to him?" Mira asked. "Maybe his car broke down or something?"

Lorenzo spoke with a few men who regarded him curiously as well, then marched toward the villa.

"I'll go downstairs and find out what's going on."

"Wait a second, he—." She turned and her friend was gone. The door slammed shut behind her. Mira searched the cars parked and didn't see the shiny yellow Ferrari she and Giovanni had taken earlier. She chewed on the inside of her jaw wondering again if he had gone for the evening. After a few minutes curiosity forced her to act. She headed for the door and stepped out into the hall. The armed man who always stood guard had gone. She'd noticed that detail first when they returned. *Just knock on the door and see if he's there. Maybe he's in there?* He clearly stated what a return visit to his room would bring. After the fourth knock it was clear he was gone. Feeling a bit silly she turned away.

"*Ciao, Bella.*"

From nowhere, he appeared. Their eyes met, and she stood frozen to the spot. "Yes. As a matter of fact I was." A warm mixture of excitement and trepidation filled her. "You left this morning without saying goodbye." To her, her voice sounded soft and needy. However, the sly smile on his face and the desire in his stare indicated he had a thing for soft and needy. She cleared her throat and straightened her back. Giovanni did his usual sweep of her appearance; his gaze lingered on her breasts before returning to her face.

When he stopped before her, she felt breathless again.

"I returned. For you."

"I see." She pretended to be unimpressed. "I..." Mira cleared her throat and spoke in a steady voice. "I didn't get a chance to tell you that Fabiana wanted to do some sightseeing with me today. Didn't want you to think I was running away again."

"You? Run? After allowing me to taste you? The thought never crossed my mind," he replied with a jesting quip.

"Oh? Good."

His gaze left her face and shifted to his closed door. "You want to come in?" he reached for the knob with one hand and placed his other to her hip to steer her toward temptation. Contact of his palm against her body nearly seduced her into complying.

"No. No." She laughed nervously reaching to touch his chest. She kept her hand there and felt the strong rhythm of his heart. *Was he excited to be near her also?* Something had accelerated his pulse. "I only wanted to see if you were free. That's all, Giovanni."

"You miss me?" He gave her hip a gentle squeeze. Giovanni pulled her up under him. She was forced to put both hands to his chest to keep from colliding with it. His hand then eased lower, and she was now secure in his hold. For some reason, he found her discomfort pleasing. The man knew the control he wielded over women, and she was sure he frequently got whom or whatever he wanted. This man wasn't one she should tease.

"I owe you lunch, don't I? It's the most important meal of the day. Though we never finished breakfast," Giovanni chuckled. Humor softened his gaze, and she dismissed her previous assessment. He was just being friendly. She noticed in this country men were a bit more forward. Maybe she had let too many boundaries down for him to understand what affect he was having on her?

"Okay." she said.

"Lorenzo has had food prepared, I'm sure. We can join him and your friend. Would that make you comfortable?"

"Who says I'm not?"

His left brow arched in response.

"I'm perfectly comfortable," she answered. "Evident by the way you have your hand on my ass."

This time laughter exploded from him. He lifted his palm and put his hands up in surrender. Mira smirked. She stayed close, however, to emphasize her point. Lowering her hands, she felt the light brush of her nipples over his chest and knew he did too. "Besides we can eat anywhere."

"I think it best we join them."

She didn't hide her disappointment. Her lip dropped in a pout. He winked at her and ran the backs of his fingers over her cheek. Funny, earlier she told Fabiana she had no intentions of being alone with the man again. Oh yes, as usual her mind and desires were at odds. She lifted her gaze from his lips to stare into his beautiful eyes again. This time she wouldn't retreat from him like a schoolgirl. Giovanni extended his hand to her. She accepted it, allowing him to lead the way. His palm was warm and large. It covered her entire hand. She felt a sense of protectiveness in the way he assumed the lead. Together they walked down the stairwell, wide enough for them to descend side by side. Below she found the hall and the dining room to be empty, but a very romantic setting with blue roses and candles were placed as the centerpiece. Mira stared at the fresh blooms, curious of their history with his family. When he drew out her chair she only half hesitated. Where were Fabiana and Lorenzo? Before she could ask, her friend sashayed in from the other end of the dining room. She blinked at Giovanni, then at her, and the romantic place setting for four.

"Everything okay?" Mira asked.

"Oh yes. Lorenzo's changing. The man was covered in dirt and mud. He said his car broke down, and he had to borrow a motorbike to make it back up the hill."

"Car trouble?" Giovanni asked.

Fabiana nodded. "He'll join us soon."

Giovanni's attention returned to Mira. Her eyes were constantly drawn to his. Fabiana's arrival was quite a relief. The wine poured and food was brought to the table on silver platters and in large shiny red and yellow ceramic serving bowls. Mira heaped pasta and a meaty sauce onto her plate, keeping her focus singular. Eat, drink, that is all. She managed it for a few moments until he spoke.

"So where did you ladies go today?"

"Everywhere. Our driver was pretty good." Fabiana answered.

She felt his stare and looked up. It was clear he could care less what Fabiana said and was more interested in hearing the details from her. "We found some boutiques and did some sightseeing."

"I wish I had the pleasure, to show you more of Bellagio." He forked a large portion of the dinner in his mouth, chewing.

I wish you had the pleasure too. Mira sipped her wine.

"Is it true? You found her purse?" Fabiana asked.

Giovanni stopped mid chew. He looked to Fabiana and his expression stilled. Mira frowned at his reaction. It wasn't a secret. Why did he glare at her friend as if it were none of her business? The silence at the table felt awkward so she interceded. "He had it brought to me. It was very nice of you, Giovanni. To go through the trouble."

He continued to eat. Fabiana shot her a quizzical look.

"I hear your family name quite a bit in Napoli. You're very respected." Fabiana began again. "One of the most powerful families in the *Campania*?"

"What's the *Campania*?" Mira asked, with a nervous chuckle. Why her friend's questions of him made her nervous she wasn't sure. It was more of an underlying feeling she got from Giovanni's silence.

"It's the region of southern Italy where Napoli is. Our new home."

"Oh." Mira feared for a moment that Fabiana would mention the mob. God, she prayed not. The tension at the table was already so thick she found it hard to catch a good breath.

"Are you the Godfather?" Fabiana chuckled.

Giovanni continued to chew, but the action seemed more mechanical than organic. His hooded gaze lifted from his plate and locked on Fabiana. Mira braced for a response.

"You think this term Godfather applies to me?" Giovanni picked up his wine and sipped. "Why do you think this?"

"I'm asking a question. Does the term 'Godfather' apply to you?"

"I've seen the movie." Giovanni sneered. He sat back in his chair and cocked his head giving Fabiana his undivided attention. "*Bella*?" It was clear when he said the word, *bella*, he addressed her and not Fabiana. Though his gaze never wavered from her friend. "We've spent some time together today. I'm curious as to what you think?" he switched his focus to Mira. "Am I what you Americans call the Godfather?"

Why is he asking me?

Giovanni waited. Fabiana gave her an apologetic shrug. Both of them stared directly at her.

Mira cleared her throat.

"I think the movie was all fiction, a story steeped in some cultural references that Americans associate with Italians. Seriously, what does Godfather mean anyway?"

"The term has meaning, for both Sicilians and Italians. Many of our families have deep roots in the Catholic Church. The Sacrament of Baptism is where it comes from. It's where the church baptizes for the remission of sin and the family appoints a trustworthy person to oversee the welfare of the most innocent, a child. S*ponsores, offerentes, susceptores, fidejussores,* this is what we consider a godparent. Am I one? I am, for many children, a blessing from many families to have been requested to sponsor the life of their child before the holy sacrament. It's my honor. Why you Americans want to sully the term and associate it with organized crime is beyond me. I guess you, *Signora*," his gaze swiveled to Fabiana. "Watch too much TV."

"She didn't mean to offend you, Giovanni, she only—"

"Let her finish her questions, *Bella*. I'm sure she's quite capable to explain what the meaning is behind them." He reclined in his chair and regarded Fabiana with open hostility. He did so in a way that Mira didn't appreciate. It was killing the sexy flirtatious banter between them that had her considering him in a new light. In that moment the man seemed quite dangerous.

"We're done with this topic. Let's move on." Mira said to them both. Fabiana gave Giovanni a gracious smile and bowed her head slightly in respect. He however continued to glare.

"Yes, let's move on." Mira said to him directly.

"Agreed." Fabiana spoke, sipping her wine, swallowing, and speaking again. "Besides, I think we are all past introductions. I was just making conversation."

"We are past it, aren't we, Giovanni?" Mira asked. He looked her way. She smiled sweetly at him and hoped whatever it was that had offended him could be forgotten. It was rude to insult the man. If she had put Lorenzo on the hot seat the way Fabiana did she would be furious. What the Battaglias did or didn't do was none of their business.

"I thought I introduced myself properly earlier." He moistened his lips and smiled her way. Mira's eyes stretched. She noticed how Fabiana watched the exchange and tried to cover her embarrassment. She couldn't be more mortified. If he even insinuated what they'd done in his room she would sink through the floor.

"Like I said the movie was just a movie. I don't have a label for you. Don't need one."

"Girl, what has you squirming over there?" Fabiana gave her a critical squint.

"*Come va!*" Lorenzo stormed into the room freshly changed. He wore a dark blue shirt and khaki-brown slacks. He yanked a chair back and sat down in a huff. Lorenzo had a flushed hurried manner about him. Wait. Was he sunburned? How long was that hike back to the villa? His face and neck was red as a beet.

"What happened to you?" Giovanni asked. "Your woman

says your car broke down."

"His woman!" Fabiana exclaimed. "Excuse me?"

Mira drank her wine and hoped her friend would let the reference pass. Fabiana rolled her eyes and laughed it off.

"Yes. I had car trouble. I had to walk then I found a Vespa unattended on the side of the road." Lorenzo dismissed the concern. He lifted a glass. "I want to propose a toast. To our lovely guests, and the next two days. May they be as promising as the first."

Mira lifted her glass. She glanced over to Giovanni who clinked his with hers. She kept her eyes on him during her long sip. The night had already started off with a bang. When Giovanni looked her way she caught that gleam of desire in his eyes again. Despite the tension earlier she relaxed and nodded his way.

****

Despite the numbness weighing down her lids, Mira woke exhausted and sensually disturbed after the day she had. There would be no hope of sleep. Blame it on the wine, her handsome suitor, or the whirlwind adventure her life had turned into since she left New York. Dinner had been nice. The conversation flowed. She even practiced a few words of Italian with everyone's encouragement. Giovanni was charming. The more time she spent with the man, the more she felt drawn to him. And just when she thought the night had promise for her to get to know more of him, he was summoned away. A tall brooding giant in a suit entered the room, said a few words in his ear and they were gone. Gone!

Frustrated, she rolled over under the coverlet and squeezed her eyes shut. Her mind refused to turn off. She remembered everything, from his touch, to his kiss. She recalled every single sensation that made her toes curl. Reaching for her pillow she stuffed it between her legs and sucked in a deep breath, exhaling slowly. Nothing offered relief.

A door slammed.

Every bone in her body stiffened. Did she hear a door slam? She glanced back over her shoulder. She was positive she heard it. What time was it? Mira sat up, her hands flat to either side of her. She stared through the darkness to her locked bedroom door. "No girl. Don't do it. Sleep. I'm going to sleep!" she grunted falling back on her pillow, and turning over. "I'm going to sleep."

Giovanni shrugged off his sports coat. He tossed it to the chair. Some vacation this turned out to be. No matter his travels, there was business to be had in nearly every hamlet. Tonight had been strange. Don Calderone, who had been enraged that his son Giuseppe missed a very important meeting with Giovanni's men, had summoned him. After the opening hostilities subsided, Giovanni felt sympathy for the old man. Giuseppe was a royal fuck up and his only heir. So he tolerated another reschedule of meetings in exchange for additional land purchases in the triangle. The old man had the nerve to try to remind him of the way business was done in the past with his father. As if he cared.

Once he unbuttoned his shirt and took off his shoes, he felt the tension drain from his neck and shoulders. The time had come to bring in his latest shipment. The Russians knew better than to interfere. He'd secured a deal that would remind all other families that he was indeed his father's son, and give him enough capital to wash his hands of blood. Move Battaglia away from the stigma of Baldementi. That was his father's dream. He sat on the edge of the bed and put his face in his palms.

At times the loneliness became as heavy a burden as managing the lives of men sworn in blood to follow him. He tired of the long nights spent alone and grew bored and disinterested with the women that shared his bed. There was no peace for him.

A soft rapping at the door drew his face up from his palms.

Who would dare defy his orders and disturb him now? Rising with his shirt open and in bare feet he strode to the door and flung it open. Mira emerged from the dark hall into view, successfully disarming him with a shy smile. She wore no makeup. It shocked him how much prettier she was without it. Blown straight, her dark brown hair with honey colored highlights faintly seen within, flowed from a center part to her shoulders and framed her oval shaped face. Her eyes were a soft hazel under a ring of dark lashes, and her skin flawless, creamy like melted caramel. Giovanni's gaze lowered. A silk belt tied neatly defined her tiny waist and gave her breasts a full lift to the deep V at the front of her robe. She rose on her small feet with her hands behind her back to look up into his eyes when she spoke. "Hi, Giovanni."

"Hi."

"Can I come in?"

Giovanni didn't speak. He was too busy staring at the sweet indention of her exposed cleavage.

"I know it's late, but I wanted, oh this is awkward, can I come in to talk?"

As if on autopilot he stepped aside, holding the door for her. The suggestion of nubile curves underneath the short robe she wore was further enhanced by the sweet sway of her hips.

No woman on the planet had a better ass than her. He smiled, surprised. Closing the door, he locked it. She would not leave.

She strolled about and stopped in the middle of his room, surveying it as if she hadn't seen it before. Of course, he hadn't forgotten her, the day they shared, the night he wished to share between her thighs. He forced himself to accept the fact that a little flirting was all he'd achieve with this one. Especially with all the bullshit he was swimming in.

"You left again. We seem to have a habit of not being able to finish a meal together. Why is that?"

So she noticed? Asked the little voice inside of his head. "It couldn't be helped, *Bella*. I wanted to stay."

"Did you?"

"I did."

She crossed her arms over the swell of her breasts. He resisted the urge to sweep her over his shoulder and take her to the bed. She smelled heavenly. Even from a distance her presence made his room soft, enticing. He took another step toward her, and she didn't back away from him.

"So?"

"Yes?" he answered.

"This can go nowhere." She opened her arms in gesture. "This thing between us. Nowhere. I have my business. I mean my business is really demanding of me now. I'm not really into dating. I don't want to date. I, just... I'm interested in enjoying myself that's all. And a friend. Maybe. Do you understand?"

Did she think he'd talk her out of this late night visit or convince her to stay? She seemed to want something, but couldn't decide on what. Giovanni dismissed her little speech. They both knew how the night would end. And right now he wanted to ease past the formalities and get to the sweet part, where she lay beneath him in his bed. The lamplight from the small dresser near the bed chased most of the shadows to the corners of his room. The drapes were drawn preventing the assistance of the moon. Still he could see enough of her. She had fine hips and shapely thighs.

"This." He pointed to her, and then himself. "Has already gone further than you imagined. It is why you've come to me. You do remember what I told you the last time we met in my room?" He stopped before her and lifted her chin with his finger. "You remember, don't you, *Bella*? That's why you waited up for me, came to me as soon as you heard my return. Isn't it?"

"We're different," she answered meekly. "I'm not talking about race. Fabiana and I are different and we're best friends. We're different in other ways."

"And that matters to whom?"

"I'm not usually this brave, okay?" She tossed her hands up in defeat. "I don't screw around."

"It's your first time. I'll be gentle."

"Oh brother, you don't beat around the bush do you?"

The saying had no meaning to him so he ignored the question. She made the first move. He couldn't be held responsible for what was to come. Maybe his sweet dearly departed mother was getting a kick out of this moment. How many women had she and Zia tried to pair him with. And it was she, Mira Ellison, a black American woman far removed from anyone they'd imagined for him. "What's under the robe?" he asked and shrugged off his shirt.

She stood motionless. He intended to ask again but slowly her arms unfolded and lowered. She reached around to the belted sash at her hip and untied the knot. The silk folds peeled away to uncover a very delicate lace negligee that barely reached past the bend of her hips. Black, lace, with a bra like bodice, it lay against her curves like a second skin. Her heart shaped hips and the dark V of her sex made him run his hand back through his hair for restraint. Even the dark extended tips of her nipples appeared.

"*Sei incredibile,*" he stammered. "You're incredible," he translated.

Mira relaxed her shoulders and the silk robe drifted to a pool of fabric at her feet. Tonight had purpose; it was no accident or chance encounter. "*Destino.* Mine. You're my fate, *Bella.*"

"I'm not sure about that." She crossed her arms across herself out of reflex. He intended to corrupt her in every way. The woman had come to tease him, seduce him, and she wanted him to think it was his idea. Giovanni chuckled.

"Something funny?" she asked.

He swallowed his smile. "No, not at all."

When she turned to go to the bed he reached and caught her hand. He brought her small palm up to his groin. Startled at first, her eyes stretched in surprise. Giovanni nipped her nose and then her bottom lip. "Touch it, feel how much I want you. I want you to know," he breathed against her mouth. Her gaze flickered down and then up to his eyes. He let his touch drift away, and her hand remained firmly pressed on the erection. It gave him a small measure of relief. Like a good girl she unbuckled his belt. She fumbled a bit and stepped closer to steady her pursuit as she lowered his zipper.

"*Che cosa desideri?*" He asked. She ran the leather belt through the loops of his pants.

"I don't understand." Mira whispered.

"I want to know what it is *you* desire?"

She smiled up at him with those round brown eyes of hers. Her voice lowered to a soft melody, which sounded purposefully mysterious. "I'd rather you uncover my desires on your own."

Mira eased her hand into the front slit of his boxers. He sucked in a tight breath when she closed her fingers over his cock. Every muscle in his dick tensed, straining towards her touch. The slow, steady strokes that followed were pure heaven. He wanted her to feel every inch of him. As if understanding his limits she withdrew her hand, rose on her toes, brushing her hard nipples over his chest as she gave him a soft kiss to the lips.

"I like," she said.

He wanted to tackle her. Throw her on the floor and ravish her, hard and fast. Instead he played it cool. He now had a full view of her backside. The black thong disappeared into shapely round buttocks. The thin lace confection of her negligee inched up to her bikini line when she walked. "I think you said, you wanted me to take it off?"

His throat moved, and he swallowed, still he couldn't speak. Slowly she eased the negligee over her head and tossed it to the side. She cast him a shy smile over her shoulder, and it was the sweetest one he'd received since they met. "*Italia* is the country of love? Right? How do you say I want to make *love* in Italian?" she asked.

"*Voglio fare l'amore con te,*" he answered.

She repeated the words.

He nodded that she did well.

Closing her eyes she found herself unable to capture a single breath. Her body had complete control over her sensibility. Her nipples tingled and extended. She ached between her thighs with constant contractions of longing and moisture dampened her thong. *Lord, why oh why, did I start this? What if I can't go through with it?* She'd only been with two men in her life. The first, misguided love for a hoodlum back in Virginia and the second, a rigid, uncompromising Chinese businessman named Kei, who had been a very controlled lover. This was as bold as she could be.

Thankfully he steadied her. His hands gently cupped her hips to pull her back, eliminating distance between them. Mira exhaled the breath she held and then found the ability to breathe again. Strong arms secured her to him. There was something to be said about a hug. From a man as tall and beautifully proportioned as him, his embrace could easily be labeled as any girl's protective dream. Visions of being a distressed damsel and her sword wielding Viking prince coming to her rescue played out in her mind.

He enjoyed holding her. It was evident in the way his large hands went all over to massage and fondle her breasts, tummy and between her tightly shut thighs. Mira released a soft sigh and inhaled. His cologne was a fresh, stimulating spice that enveloped her. His erection was as hard as a brick pressed deep between the cheeks of her ass. He moved his hips slightly to rub the rigid thickness between the halves of her butt cheeks. "Oh yes. Yes God," she softly panted.

The man was blessed below, even for his height and stature she found him huge. The hungry look in his eyes that bore down on her from the first moment they met had her so nervous with anticipation she could feel herself trembling. So this embrace was good. It gave her a minute to collect herself.

Giovanni kissed the side of her face. A deep, heavily

accented, soulful voice spoke words so decadent and delicious they warmed the inner channel of her ear and spread through each chamber of her heart. She didn't care to know the literal translation; she instead relished the feeling the sound of his desires evoked. Tonight belonged to them.

He set aside her hair, his mouth glided over her shoulder, and her teeth bit the corner of her jaw. The sharp sting of a pinch of her left nipple made her squirm and move her ass against his thickness. "Relax."

God how she wished she could.

He chuckled. His voice went hoarse and low when it whispered into her ear. "I'll make it so sweet for you, I promise. But you will have to make it sweet for me."

She nodded. "I can. I will."

Mira turned and immediately was lifted by the waist. He tossed her higher as if she weighed no more than a feather. Giddy she wrapped her arms around his neck and claimed his mouth, lips, tongue, forcing her passion on him with a deep kiss. Her breasts were mashed into his hard chest, and he squeezed both halves of her butt cheeks controlling their passion. A moan sifted between his lips. Her sex was pressed to his lower abdomen. Giovanni lowered her a fraction causing her chin to tilt and her head to go back. He maintained their kiss while he let her feel the head of his cock that had reached out of the top of his boxers. The man was so powerful he could take her standing if he chose.

He tore his mouth from her and heaved her up in his arms. "*Tesoro mio*... damn woman, I haven't wanted someone as badly as I want you."

"Show me. I'm ready," she panted.

"Indeed."

In under three steps he crossed the room with her before lowering her to the bed. She tried to pull him down with her, but he refused her efforts. Instead, he wiped his hand down his face, with eyes glued to the brazen way she lie with her sex now on display. Her knees parted. She remained in position to allow him to feast on her and feel more desired than she had in all her life. Giovanni moistened his lips. Would he kiss her there? Mira's eyes fluttered shut, and she touched herself. She hoped so. It was so good when he used his tongue. What more would he bring?

A deep groan escaped him. He had stripped himself of his trousers and boxers. His angrily veined cock curled upward and he held it with his hand. Her eyes stretched. How in the hell could she take all of him? The man was huge. And the dangerous smirk he gave her in the dark made her shudder. There would be no escape. She didn't even dare try. Tonight she'd have to go the distance.

He turned from her and walked over to the other side of the room. She could see his back again clearly. A large tattoo of some kind of tribal pattern stretched over the back of his shoulders. There was another unique tattoo stamped on his chest, and a gothic cross tattooed from the inside of his wrist to the crease of his arm. Nothing was as beautiful as the one on his back. Mira rose on her elbow. Whatever he sought he found. He returned to her. Later she'd ask him about the tattoos and the meaning. Now she could care less. One look at his erection and she was lowering back to the pillow and spreading her legs.

Giovanni captured her ankle. He massaged the center of her foot with the pads of both thumbs. It felt wonderful, relaxing all the muscles up along her calve and thigh. He then pulled her toward the middle of the bed, causing her hair to fan out behind her once she slid across the navy quilted comforter. Positioning her now in the center of the bed, he came over her. In that moment she felt almost virginal. Tonight the new and improved Mira Ellison acted impulsively. Freedom felt glorious. Bracing himself on the palms of his hands, he hovered.

Her own lips parted involuntarily, wanting his tongue in her mouth. As his face grew closer to hers, her eyelids fell shut and her exposed chest rose and fell from the accelerating adrenaline rush. His lips were so close now she could feel the heat of his breath escape his mouth washing over hers.

Gripping the sheet, she wanted it.

She needed it.

The kiss that would seal her fate.

The kiss that would make her his.

Instead, he used his left hand to gingerly stroke her hip, then his strong index finger as it hooked into the rim of her thong, easing it downward. A sharp twinge of disappointment went through her over the missed opportunity to kiss him once more. Her disappointment was short lived because his mouth brushed her lips lovingly before he drew back to sheath his dick. It only took seconds. Fire and desire struck with his tongue slowly tracing over her feverish skin to her collarbone.

He captured a nipple in his mouth and gave it a hard suck. The full eroticism of what was happening to Mira struck her like lightening. Her eyelids fluttered and her heart hammered hard and fast in her chest. He eased downward kissing the indention between her breasts. She pressed on either side of her globes and cushioned his face. He rubbed his jaws between. The scruffy feel of his cheeks sent quivers below. Not soon after his tongue circled her now tender nipple again. The warmth of his breath on her skin as his mouth closed over her areola sent shivers of delight down her spine. They traveled through her pelvis causing her hips to quake as she rotated them underneath him. Taking both hands, she ran them across the hard angles of his back. He positioned himself at her opening, and she braced for what was to come next.

Familiarize, explore, examine, you name it, Giovanni intended to possess every inch of her. Driven by an insane lust he pressed down and found her wet and ready as she ground her pelvis up against his then rubbed her slit along his throbbing cock. Her hand reached to aid his entry, which he grabbed and pinned back over her head. He intended to fuck her, love her, explore every inch of her in due time. A single thrust lodged him deep within her, and he relished the pressure he felt as her tight channel stretched to complete the fit. She arched that lovely body of hers off the bed, back bowed, and lips quivering. Damn! Is she a virgin? No pussy ever felt so glorious. "*Bella*, you're tight. For me? All of this sweetness is for me?" he asked, disbelieving how wonderful she felt. She didn't respond. Fuck he'd spoken in Italian and she probably didn't understand him. Her pussy clenched tighter. He swirled his hips and pushed forward before lifting his hips to withdraw. He screwed inside her wet heat and pumped his ass until he reached her core.

Giovanni chuckled slightly. He kept circling and pumping against her G-spot, loving the way she moved her ass beneath him in response. Sex with his sweet *Bella* was blowing his mind. She moaned with frustration once he slowed to taste her lips, and then her sweat. She clawed at his arms and sides trying to draw him down on her. He had to study her a bit longer. Then he found the control to move in and out of her again. His mouth descended on one swollen nipple, moistening it. He pumped his hips harder and faster.

"More!" she cried out.

Giovanni withdrew. He rolled her over to her belly. She raised her perfectly shaped ass temptingly at him. Her body was now glistening with sweat. Giovanni's hair lay limp with strands covering his eyes and face. Perspiration ran down his temples and the bridge of his nose. The room felt like an inferno. He lifted her hips forcing her to her knees, but she was so caught in her own emotional turmoil she slipped back down to the bed. A slap landed hard on her ass, and she shivered, obeying his unspoken command. Getting to her knees and hands, she shot him a heated glare over her shoulder. He wouldn't dare smack her ass again without permission. He kissed the tender flesh and eased up behind her, forcing her to lower her face to the mattress with the press of his hand to her right shoulder. Her arms collapsed and her face dropped into the pillow. She moaned again and again as his strokes quickened, sharpened, and her channel became drenched, easing his glide. He enjoyed the warm softness of her ass pressed to his pelvis with each thrust.

Another flurry of deep powerful strokes drove him to the brink. He licked his lips. He felt parched. This vixen, this lovely chocolate temptress, was draining him dry. The more he gave the more she took. Giovanni reached under her, covering her back with his chest, he pinched her bud and pumped hard and fast in her channel. She cried out, with her face lifting from the pillow.

Mira collapsed flat on the bed. She squeezed her thighs tight in response to the orgasmic pull he was certain was the cause for the way she trembled below and begged for mercy.

"Yes. Yes. Yes!" she wailed. "Oh yes," she exclaimed.

To his surprise, she flipped to her back and scooted out of his reach to the headboard and pillows. Unwilling to let her go, he pulled her back to him. "We aren't done." Putting her left leg over his shoulder he pushed her thigh back into her chest as he positioned himself. Re-entry was twice as sweet. It was as if their union was destined. He slid his way into her. Her eyelids half open and heavy from sexual exhaustion, she moaned softly upon his re-entry. Pulling half way out and then pushing all the way in, Giovanni closed his eyes, overcome by warmth and heat. He struggled to stay in control as he felt his body stiffen with a desperate need to possess her. Pinning her leg down he kept with his passionate thrusts, promising to go with more care the next time. He was wound so tight he needed her desperately for his own release.

She understood. Pushing him she forced him to not break their sexy rhythm but to roll. He understood and complied bringing her on top. She arched her back sliding down on him again. He held her by her right hip tightly. She threw her head back and put down a powerful up and down bounce on his cock that had tension exploding from his groin and cock.

"Fuck!" he wheezed. Placing both her hands against his chest, she rocked back and forth driving him to the breaking point. Giovanni's hips bucked two more times before all was unleashed, and hot semen filled the reservoir of his condom. Feeling his chest muscles tighten and his nails dig into her hips, he kept up the rhythmic roll of his hips, and she continued to pump her hips to control him. Together they exploded and crashed into a sexed out daze.

The woman lying next to him stirred. Giovanni's head turned. She drifted to sleep soon after their love session. An hour of staring at the ceiling trying to figure out all that had transpired between them had left him restless. He rolled to his side. There were few things in the world he needed as opposed to wanted. And nothing in this world was denied him. Giovanni decided. He would have her, for as long as this feeling lasted. The problem for him remained consistent. He wasn't sure what these feelings she stirred within him were?

With his head propped in his hand, he studied the sleeping beauty. The thick mane of curls that bounced on her shoulders when she walked had become a bit tangled and frizzy. Hair covered the side of her face. He smoothed away the tresses to reveal her delicate features.

Mira opened her eyes in response to his touch. "Hi," she said softly.

"I woke you."

"It's okay. What time is it?" she squinted at him.

Giovanni looked at his watch. "A little after three."

A frown dawned her face. "Oh, I should go to my room."

"This is your room. You will stay with me here."

She opened her mouth to object, and he silenced her with a kiss. Like the sexy attentive lover he'd found so addictive, she slipped her tongue into his mouth and overwhelmed him. The kiss came to a natural end. She snuggled up against him, and he cradled the side of her face with his hand. "It's settled."

He kissed her nose and then her brow.

Mira stroked his hip. Her hand ran slowly down his thigh. "If you insist."

"I do."

"I was thinking about you, while I slept," she teased.

Both of his eyebrows lowered. "I'm in your dreams?"

"Yes. Question after question kept surfacing in my head. One kept repeating over and over. It's how I am, I have to over analyze everything." She gave him a bashful smile. "Even things that feel good."

"Now I'm curious," he said, trying to roll her over and get between her warm thighs once more.

"Wait." She stopped him. "Don't you want to know what it is?"

"Mmm?"

"It's the question that Fabiana struggled with asking. The one that you evaded."

"I didn't evade. I answered her."

"Then answer me now. Who are you?"

"Who am I?" he laughed. "I thought you and I covered this one."

Mira laughed as well. "No. I want to know, what is it that you do exactly?"

He kissed her lips softly. His face lifted with a boyish smile so wide and pure. How could she think he could be part of something nefarious? In this moment his handsome features almost made him angelic. Still she wanted to know about him. The hard demeanor, the power he exuded among men, the tattoos on his arms and back. "Are you the leader of a Mafia family? What does that mean? Being a Don?"

"What do you think it means?"

"Don't do that."

"What?"

"Answer a question with a question. I know you aren't a drug dealer. I'm asking about organized crime. Are you really some sort of Mafia king or something?"

Giovanni withdrew from her. "Or something," he mumbled.

Mira turned to her side. "You were going to be a lawyer. You studied in America. Why didn't you finish that dream?"

"It was just a dream, and dreams aren't meant to be finished. Plus that was my mother's wish, not mine." He said dryly. "I told you my father needed me, as did my family. So that dream is over."

"That's not true, I dreamt all my life to—"

"To what? Be a dress maker?" he laughed at her. "Some dream. Making rags for spoiled pampered brats!" he spat.

Mira flinched. She sat upright. "That was uncalled for! How dare you talk to me like that?" she said angrily turning to get out of bed.

He reached gripping her arm forcefully, pulling her back to him. "I'm sorry."

"Let go!" she shouted, trying to push him away.

Giovanni overpowered her, pinning her to the bed. "I said I'm sorry!" he said in her face. "The fight is over."

She stopped struggling underneath him.

He sighed. "I overreacted. Let's not make a big deal out of it."

"Is that how you respond when you're asked a question you don't like?"

"No, no...I was wrong. Let's start over. I shouldn't have insulted you. We cannot discuss my business. It's not something that you and I will ever discuss."

"You're right, because there is no us. Now will you please let me go so I can return to my room?"

"Shit."

"NOW!" she refused to be swayed.

Giovanni released her. He fell over to his back blowing out a frustrated breath. Mira rose from the bed. She hurried to gather her robe and cover herself. She could barely stand on her feet without swaying. Her legs and back ached from the acrobatics performed in his bed. She needed a tub packed with ice for relief.

"So this is what you do? You run because we disagree?" He glared after her.

"No. Watch me walk away, and not look back."

"Wait."

"Screw you, Giovanni."

"*Bella!*" He shouted in a deep authoritative voice that stopped her cold. She glanced back at him almost in fear from the hard tone he used. But he didn't seem to be threatening her. He looked more pained than anything else.

Giovanni put his hand to his forehead and rested his elbow against his raised knee. "My mother was a sad complicated woman. She lost a lot of her happiness at a young age and gave up her family to be with my father. She wasn't Sicilian. Do you understand?"

"No."

"She asked for very little from my father, only the best for her children. She wanted me to be a lawyer. It was her dream. I wanted to be my father; that was my dream. Those two dreams could not exist in one man. So the time came for me to make a choice." He extended his arms. "This is my choice. My *famiglia*, is my choice. My business is a lot of things. And most of these things are within and beyond the law. None of it has anything to do with you and me."

Masterful persuasion seemed to be his style, but when he

spoke to her she couldn't help but recognize his sincerity. "Your life sounds complicated."

"It's extremely complicated, *Bella*; my existence is rooted in contradictions and complications. Do you know what is not complicated? Us. This that we share. Passion. I make you feel good? Don't I? You make me feel more of a man than anyone outside of those doors."

"Because of the sex."

"Because of your fire." He smirked.

Mira rolled her eyes. Still, she couldn't help smiling.

"We have a friendship, right? No strings. No need to attach meaning to what I do, if we are just enjoying each other. You appearing from nowhere reminds me of why I should not let complications get the better of me. If I do, I will miss some of the sweetness of life."

The harsh uneven rhythm of her breathing thinned. The man spoke like a poet and with his accent she weakened. Her thoughts became muddled, and she couldn't remember in that moment why they argued.

"I say what I mean, without a filter, *Bella*."

"I see."

"With you, I will be more cautious," he said sincerely.

Her memories of their shared passion were pure and clear, at the front of her mind. It made his apology sweeter. The man didn't really owe her any further explanation than the one he gave. She stared at him and wondered so many things. What did the tattoos on his body mean? What made him so angry and gentle all at once? What woman had his heart and how could she ever compete. He raised his hand to her.

"Veini qui. Abbracciami."

"Translation?" she asked softly.

"Come here, hold me." A mischievous, sly, smile tipped the corner of his mouth upward. As if the denial of his request was not an option. Mira wanted to yield to the burning sweetness that made her his captive. Her feet moved under his command. She shed her robe and crawled back over the large bed to him. "I think I like complicated," she said.

"And I think I know what else you like." He rolled her under him and her lungs dragged in deep breaths. He drew her to the edge of the bed and stood. She again was confronted with the angry long erection she longed to possess. Giovanni would oblige. His large hands smoothed over her skin and down her thighs before he spread her legs and lowered to his knees before her. She stared down the line of her body at him.

"Let me apologize properly."

Lust pushed him straight into full-on arousal. A deep groan escaped his throat as he thrust his tongue deeply into her core and his hands clenched the soft lush curves of her firm ass. Her body undulated in response and her mound pressed upon his face. If he could smile he would. *Damn.* He could dine here for breakfast, lunch, and dinner every day.

He sensed the awakening flames within her. He fucked her with his tongue, sucked and nibbled on her clitoris until she thrashed and pounded her small fists against the mattress for release, and release she did. Lapping with repeated flicks of his tongue, he enjoyed her torment.

She sat up in the bed and squeezed her thighs tightly shut while she shook hard through her climax. Giovanni peered up at her, still on his knees. He rose, lifting her legs and cinching them around his waist. Their eyes met. He found her wide gaze, full of appreciation for what they now shared. It made him more confident. He liked the way he saw himself in her eyes. He could believe himself worthy with this woman.

Intent on full possession, he drove his cock into her. He tossed his hips side-to-side to sink deeper. "So good," he groaned. "More," he said. "I like how tight you keep it for me, how you move your ass. Like this. Yes." He said thrusting in and out of her. She bucked her pelvis when he thrust deeper and he speared her with a hard glance. Though she moved the way he desired, he felt a sharp pang of jealousy that she would know so much of his needs. How many other men had known her sweet body? Who were the motherfuckers that came before him? He wanted names and address so he could send his men in to take care of the competition permanently.

"Don't stop," she moaned. Giovanni had slowed his passionate thrusts. He fell back over her and started to fuck her on the edge of the bed. A shiver racked her body and he knew she was close. Knowing his weight was making her breathless, he tried to lessen his passionate thrusts, but he soon slipped beyond control. Spiraling toward his own orgasmic ending that nearly made him weep like an infant.

Chapter Six

"**W**HAT'S THAT ON YOUR NECK?**" Fabiana asked.

Mira's hand instinctively covered the spot in question. She pulled the collar of her shirt over to hide the reddish-purple bruise.

"Oh shit! Is that a hickey?"

"What? No." Mira chuckled. She found several love bites that morning when she showered. A few bruised patches of skin also peppered her breasts, abdomen, and between her thighs. The man had a habit of biting, sucking, and licking every inch of her. "You know I bruise easily. I was showering a bit too hard this morning."

A nervous tremble went through her hand when she reached for her cappuccino, so she abandoned the attempt. It was silly to hide the truth from her best friend, but for some reason she didn't want to talk about it. She ignored the questioning look on Fabiana's face. Mira hid her sleep-deprived eyes behind the black lenses of her sunglasses. Giovanni was gone. So breakfast this morning had been served outside on the veranda facing the lake. They dined alone on an arrangement of pastries, so sweet and fresh the cream filled croissants melted on her tongue.

"I have news." Fabiana's voice, whimsical and light, matched the mood of her friend when she arrived in a tangerine sundress that Mira had designed for her three years ago.

"Sounds mysterious," Mira said, grateful for the change in subject.

"Lorenzo and I are going to date exclusively. We're falling in love. It's real."

"Oh? Okay."

"That's all you have to say?"

"Good grief Fabiana, I'm not your mother or your priest." Mira chuckled. "If you're getting close to the man, then it's okay. I only want you to be careful and use your head."

"Take off those sunglasses. I want to see your eyes when you say those words." Fabiana laughed. "Where's my friend? What have you done with her?"

Mira waved off the request. "I've only been protective of you because I love you. I've seen you disappointed too often in the past."

"He's great. Yesterday I broke the golden rule. He got a taste."

"Taste of what?" Mira asked a bit disinterested. She wondered when Giovanni would return. He left before they could finish their talk. She was even more curious about the man.

Fabiana snapped her fingers in front of her face. "Pay attention. We made love. It was more than I expected. Not to say I'm in love with the sex. It's just how he makes me feel. I can't explain it."

"Trust me I understand."

"Would you take the sunglasses off please?"

She gently removed them from her face. Fabiana leaned forward. "Sweet Jesus, girl, did you get any sleep last night?"

Mira picked up her knife and checked her reflection in the sterling blade. Her eyes were puffy, and watery with dark circles beneath. She didn't bother with makeup. "No. I didn't sleep. Not a wink."

"Why? You went to bed early enough."

Indeed she had gone to bed. Between tossing and turning and being ravished, there was no time for rest. The sun warmed her face and shoulders, still she felt drained, hollow, lifeless. Fabiana stared with an expectant look of some confession to be offered. What could she say? Every time she begged for release he had his hands on her. All night he wanted her. When his dick didn't respond he used his mouth and hands, fingers. It was never ending. Thankfully a knock on the door sent him to the shower and leaving her semi-conscious on the bed. She nearly had to crawl back to her room. The muscles in her legs screamed from the strain he put on them.

"Hello? I asked you a question. Why were you up all night?"

"Don Giovanni."

Fabiana's eyes stretched wide. Mira took another sip of her coffee, set the cup on the saucer and met her friend's questioning stare. "He returned to the villa late last night."

"And? So?"

"And I went to his room."

Fabiana sat back, her long bangs falling into her eyes. She sat perfectly still, staring, as if they'd just met. Mira averted her gaze to the lake. The water was a beautiful cobalt blue, and the waves almost sparkled under the clear sky. This place defined paradise.

"Go on." Fabiana encouraged.

"I let him... you know... we talked, and then we did more."

"Are you serious?"

"I am." Mira nodded. "All night."

"But you said you went to his room? I found you in yours this morning, alone."

"I did." Mira shrugged. "And it happened."

"Sounds to me like you wanted it to happen. Planned it?"

"Maybe. So?"

"So?"

"There's no conspiracy. You just confessed to sleeping with Lorenzo. I'm sure you wanted that to happen."

"Sorry." Fabiana raised her hands in defense. "It's not like you. That's all."

"You sound like Kei. *This is not like you Mira*, he would always say. *Has Fabiana been putting crazy ideas in your head again?*" she mocked her ex's deep voice.

"Well? Have I?"

"Everyone thinks they know me better than I know myself. And that's the thing with Giovanni, I can be me. He has no preconceived notions. It feels so good. So I say this is exactly like me. The new me!"

"Hey. I'm not saying it's a bad thing. What's wrong with you? You dated Kei for six months before you had sex with him. You are very, very particular about men, more so than me."

Mira put her sunglasses back on. "I guess I'm a bit caught up. You know. In all of this." She nodded toward the sparkling blue waters of the lake. They were in the middle of paradise.

She had a sexy Italian man showing her more passion than she'd had in years, and it's got her head spinning. Who could blame her?

"I can be impulsive."

"So he just wants sex?"

"I never said those words."

"Do you care what he wants? Is this only about you?" Fabiana leaned in and lowered her voice. "Good for you if it's about you and you only. I want you to be selfish for once. If you can forget Kei and all the stress of the past year, then that means you can create so much more. It's perfect. This is why we needed this break, so we can discover who we are."

"You are good for my inner wild child." Mira winked. "I love you."

"Who else will put up with your uptight ass? Besides I knew something was up. I mean girlfriend, who gets hickies from a washcloth?"

Laughter exploded from them both. "You haven't seen anything. I think I got some on my butt, too!"

"Whew!" Fabiana fanned herself. The laughter eased them into a comfortable silence, but Fabiana continued to grin. "Okay so I have to ask. The man is intense. Did you see the way he flipped to gangster on me at dinner?"

"He did not."

"He did too! He rarely smiles, unless you are speaking. And when you are in the room, he stares like you belong to him. Intense. Kind of intimidates me, and you know, no one intimidates me."

"What do you want to know?" she asked.

"How... how did it go down? Did you just go to his room and then bam! Sex, lots and lots of sex?"

"Don't be silly!"

"C'mon, did you seduce him? What? I have to know about this inner wild child."

"He's different. Less serious when he's with me. Sometimes. He's definitely different when he's turned on. I went to his room... and yes it was a bam, thank you ma'am!" she chuckled. "The man had me so horny after he—" Mira bit down on her bottom lip. She had no intention of sharing the details of their prelude to their sex that made her bold enough to seek him out in the night.

"He what? Mira are you comparing him to Kei? Is that holding you back?" Fabiana asked.

Mira shrugged.

"That's normal. Lorenzo's different, too. Oh and trust me, here in Italy, different is good."

They sat in silence for a moment, staring out at the sailboats drifting along the lake. Mira broke the silence. "You do know what they do, who they are?"

Fabiana shrugged. "It doesn't matter."

"Are you kidding? Having a fling is one thing, but you said you were falling in love."

"And you're not?" Fabiana tossed back.

"NO! Been there and done that. No. Absolutely not."

"I've known you since we were nineteen. I've seen you with two men in all that time. One a blind date I set up for you that you chased away, and the other Kei. You went to Giovanni last night for more than sex. You like the man."

"Like! I like him, Fabiana. That's not love."

"Whatever you say. Remember we do plan to make Napoli our home. The man practically runs the entire region along the Amalfi coast. Your paths are going to cross, over and over again. Shouldn't you get to know him outside of his bed?"

Suddenly, she felt thirsty. She reached for her water instead of coffee and swallowed down deep gulps.

"They aren't men to dismiss lightly, especially if you're having sex with them."

She released a bitter laugh. "I know this. It wouldn't hurt to get to know the man I'm sleeping with. And yes, I like him. Do you really think it wouldn't matter to you one bit what Lorenzo does as long as you have him in your life? Especially if it's illegal?"

"Are you saying that you'll end this love affair with Giovanni without finding out if there's something real there, because of your prejudices?"

"Now this is rich! I'm prejudice?"

"Of course you are." Fabiana waved her off. "We all are in some way or not. Pre-judging people makes you prejudice. You even thought Kei was tied to something illegal because of his associations. If people don't live up to the moral code your granny carved into you, you have no tolerance level for them. Everyone has to be perfect."

The accusation cut deep. She was glad for the cover of her sunglasses. She double blinked away the glaze of tears blurring her vision.

"All I'm saying is you must give Giovanni a chance, like I will for Lorenzo."

"A chance to what, Fabiana? If these men are into illegal things, what chances are you suggesting we give them?"

"If? Let's not pretend we don't see who they are. The men with guns, the way they speak, dress, nearly bow when your sexy Don enters a room. I'm suggesting that we start our life by new rules in Italy. Take a chance to discover if who these men are matters more than how we feel when we're with them. That's all. Maybe we can be better influences on them. Who knows what the future could bring."

"Dating criminals? I can't believe you would even suggest it." Mira shook her head. "You're thinking about changing who Lorenzo is to make him fit into your life. I won't play that game. You can't change a man, and you know this."

Fabiana picked up her mimosa and gestured in a mock toast.

"I get what you're saying. I don't want you to ever think that my support of you is on the condition that you are perfect, Fabiana. I'm not perfect, and I don't expect you to be."

"Fine, neither is Giovanni or Lorenzo. They aren't perfect. Let's just enjoy the time with them and see what we see."

"Right. I'm sure we'll see plenty."

After breakfast Fabiana excused herself to make a few business calls. Mira suffered a twinge of disappointment. Fabiana was far more sensitive than she. If her friend believed she was falling in love with Lorenzo then the blinders were on and her focus was singular. That could mean trouble.

A stroll is what she needed. The veranda had stone steps that led to a cobblestone path through a manicured garden. The cool serenity of the snug retreat made her feel welcome and safe. She shoved her hands down into the front of her jeans. A fresh breeze washed over her. Her oversized long-sleeve shirt, which she tied in the front and rolled the sleeves up on her arms, proved perfect for the day's weather. Her hair was up in an untamed ponytail, and her sunglasses shielded her weary eyes from the sun. She was too restless to try again for sleep.

At the foot of the path, she stopped. Giovanni was there. He had his back to her staring off into the lake. He wore a dark shirt and slacks. In fact, since she'd met him, the man had worn no other color than black. His hair smoothed back from his face covered his lapel. A curl of smoke lifted from in front of his face before his hand lowered. She saw a half-smoked cigar in between two of his fingers. Her teeth caught the edge of her bottom lip, and she glanced around to see that they were alone. Should she disturb him? She was so excited to find him she ached to do so.

When did he return? Why was he out here smoking alone?

He turned in an instant, and his gaze fell upon her. No wonder she lost her head so quickly with him. One look into his eyes, and she was filled with nervous energy. Fabiana was right. Casual would not be their thing. It had gone beyond that point. "Hi," she said.

"Morning, *Bella*. I thought that was you." He extinguished the cigar with his thumb then dropped it into the front of his shirt pocket without a flinch.

"You knew it was me?" she asked.

"It's a hidden talent of mine, eyes behind my head." He approached her. "I had to perfect that skill years ago." He greeted her with a kiss. She loved the height on the man.

"How tall are you?" Mira asked.

"Strange question," he smirked.

"You're tall, and so are your men."

He chuckled. "Blame our fathers."

"Did I interrupt you? You looked to be deep in thought."

"No, I was waiting."

Mira stepped closer. "For?"

"You. Didn't want to disturb your breakfast."

Her smile faded. He had seen her and Fabiana? Did he hear the conversation too? "Okay. So now that you have me what's next?"

"How about we go for a walk?" He extended his hand.

A shadow moved and she spotted the first of three men who remained close. She glanced around and finally recognized the others. Where were they minutes ago? Had they been there all along? Was he ever alone? The man who was less than two hundred feet away stood silent, observant. Both of them kept a reasonable distance. "Do they have to come?"

Giovanni nodded. "I'm afraid so. You'll get used to it."

"I don't think I'll ever get used to a man with a gun shadowing me."

His fingers slid sensually over hers, and she accepted the offer. *"Andiamo."*

They continued along the nature path that circled the property and drew them closer to the lake. It had the unreal beauty of a picture postcard. Tall trees and blooms nestled in dewy grass, and the lake before them under a clear sky awaited them. "Italy is so beautiful."

"I've been all over the world, and there is no place like *Italia.*"

She dropped his hand and slipped her arm around his waist. Naturally, he placed his arm around her shoulder and kept her close. "About earlier. Did you hear me and Fabiana?"

"Debate my worthiness. You ladies were quite passionate."

"Sorry, it was a private conversation."

"You have your concerns. I understand. You made me a very happy man by sharing yourself with me. I'll consider it a gift."

"And if it's more?" she smiled weakly. When his gaze

lowered to hers she looked away. "Things moved a little fast with us. And I enjoyed it. I really did. I think we should talk about what's next."

"Okay?" He stopped.

"Fabiana reminded me of a few facts. We'll see more of each other, outside of Bellagio. Napoli is a small city."

"You want to get to know me?" Lightly he traced his finger along the side of her jaw.

"You're an interesting man. Why wouldn't I?"

"I have an idea. Let's go upstairs and re-acquaint ourselves with each other." He leaned forward to pull her in, but she stepped out of his reach. A frown deepened the lines between his brows. "Something wrong?"

"Feels like it to me. I usually get to the intimacy after I know the man, not before."

"You came to my bed."

She glanced over to the men to make sure she couldn't be heard. "You're addictive."

Giovanni laughed. "Addictive?"

"Very," she smiled. "That means I'll want more, and I can tell you do too."

"Of course I want more." Gathering her into his arms, he forced her to her toes. Her breasts were pressed hard against the corded muscles of his chest. She could feel his uneven breathing and knew he was just as excited as she was. The warmth of his arms encircling her was so male, and bracing.

The hurried beating of her heart when she stood so close to him made her pant a little and lose her train of thought. This, of course, he noticed. There was a sly smile on his face. His blue eyes seemed to go dark as the lake behind him. That was another thing. The man's eye color could change with the color of the wind. How on earth could she ever back out of this attraction between them? Unlike Fabiana, the idea of turning her heart over to another man terrified her.

"We won't say goodbye." His voice held a hint of a challenge and his gaze remained steady on her.

She chuckled and shook her head in disbelief. "Are you kidding? If I want to say to goodbye I'll say goodbye."

He grunted and slapped his forehead with his hand. In fact he started to speak hurriedly in Italian. Mira frowned at the animated way he spoke with his hands. "Speak English. I don't understand you." She yelled over his rant.

"Why are you so damn confused?"

"I beg your pardon?"

"We discussed this last night. We'll enjoy each other for as long as I choose."

"You choose?"

"We choose, I misspoke," he quickly added.

Mira turned to march away, and he grabbed her wrist dragging her back to him. "There is no stopwatch keeping time on us. Why must you?" he asked.

"Why are men like you so damn arrogant and controlling?" She yanked her hand free. She dropped hers to her hip and narrowed her eyes on him. "My goodness we've known each other for a little more than 48 hours and already I belong to you? Until when? You get bored?"

"What do you want *Bella*? Reassurance?" He sighed deeply. "What is it you need to stop inviting me in and then shoving me away?"

"It's simple. You don't decide how long we last, or anything we do. I do for me, and you do for you. I want your friendship. But no thank you on the sex."

Giovanni laughed. She frowned, eyeing him. He dropped his head back and closed his eyes. A deep groan rumbled in his chest.

"No sex? What does that prove?" he asked.

"I think we can enjoy Bellagio without ripping each other's clothes off. And the attraction is what we explored. It also makes it easier to understand what's happening between us. I can keep a clear head when I'm around you. All those pretty words and seductive touches confuse me. Hard to make this light when you make me feel the way you do."

"Because losing control is a bad thing right?"

She rolled her eyes. "So what! I like to be in control is that so damn horrible?"

He shook his head, smiling down at her like a parent would a child. *"Ti penso sempre!"*

"English!" Mira demanded.

"I'm always thinking of you. Now it's worse for me, after touching you." Giovanni seized her. He lifted her by her midriff and brought her up against him. Mira didn't resist. She hooked her arms around his neck and held on with her body flush to his. Warm heat captured her mouth as his crashed over hers, and she tasted the bitterness from his cigar. He kissed her hard and strong. Caught up, she found his lips were more persuasive than she cared to admit. Breaking the passionate exchange, he stared directly into her eyes when he spoke. "You feel that?" he whispered to her. "It's me, and you can't control me, *Bella*. Do you understand?" He reclaimed her lips. Soft shivers shimmied up her spine. Mira smiled against his mouth as he spoke to her with his tongue delving. "And this." He heaved her up higher, his hands gripping both halves of her ass, and she wrapped her legs around his waist. "This is *us, Bella*. You won't control us. I see it will take more convincing. I am the man for the job."

Mira turned her face from his mouth and closed her eyes as kisses slipped down the curve of her neck. "You can't be serious." She held to him tighter.

"Look at me. Am I serious?"

She returned her gaze and stared deep into his eyes. She swallowed all doubt.

"I'm a man. Don't treat me like a boy, or one of those that work for you. Deal with me. Do you understand?"

She nodded.

"Then you must give me room to be near you. To have you."

Confused, breathless, she only nodded again.

He kissed her again. "*Approvazione,* that means you're okay with this. Say it."

"*Approvazione.*"

He lowered her, and she slid down his large frame to stand on her own two feet.

"Then we will honor this 'no sex' rule this evening. I have a condition," he said.

"What is it?" She fixed her shirt that had come untied.

"You return home with me to Sorrento. Let me show who I am. It's near Napoli."

"No." She shook her head. "I couldn't."

"You can't or you won't?"

"I have Fabiana."

"She and Lorenzo will come as well. My villa has been in our family for close to two hundred years. It's three times as large as this one. There's plenty of room. My business calls me back. I can't stay here more than a day. And I'm... I'm not ready to say goodbye."

Mira put her fingertips to her temples. Her head literally swam, and breathing was a chore with him bearing down on her. "I need to talk to her first. We're vacationing. She wanted to go sailing today, and I put her off," she lied.

"Mira, it's too late to put the brakes on when we've already taken the victory lap. You let me in, *Bella*." He lifted her chin. "I'm not going anywhere. You said you wanted to know me. The only way to know me is to let me show you my world. A small part of it."

"When?"

"I have a business meeting tomorrow, and then we can leave on my jet."

"What's in Sorrento that we can't find here?"

"The opportunity to show you how beneficial being my friend can be if you give me a chance."

The world was filled with him now. He consumed her thoughts when they were apart, and she desperately wanted to hold on to that feeling a bit more. He touched her again. His hand cupped the side of her face, and his irises were a softer shade of blue. Her mind relived the velvet warmth of his kiss. "Okay. I'll talk to Fabiana." Her friend would be game if it included Lorenzo.

Giovanni smiled and lowered his hand to capture hers. "Is holding hands allowed?" he kidded.

She laughed. "As if you need my permission."

Chapter Seven

L ORENZO CRAVED THE SHARP BURN of whisky to torch his throat. He decided on a bottle of wine from their family's private stock. He needed to have a cool head. Giovanni didn't suspect. No one did. And, dammit, he made sure no one ever would. When he returned yesterday, the men didn't question him. It would be stupid to believe his arrival on a Vespa wasn't shared with his cousin. Lorenzo drank down half the bottle. He exhaled. "Fuck. What the fuck have I done?"

Yesterday

Lorenzo slowed his car and circled the long front drive of a dilapidated, ugly little cottage deep in the east hamlet of Bellagio. Its forlorn, vacant appearance was a striking contrast to the candy-apple red convertible Jaguar parked in the tall grass to the side of it. Giuseppe Calderone travelled in and out of the hamlets in flashy cars with loud music. The motherfucker wouldn't know discretion if she sat on his face and gave him a blowjob.

He let go a devilish chuckle. But soon the humor died on his lips, and anxiety cooled his thoughts.

What if Giovanni suspected something and had Lorenzo tailed? How could he explain this meeting? His vision switched to the rearview mirror. Thanks to the overgrown cypress and hundreds of wind whipped trees flanking both sides of the single lane road he travelled in on, a car tailing him could remain unseen. Therefore, he waited.

Nothing stirred. He didn't expect this meeting to go well. Giovanni was making moves. Battaglias would soon surpass all families in the Cammora. How could he anticipate he'd try to expand their operation up through the triangle? The dealings between he and Calderone would have to come to an end.

"Fuck this shit." Lorenzo threw open his car door and got out. He tossed it shut with a loud slam. Birds took flight from the belly of tangled tree branches. The evening sun blared in the sky making everything around him bright and feverish. Perspiration spread over his brow and trickled down his sideburns. Tucking his gun into the front of his pants, he did another silent sweep of the forests. It would have been wise to clue his best friend Carlo in. To do so would reveal his mistakes, unforgivable mistakes. He had to deal with Giuseppe alone.

As he strolled around the outskirts of the property, he felt the hairs on his nape rise. Uneasy and alert, he kept his vision keen to anything out of order. The front of the cottage was boarded up but the back had been opened for their meetings over the years. And now Lorenzo tired of the side hustles and back door deals behind his family's back. He stepped through the open doorway with his hand to his gun, still tucked in his waist. Giuseppe waited alone.

"What the hell? I've been here for damn near an hour!" Giuseppe Calderone was a plump, five-foot three, well-dressed thug. Spoiled, sheltered, and tolerated by the men of their world only because of his father's notoriety. The runt had the good fortune to be the only son of Don Calderone. Lorenzo dropped his hand from his gun. Calderone wiped the sweat from his brow with his silk handkerchief tucked in his back pocket. "Well? Why the fuck did you keep me waiting?"

"You're alone?"

"Aren't I always?" Calderone sneered. "Ah, I understand now. Your half-breed cousin is in town, and now you don't trust me?"

Hackles rose to the back of his neck. Nothing made him more furious than lack of respect shown to his family. He took a measured step toward Giuseppe, and the turd actually grinned, too stupid to know how close to the edge Lorenzo actually was. "Disrespect my family again, and I'll put a bullet in your gut."

"Whoa, check out the balls on this guy. Bastardo! Baggiano! Since when do you threaten me?" Calderone took a step toward him. Lorenzo didn't flinch. "I tell you how this works. Or have you forgotten your sins and what it cost your family?"

The pressure in Lorenzo's temples pounded thickly; his throat grew tight under Calderone's mockery. The fucker would be wise not to push further. But the young spoiled jackass was just a loudmouth hothead with Lorenzo's balls in his grip. For years he did the unthinkable to bury his shame. And all of it was unraveling. The raid had opened Giovanni's eyes. It wouldn't be long before the dirty secrets of the past surfaced and destroyed his family from within.

"Nothing to say?" Calderone taunted. "Oh don't blame me. Blame the Russians, like you did before." Calderone laughed. "Your half-breed cousin spilled so much Russian blood you have enemies you cannot name. And for what? A lie. Our lie. Right Lorenzo?"

"State your business." Lorenzo ground out.

"I went into this bargain knowing you had no authority. Doesn't change the outcome. Our deal stands. I have another shipment to unload in Napoli in two days. Same Nigerians as before."

"I won't do it."

Calderone paused. His eyes stretched in their sockets and his cheeks puffed, with nostrils flared like a bull. "Figilo di puttana! What the fuck do you mean you won't do it?"

"The Albanians were using Francesco to run child hookers through my club behind my back. Then we're raided? A coincidence? I don't think so. More like a distraction to keep Giovanni off your scent. Problem is, you stupid fuck, he has shut me down, permanently, and Francesco is dead."

"Not my problem." Calderone shrugged, with a stiff upper lip.

"It is now your problem. I won't deal anymore with you or the Nigerians. You need to work the transport out another way. The Amalfi is closed."

"Bullshit! We do it my way!" Calderone pointed a finger up at him. It was almost comical considering his height compared to Lorenzo's. "My way you stupid fuck!"

Lorenzo had more respect for cockroaches than he did him. If his father wasn't feared and respected by the Cammora and Ndrangheta he'd have been put to sleep long ago. The bug actually mistook compliance for fear. Giuseppe ran his tongue over his coffee stained teeth, grinning at him. "Let's not fight. What's the point? You have no choice but to do what I wish."

"Fuck you." Lorenzo removed his gun. "I always have a choice."

Calderone's gaze dropped to the gun between them. He let go a loud gust of laughter. "You plan to kill me? Are you fucking insane? Do you know who my fucking father is? He'll fucking skin you and your fucking half-breed cousin alive and burn what's left of your fucking family to the ground. Put the gun away before I'm insulted."

"I'm the nephew of Don Tomosino Battaglia, and you made a big mistake in forgetting that!"

Calderone walked away laughing, his round belly bouncing over his stubby legs like Santa Claus. He returned his oil black eyes to him. "Forget?" Calderone touched his chest. "You are the same man that ordered his uncle's death? He wasn't your Don when you came to me, crying for rank, for power. You are that man, are you not?"

Lorenzo aimed, and Calderone's smile faded. "Don't be fucking stup..."

One shot to the chest sent the man he'd loathed and served behind his own family's back, barreling into the wall. Lorenzo marched on him and grabbed him by the throat. If Giuseppe was to die by his hand, this day, this moment, he would do it while looking him in the eye. He wanted to see the dead space fill in and the life drain from the weasel. The bullet had indeed pierced young Calderone's gut. He spat up blood. Holding him by the throat he made sure they never broke eye contact when he placed the gun to Giuseppe's heart. "Porca, puttana! For my uncle." He unloaded and Giuseppe gave a dying squeal before slumping forward. Lorenzo stepped back to let him drop. He stood over him and emptied his clip. Coughing up a wad of phlegm he spat on the bloody stump that was once his nemesis and smiled.

"Where have you been? I've been looking for you." Fabiana

walked into the parlor. He turned and forced a smile. Seeing her did help. She was the only ray of hope in the sea of shit he found himself swimming in. He drew her into his arms and kissed her.

"Forgive me. I was on my way to find you."

"Are you okay? You were gone when I woke this morning. And last night, you seemed stressed."

Lorenzo wiped his jaw nervously. Her questions were wearing on his already frazzled nerves. He would normally never speak of his problems with a woman, but he desperately needed someone in his corner. "The day is ours. No more business. I plan to treasure you." He brushed her lips with his. "Over, and over, and over again." He felt her relax against him, and damn if she didn't smell as beautiful as she looked. The woman was a dream. When he released her from another kiss, she held on to him.

"You need something, Lorenzo. I feel it. Trust me, talk to me. What is it?"

"I made a mistake once, and it cost me my soul."

"Sweetheart." She stroked the side of his face. "How?"

"I'm trying to fix it, Fabiana, but it may be too late." Lorenzo sighed.

"I'll help you, Lorenzo, any way that I can."

"You can't."

"Listen to me. You have a soul, it's why I won't stop believing in you."

Giovanni walked into the parlor and stopped. He studied his cousin and Fabiana for a moment. Mira at his side, he kept his cool in check. Today at the lake he wasn't waiting on his American *bella*. He was waiting on Lorenzo. "I need to speak with you."

"Can it wait?" Lorenzo pressed a kiss to his woman's neck. Her presence strengthened him more than he expected. He gazed down into her lovely face and reassured her with a smile. "Thank you." He mouthed to her.

Lorenzo gave him a nod and then kissed Fabiana once more on the lips, before whispering something in her ear. She drifted from his arms and headed to Mira. The ladies gave them curious glances before they left. Giovanni drew both of the large doors shut for privacy. It was just after ten in the morning, and his cousin was on his second bottle of wine.

"What have I done now?" Lorenzo asked.

"Where were you?"

"Out." he replied, taking a drink and then pouring another. Giovanni observed. Lorenzo glanced back after the answering silence. He lowered his glass. "No disrespect. I didn't want to trouble you."

Giovanni waited.

"Giuseppe Calderone has defied his father. He's working with the Nigerians or the Albanians, not sure, but I do believe he's started moving products through Genoa. I know you had meetings with Don Calderone during your visit. I wanted to make sure none of this could be tied to the family."

"You're lying."

Lorenzo sucked in a tight breath through clenched teeth. "It's the fucking truth. I need to be on top of it. Right? That's what I do. That's all I do in this family. Shovel shit to clear the path for the new Battaglia."

"I know when you're lying to me."

"I lost *Isabella's*. Francesco, the freak, is dead. This cripples me." He slammed his hand against his chest. "I have my own aspirations cousin. My own! Now I have to figure how to begin from ashes. I was trying to get ahead of you. To prove to you that I'm trustworthy. My lead fell through. Giuseppe never showed."

Earlier another meeting with Don Calderone came to a premature end. The old man was furious that his son missed the event. Lorenzo could be telling the truth. His gut churned. Something felt off.

"What have I done to have you treat me like the enemy? A mistake. The raid was not my fault. And if you say it was, fine. It's still not my greatest sin."

"Then confess. Tell me your sins. I'm ready to listen."

Lorenzo paled.

"Nothing more to say?"

"My sin is being born to Isabella Battaglia. To being second in everything you and I do. I need you to recognize my place in this family. I need you to trust me."

Giovanni grabbed Lorenzo by the face. "It's the hand we were both dealt. It's time for you to get over it. When Papa died and you brought me the Russian scum that pulled the trigger, I knew our brotherhood was destiny. But if I ever find out that you have betrayed me, I will treat you like an enemy. You are my blood. *Capsici?* I love you above all else, but never, ever, mistake that love for weakness." Lorenzo grabbed his wrists, struggling against the crushing hold Giovanni applied. He forced his cousin's head to lower and pressed a kiss to his brow. "You and me forever." Giovanni released him. He stepped back with disgust. Before Lorenzo made him act on his suspicions, he walked out.

****

The night ended too soon. Mira joined him for another walk under the moon. She shared some of her life with him. How she struggled in New York, why she thinks Italia would be so different. And like a gentleman he walked her to her room and bid her goodnight.

Giovanni closed his eyes. Lorenzo's words returned to the center of his thoughts. Could he have something to do with Giuseppe Calderone's disappearing act? Possibly. But to have done so and not tell him caused Giovanni even more concern. His cousin would never be foolish enough to weaken their bond and family this way unless there was something he had to cover up. He would never force his hand. And Giovanni could never face his father on judgment day and tell him he executed his cousin for such a betrayal. It would prove him weak and pathetic as his enemies believed his Irish blood mixed in with his Sicilian had made him. He exhaled noisily. Lying upon the bedcovers with his ankles crossed, hands behind his head, and Danny-boy, his gun, resting over to his left, he couldn't summon sleep.

What about her?

At the base of his throat a pulse beat and swelled as though his heart had lodged itself there. *What about me?* The sweetest voice whispered in his ear. *She eased over him, her hot channel pressed down hard on the sweltering tightness that was his groin. And she was nude. Her lovely breasts were a man's size, each more than a mouthful but a perfect fit for his hands. She raised her arms above her head and rolled her hips. The slender line of her flat belly under her heaving breasts made him rise for the occasion. He took her breast as a babe would, and she stroked the back of his head with a soft caress. That's right sweetie, I'm here for you.* Giovanni sat up. He had drifted to sleep. His hand went to his erection, pointed north in his pajama pants. He groaned.

No sex? Bullshit. He was out of the bed and crossing the room to the door in nothing but black drawstring pajama pants. He stepped into the silent dark hall. The man seated outside was wide-awake. He averted his gaze when Giovanni emerged. It was a good thing because he did nothing to conceal his erection. Mira's door was closed. Touching the knob sent a charge of lust through him and dismissed any doubts he should wait for an invitation. The knob turned in his hand softly, and he found it unlocked. A smile spread over his lips, and he felt the tension in his chest relax. Quiet and careful, he pushed it open slowly then slipped inside. The bed swallowed her, as did the coverlet tucked around her form. She slept on her side. Her hair was behind a checkered silk scarf; the slender strawberry red strap of her camisole could be seen half lowered on her shoulder.

It was only a dream. She hadn't come to him as she did the night before. He should turn and let her sleep. Honor her wish to court her, earn the right to be in her bed. He sucked down a breath and willed himself to do so but couldn't move. He felt trapped between his raw need to have her and his desire to win her trust and heart. It again dawned on him the power women could wield over a man. His father was no saint. His father's crimes against his mother were unforgiveable. Still deep in his core he understood the madness that made his father snatch his mother from her world and keep her with him always. Slowly he untied the knot of his drawstring and loosened the waistband to his pajama pants. They dropped to his feet. He eased back the coverlet and slipped in bed with her. Mira didn't stir. She remained on her side with her back to him. Why did she cover her lovely thick hair under a scarf for sleeping?

His lips brushed her shoulder. She responded by scooting back, directly into him. He felt her stiffen with recognition. Wiping her eyes she turned and blinked at him in the dark.

"What's going on? Giovanni?"

Giovanni brushed his lips across her mouth and spoke three words, "I need you."

He needs me? Mira tried to rise but he was easing over her. She was awake, her thighs parting, and his lips brushing hers, then her neck and lower. She pushed at his shoulders with her hands, but he was unmovable. His face lifted from staring at her body in the camisole beneath him, and those eyes of his impaled her. She softened to his touch, relaxed. "Something wrong?"

"Ti penso sempre."

The translation was simple. He's always thinking of me. He said it on their walk. He said it again when he walked her to her room. And God, help her but it was true. She was always thinking of him. "I can hold you—" Her voice faded when she felt the blunt tip of his desire press in on her. She bowed her back to lower her pelvis and slow down the momentum building between them. "Wait," she pleaded. Her nipple escaped from the front of her camisole into his mouth. "Mmm," she moaned.

He entered her with one strong thrust. His thickness filled her to capacity. She rolled her hips in response and felt a coiling tension tighten and cinch the inner walls of her tummy. She breathed deeply while he flexed his knees, thrusting in a faster rhythm. Mira bit down on her lip, squeezing her eyes shut from the pleasure tickling up through her pelvis. Giovanni held onto her hip and directed the way she responded, and matched what pleased them both.

Melting warmth drew him deeper. His teeth ground together as he flexed and pumped his hips rapidly to drive himself deeper into her. Her channel hotly fit him like a wet glove, which got tighter and tighter. There was no stopping. He knew he was a demanding lover. He'd had girlfriends in the past complain about his appetite. She never did. His breathing harsh against her ear, he quickened his pace and prayed she'd forgive his rough manner. He dropped his head and bit her shoulder to hold on. Her flesh was soft and sweet in his mouth; he balled his fists tight to keep from hurting her and breaking skin. His balls were so tight now they ached, as did every muscle in the back of his thighs, buttocks, and along his pelvis.

"Oh!" She cried out, and he summoned more control. Slowing his thrusts to push her closer to bliss and not the frenzied madness swirling in his head, everything shattered, including him.

Giovanni's face was pressed into the pillow to the side of her head. He struggled to summon his breath. She soothed him by running both hands up and down his back.

"Giovanni," she wheezed.

Immediately, he shifted his weight. Giovanni, however, couldn't release her nor escape the warmth they generated under the covers. This was the closest he'd been to heaven in a long time. The beautiful woman in his arms smiled up at him. Her scarf slipped back to reveal the natural wavy texture of the roots of her hair. He touched her face and kissed the tiny mole to the left of her nose on her cheek. "You amaze me. I could stay like this. Forever."

"Mmm, me too," she agreed. She elevated her hips a bit beneath him. Reluctant, but concerned over her discomfort, he withdrew, semi-erect, and dropped over to his left side. Mira's hand went to the bruise on her shoulder, and he felt a pang of regret.

"Did I hurt you?" he asked.

She smiled and shook her head no, and then bolted right up. "Dammit, we didn't use protection."

Giovanni reached and grabbed the scarf to pull it free of her hair. He tossed it to the floor. "Why do you wear this?"

Without a word, she escaped the bed and hurried to her bathroom. Unlike his room, her drapes were open. Moonlight bathed over her flawless body when she escaped him. He had only a glimpse of the lush curve of her backside. Touching himself under the covers, he wished his dick could get hard again, but this time she had drained him dry. He listened as water ran until his lids felt heavy with fatigue. The exhaustion of the day returned, and he felt himself slip under its pull.

"Giovanni?"

A warm wet cloth wiped over his dick. He squinted up at her. She wore a robe and again tied her hair down in a silk scarf. Mira completed her task then folded the rag and set it aside. "Come to me." He reached for her before she fully turned away. She joined him under the covers without resistance.

"Are you okay? Earlier, things got a bit intense," she said, her voice meek, almost shy of the hard edged woman she liked to portray. Giovanni didn't answer. He really was in no mood to talk. Instead he brought her body to his and curled around her curves until his leg was over her thighs and his face was buried in the sweet cushion of her breasts. She said a few more things.

Talked of how an ex-lover never made her feel this desired, things he catalogued for future reference. After listening and enjoying the melody of her voice and rapidly beating heart, he grunted a response. Sleep had never been this welcomed.

Fresh and re-energized Mira turned over with a smile on her face. She reached for her lover to find he had already gone. Her eyes flipped open. It was becoming a nasty habit. Here one minute and gone the next. She shook her head and expelled a deep frustrated breath. A sharp sting ripped through her left shoulder and she touched the tenderness. Things had gotten out of hand with them last night. He kept apologizing through the night for the bite. Though the pain was numb and not really too discomforting, the desperation in his lovemaking made her worry. The knocking at her door drew her attention. She soon realized it was the knocking that brought her out of her sleep. She covered herself and sat up on her pillows.

"Come in."

"Morning, sleepy head."

"Morning," she yawned.

"Get up," Fabiana said. She waved car keys in front of her. "The men had a meeting this morning, so I have the keys to the Spider. It's cuter than the Ferrari. Let's go have some fun."

"No, Fabiana, I'm exhausted." Mira rolled away.

"Giovanni said you were."

Mira frowned. She looked back over her shoulder at her grinning friend. Fabiana nodded. "He told me to let you sleep in. Oh and get this. He announces that we're going to his villa in Sorrento. You're okay with this?"

"The man sure does think he knows what I want," she rolled her eyes.

"Uh oh, somebody is a grumpy puss!" Fabiana teased.

"Where is he gone to now? Every night he's here, but I swear the man must be allergic to the sun because once it's up he's gone." She snapped her finger. "Just like that."

Fabiana shrugged. "He had one of his goons wake up Lorenzo over an hour ago and demand he get dressed to come with him."

Mira gave up. She sat back on to her pillows and removed her headscarf. "Oh."

"Come on girl! If we're leaving today, let's go out and have a bit of fun." Fabiana stopped at the side of the bed and picked up her tossed aside camisole. "Unless you're too tired for fun?"

Mira snatched the garment from her, suppressing a smile.

"Would you please leave? I'll meet you downstairs in an hour."

"Mira? What happened to your shoulder?" Fabiana asked.

Instinctively, her hand shot up to cover the bruise. "Nothing. Nothing."

"That's not nothing, let me see." Fabiana reached and snatched her hand down. She leaned in closer to inspect it. "Well, it looks like a hickey, but it... does it hurt?"

Mira sighed. "No. We had sex, and things got a bit rough."

"Rough sex?" Fabiana's nose wrinkled.

Quickly, Mira tried to cover. "I'm fine. Giovanni is a bit much to handle when he's worked up. It wasn't intentional."

Fabiana stared at her for a moment, and Mira held her breath waiting. Her friend smiled. "If you're cool with it, then okay. Now c'mon and get dressed. I can't wait to get behind this car." She waved the keys and walked out.

Mira released the breath she held and dropped back onto the pillows. Last night he was in pain and sought solace within her arms; she knew that. Touching her shoulder, she wondered about the dark side of her lover and wanted to know what tormented him. A softer memory surfaced. She remembered his kiss and smiled. She thought she was dreaming, but she was almost certain he kissed her this morning before he left.

****

Giovanni sat silently next to Lorenzo. The car held the curvy road that sloped upward into the mountains. It was a wet slick morning; the countryside glistened from the remnants of a fresh rain. His gaze remained trained on the passing landscape. He didn't know what possessed him last night. His hand clenched into a fist. He should have more control over his emotions, over himself. He closed his eyes and remembered how she held him. How soft and sweet her breath was against his chest when she slept in his arms. And the way she made love to him, tamed him. He had to get a grip on his desires for her. He couldn't trust it to last.

"I wanted to be included." Lorenzo's voice was tight and hoarse, demolishing his thoughts. He opened his eyes and glanced over at his cousin.

"I think it best you and Giuseppe explain what ties you have."

"Giuseppe? Ties? We have none."

"Then there should be no problem with you facing him today?" Giovanni asked with a raised brow.

Lorenzo shook his head. "I can't stand the runt."

"Are you sure cousin? Now is the time to tell me anything you have now. I don't want any surprises. Do you understand? Don't let me walk into this meeting unprepared."

"He's contacted me. Several times he's contacted me to meet over one deal or another, and I've entertained him out of respect for our families, but nothing more. When will you trust me? Must I bleed for you? Is that it? I'm loyal to you and Battaglia. No one else comes before the family."

It was a small measure of reassurance, but Giovanni accepted it. His gaze returned to his window and the countryside. He hadn't slept this well since he buried his parents. Now his head was clear. He may have to make some tough choices in the future as to his role in the family, and he needed to have Lorenzo step up if he was to ever be in his place. That meant mending past mistakes and quieting his cousin's restlessness.

****

"What about this one?" Fabiana walked out of the dressing closet. She wore a daffodil yellow dress with thin straps. The chiffon material of the skirt fell in tight pleats that moved like an accordion when she spun around. The bodice of the dress had the same chiffon material arranged in a basket weave like pattern, slimming her waistline and pushing her bust upward. Mira thumbed through racks aimlessly when she walked out. Looking over her sunglasses she wrinkled her nose in disapproval, "Not your color."

Fabiana blinked, shocked. "I like yellow."

"I never dress you in this color; it's not complimentary to your pale skin with your red hair. You look like some kind of tropical bird."

She turned her friend toward the mirror to make sure she saw her the way she did. Fabiana frowned and then her eyes stretched in recognition. "Okay. Guess you have a point."

"I know I do. I'm the designer remember?"

"Hey? What has made you so bitchy today?"

"I'm not being a bitch. You asked for my damn opinion!"

The sales woman glanced up at them both. Fabiana said something in Italian to the salesperson and then narrowed her eyes on her. She hooked her arm around Mira's and forced her to join her in the cramped changing closet. "Okay, what is it?"

"I'm worried about us." She sat in the chair in the corner of the closet. Fabiana eased down the zipper and changed back into her clothes.

"Go on. I'm listening."

"Look at us. We're businesswomen, driven and successful, but look at us. What are we doing here?"

"Having a vacation, Mira! Good grief, we have next week to return to our lives but this week is ours okay? And don't make this about us. This is about him. What happened between you two?"

"I told him yesterday we need to go slow, that we need to take time to get to know each other, and then he just shows up in my bed."

"He just shows up huh?"

"Well I sure as hell didn't invite him."

"So why not kick him out?"

Mira cut her eyes away. "I'm not angry that he came to me. Trust me I had restrained myself from going to him." She dropped her head back against the wall. "I'm not even angry that he can make my body sing. I'm mad because I woke up and found him gone, and it hurt. You know that sinking feeling you get in the pit of your stomach when you're lovesick? Pathetic! What am I getting myself into? The man just does whatever the hell he wants, when he wants, and how he wants me. What am I doing falling for this guy?"

Fabiana's eyes grew round with shock. "You're falling in love?"

"No, of course, not!" Mira hadn't realized she used the word.

"You just said you were."

"I said it makes no sense. I don't want to talk about this anymore. Let's go get something to eat."

Fabiana shook her head. "Fine, but I'm buying the damn yellow dress."

"Go right ahead, be a parrot. Don't say I didn't warn you," she called out after her as Fabiana left the changing room. She rose and picked up her purse.

Villa Calderone

"Benvenuto del Giovanni il mio ragazzo." Don Calderone rose. A short, rotund man, his face was rather long and pale under a grey stubble of a beard. He had tired eyes that suggested a hint of trouble. The men greeted him with respect. The Calderone family ran the region of Genoa, but vacationed often in Como. It was to their advantage that he too was here while Giovanni had planned a visit. The old man gave Giovanni a hug and then a kiss to both sides of his face. To Lorenzo he did the same.

Angelo, a stout man looked every bit the same as his weasel cousin Giuseppe. None of the Calderone men would win any beauty contests. The Don's nephew stepped forward. He greeted Giovanni with a respectful kiss to either side of his jaw.

"Join me." Don Calderone gestured to the chairs.

"This meeting was to occur close to an hour ago. I don't appreciate being kept waiting." Giovanni's voice was low but resonated with his disapproval.

The old man nodded. *"Scusi."* He touched his wide chest. "I was waiting on that absent-minded son of mine. He was supposed to have returned in time for the meeting. We can't locate him." Don Calderone waddled on his stumpy legs back around his desk and sat.

"*Patri*, he may still be in Genoa. He mentioned business there." Angelo dropped a comforting hand to his uncle's shoulder. All the men in the family referred to the old Don as their father, just as Lorenzo referred to Tomosino that way.

"Business?" Giovanni asked.

Don Calderone put his hand up. "Family business out of Sicily." The Don turned his attention to Lorenzo. "Giuseppe said that you two may have a very lucrative agreement in Napoli in the works?"

Lorenzo stared at the Don unfazed. Giovanni didn't read any reaction to the news. "I agreed to meet with Giuseppe to discuss his interest in hosting parties at *Isabella's*. Nothing was ever confirmed. He hasn't called to schedule."

Don Calderone smiled then reached for his cigar box, pulling out his half smoked stogie and a lighter. "I heard of your troubles," he lit the end of the cigar and pumped his fat cheeks to draw and release rings of smoke.

"Yes. The club is gone. It was an unfortunate incident and completely blown out of proportion. My cousin understands." Lorenzo answered.

"I know my son can be an *ass* at times. I keep him on a short leash, out of respect for your family and my dear friend Tomosino." He glared over at Lorenzo. "I tire of the bullshit. My son needs to keep with tradition. Traditions from Sicily. It means that you are to make no alliances with Giuseppe in or outside of the triangle without my explicit approval. No matter how tempting the offer *capisci*?"

Lorenzo nodded.

Don Calderone took a drag of his cigar. He dropped the blunt into the ashtray. "My words are not an accusation. I spoke with Giovanni and we both agree that what happened at your place was just, shall we say *fortuna difettosa*, bad luck. I want Giovanni to know that the Calderones won't be bringing any more of that luck your way." The Don reclined and puffed a ring of smoke up into the air.

The Don smiled. His nephew continued to glare at Lorenzo. Giovanni observed it all in silence. "I will go see if we can track down Giuseppe." Angelo nodded to the men and walked out. Lorenzo remained disinterested in the open animosity.

"Now that the unpleasantness is over, Giovanni, shall we get down to business?"

Giovanni gave a look to his men and they left the room behind Calderone's men. He nodded that they could proceed.

****

Mira held tight to the inside of the door. Her friend drove the flashy convertible faster than Giovanni. And along the mountainous curves it was a daredevil event that kept Mira's lunch lurching to her throat. "Could you please slow down?" She winced.

"So we leave for Sorrento! I'm so excited!" Fabiana shifted down into third gear. She eased off the gas pressing the clutch to take the upcoming curve.

"Apparently he thinks we can get to know each other better there."

Fabiana shifted up to fourth, accelerating again as she looked over at Mira, "Well it sounds like fun."

They swerved up into the drive. Mira counted six cars

parked to the front. "Looks like the men are back."

"I'm ready."

"I guess we are."

When they exited the cars, men walked out of the front doors with luggage. A few pieces looked like hers.

"C'mon." Fabiana sashayed in front of her.

Inside the place was abuzz with activity. "I'm going to take these upstairs and make sure whoever packed my bags didn't forget anything." Fabiana tossed over her shoulder, running up the stairs. Mira stopped a man who walked in a hurried fashion to the door.

"Where's Giovanni?"

"The parlor, *Signora*." The man answered and kept on his course. None of these men offered her much conversation, and many didn't speak English. She thanked his retreating back and tried to figure her way from one hall to the next to find one of the three parlors in the villa on this floor. Eventually, she found him with a room full of men. He was seated, most were standing. He listened to the man before him who talked with his hands swiftly moving. For a brief moment, no one noticed her. Then her eyes met with Lorenzo's. He smirked, and it drew Giovanni's attention. A small welcoming smile spread over his lips. He said something in Italian that silenced the room. All attention switched to her.

It felt awkward. No one spoke as he crossed the room and approached her. He leaned in to kiss her lips but she turned her face giving him her cheek instead. He looked at her confused and some of the men lowered their eyes. "Have I upset you?" he whispered in her ear.

"Can we speak? Alone?"

Lorenzo appeared. "Where's Fabiana?"

"She's upstairs packing the things she bought." Mira replied, continuing to hold Giovanni's stare. He slipped his hand in hers and squeezed it. With a small tug, he pulled her from the room and led her out. She knew he wasn't pleased with the way she refused his kiss in front of his men. She didn't care. She hoped it hurt his feelings like her feelings were hurt when he left her bed without saying a word. Taking her in a billiard room, he closed the door.

"What has you displeased today?"

Mira stepped away from him. She placed her purse in a chair and removed her sunglasses from her hair. "Had a good time last night?"

"Did you?"

"Oh, it was a blast until I woke up feeling like some cheap tramp."

"Now why would you feel that way?" he frowned.

"Let's see, maybe it's the Houdini act you keep pulling after you have an orgasm between my thighs."

"You were sleeping, I had an early meeting, so I could get you out of here to Sorrento I might add."

"Interesting." She crossed her arms in front of her. "You had no problem waking me when you wanted to make love, but you can't wake me to say goodbye?"

Giovanni rubbed his jaw. She knew he struggled with her reasoning. It was unfortunate that something so casual and addictive could be a source of frustration for them both. Mira sighed and turned away. She didn't want to make the mistakes she'd made with Kei, over analyzing emotion, labeling his actions, pre-judging the man based on her fears of abandonment.

"I'm a bit different than most men, American men, *Bella*."

She stared down at the pool table. "How's that?"

"My mother was Irish, my father Sicilian. She was his mistress just after she reached puberty. Not a story you share with a woman you want to know. I'm the product of that affair."

"Affair?"

Giovanni chuckled. "Yes, my father was married to another woman until his dying breath. And every man out there wishes to remind me of that fact. I see you struggle to find your way, to be your own person. I know that struggle."

Mira faced him. His words weighed heavily on her heart. When she opened her mouth to say so, nothing escaped her. She preferred he do the talking.

"It's okay to question my motives, *Bella*, everyone does." He took a step toward her, "I'm used to it. Inside we have some of the same fears."

"Maybe we do. Still, the more I know you, the more questions I have."

"Come closer, and I'll answer them," he said, reaching behind him to engage the lock on the door.

"Smooth," she smiled. She loved the way his dark tailored suit crisply outlined his large frame. His deeply tanned skin and the way his hair darkly framed his face was a huge turn on. She wasn't really upset anymore. She enjoyed having his attention solely focused on her. Selfish as it sounded, she would prefer he didn't speak or touch another woman after her. Mira went to him. "You liked what happened between us last night, not just the sex. After?"

He nodded that he did enjoy the intimacy. He dropped his hands on her hips and pulled her directly into him.

"You know I did," he answered.

Mira moved her face to avoid the kiss pending between them. Her breasts rose sharply as she drew in a breath. And the burn for him intensified "If you ever make me feel lonely for you again, Giovanni, it'll be the end of us." He heaved her up and half-spun her to the door. Fire spread between her thighs as his pelvis pressed into hers.

"Are you threatening me, *Bella*?"

"Yes," she panted softly.

He nipped her bottom lip. "That's my girl."

At last her lips parted and he tasted her sweet mouth. Infuriating woman. A sexy, almost apologetic little murmur of surrender escaped her. Mira wrapped her arms around his neck and returned his passionate kiss. Her tongue darted in and out of his mouth with quick little butterfly flicks that drove him wild. Giovanni parted her soft thighs with his to press in against her warm center. He seized upon her vulnerability with kisses to her neck while both of his hands cupped her ass and lifted her off the ground, pushing her higher up the door. His face went in between the separation of her wrap dress, he moved the crossed over fabric and exposed her left breast effortlessly as his lips brushed across her nipple still covered by the cup of her bra. He drew it down with his teeth. Mira grabbed his hair, wrapping her leg high around his hip to keep him close. She moaned once his tongue circled her nipple while in his mouth.

"Slow down, we can't, people are waiting on us," she panted weakly, which he ignored. Reaching for the tie of her dress he pulled on the long belt loosening it.

Nico's voice sounded on the other side of the door. He knocked hard and fast.

Giovanni let her breast go. "What is it?" he shouted. Mira pushed her breast back down inside the cup of her bra, and lowered her leg so she could fix her dress, although he refused to lift up and release her.

"Don Calderone and his nephew Angelo are here to see you. They say it's important."

"I'll be right there," he grunted finally releasing her.

Mira tied her dress and looked up at him concerned. "Let me guess, you have to go again?"

He cupped her face and kissed her. Then he turned away, adjusting his erection in the front of his pants, trying to shake off his arousal. Mira watched him pace to collect himself and walked over to him, touching his arm. "What's wrong? Who are these men?"

"No one. Visitors. Go upstairs and make sure the boys have your things. We'll leave soon." He kissed her jaw. Before she could say more he walked out, leaving her to wonder again what just happened.

Giovanni stormed down the hall. "Find Lorenzo and tell him to join us. The girls leave now. We'll meet them at the airstrip."

The men nodded and marched away.

He rounded the corner and entered the open parlor on the lower level. *"Come va?"* Giovanni asked. Don Calderone turned with his cigar in his hand. He had three of his thugs including his nephew at his side. Giovanni gave him a proper greeting by kissing both of his cheeks.

"Forgive the intrusion. We have a problem." The Don said with concern in his voice.

Lorenzo appeared at his side. Angelo seemed to tense and

focus his hostility again at his cousin. Giovanni frowned at the exchange. "I'm listening. What can I do for you?"

"It's Giuseppe. He hasn't been seen since yesterday evening. We can't locate him, and it's not like him not to check in." The Don shook his head in disgust. He glanced over at Lorenzo. "Earlier you said he was to meet with you yesterday?"

"No. I said he was to call to set up a meeting. I never heard from him."

"Where were you to meet?" Angelo asked.

"Are you deaf? I said he was to call, nothing more." Lorenzo shot back. From the rigid tension in his cousin's jaw and neck, Giovanni felt odd about the entire matter.

Angelo addressed his uncle. "How could he have a meeting with Lorenzo and be expected in Genoa the same day?" he said.

"Are you calling me a liar?" Lorenzo demanded.

Angelo's brow arched, and his mouth took on a similar mean twist. "Are you a liar?"

Giovanni threw up his hand and silenced the men. "If Lorenzo says that Giuseppe didn't call, the matter is closed. I am sure he is probably caught up handling family business, Calderone."

The Don put a hand to his brow. "It's not uncommon for him to pull these stunts. I keep telling Angelo he's worried over nothing."

"*Patri!* Lorenzo knows something. I'm sure of it!"

"*SILENZIO!*" Don Calderone commanded. "Apologize." He grabbed his nephew's arm. The move was humiliating for Angelo and his face turned a deep shade of red. Angelo looked up at Lorenzo with searing hate. "My apologies."

"No need. I understand Angelo's concern, Don Calderone. If you need anything from me or the family let me know."

The Don nodded *"Diotiguardi,"* he said, kissing both sides of Giovanni's cheek. He gave the same parting to Lorenzo and summoned Angelo to follow. Alone Giovanni returned his focus to his cousin. "Is there something I should know?"

"Absolutely not!" Lorenzo walked out.

Chapter Eight

SHE SAT CLOSE TO GIOVANNI, his hand resting on her thigh. He told her stories of places she'd only read about in fashion magazines as she sipped a small cylinder glass of *limóncello*. Apparently, the bittersweet alcoholic drink was derived from Sorrento.

Their time in the air ended too soon. She and Fabiana were whisked away in two separate cars. Alone in the limo with Giovanni she spent most of the ride trying to keep him from laying her out on the back seat. Mira laughed and giggled as she fought off his advances, flattered and horny for him herself. She rewarded his good behavior with a few kisses to appease him. Alone with him she felt like a teenager again. He excited her that much.

"Time for the lessons you promised me." She removed his hand from under her skirt. "If we're to be friends, I want to be able to speak Italian fluently."

"Shall we start now?" He eased his hand back between her thighs and under her skirt.

"Well, I think the times when I'm most curious are..." Her

voice trailed off. She blushed. His fingers reached their intended spot.

"Finish?" he said.

"You know." Again she removed his hand and this time she crossed her leg. Giovanni chuckled. He dropped his arm around her and pulled her in closer.

"No, *Bella*. I don't. When are you most curious?" he asked. "When I conduct business around you? When I'm angry?"

Mira hit his chest playfully. "No silly. When we're intimate. It's like you're having a conversation with yourself."

"Not true!" Giovanni chuckled.

"It is. I don't understand anything you're saying. I think you forget you're speaking Italian."

"It's not something I do consciously, *Bella*. Let's just say you inspire me."

Mira snuggled closer. "I'd like to be a part of the conversation, so maybe you can let me in on what those whispers are about?"

"I'll make sure to translate for you."

"On second thought, let's not kill the mood. We can talk about the translation afterwards."

Giovanni laughed again. He lifted her chin and gave her a sweet kiss. "I plan to show you a different side of *Italia*."

"I can't wait."

"Sorrento is my sanctuary, my heaven. It's not all I want to share. Tomorrow we will visit my vineyard."

"You have one?"

"In a village called San Donato which is in the Chianti region."

"Where they actually make Chianti?"

"Yes. The best vino in Chianti."

"Sounds nice. Fabiana would love to see it."

"We will do the tour alone." Giovanni said.

Mira glanced up at him. She could insist but what would be the point? Fabiana shared with her that she and Lorenzo were serious. She seemed excited about time with him on their last days of vacation. "I guess it doesn't matter. Lorenzo probably has plans for her. I love that girl with all my heart, but she is so willing to just go with her feelings in everything. It amazes and worries me."

The car slowed to a stop before tall gates. Men stepped out in front of the headlights. One spoke to the other, and they stepped aside. The car rolled along. "So this is it?" she leaned forward trying to see the details of the estate looming before them in the dark. She could tell it was huge. Block shaped with tall walls, it reminded her of a castle.

"My great-great grandfather and his brothers restored this place. Over two centuries we've added and improved upon it. This is home."

Giovanni was out the door waiting to help her step out. The evening felt unnaturally cool, so to have him draw her close felt nice. The cloudy sky shielded the moon, but still the night wasn't as dark as she would think it to be. The massive walls of the castle-like estate surrounded them from all sides.

Soft laughter from her friend echoed in the night. Men were emerging from cars. She couldn't count how many. It felt like more than a small army. One of his men hurried ahead of them. He opened and held the door. Mira walked at Giovanni's side. She crossed the threshold into the warmed over golden interior of his home. She imagined the place had so much history ghosts floated along the halls. She turned to share her joke then froze.

A stunningly attractive brunette in dangerously high spiked heels strutted straight for them. *It was her.* The young woman she saw him with at the fashion show. She was even more beautiful up close. Thanks to the elevation of her shoes she stood closer to five feet seven. She wore tight black pants and a red halter-top, which smoothly defined her slim waistline. Her hair was waist length with thick spiral curls framing her delicate features. Never had she seen a woman so striking, with skin a dark olive tan, and expressive blue eyes under long lashes, she exuded femininity.

Was he kidding? Was this his woman? Intense anger swelled in her chest. She glanced over to Giovanni who looked like a man in love. The young woman rushed him, nearly jumping into his arms. She spoke so fast in Italian Mira had no hope of understanding her. Giovanni held her to him with one arm and kissed her brow and cheek affectionately. He released the brunette but cupped her face speaking in a low voice to her. Everyone waited as he rubbed his nose over the young woman's like a father would his daughter.

Fabiana shot Mira a puzzled look. The brunette turned and her grin dimmed as shock registered on her face. "It's you!" she pointed a finger at Mira. "I love you! I buy you. I mean I buy your clothes. Giovanni brought you here for me!" Without warning Mira was seized. The woman hugged her neck chokingly tight. "You will design my wedding dress! Oh thank you, Lorenzo! Giovanni! Thank you so much! Mira Ellison will design my wedding dress!" she squealed.

"Mira, I want you to meet my sister Catalina." Giovanni made the introduction.

Sister? He has a sister? Now he tells me?

"It is so nice to meet you." Mira smiled graciously.

Catalina yanked her by both hands. "Giovanni purchased tickets to your show in Milan. He let me pre-order from your Fall line. I want the dress Zenobia wore. I will wear it at my reception. I love it!"

"*Grazie*," Mira said overwhelmed by her energy.

Giovanni rubbed his sister's back as if to calm her hyperactivity. "This is Fabiana."

Catalina extended her hand. "*Ciao*, nice to meet you," she said. It was hard to miss how both Giovanni and Lorenzo looked at Catalina with love. She was a princess among these men, and Mira imagined she was equally as spoiled.

"So you'll definitely be staying here with us at *la Melanzana*?" Catalina spun to her brother. "I can call Zia to come sooner! We can start working on the dress immediately. Can we have the lower level to ourselves?"

"Catalina. Quiet now." Giovanni touched his sister's cheek. "Mira did not come for you. She's not here to design some dress."

Confused, Catalina frowned at them both. "What are you saying?"

"She's my guest. She's here with me."

"You? In our home?"

Giovanni's brow arched. Catalina looked over at Mira and the light of admiration dimmed in her eyes. She could feel the frost in her glare.

"Oh. I see. Welcome."

His hand extended to Mira. "It's late, come with me."

Awkward as it was, she accepted. She could feel Catalina's eyes on her.

"Wait. Giovanni you just got home! I want to talk to you. Domi said you would discuss the wedding!" Catalina shouted after him. She hurried to the bottom of the steps. Mira glanced back and noticed the raw look of anger on her face.

"In the morning." He continued up the stairs. The villa of the Battaglia's was so grand her mind could barely catalogue much of what she'd seen before they entered the hall that led to his bedroom. She observed the family crest for Battaglia carved into the wall along the stairs and walked silently at his side toward two tall mahogany wood doors that were drawn shut. His hand fell from hers. When he opened the doors to a room the size of her first apartment, her breath caught in her throat. The bed of course was covered in dark chocolate bedding with soft golden colored sheets folded over it, and throw pillows in a deep magenta were mixed in. A large Persian rug lay in front of it. Giovanni walked to the left and opened doors that led to a private balcony with a long awning over it.

"My tour? It ends here?"

"Forgive me, *Bella*. I'll give you a proper tour tomorrow, I just wanted to be alone with you again."

"I see, and why is that?" she asked following him out onto the balcony. The sun was setting behind a mountain to the distance, and the sky had dark purple and orange streaks as the night ushered in.

"I'm not sure. You calm me," he said. "Not many women do."

"You seem close to your sister."

Giovanni's gaze slipped over to her. "She's my light. I adore her. But she isn't my woman. Surely you know the difference?"

Mira felt silly for even making the comparison. She avoided the intense way he stared at her and focused on the shadowy mountain in the distance. "I guess while I visit you here we will share a room."

"It's my preference." He stated.

"And if I preferred a different arrangement?"

"Do you?"

She exhaled. "No."

Giovanni chose to step behind her. She eased forward pressing into the balcony edge. Below her the land stretched and disappeared into tall trees. How high up were they? He dropped his hands on either side of her and pressed into her backside. When he spoke he did so in her left ear.

"Can I share something with you?"

"Yes."

"I've never had a woman in this room let alone my bed before tonight."

Mira tried to turn but couldn't. She strained to look to her left and read his face to see if he spoke the truth. "Are you serious? Please don't think you have to say that to me."

He stared out into the night across the hills and stretch of land she supposed belonged to him. "It's the truth. I've had women, many women. This is my family home, and this room is really sacred to me. My mother and father made me in the bed we will share. I've raised Catalina behind these walls alone since my parents' death. I'm showing you who I am and sharing myself with you."

"I'm flattered. A bit overwhelmed. We barely know each other and I have this honor?"

"Time? You keep referencing time." Giovanni shook his head in disappointment. "I wait on nothing and march to no one's calendar. I have to make decisions daily, and I do so based on how I feel, what I feel." He eased her bangs from her brow to look into her eyes. "Have I not shown you what I feel?"

"Yes." She said. She felt breathless. If the man didn't stop, she'd barricade the doors and keep him with her always. Things were too intense, and too soon. But how could she explain it? She chose to change the subject. "How did your mother die?" she asked. The answering silence drew longer than expected.

There was a knock to the door. He kissed her cheek and then released her before walking back into the room. Mira peeked inside to see Catalina standing in the doorway, arms crossed, and an angry frown to her face. Giovanni stepped out the door and closed it.

She returned to the balcony and leaned on her elbows, allowing the night air to gently cool her. Fabiana. She needed to talk to her friend. Things were happening for them at warp speed.

"What is it?" Giovanni asked.

"Why is she here?" Catalina demanded. "In our home, Giovanni? Are you... you two aren't dating each other are you?"

He grabbed her by the arm and dragged her down the hall away from his bedroom doors. He threw open the door to his cigar room and forced her inside. *"Fatti cazzi tuoi!"* He kicked the chair in front of him.

Catalina stepped back. "Don't curse me! This *is* my business, you are my brother and I have a right to be concerned."

Giovanni leveled a finger at her. "I tolerate a lot, Catalina, but not disrespect. She's a guest, and you will treat her as such. Do you understand? Do you? Say the fucking words!"

"Yes! I understand." Catalina huffed. "Do you know who she is? She's famous. Her face is in every fashion magazine. She wouldn't date you. She wouldn't even spend time with you if she knew who you were and what you do." Catalina sighed.

"You taught me to be careful of people outside of our life. Well she's American. Black American. She's from a different world and she doesn't belong here in ours. In our family home."

The accusation would make sense if it weren't Mira that Catalina spoke of. He never exposed her or their family to outsiders. To bring her into his home was a huge deal. But it felt right.

"*Cara*, sweetheart," he cupped her face and pressed a kiss to her forehead. "She's a friend and harmless. She also designs all those expensive rags you make me buy." Catalina blushed, and he let her go. Understanding her jealousy he decided to use a gentle touch. She never saw him with a woman in their home, and those that dared to get close enough to even meet her were always second to her whims. Even Lorenzo and Dominic were surprised when he announced he'd bring the designer here. But he wouldn't explain himself further. He stroked the side of Catalina's cheek. "Respect, Catalina. I've taught you better. You will make her feel welcome."

Catalina nodded.

"Good. Have our dinner sent to my room. She will be staying there during this visit."

"In Mama and Papa's room!" Catalina gasped.

"It is my room now." He said firmly. He turned to walk out but stopped himself. He glanced back to see Catalina with a sad pout. He sighed. "In the morning we will sit down and discuss the wedding. I will listen to your concerns."

The joy sparked in her blue eyes once more. "Yes! And since she's here, can you ask her about my dress? Maybe she wants to design a better one for me?"

"I've bought you three dresses so far." He frowned.

"None of them are close to a Mira Ellison original. None of

them."

Giovanni shook his head and left. He returned to his room to find the luggage had been brought up. Mira unpacked her suitcase. She glanced up when he returned.

"Little sister didn't expect me?"

"She's spoiled."

Mira smiled. "Wonder who spoiled her?"

"You hungry?"

"Famished."

"Lorenzo and Fabiana are eating out. How about we stay in? Talk. Have dinner together, privately."

She sat on the edge of the bed. Her eyes did a sweep of the room. There was nothing to see. Catalina and Zia redecorated after his mother's death. The shock of losing her so soon after his father sent him spiraling into a deep depression. Sleeping here gave him some peace. He felt close to his mother then. Most of it had been done by his mother. But this room was his, and he liked it simple. Besides the bed that had been in his family for half a century, there was a chaise chair, a tallboy, night table, and bookshelf. Mira rose and walked over to the bookshelf scanning those he read, over and over. She picked up one. "Charles Dickens? Mark Twain? Ernest Hemingway?"

"I love to read." He confessed. "When Mama took sick with grief, I read to her nightly. Those are our favorite books."

"Grief? She died from grief?"

"A broken heart. The doctors said it was her diabetes but losing my father, the way we lost him, it was too much for her."

"So she loved him? Deeply?" Mira pressed.

"Deeply. Inconceivable I know, if you knew their history, but she loved my father."

She put the books back. She turned and smiled his way.

"I'm sorry for your loss."

Giovanni blinked away the sadness clouding his vision. "Me too. Enough of my loss. What about the treasure I've found?"

She gave him a sweet smile that made him ache to touch her. But he paced himself. He had all night to explore his desires. "Thank you for agreeing to come, for sharing your vacation with me. I know you hadn't intended on things going this far."

"We have a week. One week and my vacation is over." She reminded him, wagging her finger.

"What relaxes you?" he approached. "Painting?"

"Huh? No. I don't paint. Never have."

"You sketched the lake. It was very good."

"Okay." She chuckled. "I draw, most designers do. We use that side of our brain."

"You liked the Morandi? I have some on the west wing I can show you."

He lifted her chin. "Have you tried to paint? You have the heart of a painter."

"And you know my heart after a few days?"

"I think so."

There was another knock at the door. He ignored it. "Would you paint for me? Try?"

"Sure, Giovanni. Pass me a paint brush and I'll give it a whirl." She teased. Her gaze switched beyond him. "There's someone at the door."

"Fuck them." He ran his hand down her shoulder and arm. "I like these dresses. What are they called?"

"Dresses?" she kidded.

"You know what I mean. The way it wraps around your curves and ties on the side. It's the second one you've worn. I like it."

She took a step closer. "Why? Because you like to take it off me?"

He nodded. The knocking began again. "Maybe you should answer the door."

He groaned but agreed. The visitor was probably from the kitchen delivering dinner. He yanked the doors open to find Dominic standing before him. Giovanni narrowed his gaze. "What is it now?"

"Trouble. I need to see you downstairs. It can't be avoided."

"Fuck!" he turned. Mira again was before the bookshelf. He nodded. "Give me a minute." He closed the door.

"Let me guess, you have to go?"

"Not far, just downstairs. Why don't you get comfortable? They'll bring your dinner."

She rocked on her feet with her hands clasped before her. "I understand. I'll read."

He chuckled. "Very funny. You're welcome to explore."

"I can wait for you," she winked. "I'd rather a personal tour."

Giovanni rubbed his jaw again admiring her shapely figure in her wrap around dress. He prayed she packed a suitcase full of them. They flattered her beauty so much. "I won't be long, and this will be the last interruption of the night."

"Don't make promises you can't keep."

He winked. Once in the hall he felt another pang of guilt over abandoning his guest so soon. Silly as it sounded, he needed time with her, and time was never a friend to him. He hurried down the stairs and turned left for the gathering room toward the back of his place. He found Dominic pacing. Alone. Curious he walked in concerned. "What is it?"

"Got off the phone with our contact in Genoa."

"And?"

"Giuseppe Calderone is dead. They found his car abandoned at *Le Scogliere*. There's blood in the trunk, lots of it. Also his gun and shoes."

Giovanni stuck his hands in the pockets of his pants. "A hit?"

"Angelo's kicking up a fuss; he's making accusations. Don Calderone has suffered a stroke."

"Shit." Giovanni paced.

"All his men are out on this one. Lake Como is being ripped apart. Families dragged from their homes in the middle of the night. Two have already been executed. The old man is letting Angelo call the orders on this one. They haven't found the body, but when they do..."

"You have concerns? They'll look my way?"

"Giovanni, Lorenzo and Giuseppe have been seen quite a bit together in the past few years. Between Genoa and Bellagio, many have questioned their casual friendliness."

"Lorenzo wouldn't do this and not warn me."

"I haven't found anything to connect him. But there is a weak link in Calderone's family. Do you remember Fish?" Dominic asked. "He's Giuseppe's flunky trying to make the ranks. If Lo and Giuseppe had any type of business or private feud Fish would know about it. With everything going on, I needed your approval before I make contact. I don't think my snooping around now is in the best interest of the family. Should we let the dust settle or the body to surface?"

Giovanni wiped his chin. Things could get messy. He needed to close ranks. "Return to Bellagio. We can't take him out of there. It's too risky. So you'll need to go inside for my answers. I want to be ahead of this fucking mess. Prepared. Take Carlo."

"He's too much of a hot head, Gio, he will..."

"Take him. I don't know what you're walking into, and I can't trust Lo with the truth. Not yet. You need a gun quicker than your own. You find out everything you can about Giuseppe and Lorenzo. I don't give a shit how you do it, but you fucking do it!"

"Si."

"Wait. Wait." Giovanni threw his hands up in frustration. "We receive the shipment from the Irish in two days."

"The designer, she's up and operating after your orders. I've had my men keep tabs on the workers. A staff of about sixteen working out of three floors of the building, and they are there early every day and late in the evenings. None of them have ventured to the cellars. Have you worked out that detail?" Dominic asked.

"Contact Marsuvio. Tell him I want a building inspector to pay the ladies a visit, here. We need to minimize activity at that building until my shipment is secured then moved."

"What reason should he give this time?" Dominic asked.

"Inform the women that they've broken some law. I don't give a fuck. Flavio is close to finalizing the deals in Sicily. Until then we don't need any distractions."

Dominic gave another nod and left him to his thoughts. He could be wrong. His young protégé could be wrong. Still his gut said differently. Lost in his doubts, he returned to his room. He didn't expect the scene that greeted him. Mira had taken a match to a pair of tall slender black candles in silver pedestals and lowered the lights in the room. The table was positioned outside on his balcony and the night air only licked at the flames, causing them to extend and grow brighter. She hadn't changed out of the sexy wrap dress, and he was grateful.

"Welcome back. Just in time. Dinner."

He closed the door and turned the lock. He told his men not to disturb him further, no matter the issue. The night was theirs.

Catalina had his favorite meals prepared for his return. Tonight would be the first night he dined in his room with someone special. Giovanni had to consider how many hard laid rules he'd broken since he met her. Starting with opening the doors to her boutique when he knew it didn't serve his purposes. Now he'd have to manipulate her to get what he wanted. He regretted the lie between them. She blinked at him with the most considerate trusting eyes.

"I hope you don't mind. I found the candles in your dressers when I started unpacking. I thought it would be nice to eat out here so I had them set the table for us. Your staff is nicer than the one at the Ritz," she chuckled.

"I pay them well."

The meal she delivered was of all his favorites. His mother's recipe was the first course. The room smelled of memories of her. Good ones.

"Thank you for accepting my invitation, *Bella*. For allowing me these days and nights with you."

"Will you always call me *Bella*? Is it my name from now on?" She walked around to her chair and glanced up at him from under her dark lashes. He wasn't sure when he fixated on the name for her, but it was a natural fit. "Yes." He nodded. She curled her mouth into a half-smile, and he knew she approved. She pointed at the bottle on the table. "This vino, it's Chianti. Is it from your vineyard?"

Grasping the bottle by the neck he read the black label. "It is. Shall I?"

She nodded. He poured her half a glass and she laughed. "Wait. Are you trying to get me drunk?"

"I wouldn't think of it." He poured his wine next. "I need you sober and fully mine, tonight."

He noticed how she looked at the smaller dish next to her plate. "We call it *gatò di patate*."

"It looks like... um, a quiche."

"Yes, think of a quiche. It has potato, egg, ham and cheese and is baked like a pie. It's traditionally the starter my mother would have served for us. Catalina makes a good version. She always prepares it by hand the day she knows I'm returning. My sister is very spoiled, but she spoils me in return."

"Did she cook all of this?"

"When Zia isn't here, the staff does most of the cooking. Zia is the only woman in the house who won't tolerate strangers preparing food for us. Her words, not mine. Personally I prefer a home cooked meal by the women in my family. Can you cook?" he asked. She blinked at him then nodded that she could. He felt a sense of relief. Modern women today avoided the kitchen as if it were forced servitude. He found love in a dish prepared for him by a woman who cared. He wanted to taste her cooking and more. He picked up a fork and scooped a mouthful. Mira leaned forward accepting the offering. She chewed with a smile on her face.

"Oh, it's good. Love it."

"And this." He lifted the cover of the center dish. "It's *spaghetti ai ricci*."

"What are those chunks of meat in it?"

"Sea urchin."

"Again with the sea urchin?"

"Have a taste. It's far better than what you've had before. You'll love it."

She hesitated. He ate a sample first then scooped some for her. To his delight she gave it a try. She chewed with a small smile, and then her eyes stretched. "It tastes good. The sauce, it's so sweet and tangy. Give me more?"

"Come here."

The chair scooted back, and she came around the small table to him. He opened his arm for her to sit on his lap. He stared into her eyes insistent she do as he requested. Mira straddled him and the split to the front of her dress parted all the way up to her panties. She wrapped her arms around his neck, and her lips brushed his. He could taste the sauce on her lips. "How am I going to eat this way?" she chuckled looking down between them.

"Look at me."

Her smile dimmed and she lifted her stare to meet his. "Stay."

"I plan to."

"No. Stay. Here. With me."

Mira drew back, and her brows shot up in surprise. "I can't stay here."

"Of course you can. You said you were renting a hotel room while you look for a place to buy. I'm just outside of Napoli. I have more than enough space."

"No. No, Giovanni. It's generous but I wouldn't impose. This is your family's home."

She tried to rise, but he kept a hand to her hip and forced her to stay. "I plan to spend the rest of the week convincing you why we fit."

"Then ask to date me, not for me to move in."

"Date, move in, what difference does that make to anyone when we both want the same thing?"

"I hate to sound like a broken record, but I've only known you for a few days. No one moves this fast."

"I make my own rules. My father saw my mother and loved her on sight. They were together from that day forward. I've denied myself the love of a woman. Told myself it wasn't needed. I want you." He kissed her chin and his hand eased up to cup her right breast. He gave it a gentle squeeze. "I'm a man who normally gets his way."

"Is that so?" she exhaled.

"You're here now, aren't you?" In their embrace, he could feel the rapid race of her beating heart.

"You have a point," she smiled. He reached around her and scooped *patate* to his fork and fed her. She accepted the offering from his fork. Mira chewed staring into his eyes. When she swallowed he repeated the action, until she nearly ate half in silence. She let him take care of her without objection. It pleased him.

"No more," she whispered to him forcing him to lower the fork to the plate. Her succulent bow shaped lips parted and her sweet tangy tongue slipped from her mouth to his. "I'd rather taste you," she said within their kiss. And she did. He turned away from her mouth, and she brushed her kisses along his neck. Giovanni groaned, his lids fluttered shut.

"Finish, we haven't had the main course yet."

She sucked softly at his jugular and combed her fingers through his hair, moving seductively on his groin. Giovanni's head went back. Mira began to unbutton his shirt easing her lush lips to the center of his neck and his throat. She rushed to insert her hands inside of his shirt and run her palms over his chest. The feel of her delicate hands was too much to bear.

"What are these tattoos on your body? What do they mean?"

"Growth, change, life. That's what they mean." He lifted his head and captured a kiss. It was more of a clashing of lips and tongue that had her whimpering and clinging to him. It was her turn to break the exchange.

"Each one has a meaning?" she asked, touching his cheek.

"Yes. And one day I'll tell you the story."

She brushed her lips over his. "I find you so strangely beautiful, and strong." She said against his mouth. "I can't wait to know all of you, Giovanni."

He smiled. She grinned at him. Maybe things weren't as glum as he previously thought. Maybe Lorenzo hadn't betrayed the family or started a war with the Calderones. Maybe the delivery of his guns and the transport of them back out of the Amalfi coast didn't require he hurt her business.

"What are you thinking about?"

"The future." Giovanni reached for the glass. She sipped, swallowed and accepted the dark magenta Chianti until it filled her mouth and spilled from the corners down her chin and neck. A soft laugh escaped her. Mira licked her lips grinning. Giovanni kissed her chin and tasted her. He could feel her breaths deepen thanks to her soft breasts mashed against his chest. He barely returned the glass to the table he was so eager. He seized her by her thick hair and tilted her head back so he could lick the trace of wine from her neck.

Trembling within his arms she dragged in a ragged breath and hoarsely replied, "How's this even possible? You've almost convinced me to take you up on your offer."

Giovanni chuckled and put his face into her heaving cleavage. He found her breasts to be the second softest part of her body. The first was the round ass riding his lap. "I'm still hungry," she groaned, when he finally worked her nipple into his mouth. It was too late for food. He craved her now. Rising with her on his lap he toyed with the dark swollen peak of her left breast, and she lowered her legs clinging to him. He released her. She swayed a bit in his arms but stared up at him expectantly from under long bangs, as he carried her into the room.

"A quickie, then we eat?" she bargained.

He chuckled. His balls tightened and his dick pulsed by his zipper. "Tonight, *Bella*, I'm going to fuck you. Nothing about it will be quick."

She eased down his frame. Her hand smoothly traced his abdomen as she walked around him and went to the bed they would share. Giovanni watched her. The bed was two feet off the ground with large hand carved wooden pillars at each corner and a huge intricate headboard. She leaned forward, her hands gripping the edge, and her lush ass temptingly stretching the material of her dress. He tossed up the back of her dress and almost thought she was bottomless, until he saw the tiny triangle of the thong slip into her perfectly shaped ass at the crease. He hooked his finger under the trim and tore it from her. She looked back at him with her hair in her eyes. "What are you waiting for?"

Giovanni eased down his zipper and released himself in his hand. He rubbed the head of his cock against her ass, and she turned and stopped him. Their eyes met. "It's a woman's prerogative."

"What is?"

"How she is fucked."

Giovanni released his erection and her hand touched then circled his shaft. She worked it up and down slow and easy. "Sometimes she wants to do the fucking."

"You have a saucy mouth."

Mira laughed. "Wait until I learn Italian." She stroked him harder.

He lifted his hands and raised them locking them behind his head.

"Allow me."

From the first time she laid eyes on his long dick to this very moment she wanted to ease her mouth over it. Kei loved oral sex, and so did she, giving and receiving. Kei had been the only man she'd ever did the deed with. He however, was not hung like Giovanni. The cock before her felt like velvet wrapped around steel. She could stroke its smooth hardness for eternity. Mira took a deep breath and lowered to her knees.

A quick glance up and she caught Giovanni's hard stare sharpen and narrow, shrinking into a slit. Did he disapprove? Mira blinked at him and his mouth stretched into a wide smile. He understood her intentions. He was so virile, handsome, could he get any sexier?

Tens of thousands of quivers trembled through her torso. Her nervousness and excitement made her light-headed. A ripple of pure desire coursed down her spine. Mira glanced up at him once more. Never breaking the connection they shared she traced her fingers down the veined shaft and grabbed it at the root. He stroked the top of her head and nodded his approval. She kissed the dimple at the center of the rounded tip. Using her tongue as a tease she did a swirl over the broad cap. She licked under the veined length and then took the head of his cock between her lips. Immediately she was filled with a fourth of him and taking in another inch slow and easy. Excitement seized her and was so intense she felt her hand shaking.

Giovanni moaned and clutched her hair, his hips thrusting, though she sensed his restraint to keep from ramming his cock too deep down her throat. Her hands sought his thighs, both of them thick with muscle. She remembered to breathe. She opened her mouth wider, relaxing her tongue to let him slide inside without a struggle. Her eyes fluttered shut. Her mouth watered and her blood heated in her veins. She drew air through her nostrils and inhaled his male sweat, both musky and earthy. It clung to his skin and the silky nest of pubic hairs that tickled her nose and top lip on her descent. Mira's body felt hot, her nipples hard as bullets. She swallowed him down her throat.

"*Bambina!* Fuck!" he cried out, gripping her hair, not expecting her talent to take him this far. His voice was so gravelly textured she felt herself go wet and damp at her center.

She groaned with pleasure. Mira breathed noisily through her nostrils sucking hard then slow, taking him in and out. He started to pump his hips, and press to the back of her head. He was too long for such action, her jaws caught a cramp, but she withstood. He shoved past her tongue tapping her throat so she loosened her jaws and took him deeper.

"Fuck! Fuck! Yes! Yes!" Giovanni roared.

A powerful shudder went through his thighs and she could have sworn she heard him whimper. Her big bad Don, was whimpering like a baby. He began to groan and speak in Italian or Sicilian, or were they the same thing? She didn't know. He grabbed a handful of her hair and pulled her off him, her mouth was reluctant to release him. He yanked a bit harder drawing her hair back and she liked the rough play. Dazed, she struggled for focus for a few seconds, then their gazes locked. She licked her lips and stared up at him expectantly. There was something wildly predatory gleaming in his clear blues. She had taken him to the brink. He drew her up. His dick between them, his mouth crashed down on hers. His tongue penetrating and sliding deep inside; he had to taste himself on her tongue.

"I'm going to fuck you now." He growled, throwing her over his shoulder he carried her across the room to the bed. She was tossed on top. Mira bounced and giggled. She tried to rise to undo the sash to her wrap around dress, but he dropped on her. "Leave it on. Damn dress has made me crazy all day. I want to fuck you in it." He licked her mouth and chin capturing her wrists with one hand and stretching her arms above her. He insisted he have his way, and she didn't mind. Their very first time he'd been much gentler. The second time she felt a bit of the beast of him. They were past the pretense now. She wanted all he had to give. The head of his cock found her entrance. He flexed his hips and drove inside her. A single thrust and he went balls deep into her. Her dress was gathered at her hips and the front of it pulled over to the side to reveal her left breast freed from the cup of her bra. He lifted his torso so he could see all of her splayed before him. His head lowered and he watched his dick slide in and out of her as he worked continual thrusts. Mira's eyes fluttered shut, and she gave into the glorious feeling of being stretched and filled below. "Stay with me."

She opened her eyes, and met his steady gaze.

His repeated thrusts sent heat swirling up and around her

womb. She'd never had ravishment feel so glorious. Though her lids wanted to fall shut in submission once more she didn't dare disobey his command. Instead she worked her lower half with him. His face lowered and his mouth suctioned her neck so hard she knew she'd be bruised in the morning, but he continued to deliver such pleasurable thrusts below it became a strange mix. Her legs were pinned back to her shoulders and she could barely work her hips beneath him. Then in a flash he withdrew and turned her over. Mira gasped, grabbing the sheets until they snatched free of the corners of the bed. He shot back in her and his wildly thrusting shaft stretched her channel unmercifully. His hot damp chest fell on top of her back and he fucked her fast, he fucked her slow, he fucked her with so much control she was crying out his name for release. And he did. Hot jets of sperm filled her as his cock jerked in her. She groaned and melted beneath him.

Giovanni lie perfectly still and Mira wept into her pillow. Never had she cried from such a pleasurable relief. Embarrassed by how wildly excited her body felt, she rubbed her tears away in the pillow as he withdrew.

"I think I'm in love." He exhaled.

Mira's head lifted from the pillow. His chest was heaving hard and fast with his ragged breathing, but there was such a contented smile of satisfaction on his face she smiled. The truth was, no matter how incredibly, inexplicably, uncharacteristically irrational it was of her she had fallen hard and fast for this man. "That was intense."

"It was wonderful," he said, lifting his flushed face to smile into her eyes. "It was heaven."

He lifted from her and rolled over to her side. "Hungry?"

"Yes!"

"I'll bring the food to you." He rose. She rolled to her side and studied him. He wanted her to stay. For how long? God she was tempted.

Lorenzo turned and Fabiana rolled up against his chest into his arms. He smiled and drew her into a snug embrace, his hand stroked her backside while he rested his chin on the top of her head. She was becoming a habit. One he didn't plan to break. Dinner and dancing had recharged his battery. And her sex had him wanting to touch her skin in his dreams.

What the fuck did he care about work? Giovanni had cut his balls when he shut down *Isabella's*, the gambling rooms and whores were gone. Now he was left with whatever scraps fell from the table. Hell Carlo saw more action on the front lines of dealing with business matters than him.

He closed his eyes and repressed his resentment. Fabiana had caught him by surprise. He wanted to fuck her, yes. But this, the coddling and dating was something he hadn't done since his failed engagement. This beautiful Italian American woman drank wine to whiskey with him and laughed at his jokes. Then she fucked him every way he pleased. And even now she was blowing his mind. There was nothing to worry over. The phone rang. He frowned. His room had a private line that he shared with few. He fell to his back and reached in the dark for the ringing phone. Fabiana groaned, waking she eased on top of him. To his delight she started to kiss his chest and go lower easing down under the covers to wrap that beautiful mouth of hers around his dick.

"Hello?"

"You sleep?" Carlo asked.

"No."

"Good." He heard his best friend take a drag of something he was smoking, possibly marijuana. "We got trouble."

"What else is new?"

"Calderone trouble. That is new."

Lorenzo sat upright. He pressed the receiver end of the phone hard against his ear. He didn't breathe, he didn't blink, he waited.

"They think the stupid fucker is dead. I hear rumors, Lo. Rumors Gio won't like."

Lorenzo expected the rumors. It was the truth he feared most. "And?"

"You clean?"

"What the fuck you ask me?" Lorenzo reclined back against his pillow just as Fabiana's front teeth scraped his cock. He winced. She made it up to him with her sweet licks and kisses. Damn woman was killing him. No way his dick could summon the energy to respond.

"I'm just making sure. I have your back, I have to know if you're dirty."

"I'm clean. Fuck Calderone, *baggiano*! I can give a shit what's happened to him."

The line clicked off. Lorenzo dropped the phone. It dangled on its twisted cord. He arched his back from the bed as Fabiana sucked him hard and fast. To his surprise his body responded the way she instructed. Even in the midst of mind blowing pleasure, he knew the tide had turned. He had to be careful or lose it all.

Chapter Nine

"MORNING." CATALINA CHIRPED. She sashayed into her brother's office with a tiny cup of espresso. Giovanni glanced up as the cup was set on his desk in front of him. He sat back and fixed his gaze on his sister. He'd left Mira asleep, and planned to return to her before the sun fully rose. Flavio had air-messaged documents for him to sign.

"What are you doing up this early?" Giovanni asked dryly. He closed the binder before him and eased it into the drawer he kept under lock and key.

"I was making sure breakfast was prepared for our guest. Saw the light on and knew you were in here. I am the *donna* of this house you know."

Catalina wore a long blush pink robe. Her hair was tied up in a ponytail, causing her long spiral curls to sway past her shoulders. He smiled at how much she looked like their mother when she was younger. Though her skin was a golden tan like her Sicilian ancestors, her face, eyes, and mannerisms were all Eve. She was his mother reincarnate. Softening he gestured for her to sit.

"I have a problem, Giovanni."

"Do you?"

"Franco wants to move us back to Palermo when we are married. He wants to run his father's bottling business. I want to stay in Firenze or here in Sorrento in our family home. We have more than enough room. Can't he work for you?" she asked innocently.

"He will be your husband, so you will stay where he says." Giovanni reclined back in his chair. "You know this."

"Well, that's bullshit!" she shouted.

"Watch your tongue."

Catalina folded her arms in a full pout. "I have no say in anything. I didn't complain when you said I had to marry Franco, I didn't complain when you said I couldn't have my wedding in Paris, and I didn't complain when you said that Aurora had to be in the wedding although you know I hate her! I don't want to live in no damn Palermo!"

Giovanni listened. He granted her liberties to speak to him in ways no one else in the family besides Lorenzo dare try. When he didn't give his sister the response she wanted she went for his balls.

"Did you know Mira Ellison is engaged to be married to some rich Chinese man in America? It's in one of my magazines upstairs. I can show you the article."

"I thought you were going to see to breakfast?" Giovanni asked.

Catalina rose and crossed her arms in front of her. "Promise me you will speak to Franco about Palermo? I don't want to be away from you and Lorenzo. You are all I have, no mama or papa, just you and Lorenzo."

"I will talk to him," he promised. "I want you to be

respectful and gracious to our guests. Don't disappoint me."

"I won't," she smiled sweetly.

Mira woke. He returned very quietly. She listened a moment longer and heard him release a deep sigh. The morning rays were beginning to pour in through the open doors of his balcony. She found the large double mattress bed soft as a cloud, and she usually didn't like soft beds. After playing, talking, eating and finishing two bottles of wine he made the sweetest love to her under the covers. Slowly she turned her head to see if he had closed his eyes. He stared straight ahead, deep in thought.

"Morning?" she rolled to him and he opened his arm in welcoming.

"Did I wake you?" he asked his voice hoarse and gruff.

"No. I was waiting for you," she lied.

"Forgive me, *Bella*. I promised to be here when you woke."

She looked up at him. The joke fell flat. In fact it kind of stung. She wasn't so needy that she'd pitch a fit if he wasn't there, though she did give him a hard time before. "What is it? What has you leaving the room constantly and looking so worried? Can't you share your troubles with me?"

"No." He scooted down the covers and faced her on his pillow. "I have a question for you."

"Mmkay," she said kissing his nose.

"Are you engaged to be married in America?"

Mira double blinked. "Wha-um-no. No. Who told you that?"

"Doesn't matter. I believe you." He then kissed her softly. "Are you ready for a trip out to Tuscany? Just you and I?"

"Yes."

"Let's shower and make love. Then we can join everyone for breakfast."

"I thought breakfast wasn't a tradition in Italy?"

"My mother is Irish. Breakfast was always served from her table. Besides my little sister loves America. She spends a lot of my money in New York City. Breakfast is her favorite meal of the day. Catalina knows what is proper; she will feed you." He kissed the tip of her nose. "After breakfast I will show you another side of my life. Remember my goal is to keep you with me," he kidded.

"I can't wait."

Fabiana sashayed out of the bathroom and paused. Lorenzo placed the receiver back on its cradle. It was the third phone call he'd accepted that morning. She knew something was wrong. She could feel it. But her guy told her nothing. He showered her with gifts and sweet talk but gave her little of himself. In the harsh light of the new day, their arrangement didn't feel as appealing as before.

"I'm thinking I might go to Napoli. Visit the boutique today to check in. We have two floors with employees running our business, and we haven't been back since the show in Milan."

"No." he rose. He wore dark slacks and no shirt.

"No?"

"We have such a short time together. I don't want you to go."

Fabiana cut her eyes. Not believing his bullshit.

"Something wrong?" he asked.

"Yes, with you, not me. We get close and then you shut down. You can trust me Lorenzo. Talk to me. I can see you're stressed. Maybe I can help."

Lorenzo smiled. "*Cara*, I'm enjoying every minute with you. That is all you see."

Fabiana uncrossed her arms. She had to get out of her own head. It was *she* who asked so little. Mira warned her about being eager with men. This one she liked, a lot. She felt the heartstrings connecting with his. It could be the makings of love. "For starters your life. I know you aren't married, and you never mention any family outside of this. Where is your mother? Your father?"

"Come here." He sat on the edge of the bed and patted his lap.

Fabiana walked over in bare feet. She wore a summer dress with thin straps and a long split. He pulled her down to his lap and kissed her under the neck. "My mother is dead. She died of breast cancer, many years ago. My father died when I was only twelve. He was murdered. I was raised with no siblings, just Giovanni and Dominic. Then came Catalina. You've met them all."

"Right. I have. But who are you Lorenzo?"

"Who am I? I'm second. Second in everything."

"That makes no sense."

He let go a gust of laughter. She thought he was kidding, but the pain in his eyes said differently. "*Si.* I'm nephew not son, cousin not brother, *capo* not *consigliere*, never first *Cara.* I've competed with being first for a very long time. Then I met you. I look at you and I don't feel second. I feel chosen. You have chosen me no?"

Stunned she nodded.

A sly smile moved across his lips. "*Sei bellissima. Grazie.* For being mine."

His lips, soft, lush and persistent brushed hers and started the kiss that swept her breath from her lungs. He lowered her to the bed, and she held to him, to the feeling of having him. The kiss came to a natural end, but his forehead pressed to hers. "I'm in need of a favor."

She frowned. "From me?"

"An inspector will come in the morning. He will tell you and your friend that your business is closed again. This time you won't question it. *Capisci*? You will explain it to your friend and help her accept it. Then you will convince her to stay here."

"Lorenzo, I..."

"Not permanently. Just a few days longer than you intended to stay. A week, no longer, I promise. C'mon, you know who I am. What I do. Trust me. This trouble will pass in a few weeks. Until then you and her are safest here. The phone call was my cousin. You know what power he has."

"Yes, I have no illusions of who Giovanni Battaglia is. The head of the *Cammora*, of your family."

"Very good. This is his wish, and we have to abide by it."

"Then why can't he just be honest with Mira? She's my best friend. I won't manipulate her for him."

"Then will you do it for me. It's in her best interest and yours. It will only cause her undo worry. You run her business right? Right?"

"Yes, but Lo—"

"Shhh, consider this another business negotiation. I haven't told you the best part. You do this, convince Mira to stay here with my cousin for a longer vacation, and he will get your business visa cleared. You can buy property, cut through all the negotiations with that useless solicitor. Tell me this isn't a deal worth making. Huh? Tell me?"

"It could help us. Are you sure he will do this?"

Lorenzo nodded. "He's taken with her as I am with you. He doesn't want our business to interfere with your lives. This is a good deal for you both. Can you do this for me *angelo*? Can you do this without question?"

"Will it help you, be more than second?" she reached up and touched his face.

His dark sapphire blue eyes narrowed on her. "*Si*. It will help me."

"Then I'll do it. I'll figure something out for our workers. I can handle Mira."

Lorenzo smirked. "I'm hungry, let's join everyone for breakfast."

He held her hand everywhere they went. The brief tour of his home was a bit overwhelming. He covered the front wings. There were lower levels and wine cellars she hadn't seen. The place had two kitchens, one used to prepare formal dinners with four stoves, a walk in freezer, a drink refrigerator, a wine closet and other top chef appliances. The other kitchen was a bit smaller with a gas stove and a brick layered oven heated by wood and coal, and a small white fridge. It reminded her of a cozy home atmosphere with large tin pots and skillets. He said the larger one was built for his mother but she refused to cook in it. To this day Zia and Catalina cooked out of the smaller one. Finally he brought her to an outside terrace that faced one of the most spectacular views. There was a pool with a roman statuesque fountain that looked strangely authentic. Also a two-story cottage down a garden path, and mountains everywhere.

"Morning sweetie," Fabiana bit into a pastry, seated before a vibrant spread of bright red, lime green, yellow and purple slices of fruit and fresh baked pastries.

Catalina looked over her shoulder at Mira and then cut her eyes, mumbling a greeting.

"Hi everyone, good morning." Mira said, as her guy pulled out a chair for her and she sat. A few men, possibly under his employ rose from the table taking their cups of coffee with them. Mira made eye contact with Catalina. Even without makeup she was gorgeous. She decided to make an attempt at being friendly. "So I hear you will be married soon."

"I will. It's difficult because," she glanced over at Mira. "Still looking for the perfect dress."

"You have two dresses being delivered this week. Enough talk of this dress. You will choose from what we bought." Giovanni said sternly.

Mira was grateful. It was her vacation and a short one. In another week this fantasy would end and she'd be in her shop working hard on next season's line. Designing a wedding dress for a spoiled little Mafia princess, didn't feel appealing. She reached for a pastry and some of the sliced fruit on the platter, turning her attention to her friend. "What are you doing today?"

"Horseback riding, here at *Melanzana*."

"You have horses?" Mira asked.

Giovanni winked.

"Oh. That's nice. I didn't know you had horses." She glanced down to Giovanni. He sipped his coffee, returning his attention to the newspaper he had unfolded to read.

"We have over three hundred acres of land. I wanted to show it to Fabiana. You and Giovanni can come."

"No. We have plans." He announced. Lorenzo's gaze switched to Mira and locked with hers. There were times his sly smiles made her uneasy. But again she suppressed that feeling. They ate breakfast and enjoyed light conversation.

"Where is Domi? I've been waiting for him all morning." Catalina asked.

"I sent him away on business. He'll return."

"What! Why? He... he and I... we had things to do."

Lorenzo chuckled. "Yes, Gio. Domi is better suited running errands for little Catalina than tending to our affairs."

Giovanni gave Lorenzo a silencing glare. "He'll be back tomorrow, Catalina."

The young woman let loose a few angry words in Italian and stormed off. Mira found her reaction interesting. She and Fabiana exchanged looks but said little.

"Are we ready to go, *Bella*?" Giovanni asked.

The breakfast was sweet and fresh. The pastries had to have been homemade. She nodded and rose and followed him out. Outside parked in the circular drive was a box shaped jeep with an open top. She eased on her sunglasses and silently wished she hadn't spent so much energy straightening her hair. The wind would have it wilder than an Angela Davis afro.

"After you." He extended his hand to help her climb up into the elevated seat. Giovanni took the time to secure her belt around her, before kissing her cheek. He walked around the front of the vehicle and slipped inside with a gun in his hand. When did he pull a gun? She stared as he tossed it into the glove compartment. She assumed he had it on him since they left the room.

"You take a weapon with you everywhere you go?"

"I call him Danny-boy." He answered. She watched him put on a dark pair of sunglasses, his tone matter of fact.

"You named your gun?"

"He and I have been through some tough times." Giovanni fired up the engine, and they were zooming out of the drive toward the tall gates. As she expected the wind whipped over them tossing her hair wildly in her face. The drive out of Sorrento was magnificent. They arrived under the cover of darkness. Today, in the sunlight, she saw the coast. To her right, homes and stores stretched up the mountain, and down to the left the cliffs that led to the coast had the same homes and roads. The sea sparkled as if filled with blue diamonds. The sky was clear of clouds, and the sun burned brighter than she'd ever known. Mira observed it all in silent awe, until they arrived into the congested streets of Napoli.

"We will fly into Firenze, and drive out to Chianti."

"Fly?"

Giovanni smirked at her. "In my private plane."

She relaxed, imagining making love to him in the clouds until they arrived at the airstrip and she saw the tiny three-seater. "We aren't flying in that!" she exclaimed.

"I'm a pilot. You're safe with me." He exited the jeep.

"Giovanni! No!" Mira shook her head fiercely. She wasn't afraid of flying, but she was terrified of flying in that propeller contraption. And was he serious? He's a pilot. Bullshit!

He helped her out and cupped her face. "I make this flight often. You trust me? Don't you?"

"But..."

He kissed her. "Trust me."

If he cared about her objections, he didn't let on. He just dragged her by the hand and spoke in Italian to some man with a clipboard. Mira glanced around timidly and begrudgingly climbed inside the small cockpit. Giovanni carefully strapped her inside and gave her a headset. "You are my co-pilot."

Fear seized her gut, and she couldn't speak. He winked, slamming the door shut. As he turned the ignition the man out front gave the front propeller a spin and the plane grumbled to life. "Oh sweet, merciful God. Please be with me." Mira said. She glanced over to her lover. He looked so happy to be flipping switches and speaking into the microphone piece. "Ready?"

She put on a brave smile and nodded. They drove down the runway and slowly they picked up speed. Mira squeezed her eyes shut just as the plane lifted to the clouds and her stomach lurched to her throat. She grabbed his thigh, digging her nails in.

"Open your eyes, *Bella*. Really see *Italia*."

Slowly she did. Her gaze swept the buildings and then the coastline. Nothing had every appeared so beautifully serene. And soon she was relaxing into her seat. They coasted through the sky. He spoke to her through the headset, showing her Mount Vesuvius, one of the few active volcanoes in the world, and flew past Pompeii, so she could see the ruined city. It was magical being with him. The flight ended too soon. When they landed, he kissed her before he turned off the plane, and Mira felt such a profound new feeling of love in that kiss.

They were ushered next to another waiting vehicle, a small convertible two-seater car that had speed. Giovanni looked so handsome driving them through the coast with the sun bronzing his olive toned skin. They travelled roads that were more scenic where street vendors sold everything from leather to fresh fish. And soon she understood his choice in vehicle. A bumpy course of cobblestone had her jostling a bit in her seat. After a few hours he told her they were entering *San Donato*, which was named after *Saint Donata*, translating into a gift from God. He shared the history of the village. It dated back to the Romans. In the 4th century Christian soldiers from *Arezzo* stumbled into the vast hills and took up post. The men built the village because of its abundance of fruit and fertile soil. They made a fortress out of it. Afterwards the village was given the name *San Donato* after their bishop.

San Donato stood frozen in time, a relic of what once was. Approaching from the distance she noticed a small modest old cement block church on the left side of the country road. Giovanni eased on the gas and the car slowed to a stop. There was no traffic in either direction. Above the pointed roof was a block wall structure with a rusted bell and it appeared older than anything she'd seen thus far.

"It's beautiful."

"You should see the inside, *Bella*, it actually dates back to 1000 AD. When the Romans discovered it, they uncovered numerous art treasures still inside."

Mira smiled at him "What kind of art treasures?"

"The front of the church has a mural painted by Giovanni della Robbia. It depicts the life and death of Giovanni the Baptist. The Romans also found a crucifix to *Taddeo Gaddi*, two altar pieces by Giovanni del Biondo, another by Bicci di Lorenzo, and a 15th century Florentine chalice."

"Giovanni and Lorenzo? You have got to be kidding me!" she laughed.

"Our names are as old and steeped in tradition as that church there."

She stared with eyes stretched in wonder at the church. "I suppose it's not in there now for me to take a peek?"

"On the way back I'll walk you inside to see the mural. The other treasures are long gone," he said smiling, shifting into first gear and driving away.

"How do you know all of this? Seriously as historical as Virginia is back home, I'd barely be able to tell you any of it, and I grew up there."

"My father would make this same drive to our vineyard when I was a boy. He'd stop along the way and we'd visit families, pray at that church. He'd always share tales and make us recite history to him. He was a man that loved Italian and Sicilian history. He instilled that pride in us. I think he was destined to return to *Italia*. He met my mother in *Firenze*. Kept her nearby until she became pregnant with me then brought her to Sicily. He said he knew I'd be born a boy and he wanted my birth to be on Sicilian soil. His family was in Palermo, but Mama lived in Mondello Beach."

"Mondello Beach? Sounds nice."

When he didn't respond she glanced over to find a sullen frown denting his brow.

"You said that you were born in Mondello? Right?"

Giovanni nodded. "At the time of my birth there was conflict within the family. My father at first wanted me born in Palermo where he was born. But for my mother's well-being he decided on Mondello."

"What kind of conflict?"

"We'll talk about it later." He veered off the main road across a grassy one barely mowed. Mira looked up to see the fields painted brilliant colors of purple and yellow from the wildflowers that bloomed all around and found it captivating. But to be honest their travels into Tuscany had become as freshly exciting as her new love affair with this complicated man.

"This is it?" she asked. She pointed toward the land and the vineyard fields stretching for miles. She saw several weathered barns and a small ranch style farmhouse between them.

"Yes, this is it. We will have to walk the rest of the way. My uncle doesn't like vehicles driving up to the winery, spewing what he thinks are toxins that poison his land from their exhaust pipes."

Mira smiled, opening her door. A quick glance back and she caught a glimpse of his gun as he retrieved it. Out in the middle of nowhere she had a newfound appreciation for his Danny-boy. If he felt it was needed, she wouldn't dare question why. A fresh vibrant fragrance of wild strawberries unfurled all around her. "I smell strawberries. That's weird."

"It's called *Sangiovese*, the work horse grape of Chianti. When it blooms and ripens, it smells like strawberries," he said after taking her hand and helping her from the car. He leaned in to brush his lips across hers.

"What is that for?" she touched the side of his face, staring up into his eyes.

"It's hard for me not to touch you." He kissed her again, and she rested her hands on his sides. It was a soft gentle pressing of their lips and a sweet exchange of their passion. The breeze rustled the leaves of the trees and swirled through the tall grass. She lifted her arms and reached her hands around his neck to kiss him more passionately. She lost all sense of time and space before he broke away. Together they walked along the road, to the gate. Giovanni let go of her hand once they arrived. Tall grass and weeds were tangled around the rusted links of the fence. He slipped a key into a large lock, opened it, and then pulled the chain loose. He yanked the gate open. "After you fair lady," he smiled.

"Why, thank you," she said.

She had to trudge through some of the grass and felt tiny pricks and stings on her bare legs. Giovanni insisted she wear another wrap around dress. She only had three in her luggage, and this one was of fine grape purple silk that clung to her legs and hips. She chose a pair of flat open toe thong sandals to wear with it, and now she regretted this choice. Once he led her from the grass to make the climb up the slanting dusty cobblestone laid road, she wished she had worn sneakers instead.

"Careful, *Bella*," Giovanni pulled her under his arm, helping her move over the rocks, smiling at her struggles. "Do you like Chianti?" he asked

"I'm not really into cabernets. I called it a merlot, but it's really a cabernet, right?"

"Right. So you prefer merlots from Napa?"

Mira shrugged. "I guess. I've drunk so much wine since I've arrived it's a mix for me."

"Well, it's okay because Chianti doesn't stand well on its own. With the right meal, it's the red wine of lovers. Not an expensive wine compared to some I'm sure you've had, but its taste lingers along the palate and arouses your senses in sensual ways you will come to appreciate," he said kissing her forehead, draping his arm around her shoulder to keep her close. Mira glanced over to the violet colored blossoms on the vines.

"Those flowers are beautiful."

Giovanni nodded. "When they bloom, swollen grapes the size of coins drop down."

Letting go of his waist, she walked over to the vine and pulled a full bloom. Biting into the round tiny fruit, she frowned. His laughter boomed in the air. Her mouth was filled with a sour burning flavor that must be the same as the taste of battery acid.

"Bitter is it?" he asked.

"Extremely!"

"It takes time to mature; the longer it's allowed to ripen the sweeter and higher the alcohol content."

Mira put her hand behind her back and dropped the grape innocently.

"I saw that," he chuckled

"It was nasty." She kissed his lips. "Mmm, now this tastes better."

Giovanni laughed, pulling her in his arms "Let me taste, again," he slipped his tongue inside her mouth. Wrapping her arms around him, she kissed him back, feeling his hand go down her back, cupping her below.

"Il mio ragazzo! Il mio ragazzo!" A short man who looked to be covered in wrinkles from head to toe yelled out to them. He wore blue jean overalls over a short sleeve white t-shirt and a cap pulled down low, shading his face. Giovanni let go of the kiss. "Here comes my uncle Rocco. He's a bit of a flirt. Be careful how close you stand to him."

Mira watched a peculiar bowlegged older man with a wide grin rushing toward them. He flashed her a toothless grin. His face deeply wrinkled, his hair thinning and grey. She guessed his age around seventy, at the very least.

"Giovanni!" he shouted. He pulled Giovanni down into a hug, giving him kisses to his cheeks.

"Rocco! Where are your teeth this morning? Did you not get the call we would be visiting?"

Rocco laughed. His gaze volleyed over to her and snagged. *"Chi è questa belladonna?"*

"Speak English, old man. She's American. Her name is Mira."

Rocco took Mira's hand and kissed it. Rubbing his gnarled fingers over her soft skin, smiling he said, "Welcome to *Vigna di Battaglia*."

"*Grazie.*" Mira smiled and the old man embraced her. Once they parted she was almost certain his hand brushed her backside.

"Rocco, she's with me," Giovanni pulled her back to him.

Rocco nodded. "I still got it, Gio," he boasted.

"Well, keep it away from my girlfriend *capisci*?"

Girlfriend? Did he just call me his girlfriend? Mira slipped her arm around Giovanni smiling. Her hand hit his gun, and she flinched, pulling away. He looked at her confused, but Rocco immediately interrupted. "Come, come, Carlotta will be so pleased."

"If it's okay, Rocco, I'd like to give Mira a tour of the old cellars so we can do some tasting."

Rocco nodded. "Of course, Gio. I will set it up." He shuffled off excitedly.

"I don't want to impose. If he has work to do today we can—"

"Nonsense. Those are my cousins, the workers," he nodded to the vineyard. She could see two men on top of a large truck, and others in the distance. "They will handle the business, and we'll tour the old wine cellars."

"How old is this place?"

"Over a hundred years old, before Mussolini. My grandfather bought the land, and Rocco and many other family members made it fertile."

Rocco waved from a distance signaling for them to follow.

She walked a bit ahead, around the mowed path to an older building made of wood instead of stone. When she entered the cool atmosphere it made goose bumps rise along her arms. Mira took note of the dark stone walls and large barrels lined up in the center next to blocks of steel containers for crushing grapes. She inhaled the acidic smell of fermentation and was overwhelmed by the odor. She glanced back to see Giovanni pick up a very crude looking pair of sheers with a long wooden handle. He inspected them closely.

"What's that?"

"My uncles would use these to cut grapes free from their vines. They'd fill barrels that they wore strapped to their chest and then haul them in to be picked free of stems and leaves."

"Wow, that seems like a lot of work."

Giovanni hung the sheers back on the wall. "It was." He nodded goodbye to Rocco who closed the barn door giving them privacy. "Until we bought those."

Mira looked over in the direction he pointed out the window. She saw a tractor looking vehicle with a large container in the front and two mechanical arms that had sheers on the end.

"That is a *mietitrice meccanica,* what you would call a mechanical harvester. It fills those containers with the amount of grapes ten harvesters could haul in within a matter of minutes as opposed to hours. They are brought into a room like this and dumped into crushers."

The more he talked, the more he touched her. First his hand reached for hers, and then he stroked her arm. Now he was behind her, running his fingers up and down her hips. Mira relaxed against his chest as the low timber of his voice spoke smoothly against her ear. In her mind's eye she saw a family of brothers, relocated to Chianti from Sicily, out in the fields doing honest hard work. How did that life lead them down the path of a life of crime?

"Sounds interesting," she said, folding her arms and pressing into his tall frame.

"The crushers?"

"Yes. I thought most of it was done with their feet?" she asked softly as he kissed the inside of her neck.

"Would you like to?"

"No," she chuckled.

"I think it'll be sexy to see you stomping grapes for me." He let his hand ease from her hip down the front of her thigh.

"Is that so?" she sighed.

Giovanni let her go, and Mira collected her thoughts again. She stepped away from temptation to get a closer look at the large containment barrels, as if she cared.

"Come with me. The tour isn't over." He again captured her hand and led her to the back of the barn to a closed wooden door. He opened it, and she saw the stone steps that went to a dark cellar. Hesitant at first she braved the steps, careful to follow close in the dark cramped hall. An unknown light source beckoned them at the end. They arrived to find it to be from a single bulb in the center of the wine cellar, and walls of bottled wines, some covered in cobwebs. There was a small bench and table at the back of the room with a ceramic bucket used in tastings to pour out excess wine. To her left there lay a thick yellow quilt with a white picnic blanket on top. She counted three bottles of wine and a tray of meats and cheeses. Giovanni led her over to the large blanket.

"You planned this?" she asked. "A picnic in a wine cellar?"

"Zia honored my wish. You will meet her soon. Shall we?"

he said.

She smiled at how sweet and secluded the setting was. With him a dusty wine cellar felt like the Taj Mahal. He reached behind his back and removed his gun. He turned to put it up over on one of the shelves. Mira dropped to her knees. She picked a bottle with its black lettering and read the family name across it. "It's a 1987 Chianti. Only two years old?"

"It's from our best harvest. Mark my words, ten years from now people will proclaim 1987 the best crop Chianti has ever produced."

She liked how he spoke of wine, how confident he was. It was the kind of strength most women found attractive in a man. After the long drive, she was a bit hungry. She lifted the lid to the basket to find fresh baked bread wrapped in red napkins. "What's for lunch?"

"*Prosciutto* and *soprassata*. Think of it as different salamis and cold meats. The cheese is fresh. Zia makes it and the olive oil too, from scratch. This here is *raveggiolo* cheese you should spread across sliced bread." He stretched out and laid down on his side, observing her. She took the lead to fix their tiny plates and spread the cheese as he suggested over the sliced loaves. She found a container of plump olives, her favorites, and fed him one from her fingers.

"I like when you feed me, care for me," he winked.

"So you're the kind of man that wants a woman to take care of him?"

He nodded.

"That's not attractive in the States," she smiled.

Giovanni looked as if he could give a shit about what men in the States preferred. "You know what I would really like?" he asked as he poured them wine, and she tasted everything she could sample from the trays. She stopped mid-chew and looked to him. Swallowing she blinked curiously. "What?"

"To taste Chianti from your nipples."

Mira laughed thinking his request no more than one of his saucy jokes. He'd made a few since they became lovers. In the shower he talked of her pussy as if it were a fruit and constantly made references to the softness of the skin between her thighs. At first she blushed inwardly at his frank manner. Now the words were warm and enticing. "Are you serious?"

"About your nipples? Yes."

She rolled her eyes, shaking her head. But when she looked around, she couldn't deny how isolated they were. And God help her, but she loved the way he sucked her nipples. Rising she dusted off her hands and chewed what was left in her mouth. "Fine. It's a deal. And if I let you, then you must do something I want."

He drank from the bottle staring at her breasts.

"Do you agree?"

"What do you want?"

"To know the story of your parents. How they met, how they died. The entire story of their love affair."

Surprise siphoned the blood from his face. He stared at her silent for a pause before speaking. His body language sent her a private message to be careful how far she pushed him. Doors once open cannot be closed. What could she gain by unlocking the mysteries of his past, how far did she want their lives to intertwine? She considered taking back the flirty challenge. But the words didn't form. Giovanni's gaze shifted away. "To gain my pleasure I must exchange my pain, is that your proposal?" He sat upright.

"Is it that painful of a tale? I don't want to pressure you

into anything. I only wanted to know a bit more, after meeting your family. You've shared so much, I only... I guess I'm curious to know more."

The dim lighting within the wine cellar covered his face in partial shadows. Still she could read his pain, feel it, and part of her even understood it, though a full understanding wouldn't come until much later. "I will tell you the story of my parents. Now undress for me."

It had become clear why this man had a preference for the flimsy silk wrap around dresses she owned. His insistence that she wear this dress in particular today would soon prove essential in her seduction of him. She untied the belt and parted the fabric to reveal her black bra and panty set from her intimacies collection. The unveiling of her body underneath made his beautiful eyes sparkle like crystals. The lacey black bra cups housing her medium sized breasts were connected by a thin satin bow. The same tie was knotted to the left and right side of her panty, keeping them snug and low on her hips. He drank more of the wine from the bottle with his gaze sweeping over her body.

"Undress." He ordered.

She smiled. "This is a wine tasting. My nipples yes, my navel yes, nothing more. My panties stay on."

"I want the knickers off." He frowned, his eyes level under drawn brows.

"Not part of the deal."

He stared at her for a moment then nodded that he agreed. Mira untied the bra in the front and shook it off her shoulders. Giovanni moved the food. The wine glasses and the basket of food were set aside on the cool concrete floor. His hand reached for hers, and she allowed his help to lower her down to the blanket and stretch out before him.

She was gorgeous. Undressing her had become his favorite thing. However, there was nothing more exciting than having her undress herself. She laid on her back before him with one knee raised, beautiful, submissive and dangerously sexy. Her smooth, brown skin, hair thick as sable, and smoky eyes made him a bit hesitant. What if he gave his heart to this woman and she never truly felt for him what he felt when he was with her? Was the risk worth taking?

Her mouth and lips, begged to be kissed. If he did he'd climb on top of her and take her as he had done the night before. Lying before him now he was once again reminded of the Egyptian goddess statue they saw in the gardens of *villa Melzi*. Giovanni reached for the dark bottle of wine and her gaze lifted to the action as it hovered, then he poured magenta grapes to the center of her chest. The stream slid downward to her neck so he had to pour with a more concentrated attempt over her left then right nipples. Wine splashed and her chest heaved, causing the crimson drops to spread and drip along the underside of her breasts, down the slender curve of her belly.

"You're pouring too much. I'll be all sticky!" she squealed.

"Trust me, not one drop will go wasted."

Licking her lips, she laid perfectly still waiting for whatever was to come next. Giovanni took his time tracing his trigger finger around her areola. He pinched her stiff nipple. She sighed. The sexy tension stretched tighter between them. He hadn't shared why this cellar of all places would be a place he wanted to bring her to. Often he'd fly his plane out here, drink wine, and think over his troubles, away from those that needed him. He loved the quiet isolated feel he got here, much more than at the wine cellars he had on his estate in Portici. And he had grown equally fond of the peace and contentment she'd given him in the short time they'd known each other.

His face lowered for the first sample of her skin laced in his family's wine, and his focus became singular. He brushed his lips over her warm skin, and then flicked his tongue at the dark berry while using his free hand to ease down her damp, sticky tummy over her mons. She parted her thighs an inch and his pulse accelerated. He aided her by cupping her pussy in his palm. Now he was ready to taste her. Holding her intimately he swirled his tongue over the circumference of her nipple then licked and tasted the swell of her breast. He could feel her core grow hot and damp against his palm as he used his tongue to swipe her right breast clean of Chianti. His gaze flickered up, and he could see the frozen gasp of pleasure on her parted lush lips. Caught between wanting more and suppressing the urge to say it, she was his goddess and he her King.

Descending into undiluted pleasure, he tasted everywhere he could along her chest, grateful for the privilege. Easing aside the seat of her panty, he eased two fingers into her tight channel. The soft walls of her inner channel warmly stretched and accepted his invasion. She immediately brought her hand to his as if she had the strength or will to resist him. Giovanni let go a deep chuckle when she failed to maintain her grip and shuddered as he masterfully fucked her with his fingers. He latched on to a quivering nipple and sucked harder. Mira's hold on his wrist weakened and dropped away. She rolled her ass and parted her thighs to pump her pelvis upward. He longed to strip down to nothing and fuck her raw, no condom. He wanted to desperately ram every inch of his manhood into her and fill her womb with his seed. What was he thinking? How dangerous had this affair become? She was now his new weakness.

Instead of resisting her hold on him, he used his fingers to elicit a soft chant of submission from her plush lips. While Giovanni observed her climaxing under his watchful stare, she opened her eyes and locked onto his.

He kissed her. Soft, and then hard, her lips and his tongue begged for a union far beyond sex. Neither of them could comprehend the implications this early in their courtship. Still he kissed her like a man would his woman and made a silent vow. He'd do anything to ensure no other man ever knew the pleasure loving her could bring. She returned his kiss with a hunger that belied her outward calm. He moved his mouth over hers, devouring her softness until she weakened and became his again. His lips left hers, and he stared into her lovely face.

"Are you okay, *Bella*?"

"Always, with you always," she said softly.

"We can take the lunch with us."

"Where?" she half-moaned with her lids sliding shut as he rubbed the sensation of her quaking orgasm into her pussy.

"I've shared my pleasure with you. You asked to see my pain. For that we must take a short drive."

Her eyes flashed open again. "Mmkay."

She dressed after using napkins to clean herself. He hadn't intended to take her to *Villa di Luce* when they embarked on a visit to his family's winery. Her request to know more about his mother threw him. But now he wanted to share his history. For the first time since his parents' death, he felt okay with explaining to a stranger why he was who he was.

As she packed their lunch and he folded the wine soaked

quilt, he cleared his throat. "What's your mother's name?" he asked.

"Melissa, everyone called her Lisa," she said confused by the turn of the conversation.

"How did your mother die?" Giovanni asked. She froze, her gaze lifting to him from her crouched position. She stood with the basket. "She died from an overdose of heroine."

Giovanni couldn't imagine that to be her mother's fate. Mira shied away from him, busying herself with tidying up the space of their brief picnic. He ached to comfort her, to tell her it was nothing to be ashamed of. But he declined. He hated what drugs did to those he knew and cared about over the years. Men he trusted as brothers who wasted away.

They headed up the cellar stairs through the old barn and out into the fresh air. Her mood seemed to lighten under the noon sun. He dropped his arm around her shoulders and walked at her pace, answering her questions about the land and the products sold there. He loved her curious nature, though it would prove troublesome if she didn't understand and appreciate the times when he would need to remain silent.

Zia, having seen them through her front windows, came to the door to watch their approach, all of which was pointed out to Mira by Giovanni. His aunt wore a forced smile. According to Giovanni she'd never seen him bring a woman to their vineyard for a visit. His visits were always alone; only Lorenzo knew of his need to come to the vineyard and disappear at times.

In the past Zia had set him up on many ambush dinners with local girls. Other than sex, Giovanni had no time for romance. Her lingering stare on Mira was uncharacteristically critical. However, his *Bella* was uncharacteristically different.

Still Mira was gracious and polite. He couldn't tell if it mattered to her that others regarded her with suspicion and scorn because she was different than them, just as his mother had suffered the same looks of contempt over her red hair and ice blue eyes.

Zia spoke with her limited English. She invited them both for dinner. Mira looked to him expectantly. Her smile indicated that she'd be willing to stay. He passed on the temptation before he lost his nerve. They would visit his mother's villa, and he'd face his demons with her.

"No." Giovanni simply stated and his aunt glared at the lack of respect. To refuse her, was an insult. He had no time to explain his intentions. Mira would be his and only his this evening.

Zia took Mira by the hand and told her she would refresh their basket with food from her oven. Mira appeared enchanted with his aunt's tiny kitchen. She found a way to communicate as they packed away a fresh basket of thinly sliced meats and cheeses for the wine, along with pasta he knew his aunt hand rolled.

"She's a beauty." Rocco said in Italian. "Is she yours?"

Giovanni understood the reference. His uncle had leered at his woman since they arrived. He wanted to know if she was his mistress or plaything. He chuckled. "No Uncle, she's an American friend."

"You said girlfriend?"

"*Si*, an American *raggaza*."

Rocco leaned to the left to get a clear look at Mira in the kitchen. Giovanni shook his head and let it pass. The women returned and Mira allowed Rocco's farewell embrace, though it lingered too long with polite kisses to her left then right cheek before he brushed his lips over hers. Giovanni put a hand to his shoulder to remind him to show respect. Zia shooed him away and kissed Giovanni goodbye.

"Your uncle felt me up. Twice! And he kissed me on the mouth in front of his wife!"

"I apologize. He's harmless."

"Well he's fresh, really fresh."

Giovanni chuckled. "I'll talk to him. It won't happen again."

Once outside he walked her over to his motorbike. Mira stopped. Her eyes registered shock, but she didn't question him. He took her basket and secured it in the back hutch, then put a helmet on her pretty head. He couldn't wait to feel her pressed against him as he drove out of Chianti.

"So are we dating now, Giovanni?"

He slipped her a sly smile and eased on his sunglasses. Giovanni climbed on the bike first and got it started. Mira used his shoulders to climb behind. "My dress, it'll fly open on this thing."

"Keep your thighs close to me and sit on your dress."

She tucked the center of her dress hem under her and between her thighs. Her arms circled his waist and he again felt more alive than he had in months. Soon they were racing out of the vineyard toward a new destination. He could feel her nervous energy in the way she clung to him. He tried to tell her he'd be extra careful, but she wouldn't lift her face from his back.

The road to his mother's villa turned into a long one-way stretch of dirt, paved, and then cobblestone strips mowed through browning grass. After travelling for over thirty minutes he relaxed on the speed, and Mira lifted her head to look around.

"Where are we now?" she said loudly.

"Fiesole," he answered dryly. "There it is!" he pointed ahead to the aged block shaped lemon yellow building trimmed in plum colored purple, over the hill. The tall grass had rose red wildflowers blooming. Giovanni drove the jeep up to the front of the villa and parked. "This is where Mama lived after we returned from Ireland until Catalina was two. I was fifteen when we were brought here. Catalina wasn't born until a year later. After that Mama stopped running."

"Running?" Mira asked into his ear, holding him again tightly around the waist. "What do you mean running?"

"Papa would have preferred to have her in Sorrento, but she resisted this for a while. She was kept here under guard. Here he could have access to her without interference. He couldn't be separated from her."

"But why, did he do it by force?" Mira asked.

"Let's go inside."

He drove them to the door and held the bike steady while she got off. Giovanni dropped the kickstand and collected the basket and wine. He watched her stroll toward the doors removing her helmet. Giovanni had forbidden Catalina and others from going to the once dilapidated cottage. Just recently he'd had the place painted and the roof replaced. He had to admit he missed his mother intensely whenever he dared to venture here alone. Mira waited for him at the steps. She accepted the basket while he fidgeted with the old lock and forced the wooden door to creak open. Immediately they were overcome by the strong pungent odor of stale air and mildew. To his relief Mira set aside all that was in her hands, drew the curtains back, and opened the dusty windows to allow fresh air in.

When Mira turned he walked away with a large ball of sheets trapped in his strong arms. Every piece of furniture including the mirrors was covered. She brushed the pads of her fingers across the film of dust on the mantle and wondered how long the place had remained untouched. It was then she noticed a portrait in a large silver frame on the mantle. Giovanni continued to open windows on the lower level. She could hear him groan and struggle with a stubborn latch.

Careful of the delicate silver frame she handled it with one hand and wiped the dust off the glass of the frame. The man in the picture had to be his father. He was a strikingly handsome man with jet-black wavy hair that greyed at the temples, and a perfectly shaped mustache that reached his chin. He had hard eyes. They were so dark the irises appeared black in the portrait. He wore a navy blue pinstriped suit and a blue tie on top of a white shirt. In front of him sat a beautiful woman with paler skin, dressed in a matching blue dress. Her hair bright red, long and wavy hung past her shoulders. She had kind eyes. Clear blue like Giovanni's, there was such a sweet beauty to her. Though the portrait was aged she could see the details of her dress, the freckles on her cheeks and the sweet baby in her arms in a christening gown. To her left stood Giovanni as a teenager, no more than sixteen, wearing a pensive look.

Giovanni spoke behind her, and she jumped. She turned and revealed what had her so mesmerized. He accepted the frame from her. "Papa was so happy when we took this photo. He had a local artist transform it into a painting. It hangs in Mondello now. Mama placed the replica here."

"You don't look happy," Mira said.

"My mother never spoke ill of him, but I was a teenager at

the time this picture was taken. I had no delusions of who my father was."

"It's hard relating to our parents as teens."

"More than hard, *Bella*." His gaze lifted to hers, the blue had dissolved to a soft violet and she could see tears glisten. He blinked and the illusion of tears cleared, but the beauty of his eyes remained. "Mama took me with her when she fled Sorrento and hid with her cousins in Ireland. Her mother and father wouldn't have anything to do with her, because of me, but her cousin took us in. She was happy for a short while. We were dirt poor, and she was happy."

"You weren't?"

"I knew nothing about poverty. As Don Battaglia's son I always had the best of everything. I didn't understand why we had to eat scraps from the dinner tables of others, and wear rags. Mama could barely make enough to keep us fed through winter with her washboard. Still she acted as if we were free. I felt like we were in hell."

"You were a boy, confused."

"After two years in Ireland my misery got the best of me. Kids that I didn't fit in with taunted me. I defied my mother and called Sicily for my father. I told him where we were."

Mira held her breath, transfixed by the story. "What happened?"

"He arrived. Our little one bedroom cottage door opened one day and he and his brothers walked in." Giovanni smiled, but there was no pleasure in this smile. "My mother knew immediately that I had betrayed her. I'll never forget the look of pain and hurt on her face. It haunts me now. He walked in and kissed her, told her to collect our things. She did as he said without objection. We were immediately taken back to Italy.

Soon she was pregnant, and the fight in her was all gone. She never tried to leave again."

"I don't understand. He was her husband. Why did she leave him?"

"I told you they were never married." He said bitterly. Mira realized he had shared that truth with her, but she didn't find it scandalous. He spoke of it as if their love was some mortal sin. She opened her mouth to apologize and he shook his head. "Don't. I'm sorry. I didn't mean to be cross."

"Your mother made a sacrifice for you. For your sister?" Mira asked.

"Yes."

"She loved you."

"She had no one but us. Even in Ireland she was treated with scorn." He sighed, dropping on the sofa. Mira sat next to him. "My mother arrived in Napoli with her parents at the age of fourteen. Her dad wanted to open up his textile business there, and hearing that they could prosper better than in poverty stricken Ireland, he relocated the family. At the time my father had gained prominence within Mussolini's Republic. He had a lot of influence." He ran his hand through his hair and sucked in a deep breath as if the weight of the tale constricted his breathing. Mira ran her hand across his chest to soothe him through the telling.

"I don't know when he first laid eyes on my mother, but he did. He said once that he'd never seen hair so red on the head of an angel. He said he fell in love at the sight of her."

"She was a child, only fourteen."

Giovanni wiped his hand down his face and slouched in the sofa seat. "Yes, she was a child."

"I understand, you don't have to—."

"I'm not done." His tone was flat but assertive. "He commanded a lot of respect."

"As do you?"

Giovanni glanced over to her with a curious frown.

"You helped me with opening the doors to my boutique when we were closed down. Seems that your family's influence extends throughout southern Italy."

"It does." Giovanni chuckled. "To insult a man of my father's prominence is a grave mistake. The McHenrys didn't know this. My grandfather challenged Papa openly for touching his daughter inappropriately during a visit to their store. He threw him out. My father left without any complaint. This part of the story was told to me by my cousin, as part of my shame."

"Why is it your shame?"

Giovanni stared down at the picture. "My father ordered his brothers and men to leave the McHenrys alone. No punishment was to be extended for the insult. It confused them all. One thing Don Tomosino wasn't was a charitable man. But he had other plans for the family. He had other plans for her."

"What did he do to your mother?"

"The unthinkable. He raped her."

Mira froze. Had she heard him right? He used the word rape as casually as a man would say the word love. She looked down at the picture of the family with a renewed understanding. It pained her to hear the fate of an innocent girl by the hands of a lustful, calculating man twice her age.

"How did he get her alone?"

"My mother attended a school in the hills during the day, while her mother and father worked to get the business off the ground. They had a driver pick her up each evening and take her home. She once told me her dream as a young girl was to be a nun. Her father had taken her to Vatican City and she believed in her calling." Giovanni chuckled bitterly. "It was not to be."

"We don't have to talk about it."

"We do. I want to. Papa learned of her school schedule and interceded. He had her brought to him."

"Did your mother tell you she was raped?"

"No. I'm a man now. I know how this works. Whether she understood or consented to what happened to her that afternoon, she was a young sheltered girl who had no idea of the consequences. After it happened she tried to cover her shame and avoid him, but Papa convinced her that she would have to continue to let him have his way with her or her family would be disgraced. Soon she was pregnant with me and her world fell apart."

"I know the rest of this story." Mira said sadly. Her stomach soured. She didn't want to hear anymore. "Her family threw her out. Didn't they?"

He nodded. "As my father knew they would. Her parents were sickened and enraged to learn that the affair had been going on under their nose. To them it was the most unforgivable sin. My father being a married man made it all the worse. She fled to him for protection. Because her father felt wronged, he went to a feuding family that he heard customers whisper were enemies of ours. He asked the Don for revenge. In exchange he would give him part ownership of his textile company. That was a direct insult to my father since he had given my grandfather a free pass in his city. Blood spilled in the streets over this feud, and until this day many blame the Battaglias for this. Mama's parents fled in the night to Ireland with nothing but the clothes on their backs."

They sat in silence.

Mira put her hand over his. He turned over his hand and captured her palm, intertwining her fingers with his. "Then came you?"

"Papa's wife was barren. To Papa the union was a fraud. He felt cursed to be joined to her and treated his bride horribly. Mama was her replacement. She gave him what he always wanted, what none of his mistresses were able to achieve. A son."

"Does he have other children outside of you and your sister?"

Giovanni sighed. "I don't know. None have ever come forward."

"Then why not divorce his wife and marry your mother?"

"Divorce?" Giovanni's nose wrinkled. He glared at Mira. "We're catholic. Divorce is not an option."

"But he had affairs. Adultery is a sin."

"Divorce from men like him, like me, would never be an option."

Mira withdrew her hand from his, understanding his message loud and clear. Giovanni's gaze returned to the portrait. "His wife was madly jealous of Mama, the Irish woman with the bright red hair who had charmed her husband away. Even though my mother was a child herself, she hated her on sight. She made Mama's life miserable during the last months of her pregnancy. Even in Mondello the people shunned her. When Papa came for us, I was two months old and Mama was heartbroken."

Mira didn't know what to say. She looked back at the picture, "What's your mother's name."

"Evelyn, but he called her Eve."

"Did she ever explain why she stayed with him?"

"I suppose she loved him, or learned to love him as some prisoners learn to love their captors. Because in spite of everything he put her through, she was a devoted woman to her faith and her family. We were moved to *Melanzana* and she became the *donna* of our family."

"But you said she ran from him?"

"Even a saint has her limits." Giovanni dropped his head back and told the rest of the tale with his eyes closed. "She watched me and my cousin grow in the image of our fathers. The way we worshipped them and our lifestyle as teenagers became too much for her. When Lorenzo's father was killed, Mama took Lorenzo and his mother in. The competition between my cousin and me worsened and Lorenzo's mother constantly worked to drive my mother from my father's heart. To do so would mean I wouldn't be a Battaglia heir. Lorenzo would fill those shoes."

"Oh, okay."

"So my mother went to my father and asked that Lorenzo and I be schooled away from Italy, that we not know the brutality of our family's history. My father refused. He told her that I would carry on the traditions. I was his son. She packed our things and bought us a ticket out. Telling my dad she wanted to purchase things for our upcoming visit to Mondello, we slipped past him and the guards."

"Then you told him where you were?"

"And he came for us. I later learned that she made him swear to send me to college in America, to give me a different life. He told her she could never leave him again and would give him another son. That's why he put her here. Her open defiance wouldn't allow for him to bring her back to Sorrento.

Catalina was born. Having Catalina healed my parents. They changed. She and my father were inseparable from the moment Catalina entered our lives."

"What happened to her, after your father's death?"

"When he was shot and I accepted an oath, the ordeal broke her heart. She pleaded and cried at his bedside to release me. Mama actually thought I'd be some great lawyer and leave this life. He refused. We fought; I didn't show her the respect she deserved. I was too hell bent on avenging my father. I'm not proud of the things I said to her. Less than six months later she took ill. I believe she stopped taking her insulin. She died soon after."

Mira pulled his face to hers and kissed him. He reclined her on the sofa and she parted her legs continuing the kiss. With him on top of her, she felt the weight of his burden. She clung to him wrapping her legs around his waist. Giovanni's mouth was the most persuasive. The kiss pulled her under his spell. His lips grazed her cheek and then went down to her neck while he worked the zipper on his pants and freed himself. He lifted and raised himself by gripping the arm of the sofa above her head. The folds of her dress had parted and slow and easy he untied the ribbons to her hips to release her panty. Afterwards he was thrusting into her hard and strong. He pressed his forehead against hers and they breathed in unison as he drove both pain and pleasure into her until her body melted beneath him and she cried out her release. He lay on her panting against her ear with his face partially covered by her shoulder and the sofa seat. Mira stared up at the ceiling thinking of her own sad tale. Should she share it? Could she fathom the sad life her mother too shared with a man that led to her misery and then her conception?

"My mother ran away from my grandparents when she was sixteen. With a boy from our town to God knows where."

Giovanni withdrew from their intimate connection but rested on her breasts, close to her heart. She stroked his head to share what she did know of her mother. Her intention was to lessen his suffering but the more she talked of her mom, the more it lessened her pain as well.

"She came back ten years later with me in her arms. My grandmother said her eyes were dead. For old people dead eyes meant the person had lost their soul. The bracelet you found with my purse was attached to my wrist. My mother would not speak of who my father was, but Me-ma said it wasn't James. Later they discovered she had overcome a bad drug habit. Something she confessed in my grandfather's church. She found a way to remain clean. After a month she asked my grandparents to take care of me. She said she had left her heart somewhere else and it was time to go claim it. My grandmother begged her not to go. She couldn't believe her daughter would run out on a new baby for a man. My mother swore that wasn't what she meant, but she never disclosed the truth. Four months later she died of a heroin overdose in Chicago." she said bitterly.

His head lifted. She touched his face. "You see, your sorrow is mine as well."

He nodded and relaxed against her breast. Mira closed her eyes. Before long they were asleep.

Chapter Ten

DOMINIC REMOVED A PAIR of slender black gloves and slipped one on his left hand then the other on the right. A perfect fit. His gaze lifted to the mirror. He didn't possess the features of the Battaglia men, namely Lorenzo and Giovanni. Both were giants in personality and height. Dominic barely stood over six-feet. His hair, unlike theirs, was curly, his skin a richer shade of olive and his irises a deep chocolate brown. Still he loved them both like brothers. Papa Tomosino had been the only father he'd ever known. Giovanni told him they shared the same blood within *omerta* and that was enough. It was Dominic's brain, quick decisive actions, and carefully laid plans that always bore results and earned him his respect. Tonight he would keep a cool head. Get the information his Don needed and return to Napoli before the sun rose.

The whimpering drew his attention from the mirror. Maria Bottego, daughter of Sal '*il sarto*' Bottego and Fish's whore, sat on the edge of the bed sniffing. She was a beautiful young thing. Her dark hair cascaded down her shoulders and shielded the tears streaming down her face. He could understand why

Angelo and Fish constantly fought over her.

Dominic walked out of the bathroom into the bedroom. He'd arrived to find her in a skimpy negligee, satin and pink. He told her to cover up before he signaled for Carlo to enter. Dominic was a gentleman; Carlo on the other hand didn't have such grace. It was evident from the smells from the kitchen she was expecting Fish for dinner and dessert.

He stared at her. The woman found it hard to make eye contact. Her mascara ran dark tears down her cheeks. A few black tears dropped to her lap. He removed the gun from the back of his pants and screwed on the silencer.

"Why the fuck is she crying? No one has touched her." Carlo sneered. He glared at the woman from the corner he leaned in, a toothpick swirled on his tongue between his pressed lips.

Carlo was mean. It was the only word to describe him. He was another giant among men. Stood as tall as Giovanni and Lorenzo, and chose to dress like a businessman instead of the thug his reputation proclaimed him to be. He hated to have him on a mission of discretion, although Carlo's thirst for respect and blood could prove handy if Fish didn't cooperate.

"We do this clean." Dominic approached Maria. He curled his index finger under the young woman's chin. "*Tutto a posto.*"

She sniffed and blinked up at him. Her hands trembled in her lap. The corner of his mouth lifted into a small smile.

"Be a good girl for me. Stay in here and stay quiet. Carlo will behave unless you give him a reason not to." Dominic glanced up to Carlo to emphasize the order.

She nodded that she would obey. On cue the door to the front of the small cottage opened and slammed shut. "Maria! Get your ass out here. I've been calling you."

Dominic winked. He brushed his index finger along the side of her cheek affectionately. He shot Carlo a look and the enforcer removed his toothpick flicking it to the floor. His hooded gaze narrowed in on Maria and the woman pleaded with Dominic with her eyes to not be left alone with him. Dominic waited a beat and Carlo nodded his obedience. Satisfied Dominic walked out of the bedroom. He could hear Fish in the kitchen, possibly sampling the dinner his woman had prepared for him. He chose to go left to remain in the shadows toward the enclave that separated the family room from the bedrooms.

"Maria? You here?"

Dominic watched and waited for Fish to leave the kitchen for the bedroom. He did. Fish was only five-foot six, but not chubby like the Calderone men. He had a slender frame and a nasty scar under his neck that stretched from ear to ear. He dealt in knives after having one used on him as a preteen. Everyone knew no man could survive a one on one knife fight with Fish.

And that wasn't the best of his talents. Fish was best in explosives, which was why Dominic kept the gun steady and ready. The Calderones and the *Ndrangheta* were best known for firebombing and blowing up their adversary.

Careful, Dominic slipped behind Fish once he passed. Unfortunately, his shadow gave his presence away, and Fish was ready. He swung with a blade in his hand. Where it came from Dominic wasn't sure but he countered by leaning out of the strike reach just as it swung up to run through his throat. He hit Fish hard and fast in the gut and then shoved his fist into his throat. The deft move brought Fish to his knees. *"Salve."*

Fish gagged.

"Surprised to see me?"

The hacking man with watery eyes looked up to his attacker and the light of recognition drained blood from his face. Fish's eyes stretched once his mind made the recognition.

"It's been awhile. I'm disappointed. You don't write, you don't call."

"I... why are you here? What have I done?" Fish dropped the blade and rubbed his sore throat.

Dominic smiled. "My Don deserves answers, and you are going to give them to me."

"I won't tell you shit!"

Dominic nodded. "Then that's a shame. I left a present in the room with your *puttana*. Shall I tell you *who* it is?"

Fish looked back over his shoulder. "Is Carlo here? With Maria! Maria!" Fish staggered to rise to run to her rescue. Dominic forced him down with a hard grip to his shoulder. Fish returned to his knees, his eyes wide with panic. He placed the silencer between Fish's brows. "Let's have that talk."

****

"Couldn't we have stayed the night?" Mira asked. She really wished they had more time to talk and share with each other. But a stranger appeared at the door, and Giovanni left their warm bath. Curious, she stood in the tub and leaned over to the windowsill, dripping wet. She stood on her toes and held to the sill; afraid she'd slip and break her neck in the claw foot tub. She couldn't see Giovanni but the visitor stood off from the step. He appeared to be a young kid of sixteen who had arrived on his bike. He gave Giovanni a phone from the front basket on his bike.

Mira left the tub and wrapped a towel around her damp

body. She crept downstairs just as the conversation ended, and Giovanni reentered the living area. She watched him plug the phone into the wall. As soon as he did the phone began to ring. Giovanni took a call and paced. He spotted her, and she bolted back up the stairs, her heart racing. Later he found her. Neither mentioned what she witnessed. Instead they shared a lovely dinner. They made love with her pressed down on the table where they had dined and his long hard cock ramming into her from behind. Again Giovanni sank his teeth into her shoulder, back, and when he flipped her over and he laid her out on the table to ravish her more, he bit into her breast. Sweet merciful God, she loved every minute of it. Until it ended. He told her to dress and they were on his motorbike racing along the roadways at a very dangerous speed back to the airport. Once they landed in Napoli he whisked her away in a car to Sorrento.

"It could not be helped."

She realized she was pouting and corrected the action. It was crazy to be so needy of his time. Even with Kei, the attraction between them wasn't this strong. The cold hard reality was that eventually she and her Don would have to return to their separate lives. She dreaded the day. However, it was best to accept the truth of what they were and weren't now rather than later. To her disappointment they drove up the winding road directly to the Battaglia gates and the truth waited.

"I had a lovely time today. Thank you," she said. He cast those jeweled eyes at her and gave her a sweet smile. She leaned forward and kissed him. "And thank you, Giovanni, for sharing your story with me."

"*Prego.*"

She opened the door and hopped out of the car. They left

the picnic basket and wine in the back. As soon as they crossed the threshold, the sounds of a young woman's wails filled the foyer.

In a flash Catalina rushed through the hall into her brother's arms, weeping. Mira stood frozen watching the scene. A petite woman in a long skirt with a messy grey bun to the back of her head hurried down the hall after Catalina. Giovanni wrapped his arms around his sister as one would do with a terrified child and comforted her. He kissed the top of her head, trying to understand what had her so distressed. "What is it?"

"It's awful, just awful!!"

Giovanni gave Mira a desperate plea with his eyes to free him from the entire matter. So she addressed the older woman who appeared to be at the center of the drama. "Can I be of any help?"

The woman looked Mira up and down. She then glanced to Giovanni and spoke in English to be clearly heard. "Donatella is unable to make the dress exactly as requested; the one she sent is all wrong. We have a week before the wedding."

"A week?" Mira looked to Giovanni surprised. She knew there would be a wedding, but in a week? Catalina let go of her brother shaking her head. "It's ugly, I hate it! I will look like a fool, Giovanni. And she didn't even send the second dress. We paid for two dresses. All I got is one horrible thing!"

"Do you mind showing me the dress? Maybe I can help?" Mira offered.

"Can you?" Catalina asked wiping her eyes.

"Of course, it's what I do, remember?"

Catalina smiled. "*Grazie.*" She looked to her brother for approval. "Is it okay, Giovanni? Can she help me?"

"Thank you, *Bella*," he mouthed.

Catalina took her hand and pulled her toward the stairs. She glanced back once more and Giovanni winked at her. She returned the wink. Together they ascended the stairs and met Fabiana at the top. Her friend looked at them both curiously. "What's the hurry?"

"My dress! She will design a new one." Catalina beamed.

"Wait, I only offered to—."

"I'm so excited."

"What dress?" Fabiana asked.

"This way!" Catalina announced. The woman who had to be an event planner shoved her way past Mira and Fabiana heading down the hall after her client. Fabiana gave Mira a puzzled look. "Please don't tell me you agreed to do a dress for her?"

"How could I say no?" Mira whispered. They both started walking.

"Just say no." Fabiana whispered back.

Mira chuckled. "It can't be that bad. She said Donatella sent it."

"Wait." Fabiana grabbed her arm before she entered the room after Catalina. "You can't work on another designer's dress. Are you insane? You know better."

Mira sighed. "Let's look at it. Okay?"

As her business manager, Fabiana never let her do personal designs without going through her. Everything she touched was viewed as a business deal. Reworking another designer's piece was a complete insult and a definite no-no in the industry.

Giovanni was in no mood for his sister's hysterics. He

walked through his home and out the back doors. In Sorrento he kept his family safe and contained, but the times business called it would always take place in the *Villa Rosso*. It was the cottage his father ran his business from and the place he took the oath of silence and accepted his role in the family. Necessary matters were only conducted behind those doors. The women knew to never venture in when he and the boys were meeting.

He glanced back over his shoulder. On the third floor of the villa he could see the lights to Catalina's room flicker on. He hoped the dress matter would be resolved soon and Mira waiting for him in his room when he returned. A wishful thought.

The inside of his two-story cottage was dark and silent. His men patrolled the grounds, but no one had entered before him. He smelled the deep ingrained aroma of his favorite cigars and frequently consumed malt embedded in the walls and floors. It was indeed a meeting place of men. Giovanni flicked the light switch and closed the door. He crossed the gathering room and headed to his office in the back. Above him was a single bedroom and shower. Many nights he chose that room over his own bed.

Not long after he entered his office and sat behind his desk, he heard the outer door open. He lowered as his visitor crossed his threshold. "Did you leave him alive?" he asked.

"Barely."

Giovanni dropped back in his large swivel chair and gazed up at Dominic. "Will he name you?"

Dominic chuckled. "We made sure he has amnesia when it comes to our visit. This is hard for me to say boss. I chose to question Fish away from Carlo, because I feared...I... I haven't shared this with any of the men."

"Speak."

"I believe Lorenzo killed Giuseppe."

"And you believe this why?"

"No one, not even the Nigerians would have done away with Giuseppe this way. You know how this works. Sure they would have wanted to send a message, and maybe even teach the old Don a lesson, but Giuseppe played against his father's best interest. We all know what he was trying to move through the triangle. It just, it doesn't feel right. And Fish confirmed it. He said Giuseppe and Lorenzo met frequently in Como and often in Genoa."

Giovanni sighed. "Where's Lorenzo?"

Why would Lorenzo betray the family this way? For drugs? Did he want to force his hand, force him to make an example of him?

"Fish can be useful." Dominic's voice rose above his thoughts. "He can throw the Calderones off the scent. He wants to deal. He knows when the old man's grief takes him down after the body is discovered, the family will disintegrate. Revenge will overwhelm them."

Giovanni closed his eyes and remembered how revenge almost destroyed his family as well. It was Lorenzo who found the Russians who put the hit on his father. His cousin helped him channel his angry grief into the final act that made him the boss of all bosses. Their Don. He refused to believe that Lorenzo would betray him now or ever. There still wasn't any proof. His cousin loved his Bellagio home, and he frequented the pussy holes, where men gathered. Calderone's gambling house in Genoa was one of them.

"Go on," Giovanni sighed.

"Fish will work with me, only me. Provide me updates and do your bidding. He'll even put a bullet in Don Calderone if you want it."

"Now why would he do that? He has no allegiance to the *Cammora*."

"Angelo." Dominic answered. "He hates the fucker. Doesn't want to work under his command. There is a long standing feud between the men over his woman Maria. We have her and Fish will do anything to get her back." Dominic's grin was half sneer, half humor.

Giovanni sat forward. He clasped his hands together on top of his desk. It always came down to pussy for men. Pussy and greed were every man's Achilles' heel. That's why he fucked nameless faceless women. Except for her. Now he too had a weakness. He'd welcomed a woman into his home and bed that he'd barely known a week.

"Boss?"

"Sounds like we can use him." Giovanni answered.

"If it's going to be war boss, we need an inside man," Dominic said. "Whether Lo did the crime, we both know what Fish has seen others have as well. It won't take long before Angelo and the Calderones drag us into this shit."

****

Mira sat on the bed waiting for Catalina to come out of the bathroom in the wedding dress. She soon became distracted with the way Fabiana lingered near the window. She figured she was holding her tongue for what she was about to do, but honestly a wedding a week away left her no real choice.

"What's wrong?"

"Huh?" Fabiana asked.

"You don't want me to fix this dress?"

Fabiana smiled. "Oh no, it's not that. We can do something with it. The girl has a wedding in a week."

"How was your day with Lorenzo?"

Fabiana's smile wasn't as bright as it was before. Still she was lovelier when she let her inner charm come forth. "We went horseback riding, had sex, went to lunch at this little pizza spot in Napoli, had sex again at an apartment he has there, went for gelato and came here for more sex."

"Sounds like fun."

Fabiana shrugged. Catalina walked out of the bathroom with the woman from earlier following closely. Both Fabiana and Mira looked at the dress that was definitely a size too big and sloppily cut. The short puffy sleeves and too wide waistline were too low for her tiny frame. The front of the dress was raised too high and the train fell awkwardly behind. The entire dress had woven white beading on top of heavy satin material that would make re-cutting the fabric a nightmare. All in all Mira got a headache from one look at the monstrosity.

Mira sucked in her breath and then cleared her throat, "Donatella Versace sent this over for you?" she asked in complete disbelief.

The lady next to Catalina flashed Mira an irritated smile, "It was from her private line, not her brother's. She's starting to do more designing for him." Catalina nodded.

"Her private line of shit," Fabiana said aghast at the way the dress looked.

Catalina burst into tears again. "Oh sweetie, I'm so sorry. I run my mouth sometimes. Forgive me."

Mira walked over to her. "We can make this into the dress

of your dreams please don't cry."

The woman started speaking to Catalina in Italian to soothe her, and Mira wondered who she was. Catalina saw the curious look on her face and explained.

"Forgive me. Fabiana and Mira this is *Signora Clara* my *Masciata*."

Mira glanced to her friend for translation.

"She's her matchmaker."

"Matchmaker?" Mira looked at the woman and then Catalina. The young girl was in an arranged marriage? Really? Mira extended her hand. "Nice to meet you, Clara."

"She's also my wedding planner. You know the one that makes sure the wedding follows our traditions."

Fabiana extended her hand and greeted Clara as well. "Nice to meet you."

Mira addressed Fabiana. "Can you go get my kit that you packed away with your things? It's obvious that we'll need to go to our office tomorrow and get some fabric and other things I need."

Fabiana nodded and walked out. Catalina let go a sigh of relief, "Thank you so much, Mira. I really appreciate this."

"It's no trouble. I'm excited for you. Tell me about your guy." Mira smiled.

"Franco?"

"Is that his name?" Mira accepted her hand and led her to the bed in the room where they both sat. Clara stood off, observing them silently.

"Yes his name is Franco Minetti," Catalina beamed.

"Where did you meet him?"

"The first time I met him was at my christening, Giovanni said he put me in the crib with Franco and even though we were babies we held hands," she grinned. Mira tried to keep the smile to her face. Catalina placed both hands in her lap and continued with her tale. "Then we met again my graduating year in school at my cousin Aurora's wedding. It was a year ago. Giovanni said it was okay if I wrote him, so we wrote quite often until I graduated. That's when Giovanni let Franco come here for a week. We swam, rode horses, and did things."

"What kind of things?" Mira asked.

"You know, date and things. All of it supervised by Domi of course," she blushed and looked away.

Mira smiled. "Okay so you fell in love with him?"

"*Si. Amore.* Giovanni sent me to Palermo, and I got to spend a week with his family. Domi came too. He was right by my side. I hate Palermo. Have you been?"

"No sweetie I haven't." Mira glanced over to Clara who continued to watch over them with a critical squint.

"Catalina are you saying this marriage is arranged?"

Catalina frowned at the term.

"I mean was it setup by Giovanni and Franco's family?"

"Of course. That's what I'm saying. *Signora* Clara knew Mama. She has governed our lives always. She is here to make sure we follow the traditions," Catalina smiled.

"This is something you want?"

"Giovanni said—"

"I'm not talking about your brother. I'm talking about you, sweetie. You are the one getting married. Is this something you want? Marriage is serious and something you should do with a person you love. You do know that don't you?" Mira asked, taking her hand and giving it a squeeze.

Catalina looked down at Mira's hand and then to her eyes. "Why did you ask me that? Of course I know this. Of course I want my marriage! Don't you dare tell Giovanni I don't!" Catalina snatched her hand away and rose.

"I didn't mean to insult you."

"You think I'm young and stupid and can't handle getting married?"

"No, of course not."

"I'm the *donna* of this house. Not you! I take good care of Giovanni and Lorenzo, and I will be a good wife to Franco. I've done nothing wrong!"

"Sweetie calm down. I just asked you what you want. If Franco is who you love, then I'm happy for you."

Catalina folded her arms and glared. "Franco is what I want, it is what God wants. Don't you dare say anything different."

Fabiana walked in with Mira's sewing kit. "Found it!" she said smiling. Looking at the women she frowned, "Something wrong?"

****

"I took the liberty of ordering. Not big on wine like you and these Italians."

Lorenzo locked eyes with the large Nigerian seated at the table. The man had skin as dark as coal and a shaved head and face. He wore a stark white shirt that appeared brighter against his skin. Lorenzo found him dining alone in a hotel suite crowded with heavily armed men. He felt no fear. He'd shoot every motherfucker in sight if he had to and walk away from this meeting. It was his false bravado that time and time again proved to be his weakness.

"Why did you ask to meet?" Lorenzo asked.

"We haven't been properly introduced. Name is Enu."

Lorenzo glared as the African wiped his mouth and extended his large palm in greeting. After a moment Enu slumped back in his chair. "I will admit this is awkward. I have a lot of respect for your family. Actually the *Cammora* in general. Unlike the *mafioso* you men understand there can be alliances outside of Sicilian blood ties. You're much more progressive."

"We aren't that tolerant." Lorenzo scoffed.

"Giuseppe was. In fact he was quite accepting of new ways. Of change." A beautiful black woman in a traditional wrap of green and gold brought a fresh drink for the Nigerian. She blinked her large brown eyes up at Lorenzo and then shied away. Lorenzo refused to touch his glass of wine. "Giuseppe's missing, and this presents a problem."

"Not for me," Lorenzo sneered.

Enu chuckled, his dark eyes gleamed like those of a cobra with prey in sight. "I hear your boss is expanding the family business."

"That's none of your concern."

"You sure about that? Not only does Giovanni Battaglia own the coast of the Amalfi but now he strives to extend his reach along northern Italy?" Enu raised his glass in a mock toast. "He does have balls."

Lorenzo glanced at his watch. On the verge of dismissing the bastard he summoned restraint.

"He does understand that his interests have now become my own?"

"Fuck no."

"Then you should help him with this understanding. Considering Giuseppe's disappearance has many pointing a finger your way. In a time of war we can be quite useful."

"The Nigerian Mafia? An alliance because that runt Giuseppe missed dinner?" Lorenzo spat out a burst of laughter. The humor drained from Enu's face and his features hardened like stone.

"Are you fucking kidding me, Eboo?"

"The name is Enu and I never kid. Yes, I propose an alliance because Giuseppe Calderone didn't just miss dinner. He's dead. You killed him."

Lorenzo's jaw went tight. He narrowed his eyes on the man before him.

"Giuseppe ran his mouth. The stupid fuck never knew when to shut up. He talked of you often. How you were his bitch." Enu chuckled. "Didn't like you much."

"Feeling was mutual."

"He also had a nasty habit of taping men." Enu's gaze flickered up and latched on to Lorenzo. "I hear he has tapes, very interesting tapes, of conversations he's had with you."

Lorenzo felt his hand tighten to a fist, but sat rigidly still. Was he bluffing? Did Giuseppe tape him the fateful night he spoke words that brought about his beloved uncle's death. No. If Giuseppe had a tape of their conversation he would have leveraged it by now. It had to be a bluff. If this African knew of his part in Tomosino's hit he would have played that card by now. At this point the bastard was simply feeling him out. "Giuseppe's not my problem. But you have one. The same tall tales he told of me and my family he spread about you and yours. Said the Nigerians sucked his dick to pass their women and drugs through the triangle. He said you *moolignons* were under his command. And now Don Calderone knows of your deals. The war isn't with the Battaglias. It'll be at your door."

The Nigerian broke the whiskey glass in his hand. He didn't flinch at the glass slicing his palm or the blood splatter on the linen of the table. His dark irises went darker than coal. He snarled when he spoke. "You made a big mistake dismissing my offer of friendship."

Lorenzo drank from the wine and set the glass back on the table. "Enjoy the *raglione*." He said rising and walked out. He didn't bother to look back. He needed to get home. Things were falling apart, and Giovanni would be on to him soon.

****

Catalina stood with her arms out as Mira measured and stuck pins in the dress before going back to her pad to write down her measurements for cutting the fabric. Clara paced nervously in front of the women, not sure what to make of all the pins and tape she saw covering the dress. Wringing her hands she finally spoke. "No cleavage must show and the hem must touch the floor."

Mira looked over at her and smiled. "I'll take care of her."

Catalina stuck out her bottom lip. "I want some cleavage to show. It's my dress!"

"Hush you silly girl!" Clara clapped her hands together to silence Catalina.

Fabiana frowned at the older woman. She and Mira exchanged a look. Fabiana rubbed her hands together, and tossed her long hair before approaching. "Clara, how many weddings have you been the *masciata* over?" Fabiana asked. She draped her arm around the woman's shoulder.

"I've placed Italian brides with their chosen mates for over 50 years."

"Fifty years huh? Impressive. And in fifty years how many dresses have you made for these brides?"

"I beg your pardon?" Clara snipped disgusted. "I may not be a dressmaker like *Signora* Mira but I know what's proper for Catalina, and what's expected of her from Don Battaglia." She announced.

"Of course you do. I wouldn't dare suggest you didn't." Fabiana guided the old woman's steps toward the door.

"*Signora* Mira, as you called her, is more than a dressmaker. Just as you find yourself qualified to orchestrate this wedding from your fifty years of experience, Mira finds herself qualified to dress a bride from her many years of experience. Experience that I might add produced a multimillion dollar company on dress making alone. Now why don't we let her get to it?" Before Clara could counter the argument Fabiana opened the door and pushed her out. "We'll let you know when we're done!" she said smiling nicely and closing the door.

Catalina laughed. "Thank you! She is such a pain in the ass!"

Fabiana turned with her hands to her hips. "Tell me about it. Don't you have any aunts or cousins that could help you with your wedding?"

"Yes, but they don't really like me and Giovanni." she said softly.

Mira glanced up and then made eye contact with Fabiana. She knew of the relationship Catalina's parents shared. Tradition with the Sicilians must have made them outcasts within their own family. "It's okay sweetie, because you got us." Mira winked.

Catalina nodded, eagerly. "*Grazie* Mira. I'm sorry for being a brat. It was weird seeing Giovanni with someone."

Fabiana went back to the bed, sitting down. "Giovanni and Lorenzo never bring women home?" she asked.

Catalina shook her head. "Lorenzo had a sweetheart once, and everyone thought they would get married, but she broke up with him. She married someone from another family. This was before Papa died, but I remember it of course. Lorenzo was very upset."

Mira lifted her eyes while working to see Fabiana's face. She noted how tense her friend was and wondered again what had her on edge. "You okay?"

Fabiana nodded "I'm fine."

Mira rose. "That's it. Let's get you out of this, tomorrow we will go to my store and get the things I need to redo the dress."

"I feel like a porcupine." Catalina laughed. "Can you get rid of the puffy sleeves too?"

Mira smiled. "That's the first thing I plan to do."

Fabiana shook her head. "There is no way in hell Donatella Versace designed that dress. I think *Signora* Clara is full of shit."

"Fabiana!" Mira warned.

Catalina looked over to her, "Why do you say that?"

Mira began to work down her zipper. "Ignore Fabiana, she doesn't know anything." She reassured her. "Now go take this off."

Catalina agreed. *"Grazie,"* she said rushing to the bathroom.

Mira turned on Fabiana as soon as the door closed. "Would you cut the wise ass remarks?"

Fabiana shrugged. "Please. You know that dress didn't come out of the house of Versace. That woman is just controlling that child. She probably took one look at the dress Donatella sent over and the rest of her hair turned white. She replaced it with that tacky mess."

It was what Mira felt as well. She could see where the inside label had been cut out. "I checked the inseam and material. It's a store bought dress alright, which explains why it doesn't fit. I think you're right. Clara got rid of Donatella's dress and fitted her with that one."

"Why the hell would Giovanni and Lorenzo allow the manipulating shrew near that girl?" Fabiana asked.

Mira shook her head, "She isn't the only one controlling her."

"What does that mean?"

"You heard her. She's been given over to a matchmaker. Do they still arrange marriages in Italy? It's almost 1990. They can't be serious."

"I think with certain families it's a tradition. It's none of our business. Catalina seems very excited about it. To suggest it's barbaric or anything other than tradition is an insult to them. You remember that." Fabiana cautioned.

"Catalina doesn't want to disappoint her brother. You should have seen her reaction when I questioned her, and she couldn't say she loved this Franco person, which to me...."

Catalina came out of the bathroom with the dress. "Okay here you go," she said smiling, bringing it over. Mira accepted the dress.

"Thanks sweetie, I will start on this first thing tomorrow.

****

Lorenzo handled the narrow, curving roadway in his car

like a daredevil. The coastal villages zipped by as the speedometer climbed to the point of dipping into the red zone. Still he drove faster.

He also had a nasty habit of taping men. I hear he has tapes, very interesting tapes, of conversations he's had with you.

Anger gripped him so tight he could barely suck down a breath. It was a lie. There was no tape. He remembered sitting in the bar drinking, bemoaning his existence and Giuseppe feeding his ego. When did the slug have a chance to tape him? Which conversation did he record? The one where he joked that Don Tomosino's death was the only way he'd have his birthright? "No dammit! No!" he hit the steering wheel. There was no tape. The fucker was lying.

What he'd done because of his pride and jealousy of his cousin could destroy everything they've built. He could feel time and plausible excuses slipping away from him. His life was spiraling out of control, and he was powerless to prevent it. Making a sharp turn the car engine revved then sputtered. Lorenzo frowned, checking the gauges. He rarely drove the car and had it tuned regularly.

Soon he arrived at the Battaglia gates, avoiding a roadside stall in his favorite sports car. The men opened the gates and granted him entrance. No one came or went without a face to face. He drove up the drive and parked behind an American made motorcycle. He wondered which of the boys had bought the toy. Outside of the car with the door slamming shut behind him, he approached it.

"Nice, isn't it?"

He glanced to his left. Carlo flicked his hand rolled cigarillo and smirked. "Been waiting."

"Need you to have someone come pick up my car to have it

tuned. The engine sounds funny." He was in no mood for questioning from his friend or anyone. He just needed to get somewhere and cool off to think of his next move.

"What the fuck I look like, your errand boy?" Carlo asked, catching the keys tossed to him mid-air.

Lorenzo didn't break his stride. He entered the house and beat a hard path to the lower rooms. He heard the soft sounds of laughter. He slowed and looked to the left. It was a woman's laugh.

Smoothing out his hair he sucked in a deep breath and walked into a sunroom that led out to the open terrace. Seated around a table was Mira, Catalina, and Fabiana eating and drinking wine. Fabiana's eyes lifted and locked on him. She rose from her seat and came to him immediately. "I was wondering when you'd come back." Lorenzo pulled her into his arms, grateful to feel her. She kissed him sweetly on the lips then offered him more. Amazing how calm he felt after one kiss from her. Fabiana withdrew. She turned and grinned at the women while holding his hand. "Mira and Giovanni brought back some wine from the vineyard. Do you want some? Have you eaten?"

Lorenzo looked at the ladies staring at him and then back at Fabiana, "Where's my cousin?"

"*Villa Rosso* probably." Catalina said.

The night dragged on without him. Laughter, wine, and the excited chatter of the pending nuptials from Catalina filled the evening. Several times she caught Lorenzo checking his watch. She wondered about this place called '*Villa Rosso*' and why Lorenzo didn't go there to summon Giovanni. He never did. Eventually he and Fabiana retired for the evening, and she was left alone with Catalina.

"Where is this *Villa Rosso* place?" Mira asked.

Catalina lowered her wine glass, her nose wrinkling. "Outside. It's the cottage Papa built at the end of the garden trails. Giovanni lives there mostly. Sometimes for days." Catalina gave an eye-roll. "I try to keep it nice, for him and the men, but he won't allow me in there without his permission, and they make it messy always. The staff is never allowed there. It smells of whiskey and his stinky cigars." She shrugged her shoulders. "He's like Papa, likes to be there alone, no matter the state. Mama had a kitchen and bedroom made up in there so he's fine."

"Days? You said he lives there? Not here?"

"When he wants." Catalina smiled. "Don't worry, he'll come back. He always does."

She felt a presence behind her, the deep blush to Catalina's cheeks made Mira turn to see who had entered. The one Giovanni called Dominic stood in the doorway. He wore a look that Mira recognized, a mixture of love, lust, and shame. She saw that look in Giovanni's eyes after he ravished her in the bed and caused the bite to her shoulder. Mira's gaze swiveled between Dominic and Catalina, and her brows lowered with concern. Dominic was staring at the young bride to be.

"Good night, Mira. I have to talk to Domi."

Catalina was out of her chair sashaying toward the door. Her dark curly hair swayed across her shoulders. Then she was gone.

"Stop, Mira. Mind your own business. The man is too old for Catalina." She reasoned, dismissing what she thought passed between the two. She sighed. What was she doing there? It felt ridiculous to be held up in this massive estate to only spend evenings in this man's bed. She understood he had work to do, but so did she. Maybe she'd talk to Fabiana about cutting this visit short. It didn't mean that their affair had to end. She just needed her life back. Working on Catalina's dress had sparked the urge to do more. She rose and walked out. As she approached the stairs she considered what Catalina said. The man wouldn't disappear on her if it wasn't serious. What if he needed someone to talk to? Uncanny as it was, she felt such a tie to him now. She couldn't dismiss it.

Mira turned left instead of right, lost in her thoughts. Passing through two open rooms she stopped and looked around confused. The stairs had to be in the front of the house, so she tried to double back.

She heard a woman's sigh. Mira stopped. It could have been the wind. The longer hallways carried drafts from all the open windows to the front of the villa. She listened and heard nothing. Glancing back over her shoulder the sound drifted to her ears again. A sweet mixture of soft sighs and moans that sounded feminine in nature. She stood alone in the hall. Curiosity seized her sensibility, and she began to trace her steps back the way she came. She stopped at a door drawn partially shut. She heard a crash and a giggle. It was Catalina. Silent and careful she positioned her left eye to the crack in the door and peered in.

Dominic advanced on Catalina who stepped back with a sly teasing smile. Mira pressed closer to the door to see, and it eased open a sliver. Dominic drew Catalina to him in a gentle manner with his hand to her hip. It seemed innocent enough if it weren't for the glazed look of awe and desire on Catalina's face. Mira held her breath. What was unfolding? Dominic said something. He had a deep timber to his voice that reminded

her of a rhythm and blues singer—husky and sultry. Mira
wished she knew the translation. Soon she needed none.
Catalina threw her arms around Dominic's neck and giggled.
He spun her in his arms, and she hugged his neck tightly. What
seemed like simple flirty play soon changed to an embrace of
lovers. In one deft move Catalina was pressed up against the
wall bookshelf. The couple kissed and clawed at each other's
clothing. The front of Catalina's dress was yanked down and
Dominic's face was buried in her cleavage. Catalina responded
by working on his zipper. Soon Dominic's pants were riding at
his hips, belt undone. Catalina's right leg draped over the crook
of his arm opening her for his thrusting cock. Catalina gasped
clenching his shoulders, her head rolling back in pleasure. The
bookshelf shook, a few books dropped to the floor. Dominic
fucked her with slow measured thrusts. Mira covered her
mouth. Dominic stopped his thrusts and lowered, sucking her
nipple then going down between Catalina's thighs. She
dropped her leg over his shoulder and gripped the top of his
curly hair to grind her sex against his plundering mouth.

Mira couldn't tear away from the scene.

Catalina moaned in ecstasy. Her eyes opened and her head
turned. She locked eyes on Mira who had inadvertently pushed
the door ajar a bit to reveal the scene. Embarrassed Mira fled
for the stairs.

Giovanni rose from his chair. He walked over to the bar
and picked up a bottle. No matter how he digested the news of
his cousin's involvement with Giuseppe Calderone he couldn't
accept it. They'd taken an oath, and it meant more than words
and blood, it was who they were. They believed in family and
loyalty above all else. Lorenzo would not jeopardize it all to be

some drug pusher. There had to be another reason for his lapse in judgment. But what?

He turned up the bottle and took a long swallow until his throat felt torched and his chest aflame. He wiped the scotch from his lips. His eyes fell upon his gun. He remembered when he first used it. How he felt. What he'd done. Could he use it again? On the man he called brother?

February 16, 1983
Napoli, Italy

"Count minchione!" Lorenzo shoved the nozzle of the gun so deep into the man's mouth he gagged. Others stood around watching, waiting. "Figlio di puttana!"

Two Russians lie dead in the freezer, both with their throats cut and bullets to their backs. Giovanni still had blood on his hands, pants, and shoes. His chest bulked. He wanted a confession. He needed a confession. And though he should be nowhere near this bloodbath, he intended to see it through. Lorenzo knew this. Felt his need for revenge that ate away at his soul like a cancer. His cousin had found the bastards and tied them down in the bakery. He summoned him without the men. Fed the monster in him that made him Don Tomosino's son.

Lorenzo glanced back to him. "He's the one, Giovanni, the one who pulled the trigger. He's the one who took Papa from us."

"He's mine!" Giovanni said.

"No." Flavio entered the freezer with Dominic and Carlo behind him. Giovanni was in such a murderous daze he didn't hear the old man speak. He gripped the gun tighter. "Don't do it, Gio."

Lorenzo removed the gun from the man's mouth. He glanced back at the men then to Giovanni. All of this unfolded as the Russian dropped his head, gagging and gasping for breath.

"Gio?" Flavio said, he walked over, stood before him. "Listen to me. Your word is law. You do not have to do this. Let the boys finish him off. Bring you his head, his hands, and his feet. But you must remain clean."

"He deserves vengeance!" Lorenzo shouted.

"We all do." Carlo spoke out of turn.

Giovanni breathed through his nose. He tracked the Russian with his eyes as the coward backed away on his knees.

"And he shall have it! That is why you are number two! It is your job to do this for your Don! Do you hear me!" Flavio snapped. He eased the gun from Giovanni's hand. "Lead these men, Gio, don't become one of them to do it."

Giovanni remembered the gunshots. How his father fell and blood pooled like a river of red draining from his body and running streams down the streets. He remembered the suffering of his poor mother, how confused and desperate she and his sister had become. Together they wept at his father's bedside. Eventually his mama had to be medicated in order to be taken out of the room. He remembered Catalina crawling into bed with him shivering, begging him to make Papa well again. And he remembered the day they lowered his father into the ground. All of it boiled up into a storm that strangled his heart. He shoved Flavio from in front of him. He grabbed the two ice picks on the steel freezer and charged the man. The Russian didn't scream, he didn't beg for mercy. In fact Giovanni could have sworn as he charged him the man knew his fate and smiled. Without delay he shoved both ice picks into his eyes and pinned the murderer to the ground. Men converged on him and he managed to throw *them off in time to get his gun, the one given to him by his grandfather. The one called 'Danny-boy'. He unloaded the clip into the dead man.*

Silence fell over those in the freezer. Giovanni stumbled back, rising from the darkness that had engulfed him. He saw the carnage, the one he'd committed and suppressed the gag in his throat. He'd killed men. He'd done it with his own hands. He'd become what his mother always feared. When he glanced up he could see the dark approval gleaming in Lorenzo's eyes. He could see the satisfaction in Carlo's smile. And he could see the profound disappointment in Flavio's scowl. Unable to stomach it he turned and walked out.

Giovanni sucked down a deep breath. Lorenzo wouldn't betray him. There had to be an explanation for all of this. His cousin was loyal. They all were. They had to be. He stared at Danny-boy. Otherwise he'd have the final word.

Chapter Eleven

MIRA SLIPPED ON HER GOWN. She looked at her frizzy hair and felt tired from the sight of it. She showered and tried hard to forget the scene she witnessed. Catalina and Dominic? What had she seen? Mira flipped off the light switch and walked back into the room. Catalina stormed into the room and paced by the bed. Her face was streaked with tears.

"Please! Please don't tell him. Please! He'll kill Domi. Please!"

Stunned, Mira froze.

"I can explain. I can..." Catalina gripped her hair on both sides, pulling until her eyes stretched. "It's not Domi's fault. He didn't want it. He never did, but I wouldn't stop. I've loved him since I was two. I've always loved him. He's a brother to Giovanni and Lorenzo. He was raised by them. They will see this as incest, but it isn't. We aren't blood related. He's adopted. It's not... and... oh my God. Oh my God, Gio will find out!"

"Calm down." Mira hurried to her. She drew her into an embrace. Catalina clung to her, crying into her shoulder. "I didn't tell Domi you saw us. He is guilty enough. He'd be foolish and confess to my brother. They'd kill him. Please, Mira."

"Okay. I won't say a word. Listen to me. It's okay." She pulled her face from her shoulder and cupped it in her hands. "It will be okay."

Catalina nodded. Mira guided her to the bed and let her sit. "Are you in love with him?"

"Yes. And he loves me."

"Then why not go to your brother and tell him?"

"I couldn't! I can't! I'm to be married."

"Marry Dominic?"

Catalina frowned. "It doesn't work that way. Giovanni is following my father's orders. He always does what is expected and so do I. That's how it works. He's in danger constantly, Mira. The families, well they don't respect him. He has to do things to keep his respect or it's the end of us all. And if the families found out about me and Domi, and I backed out on my wedding then Giovanni will be shamed. The entire family would be. Don't you understand? We can't be together. Ever."

"When did this start? When did you two begin this affair?"

Catalina looked away. Mira rubbed her brow. She didn't know Giovanni long, but she knew one thing, loyalty was a big thing with him. If she kept a secret like this there could be consequences. She had to know more.

"When he took me to Palermo for Aurora's wedding. He was my chaperone when I went to meet Franco and his family. I was so upset after the first meeting. Franco is, well he isn't pleasant on the eyes. Not like my Domi. He's short, crude, he smells of dirt and cigarettes. He has a gap between his front teeth!" Catalina tapped her front tooth to emphasize the point.

"Domi saw I was disappointed. He tried to cheer me up. I was only seventeen. That night he took me to dinner and though we have family in Palermo we aren't..." She cast her shy gaze to Mira. "We aren't welcome to stay. Only when Giovanni is there do they show respect. So Domi and I stayed in a hotel. And we talked, drank wine, played cards... it happened."

"You have to stop the affair with him! If one of Giovanni's men had seen you. Do you know how risky that is?"

Catalina didn't look her way this time. She stared straight ahead.

"You have to end it. For good."

"Will you keep my secret?"

Mira struggled with her answer. It wasn't her business. She didn't want to be involved. But she had seen it, and she had to decide what she'd do with that knowledge. "Yes."

Catalina threw her arms around her neck. "Bless you! Thank you!" She released her. "You want to see my brother, don't you? I'll help you go to him."

"No. He's working, I won't bother him."

"No he isn't. I spoke to Domi. He's alone. And if he's alone, he's miserable. Something is wrong. Something is going on with the other families. Go to him."

Mira felt it too. Catalina rose. She went over and found her satin robe. "Wear this. You have to be covered when you go out there. When you see his men tell them that Giovanni sent for you. Stand your ground with his men. Demand respect and look them in the eye when you speak. *Prego.*" She helped her into her robe. "They'll let you in."

"Maybe I should give him space tonight. If he wanted to see me, he'd have sent for me."

Catalina shook her head fiercely. "He's never brought any

woman home. I've seen the way he looks at you. You are changing him. He seems... happy. And trust me a happy Giovanni is what we all need. So go to him. *Prego*. And we will forget this whole matter with Domi, right? It's over. That was us saying goodbye. We're done." Catalina grinned nodding through her lie. Mira knew she was being manipulated, but she relented.

"Where is this villa again? How do I get there?"

"Let me show you a different way, to avoid Renaldo and Carmine. They are the worst. The others you can manage," Catalina said. Mira quickly tied down her robe. It was about the length of her dress she wore today, barely touching her knees. She and Catalina crept out into the hall and down to the lower floor unseen. "There, take that path and it will bring you to his door." Catalina kissed her on both cheeks. "*Grazie*, for listening and keeping my secret. We're friends now. Best of friends. *Si*?"

"Catalina, I...."

"*Grazie!*" she waved and hurried off. Mira did as instructed and walked a path through a manmade garden that circled the pool. Soon she saw the cottage and realized the name given to it was due to the rust colored paint that covered its stone walls. Wild vines and ivy grew along the windowsills, wild red flowers blooming about. It looked unkempt compared to the rest of the estate. Still it had such an overwhelming masculine quality to it. There were three men smoking outside of it that didn't seem happy to see her.

One of the guys glanced to the other confused by her arrival, but the other just checked her out. Finally another English speaking man spoke. "*Signora?* Please return to your room."

"Can you tell him I'm here? Please?" she asked.

Another man leaning against the wall exhaled a stream of smoke. He was taller than the ones glaring at her, but had an intense gaze that made her feel vulnerable in the night. Mira crossed her arms against the hard stare.

"And who are you?"

"*Mi chiamo Carlo.* Back off boys. I'll tell the boss you're here," he winked. She nodded her thanks and waited. Carlo did as promised. He was in the cottage for under five minutes before he opened the door for her to enter. The darkness closed in on her. She wished she could find a light switch. The front door to the cottage closed behind her. After a few minutes her vision adjusted to the shadowy atmosphere. She bumped furniture, walked towards a door to the back of the place and wondered if she should instead climb the stairs. The knob felt cool to the touch. She turned it slowly. Again more darkness. Was he in there?

"*Che vuoi da me?*" A deep man's voice said to her left. Mira wasn't sure but she believed that he asked what she wanted from him. A bright orange glow of a half smoked cigar was all she could see, until the orange red flames dimmed.

"I've been waiting, looking for you. Why are you sitting in the dark?" she asked. The moonlight defined his frame, but his face was covered in shadows.

"Why would you walk out here in the middle of the night dressed like that?" He sat upright. Part of his face became clear in the shadows. His hard tone and stare stopped her heart.

"There's nothing wrong with what I have on." She looked down at herself. "This robe stops no lower than the dress I wore today."

"You shouldn't be parading in front of these men in underwear! Show some got damn respect," he yelled.

Mira stunned, turned and headed for the door. Reaching for the knob her anger stopped her. She glared back over at him, seeing him. He drank from a bottle instead of a glass. He made no attempt to stop her or explain himself further.

"What the hell is wrong with you? Why are you acting like a mean jackass? How do you say asshole in Italian?"

He chuckled. *"Briccone!"*

"Yes! That's what you are. A mean *briccone*! There's no reason to attack me the way you did. I came out here out of concern for you, and you all but called me a whore!"

Giovanni rose in the dark, the bottle clutched by the neck in his left hand. The other balled into a fist. He stalked toward her. She stood her ground, with folded arms, though her hands trembled with nervous energy. He stopped with barely a foot of space between them. He reeked of tobacco and the strongest stench of whiskey she'd ever smelled. "Leave," he said. "I won't stop you. Go back to your pampered life. I won't beg you to stay." His voice held a shaky uncertainty that she couldn't help but recognize as weakness. He turned up the bottle drinking more, his gaze never shifting from her.

Mira ran her hand back over the wall to her right, never breaking his stare. Her fingers brushed the switch and flipped it up. The state of him was just the beginning. His eyes were glassy and bloodshot red. Still he managed to glare down at her. She got a good look of the destruction he had to have done to the room. His chair was all that remained upright. Glass and broken furniture was everywhere. A desk that looked to weigh over 200 pounds was flipped over on its side and the walls had stains from bottles of liquor from the bar being smashed against it.

He walked away. She stepped over what she assumed used

to be an office chair and almost lost her balance. Shaking her head she walked over to the side of him studying his face. Reaching she touched his hair and he snatched away. "I won't ask what this is about. It's none of my business."

Giovanni took another long swallow from the bottle. Mira reached for it and gently removed it from his hand. "Please stop drinking."

He glanced down at her.

"Have you decided? Who I am? What I am? Have you decided on whether we can be friends or are we just fucking?"

"You know we're more than that." Mira said.

"So you've decided to stay?" His eyes stretched.

She opened her mouth to object, but something in his tone and the look he gave her made her waver. He was on the edge in the moment and rejection was something he wouldn't tolerate. Men were such fragile babies when it came to pride and ego. "Is there a... room here? Some place other than this where we can be alone? Talk?"

"Upstairs," he sighed, rubbing the fatigue from his eyes.

She stepped to his side and eased her arm around his waist. "Show me."

Giovanni dropped his arm around her shoulders and together they walked over the destruction to what was once his office.

Giovanni allowed her to hold him steady so they could climb the stairs together. Making it to the landing, he took the lead and her hand to go towards the only two bedrooms in the cottage. One was a disaster, and men would often visit and crash there. But he kept the other tidy and neat. He didn't realize how tired and drunk he was until he lowered to the bed.

He could barely reach for her before his brain became a dull fog and sleep fell on him like an anvil.

Mira frowned. Was he snoring? *He'd passed out on her!* She looked around the room and realized that this was it. This was his life and she could run now or be caught up in this tangled affair. Releasing a burdened sigh she picked up his long heavy legs and brought them over to the mattress making him lay horizontal. Giovanni moaned saying something in Italian. Mira swore that she'd take damn lessons. She was going to learn this language and soon. Part of her could have sworn he called her out of her name. But she couldn't be sure. Maybe Catalina could teach her the curse words so she could be a step ahead of him.

She removed his shoes, pants, and struggled with unbuttoning and pulling his long arms out of his shirt. Exhausted she decided to leave him in his t-shirt, underwear and socks.

Hot from the stuffiness of the room she reached up to the cord hanging from the ceiling fan, yanking it. A soft breeze cut through the air as the long blades whipped around in lazy circular moves. Taking off her robe she put it over the chair in the corner of the room before stepping out of her slippers. Mira then went to the window in the room and threw it open to let fresh air inside. She looked down and saw the same three men milling around and shook her head. It was this life that had him drinking himself into a stupor, and made his sister terrified of him enough to keep an affair behind his back. Her head turned to look back at her lover. He had rolled over to his side. Hair that was normally combed back was now covering his brow. He looked like a sleeping giant.

Her heart ached for whatever stole the joy from him that they'd experienced earlier in the day at the vineyard. Stepping away from the open window, she went back to the bed and worked the sheets from under him, moving in close and lifting his arm to allow her further access as she kissed his nose sweetly.

Immediately feeling her next to him his heavy bloodshot eyes opened slightly and he looked at her, half smiling. Grabbing her butt cheek and squeezing he pulled her closer, kissing her. She tasted the whiskey and cigar on his breath and turned her face away. "Sleep it off and we can talk in the morning."

He began to kiss along the side of her neck pushing her nightie up and slipping his rough hand in her panties. His voice was muffled but she was sure he spoke. Feeling him try to roll her over as his hand moved to the front of her panties massaging her between her legs, she shook her head and struggled underneath him. "Sleep it off." She refused him.

He let her go and rolled back over to his back with an angry grunt. His hand shot up to his forehead. Mira slid her arm across his chest, snuggling him.

Giovanni fully woke. He lifted his hand from his face and peered down at the top of her head. He raised his other hand and smoothed over her thick hair smiling to himself that she was at his side even now. She was his *donna*, and didn't even know it. He desired her, needed to be inside of her, but after the way he treated her he decided not to push it further. Instead he let go of his anger and drifted off into a fitful sleep.

Later that night

Giovanni felt his stomach clench. He opened his eyes in time to suppress the urge to gag. Mira had rolled over to her side of the bed and was resting peacefully. He sat up, feverish with his own sweat. A wave of nausea overtook him, and he knew he had to get to the bathroom. He rushed in time to spill his guts in the toilet. He'd drunk so much with little other than cheese and sliced fruit on his stomach. He was surprised he hadn't suffered from alcohol poisoning.

Flushing, he went to the sink grabbing the spare toothbrush and reaching for the toothpaste. As he began to brush his teeth, he felt his stomach settle, and control over his body was restored. He'd done damage like this before, and his body knew how to self-medicate.

"You okay?" a sleepy voice whispered behind him.

Looking up to the mirror, he saw her standing behind him, her hair tussled around her head, rubbing her eyes. She was a vision of beauty as always. Giovanni turned and stared down at her with a sly smile. "What are you doing up? Go back to bed, *Bella.*"

Mira blinked at him and said nothing. Giovanni saw the questions in her eyes, causing him deep pangs of guilt for yelling at her earlier. Avoiding the tension between them he turned back to the sink to finish brushing and rinsing out his mouth. Grabbing a hand towel from above the toilet he wiped at his face, "I'm sorry for earlier," he said softly.

"I am too."

Surprised he looked at her. "Why are you sorry?"

"I'm sorry that I couldn't comfort you."

"That's not true," he said, tossing the hand towel to the sink.

"It is true. If it weren't, I wouldn't have had to come out here to find you," she said before turning to leave.

Reclining back on the sink, he rubbed the tension from his jaw. Catching the remnants of blood on his hand he looked back at the door she disappeared from. At some time during his rage he cut his hand in the palm. He didn't want to expose her to his world, but his world was inescapable. Giovanni tried to scrub his hands free of the blood and wash away the violence of the night. He was good at being in control, but he failed at maintaining control when his heart was struck. He didn't know how to be vulnerable to anyone, especially her. "Fuck." Drying his hands off he walked back down the hall to the bedroom and found her in bed with the covers pulled up over her. Leaning in the doorframe, he watched her.

"Are you asleep?"

"No," she answered.

"Can I join you?" he asked.

Mira pulled back the covers and extended her hand to him. He walked over to the bed. Standing at the foot of it, he removed his t-shirt and boxers. He eased in with her, and this time she didn't resist his touching her. "Should we talk?" he asked.

"I don't want to argue with you, so I'd rather go to sleep."

He ran his hand over her back to her bottom and kissed the top of her brow. "Then maybe you can let me hold you," he said pressing into her and kissing her shoulder. Taking his hand he rubbed her hip pushing up her thin gown. Sliding his hand around and upward he massaged one of her breasts, grinding his stiffening manhood into the back of her.

He felt her go stiff, and knew if he pushed for more, she'd resist. So he willed his erection down and held her. Sleep was a welcome event for them both.

"*Bella?*"

Morning came. His lips brushed hers, and her lids parted to a room full of light. She squinted against the brightness. The bed felt so warm and soft she literally felt as if she were floating. Her vision cleared and his face normalized. Mira raised her arms and wrapped them around his neck. "Mmm," she said, sparing him her morning breath. He however had brushed his teeth, again, and she could smell his fresh clean male scent. When had he showered? How long had she slept?

"It's after ten," he said. "An inspector is here to see you."

"Me? Why?"

"I went back to the villa and got your things to wear, so you can dress." He rose from the bed. Clutching the sheet to her breast she looked at him confused. "Why is an inspector here to see me?"

"I think it has something to do with your building." He buttoned his shirt. "Don't worry. Fabiana has met with him." Giovanni leaned over, sitting on the edge of the bed and smiled, his hair disheveled and in his eyes. "Thank you for last night, for coming here. Are we okay?"

She nodded they were. Trying to smooth her hair, embarrassed by her state, she escaped the bed, bringing the sheet with her. He'd picked out a plum colored wrap dress and matching bra and panty set. She glanced over at him. He had to rummage through her things to find it.

"I like you in this. Will you wear it?"

Mira nodded she would. Picking up her clothes she held

her tongue. She wasn't ready for the day, let alone for how overwhelming his needs had become. All of it could wait. She felt anxious over having a visitor, especially concerning her business. She heard him leave the room as she entered the shower. The warm water against her skin, and the rising steam cleared her head. The night had been strange. She hadn't forgotten what she'd seen between Catalina and Dominic. She hadn't forgotten what she discovered when she found Giovanni, the blood on his hands, the pain in his voice. None of it. Not since she left Virginia had her life been so complicated. With Fabiana and Kei she always felt protected, almost sheltered in normalcy. Standing next to Giovanni, as his friend and lover, she felt a greater sense of responsibility. What it meant escaped her.

After she showered she dried herself, dressed, and finger combed her hair into a messy French braid. She found Giovanni downstairs. He was in his office with large plastic bags picking up the debris from the angry tantrum he'd thrown in the night. Still the room looked like a horror story.

"Hi?"

He glanced up. He straightened and smiled at her. "You look beautiful."

"Thank you. Need help?"

"I have some men coming to finish, just wanted to get up some of the glass," he said with a sheepish grin.

"I have a question."

Giovanni glanced her way. Mira stepped forward. "It's about your sister."

He smiled. "She's really happy you are helping her. The dress will be pretty? Right?"

"That woman you hired, Giovanni, Clara. She's not working

in Catalina's best interest."

Giovanni ran his hands through his hair shaking his head. He really had so much on his mind today he didn't want to debate the semantics of a wedding. He paid people for this. But seeing her take a genuine interest in his sister and the coordination of this event was endearing so he tried to be patient, "What has she done?"

"She sabotaged the girl's dress. You should have seen what she tried to force on her."

"*Venuto*," he reached for her hand and pulled her to him.

Giovanni reached for her hand pulling her to him "I think it's wonderful that you care about my sister and are helping her. I trust you, *Bella*. And I need a date for the wedding. Will you be my date?"

"I... okay, but, well this woman."

"You and Catalina listen to *Signora* Clara. She's a wise woman. Catalina will have a traditional Sicilian wedding, and Clara will see to it. If she objected to the dress, then there must be a reason. My sister will not flaunt fashion over our faith. I want her to be beautiful, can you make sure she is?"

"I will try. Giovanni, why an arranged marriage? Catalina is so young, why not send her off to school? Or let her fall in love on her own."

Giovanni frowned. "Where does this question come from? Has my sister said she doesn't want to marry Franco?"

"No. No. It's just, I didn't know arranged marriages were still done. I guess it's my ignorance."

He released a gust of a laugh. "Well it's not always done. But in our family it is. My father arranged this marriage between our families, and Catalina is happy with the choice.

Now enough of this." He kissed her cheek. "You have a visitor waiting."

****

Fabiana looked up when her friend walked in. She felt her heart sink. Mira smiled sweetly at her, and she looked away. The idea of lying to her made her stomach clench and her heart hurt. She sat silently as Lorenzo introduced the building inspector to Mira and barely listened when they told Mira that their boutique would be closed for the coming weeks until the building is up to code. Her friend asked the usual questions, panic in her voice and face. Fabiana couldn't speak. She couldn't say a word.

"Fabiana? What are we going to do?" Mira asked.

She gripped the chair, her gaze lifted to Lorenzo and his stayed on her. She glanced over to Giovanni who watched her as well. She should say to hell with them and call bullshit on it all. Grab her friend and walk out. Last night Lorenzo confessed something to her that had her terrified for him, for them all. He needed her help. To save his life she'd have to risk a friendship that meant more to her than anything in the world. What was she to do?

"Fabiana? What should we do?" Mira repeated.

"Don't... don't panic. This is only temporary," Fabiana's voice cracked and she cleared her throat. "I made some calls while you were with," her gaze shifted to the Don and away. "Giovanni. Angelique is going to bring over your designs. He's agreed to give us space to work here. Until this matter is cleared up."

"You did? How could you do that if he just told us the

building was closed?" Mira frowned.

Fabiana stammered over her answer. "I found out about the problem late in the evening. I um, asked the inspector to come here. I didn't want to worry you."

Giovanni took her hand and kissed it. "I want to help. Let me."

"What about our staff? Where will they be?"

She forced a smile. "Sending half of them to New York and the other half to Milan. We can join them in a few weeks. Setting things up now. See. No problem. We'll handle it."

Mira felt it. Something was off. Giovanni kept her hand in his, and Fabiana could barely make eye contact with her. The inspector needed a translator and again she felt like the only person in the room not in on the truth was her.

The inspector picked up his hat and situated it on his head. The man said a few more words in Italian to Giovanni and then left. "Are you okay with this? With us staying here?"

Giovanni smirked and she knew he was. In fact it played right into his request that she stay longer. Mira rubbed her temples, pacing. "This can't work. This is wrong. It's wrong."

"*Bella*? Look at me."

She stopped and looked at him. His smile melted her anxiety. "I will do whatever it takes to put this in order. Trust me."

She glanced to Fabiana and Lorenzo. She had no reason not to trust them. Her gaze returned to Giovanni. Especially him. Her heart had grown fond of him. She nodded. "Well I'm yours."

He kissed her cheek and whispered in her ear. "Yes, you are."

He then signaled to Lorenzo to follow him and the men walked out. Fabiana rose to leave behind them. "Freeze. Don't you dare leave."

Fabiana flashed her a pretty smile. She wore her hair in a slender ponytail. She'd chosen a pair of khaki colored capris and a sheer pink shirt with oversized sleeves that were adorned with tiny sequined beads circling her collar. Her friend smiled and stopped.

"What's going on? How bad is it? Do we need to find another building to lease? Have you called our solicitor? Teddy?"

"Hey! Slow down!" Fabiana laughed. "It's a setback. We can manage it. I can manage it. You know me. When I panic then you panic. Okay?"

"Mira! There you are!" Catalina hurried in. She and Fabiana froze. Catalina, in an all-white sundress, looked completely virginal compared to the seductress she saw having her way with her adopted brother. "I've been looking for you."

Signora Clara was on her heels. She scowled at Mira then Fabiana. "I thought we were going to Napoli to your store. So you can finish my dress."

"Change of plans sweetie." Fabiana said. "We will have some things brought here. Looks like you have house guests on an extended stay."

"I don't understand." Catalina frowned.

"No worries. I will finish your dress. We can still drive into Naples and check for a few things." Mira smiled.

"Great!" Catalina clapped. "The driver is out front. *Signora* Clara is coming too. Come on. Let's go."

Mira touched her messy hair and considered running upstairs for a comb and brush. "We'll meet you out front. Let us get our purses."

Catalina smiled and flounced out. The old woman shot them both a warning glare, turned up her nose, and followed. Mira rubbed her temples. First she had to deal with the mean tempered Don, who could turn into Casanova in a flash, and now her store doors were closed.

"You really up to doing this dress?"

"I can't get out of it, now can I?"

Fabiana laughed. "Guess not."

"Let's go."

Her friend grabbed her hand when she passed. "Mira, trust me. I know what I'm doing."

Mira hugged her. "Of course I trust you. Always."

Giovanni strolled ahead. When they entered the billiard room he stopped. Dominic waited with Flavio Pricci. Thirty years his senior Flavio was a man of great respect and importance in Sicily, and now within the *Cammora*. As Giovanni's *consigliere* he was the third most important man in the family.

"Lorenzo?" Flavio stepped toward him smiling. He was of average height, but very cleanly dressed and groomed. He looked ten years younger than his age, and Giovanni knew personally that Flavio had more women than one man should handle. But he remained a bachelor with no kids or entanglements. His focus was and had always been the family.

"Flavio!" Lorenzo greeted him warmly, kissing both of his cheeks and then giving him a welcoming hug. "I thought you were in Sicily?"

"I was." He cut him a sly smirk. "Gio summoned me yesterday evening. Said we might have trouble."

"Trouble cousin?" Lorenzo feigned shock. "Is it Calderone?"

Giovanni didn't answer. He continued to glare.

"Flavio!" Catalina squealed. She rushed into the office, arms flung wide. She crashed into Flavio causing him to lean back in their embrace. He hugged her tight, cupping her face and kissing her brow. Lorenzo watched as Flavio spoke in Italian to her, soft whispers of how beautiful she was becoming, and how proud he was to hear that the wedding plans were progressing. It was enough of a reprieve for him to turn his focus to Giovanni. For the first time since he'd arrived in the billiard room Giovanni was not glaring at him. His heart raced with indecision. Should he confess? Deny? What would be the preemptive move that would save his life?

"I knew you'd be back in time for the wedding." Catalina gushed.

Mira appeared with Fabiana. Her presence among the women made Flavio's brow rise. He narrowed his gaze on her. Lorenzo watched, mildly amused. Flavio was old school. Lorenzo suspected he wanted Giovanni free of the entanglements of women, to mold him further into the cold bastard Tomosino was. "You ladies leaving?" Lorenzo asked.

Giovanni winked at Mira and she crossed the room going to him. Flavio tracked her with his eyes and released Catalina to openly stare at her.

"Flavio, meet Mira Ellison. She's my guest." Giovanni said.

Mira extended her hand. "*Ciao.*"

After a pause he accepted her hand and kissed her knuckles in greeting. He never spoke. Mira shyly stepped back to Giovanni's side.

"She's going to design my wedding dress!" Catalina proclaimed.

A light of understanding sharpened the steely grey stare he fixed her with. The old man actually looked relieved. Lorenzo shook his head at the scene.

"Time to go. We have some things to get before we start today. Are you staying for dinner? Please say yes!"

He nodded and patted Catalina's cheek. Mira said something Lorenzo couldn't hear to Giovanni and he chuckled. He kissed her in front of everyone before the ladies left.

Giovanni noticed the old man's reaction to Mira. He'd address it privately. His attention switched to his cousin. Lorenzo met his gaze dead on as if there was nothing to hang his head in shame over. Again anger boiled his gut and made his chest tight. "Leave us. Flavio and I have things to discuss," he said to the room. Lorenzo looked around, confused at the short reprieve. If Giovanni had learned nothing over the past years, it was that his emotions could never rule him. He let that happen once with the Russians and his men saw his weakness for his father. But his father was gone and that weakness was shelved. He could not and would not show the same irrational rage toward Lorenzo.

One by one the men left as he requested. Lorenzo was the last to draw the doors to the sunroom shut.

"They have not found Giuseppe's body yet. We need to get to that body and make sure it's never discovered."

"So it's proven. Lorenzo pulled the trigger?" Giovanni lowered to the chair.

"Dominic's information is solid. I checked with some of the families in Sicily. Lorenzo and Giuseppe did business. No one knows for how long or for what. Your father is turning over in his grave."

"Good. He can make room for Lorenzo when I bury him."

"Is that how you would do it? Kill your cousin?"

"Do I have a fucking choice? If he's betrayed me, this family, he has left me none."

"If? That is the word you must consider before you act. If he betrayed the family. Lorenzo is a hot head, like his mother. She should have been born a man." Flavio chuckled. He lowered to the chair across from Giovanni and crossed his legs. The gold tiepin sparkled against his all black attire. His salt and pepper hair extended to his neatly trimmed beard, and his grey eyes were vibrant with life and wisdom. Giovanni trusted him above all else.

Flavio smiled. "You are your father's son."

"My father wouldn't have tolerated this insolence. He wouldn't have stood for it."

"Your father was a man of great strength. However, family was the source of that strength. Do you think he could have built all that you have without family?"

Giovanni's eyes swept the room.

"No." Flavio uncrossed his legs and leaned forward. "He chose you son. The day you were put in his arms he chose you. He didn't care about your mixed blood. You are his son."

"He tested me." Giovanni said bitterly.

"As a father should test a son." Flavio nodded, and again Giovanni had to accept abuse for love. "He gave you a new name. Battaglia. A family within the *Cammora* that even the Dons of Sicily bow their heads in respect to. This was no easy feat."

"Spare me the history lesson. I know it!"

"Do you?" Flavio's gaze lifted as Giovanni rose and began to pace. "History is what we play our hand from. It's what guides our future. You are stronger because of the men that are sworn to you. Lorenzo's actions could work in your favor. If you are wise enough to know how to use it to the family's advantage."

Giovanni closed his eyes. He knew Flavio spoke the truth. Still Lorenzo defied him. The only explanation for the alliance to Giuseppe was to feed his greed. How could that go unpunished? Giovanni stopped. He cast his gaze to Flavio. "You want us to go to war with Calderone?"

Flavio smiled. "Think of it. No more begging the old Don for land purchases. You, Gio, can own the triangle. Genoa, Turin, Milan. All of it yours, unchallenged. And I'm speaking of legitimate business, not the squalor. The *Cammora* has no reach in northern Italy. This is your way."

"A war will mean lives, bloodshed. For what? To make me as greedy as my cousin?"

Flavio waved it off. "To make you omniscient. It's time for you to become what your father had been working for. Don Calderone is barely recovering from his stroke. He will act irrationally. He will spill blood first. A war is here, how you win the war is for you to decide."

"Lorenzo should not go unpunished!" Giovanni slammed his fist into the palm of his hand. Flavio nodded his agreement.

"Lorenzo is impulsive and reckless. He's never been satisfied with the title of underboss. This was bound to happen. I advised you years ago not to give him the gambling houses or the whores to manage. It was too big of a responsibility and temptation for him."

"Well, obviously, you were right." Giovanni mumbled.

"What you must consider is not the betrayal, Giovanni. We can deal with his flagrant disregard for the rules. See the bigger picture."

Giovanni closed his eyes and sighed. "And what of respect, loyalty, honor? How is *omerta* held sacred without those three?"

"No kingdom has been built on flowers son. You need a strong foundation, hard muscle, and an unwavering message to all of your enemies that you will control both worlds. Then your enemies will respect you. The men you lead will be loyal to you. And Lorenzo will learn the meaning of honor."

"What do I do?"

"What you must. Tell him what you must. Tighten his leash, and when things settle we revisit this conversation of respect, loyalty, and honor. If he must be dealt with, then you put the family in order first."

"I want to forgive him, to right this. I don't know how." Giovanni said.

Flavio smirked. "It'll come."

"Send for him." Giovanni said. "Make sure the women are gone before he enters." He removed his gun and put it on the table. Flavio stared at the weapon for a moment, and then lifted his dark gaze to him.

"A cool head, Gio. Remember."

"I will try."

He watched the old man leave. Waited until he returned with both Lorenzo and Dominic. Tomosino's boys, as the three of them were often referred as. His father had a hand in the men they all had become. And it was true he could see the best and worst of his father in him and Lorenzo. Today he'd have to rise above his pride for the greater good. One look at his lying cousin and that became an insufferable task.

"I'll ask it one time." Giovanni began. "Careful of your answer. Why did you kill Giuseppe Calderone?"

Lorenzo heard the door open behind him. He didn't have to turn to know that Nico and the boys had arrived. Things would get ugly before it settled. He eased his hands into his pockets and gave a one shoulder shrug. "I did it for the family."

Giovanni smirked. "Is that so?"

"You were right to close *Isabella's*. We didn't know that the Albanians had young girls, or if it was Francesco who soiled our business. The family and our honor were jeopardized because of it. You were right cousin and I was wrong. But there's something you don't know." Lorenzo swallowed. He thought of Fabiana's words to him. Last night he confessed. He told her of how his jealousy got him to drinking in Genoa one night, the night he stumbled into Giuseppe's club and bitterly told his tale of being rejected by the Don. When he learned that Don Tomosino had no intention of letting Giovanni go, but would bring him back and make him next in the line to lead Battaglia. That night he and Giuseppe commiserated over how they loathed their fathers. And whether it was a joke or boastful bragging, they suggested taking a shot at each other's Don to free them. Lorenzo didn't mean it. But Giuseppe hired some Russians to do the job. The bastard set it into motion, and Lorenzo could do nothing to stop it. He confessed this shame to Fabiana and she held him, took his burden and swore to help him through it. Now he had to remember her advice to not falter, not waver from his truth, but to do anything to keep the nasty details from his cousin.

"Continue." Giovanni said. "What is it I don't know?"

"The real threat that I've kept from you is the Nigerians. They've started moving drugs along the Amalfi, and Giuseppe helped them. He tricked me."

Giovanni tapped his fingers on the arm of the chair.

"I was trying to gain some advantage in Genoa. I had agreed to let Giuseppe import through my line of the coast."

The Amalfi was hard to move in and out of without being stopped by patrols. Giovanni never had this problem because of the people on his payroll. This gave Lorenzo the freedom to take liberties that he shouldn't have. A coil of rage tightened his lungs, and Giovanni breathed slow and easy to remain calm and hear the tale. He nodded to Nico, and his enforcer stepped directly behind Lorenzo.

His cousin wiped his jaw, his gaze unsteady as it switched from Giovanni to Flavio, then to Dominic. "Rare antiquities that were being put in the market. Giuseppe wanted to deal with the Nigerians to handle it. Players we don't know. I believed him, at first. Then I checked a shipment myself. A small bust broke and inside was drugs. When I confronted the worm, he admitted to bringing in drugs. I was outraged. We argued, he insulted Papa, you, and our family. So I killed him."

"Albanians, Russians, Nigerians, what the fuck is this, Gio, the UN of thieves? Why are all these outsiders circling? And why, Lorenzo, did you not think to tell any of this?" Flavio asked.

"I had it under control."

"You figured." Giovanni nodded. "You decided for all of us."

"I made a mistake. I tried to rectify it, Giovanni."

He rose from his chair. He stood before the gun and Lorenzo. Every man in the room tensed. Lorenzo's voice broke the stand-off. "I am guilty, but is it worth my life, Giovanni? What do you need from me, cousin, for me to gain your forgiveness?"

"It is not worth your life." Giovanni half smiled. "I couldn't do that to Catalina. But you have lost all privileges. Including the house in Bellagio. Dominic is now my left hand."

"Giovanni!" Lorenzo barked. "That is not just!"

His lips curled into an angry snarl. "It is the only justice today for what you have done!" he yelled.

"And? That's it? I'm an errand boy?"

"You're alive. Show some gratitude." Flavio warned.

Lorenzo turned to respond, but Nico delivered a hard punch to his spine. Unexpectedly, Lorenzo's knees buckled, and he dropped on all fours. Renaldo grabbed Lorenzo's hair and yanked it up as Nico stepped in front of him and started to pound his fists into his face until blood spewed from his nostrils and mouth. Semi-conscious Lorenzo fell over to the floor, and all four men began to kick him in the chest, back, even to the face. Giovanni glanced up to Dominic who had fear in his eyes. He nodded that the beating could cease. Dominic yelled for the men to stop and shoved them several feet away from Lorenzo. He went to his knees, checking on him. Giovanni walked back to his desk and sat behind him.

"Clean him up. Don't let Catalina see him that way."

They carried him out. As angry as he was with him, he loved him still. Killing him at the end of this would be the hardest thing he would have to do. Yet the lessons learned from his father and his uncles made him a man capable of it. Lorenzo knew this. They were all on borrowed time.

Chapter Twelve

SHOPPING HAD ONLY TAKEN a little over an hour. They were back to find the villa buzzing with activity. There appeared to be more men now than before they left, and Mira could sense the tension between all of them stomping around the grounds. Catalina was given an update from her staff in Italian, and she spoke to Fabiana in Italian. Mira tried not to take it personal, but it irked her. She was then led to the third level. Mira was shocked to see a lot of her equipment from the boutique had been brought in.

"How is this possible?" Mira asked.

Fabiana smiled. "I told you I'd make it work. Lorenzo pulled some strings."

Mira found her kits and felt like she could breathe again. Suddenly the heaviness on her heart lifted. As Fabiana gave some instructions on where to set up her cutting tables, Mira drifted to the window. It faced the back of the estate. Giovanni was below. He was near the pool pacing with the man he introduced her to earlier. Frowning, she moved closer to the window observing his body language. Something was wrong with the way he kept smoothing his hair back. He was angry again.

"Mira, where do you want this?" Fabiana asked.

She turned from the window and tilted her head to the left looking at the table "Over there in the corner," she said then turned back in time to see Giovanni heading to the cottage they called *rosso*.

"Come here, sweetie." Mira said walking over to her portfolio that they'd delivered. She tore a clean sheet of paper free and found a sharpened pencil in the side pockets. Clara, Fabiana, and Catalina all stood riveted as Mira sketched the idea of the dress before them. In under ten minutes she had the concept completed. Catalina clapped with delight.

Clara paled.

"It's perfect. Can you do it in time? Can you?"

Mira tried to match her excitement, but images of Catalina and Dominic kept flashing to the front of her mind. She nodded that she could.

"No. No. No. No!" Clara said. "The cleavage is wrong. And it fits too snug below the waist. It won't do."

"I want this dress! This one!" Catalina protested.

"Time out!" Fabiana said. She took the woman by the elbow, and they spoke in Italian. Their voices rose and Clara moved her arms animatedly, gesturing at Fabiana. The old woman reached her limit and stormed out.

"What did you say to her?" Mira asked.

"Don't worry. You work on the dress, and I'll handle the matchmaker from hell."

Catalina grinned. "Thank you both, so much."

Mira forced a smile. "This is your wedding, what you want, so we will make it perfect."

Catalina nodded. "Yes. It's what I want."

Giovanni entered *Villa Rosso* with Dominic and Flavio following. "The Minettis will be here tomorrow. We will not have this unrest around the wedding."

Dominic nodded. "I've already reached out to Angelo along with the other families to offer our assistance. Fish says the Calderones are divided. The old man is convinced it's the Nigerians, but Angelo keeps questioning Lo's involvement. And with the old man on his back, Angelo is calling the shots. "

"I want this contained until after the wedding and our delivery from the Irish. We need this week." Giovanni said, and the men nodded in agreement. Giovanni knew his cousin was reeling now. He'd cut off his balls. He should be on his knees thanking him for not taking his head as well.

Dominic headed for the door. He stopped. "I think you decided fairly, Gio. Lo is a brother, our brother. He deserves this chance." He opened the door and left.

"Well it's been an eventful morning. I need to make some calls." Flavio rose from his chair.

"Wait." Giovanni said.

He turned and looked over his shoulder, "Yes?"

"Mira Ellison, she's staying here."

"I see." Flavio's brow arched. "I hear you arranged to have her things moved in."

Giovanni's gaze lifted. "She's important to me. I want her treated with respect."

"How important?"

"Important."

"She's American, black American. She doesn't belong here, Gio."

"But she is here." Giovanni said flatly. "And I say she belongs."

"Does she know who you are?"

"She knows enough."

"And?"

Giovanni didn't answer.

Flavio nodded. "We will talk more on this later."

"No, we won't." Giovanni stood. "I won't discuss her with you or anyone, and you won't interfere with our... friendship. It's non-negotiable. Are we clear?"

Flavio nodded. "Of course."

Catalina sat on the stool next to Mira, watching as she ran the fabric through her sewing machine, reattaching the seams. She taught Catalina different ways to work with silks and satins. The young woman was a quick study. In return, Mira got some of the Italian lessons she'd been wanting.

"Who taught you how to sew?" Catalina asked.

"My grandmother." Mira answered.

"Really, I never knew my grandmother." Catalina returned the smile.

"What about your mother?"

"Oh, Mama sewed too. She made me dresses, but I never took the time to learn. I wish I had." She said in a sad voice.

Mira looked over at her, "You miss her?"

"She was supposed to be here for this... I'm getting married and neither of my parents will be here to see it."

"They're here, just not in the way you would want."

Catalina smiled. "You think so?"

"I do."

Fabiana rose from her perch on a stool. "It's getting late.

I'm going to go find Lorenzo." She smiled.

Catalina stood to stop her. "Tomorrow is my serenade. Make sure you are up for it."

The girls looked at Catalina confused. Fabiana voiced the question first. "What serenade sweetie?"

Catalina beamed. "Franco and his family are coming. It's a tradition that we will do. A surprise for Giovanni. Franco serenades me as his new bride. It will be right outside my window on the west side of the villa, around 7 in the morning. I'd like you to be there."

"He comes here and sings to you?" Mira asked.

"Yes, part of the tradition is that we do not speak before the wedding. This is his way of communicating his love for me."

"Damn, that's hot!" Fabiana laughed, "I like it!"

Catalina nodded in agreement. "It's really sexy. He comes here with his brothers and relatives, serenading me with either a violinist or someone on guitar outside my window. After the serenade my brother, as my guardian, is supposed to offer a ceremonial dinner to Franco's family, thanking and welcoming them. *Signora* Clara has arranged the breakfast feast, but I wanted you two to be in the room with me when he comes, if that's okay," she grinned at Mira.

"I'm honored." Mira looked to Fabiana, and both women blinked their surprise.

Catalina touched Fabiana's arm. "You too, you have to be there."

"I will set my alarm clock, sugar. I'm right there."

"What other traditions will you be practicing?" Mira asked, continuing with her stitching of the fabric.

Catalina's face beamed with excitement. Mira again had to

wonder if the scene she saw between her and Dominic was real. The girl didn't look torn over the wedding. She was bubbling with excitement.

"In America your custom is for the bride to have four things, something old, something blue, something borrowed, something new... right?"

"That's right." Fabiana answered.

"Those are customs borrowed from us Sicilians."

"They are?" Mira asked surprised.

"*Si.*"

"So you have the same traditional things required." Fabiana said smiling.

"I do, but ours have meaning."

"What type of meaning?" Mira asked.

"I get five, not four. The first is something old which symbolizes the life I will leave behind. Giovanni gave me the pearls that Papa presented to Mama when I was born. They belonged to my nonna."

"I bet they're beautiful." Mira said.

Catalina nodded. "They will look so nice with the bodice of the dress you're designing. Absolutely perfect."

Fabiana went to the chair across from them sitting back down. "What's next?"

"There is something new which symbolizes the new life I will have. I was thinking of my wedding band; it's all diamonds. I decided it will be the new. Franco has the solitaire on him that matches it."

"That'll work." Mira nodded. Turning to find the fabric pieces she cut earlier. "Go on."

Catalina scooped her locks behind her ear and smiled. "Then there is something borrowed which represents the people dear to me who will be at my side as I move from my old life into my new one."

"I have my pearl earrings with me, I'll let you wear them." Fabiana winked.

"Would you?" Catalina asked her eyes growing wide with excitement.

"Of course, they will work perfectly with your nonna's necklace."

Catalina clapped, excited over the gesture, and the girls laughed as her excitement spilled over to them. Mira had never been this close to planning a wedding, and she was falling in love with Catalina and her enthusiasm. "There's something blue! In ancient Roman times blue was the color of purity, and it was also the color of wedding gowns."

"Women married in blue gowns?" Mira asked.

Catalina nodded. "Oh yes! It was a great honor, but a pagan custom. With Catholicism, tradition changed the gown into white as virginal, so the royal colors of blue and yellow were dropped from tradition; which is why the bride still holds onto something blue for good luck. You Americans adopt our customs and don't even know it," she boasted.

Mira counted. "Well that's four, the same things we American brides have to have. What's the fifth?"

Catalina walked away and turned to face them smiling sweetly. "Something she has received as a gift from her papa. In this case, it will be Giovanni. It's to remind me of the people that love me when I leave home with my husband. Giovanni hasn't told me what it is, but I know you can find out."

Mira put up both hands. "No way. Your brother is as old fashioned of a man as I have ever met; there is no way I'll spy for you. He'll kill me."

"I can't figure out what it is! Please!"

Fabiana looked at Mira "We girls got to stick together. You can find out, Mira."

"Fabiana!"

"Aww, it's not such a big deal. Really, I won't say anything, and I promise to be surprised." Catalina chided.

"Not going to do it."

Catalina poked out her bottom lip. "Fine."

"How about a compromise?" Mira said placing down the sheers. "I confirm that he has it and whether it's big or small, so you will have a general idea."

Fabiana smiled at Catalina. "That sounds fair. What do you think?"

Catalina cheered. "*Perfecto!*"

After sunset and her fingers were cramped, Mira too gave up and found her way to her room. She showered alone. She was dressing for bed when she heard the inside door open. She peeked out to see Giovanni arrive. She watched him go over to the bed and drop down on the edge exhausted, putting his head in his hands. He didn't even look up to see her watching.

"Tough day at the office, honey?"

He looked up at her and smiled weakly. "Cute."

"Want to talk about it?"

Kneeling in front of him she parted his legs so she could ease in between them and look up into his face. "Maybe I can help?"

He lifted his face from his palms. Their eyes met. A small smile curled the corner of his mouth. "You are helping, by being here." Giovanni sat upright. Bringing her from the floor to his lap, he kissed the inside of her neck. "I'm sorry your store is closed."

"I have plenty of stores." Mira smiled. "Besides, it's only a setback. We might need a different building."

"You accept things very easily, Mira, without question. That's why I'm so fond of you."

"Fond?" She brushed her lips over his. "Only fond of me?"

"I'm falling in love with you." He said.

Mira drew away. "Love?"

"A man knows his heart, and I know I have never desired, trusted, wanted a woman more than you." He stroked the side of her face. "Tell me that isn't love."

Mira escaped his lap. She nervously shook her head. "That's too fast. I, we, that's too fast."

"For what? For you to accept us as a couple? For you to trust me?"

Mira paced. She and Kei had been together a year before she even said the word. How the hell could two weeks turn into love? It's the country, the romance, the sex. All of it had her head in the clouds, but she wasn't reckless. She loved her newfound independence, her freedom to do and be whoever she wanted. She didn't come to Italy for love. When she looked back to him her entire being seized with the emotions she discovered in his arms. "Let me ask you a question, Giovanni."

He nodded.

"What is expected of... a woman, your woman, a woman in your life?"

"Expected?" he frowned.

"Let's not pretend here. I sure as hell can't. You are a complicated man with a complicated life. What happens to a woman you fall in love with?"

He rose. "What's expected of any love? It grows."

"And?"

"And eventually we marry."

Mira looked away.

"If you love me, we marry. As my wife you'll have my *bambinas* and take care of our home. You will support me unconditionally."

"I can't do that... I'm not ready for marriage, kids. I don't even know if I want kids."

Giovanni laughed. "It doesn't happen tomorrow, *Bella*." He took her hands. "But it will be the future I want with you. I am a dangerous man, and I deal with dangerous men. My business remains secret because in that secrecy is your protection. Contrary to the movies and what you think, there is only one way I leave this role. That's death."

"Are you telling me that you won't ever walk away from this lifestyle, no matter what the circumstance? Not even for our love?"

"Yes."

He dropped his forehead on hers. "That's my future and yours if you accept me. Tonight, all I want is you."

"I don't know what to say."

"Say nothing." He captured her mouth with his. Her arms lifted to his neck to hold to him, and he carried her to the bed. Everything about him was gentle and caring, the way he laid her upon the sheets and stroked the side of her face. She stared up into his eyes and the blue dissolved into the sweetest shade of violet. She smiled and knew that was the color of his love. Beyond the heart-pounding pleasure she found when he made love to her, she also felt safe, and protected enough to trust her feelings for him. Was it love? She had no idea, but she knew she cared deeply for him. She knew she could never abandon what was happening between them. His mouth crashed upon hers. A kiss strong and demanding drained her resistance. She clung to him and fought to breathe through their shared passion. When he released her from his kiss, her mouth and heart ached for more. Giovanni untied her robe. His lustful gaze seemed to flame with excitement to find she wore nothing but a thong panty beneath.

It was unfair to confess his heart to her so soon, to claim her from her life and barricade her within his. But he was a selfish man, completely when it came to her. He'd never let another man take her from him. She'd be the mother of his children, the wife he didn't know he needed, and if it took a year or more to convince her, so be it.

Giovanni stared down at her. Her kiss-bruised lips parted and her eyes gleamed with passion. Her body was flawless. Slowly he eased her thong from her hips and down her smooth brown legs. She lifted her ass from the mattress to aid him, and then sat up to shrug her arms out of the sleeves of the robe. When he made to move on her, she stopped him with a hand to his chest. "I do have feelings for you. I'm not ready for anything more than friendship now. I need time to know you. Okay?"

He stared into her eyes and lied. "Take all the time you need, *Bella*."

She relaxed, lying back, and he smiled. The bastard in him didn't care what she told herself to reason away their bond. He would remove any obstacle that kept her from him, and he already had. He shed his clothing in a hurried manner but took the time to run his tongue from her knee to her decadent center. He found her scent invigorating and buried his face between her thighs. Her hand stroked the top of his head as his tongue gave light swirling licks to her swollen bud. Before long she was bucking her ass off the mattress and pressing down on the back of his head to speed her orgasm along. But he wanted to be inside of her when she came. And again he'd do so without protection.

Giovanni positioned himself and slid his length into her while he held her hips steady.

"Ah!" she exclaimed.

His eyes blinked slowly several times and then closed as he sank into her velvet warmth. "Fuck!" he cried out shuddering and struggling to keep control. Faster and faster he thrust into her until his breath was reduced to ragged gasps for air. Her breasts shook and her bottom half pumped up at him, driving him to madness. He forced his eyes to open, to look upon her face as he moved with more control. Her expression was regal. Her well-shaped nostrils flared slightly and she drew in a deep breath and released it slowly as he gave her another measured thrust.

Caught between rapture and self-loathing hell, he dropped on her and clung to her desperately as he released his seed into her womb. He wanted this. Desperately. He needed this, her, like he needed air to breathe. Fuck her timetable. She was his.

Chapter Thirteen

"Giovanni?"

He opened his eyes. Mira laid close, her arms around him and her face tilted up to stare up at him. How long had he slept? The room was still dark, but the drapes were drawn. "Yes?"

"Catalina's wedding is soon. She says today you'll have your family here."

"Mmhm."

"I know you have traditions, family traditions that you believe in. I just..."

He sat up a bit and tugged her up into his arms. "What is it?"

"Catalina. Have you ever asked her if she understands marriage? The commitment she is making?"

Giovanni chuckled. "You're worried about my sister and her wedding? I thought something was wrong."

Mira drew away from his embrace. "She thinks it's a big party. Her party. But I don't think she understands what happens when the party is over. She's about to be married, and she's only eighteen. I remember when I left Virginia at seventeen, and how confused I was at eighteen. I think you should talk to her and be sure she knows what she is doing."

"You talk to her."

"What?"

"You're a woman. She needs a mother. Talk to her."

"That's not what..."

"Come here." He brought her down to his chest. He kissed her forehead. "My sister is young and spoiled but she is marrying a boy who will love and cherish her. I made sure of it. This is the life she wants. Trust me."

"If you say so."

****

"Fabiana? What's wrong?" Mira walked into the sunroom. She had escaped there to be alone with her thoughts and the tears came expectantly. At the sound of Mira's voice she turned from her and tried to wipe her tears away to keep the anguish from her friend. Regret squeezed her heart as she thought of the lies she'd told. How could she confide her worry now, without revealing her part in the scheme to keep them in this house of lies and secrets?

Last night was a disaster. After pacing the room waiting for Lorenzo's return he was thrown inside, severely beaten. Panicked she fled the room and demanded they help him, call for medical assistance. The man she faced in the hall issued a chilling warning. *Keep him out of the Don's sight or we will return to finish him.*

Fabiana spent the night nursing the bruises and wiping away the blood. She pleaded with him when he was conscious to leave with her, to go to a hospital. Instead he told her the entire story. His confession would haunt her for the rest of her life. Who he was, what he'd done, and the secrets he carried that would end his life if ever breathed to another soul.

"Hey, talk to me? What is it? Something happen?" Mira forced her to face her. "I was looking for you and they said you were in here. Where's Lorenzo?"

"Recovering."

"Recovering?"

Fabiana sat. "He's been hurt."

"How?"

If she told her the truth, it would make her as guilty. She thought she was helping the man, but all she was doing was burying them deeper in this place. She had to get a grip. "I think he got into a fight. I don't know."

"Fight?" Mira drew away. "Is he okay?"

"He is now."

"I'll tell Giovanni and he—"

"No! Don't say anything."

Mira sighed. "Why do I get the feeling that you aren't telling me everything?"

"Because I'm not. He's in trouble and I can't talk to you about it. These men, they're impossible to understand. You know what I mean."

She paced the floor. "I've heard enough. I don't know what happened to Lorenzo, and I don't want to know. I'm concerned about you, us, the way we've pretty much lost control of our lives. I don't think we should stay here much longer, Fabiana."

"It's barely been two weeks. We're on vacation." Fabiana said.

"Are you kidding me? This isn't a vacation. Not for me anymore. It's a seduction, and it's working. You, Lorenzo,

Giovanni, and I are caught up in this... I don't know what to call it. The man says he loves me. You look terrified, and I know it's connected to him. What am I to think?"

Fabiana's head dropped and she shook it sadly. "It's all my fault."

"Nonsense. We agreed to come here."

"You don't understand."

"I do. That's why we need to step back and get some perspective."

The anxiety she carried since Giovanni said he loved her left her struggling to find the words. She realized she too had fallen in love, and her judgment felt impaired. The violence and secrecy in this family wasn't as appealing as her new lover's touch. They needed to regain focus.

"Think about it. We have the fashion debut of my career, and I haven't done any more press-ops or met with our investors. I know we said a vacation, but we're here now. And my store doesn't have anything to do with it. We're here because we've become distracted with feelings for these men. It's too much too soon. I can't help but feel out of focus."

Fabiana nodded. "I feel it too."

"Good! Thank God! I thought I was losing it or something."

"No." Fabiana smiled, "We are out of sync. I've let things get out of hand." Again Fabiana avoided looking her in the eye. "Let's help Catalina with the wedding and then I will make some calls. We can fly out to New York next week."

"Okay. Okay." Mira nodded. "I'll explain it to Giovanni. You do the same with Lorenzo."

Fabiana embraced her, and Mira felt a bit at ease. "Is he okay? You said he was hurt?"

"He's better. I just came down here to get my head clear."

"C'mon let's find Catalina."

"That's right!" Fabiana forced a smile. "I want to see this serenade."

Together they walked in silent contemplation to Catalina's room. Mira was curious about Fabiana's news that Lorenzo had been in a fight. She kept the questions to herself. When they entered Catalina's room, they found her at the window. She looked back with tears in her eyes smiling then signaled for them to move closer. Mira and Fabiana eased in behind her and became enchanted by the heartfelt song bellowing out of the young man who played the guitar himself. Beyond him were 12 other members of his family watching proudly. Mira found him relatively attractive. Maybe not as charismatic as Dominic but not the ogre that Catalina described him to be.

Signora Clara and three other ladies were present, one of which was Zia from the vineyard. The old woman wore a blue dress, her silver hair pinned neatly behind her head. She stared intensely and didn't speak. When the song was done, the girls clapped and the family below cheered.

"*Ciao!*" A beautiful woman said, stepping to Mira's left. She was almost Catalina's twin. "I'm Aurora, Catalina's cousin."

"*Ciao.*" Mira said shaking her hand.

Signora Clara announced something in Italian and the women lit up with smiles and applause. Catalina spun in her dress, smiling brightly at them.

"She said it's time to meet the guests. It's Catalina's day." Aurora translated. "She'll be more of a spoiled brat than usual." Aurora chuckled, but Mira detected a hint of envy in the tone. "You're that designer. Mira Ellison. I saw your fashion show on the TV. I speak English really well."

"You do. And nice to meet you." Mira said.

Catalina's eyes cut over to Mira and Aurora. They narrowed on her cousin, as if she had taken away her favorite toy. She marched over and tugged Mira away. "These are my aunts *Zia Tadea* and *Zia Pagna*. This is also my *Zia Carlotta*." Mira nodded to the women and smiled at Zia who forced a smile in return. "Oh and that's Aurora my cousin." Catalina said dryly.

Signora Clara again spoke in Italian and the women nodded in agreement. Fabiana answered the woman and sneered. Whatever was said the tension in the room raised a notch.

Thankfully everyone began to walk out. Mira caught Catalina's hand and delayed her. Fabiana closed the door, getting the message that they needed to be alone. "It was very lovely, the serenade. He's a charming guy."

"Franco is excited. He wrote me a letter." She went to her dresser and got the letter. "My *zia* gave it to me this morning. Really sweet."

"I want to talk to you honey."

Catalina nodded.

"I spoke to your brother."

Catalina's smile faded from her lips. "Why?"

"Don't worry. I didn't tell him about Dominic."

"Shhh!" Catalina gasped, her eyes switching to the door. She pulled the drawer open on the dresser. "There's nothing to tell. We said we wouldn't discuss this anymore!" Catalina slammed the dresser door shut.

"Yesterday when you helped me with your dress I saw how talented you are. Really talented. Maybe you could go to fashion school. Learn a bit about designing."

"Me? Really?"

"Sure. There are schools in Milan and New York."

"School?" Catalina frowned.

Mira nodded, "I will be between New York and Milan. My store might not open in Naples. You can do your apprenticeship with me. I think it would be a great way for you to come into your own."

"Franco will not want his new wife going off to school."

"That's why I spoke to your brother..."

Catalina's eyes stretched with alarm. "You didn't tell Giovanni this?"

"No. I just suggested he talk to you. To hear what you want."

"Why? Why won't you listen? Stay out of it!" Catalina snapped.

Mira blinked at her, shocked. "I'm just trying to help."

"Giovanni is not stupid. You keep meddling he will catch on. Stop interfering. It's not your damn business. You aren't my mother!!" Catalina shouted at her, her eyes glistening with tears.

"Catalina? I'm sorry."

"I am marrying Franco and that's it!" she stormed out of the room and slammed the door.

****

The place was beautiful. Mira found the lower level decorated in yellow and blue flowers and trimmed in ribbons. The floors shined. Light poured in from every angle, and no door was closed. So many people moved about she recognized no one. In the left corner of the foyer was a string quartet playing a romantic melody that welcomed the guests and family members as they poured through the door. Mira glanced up to the top of the stairs, wondering where Giovanni was.

She decided to go to the outside terrace and try to locate a friendly face. Then a touch came to her hand. Her head turned. "Morning beautiful," he whispered in her ear. His voice was just one of the things she loved about him. Inhaling his scent and feeling his strong presence envelope her, she smiled to herself once again.

Giovanni ran his hand across her lower tummy slowly then to her hip, turning her in his arms. She opened her eyes to see him dressed, shaven, and looking strikingly handsome. She also sensed the open stares of people. Some stopped their conversations to watch them.

"I think we have an audience," she said about to lower her arms. He drew her even tighter into his embrace and kissed her softly on the lips. Mira's eyes stretched. She felt her cheeks flame with a blush, but she didn't turn away.

"This is Catalina's day. Let's not be a distraction." She lowered her arms and gently pushed free of his hold. He glanced up and those staring looked away or walked off.

"You're right. But you are mine, and I don't care who knows it."

A woman approached. Mira noticed her first. Tall, with dark flowing hair that feathered away from her pretty face. She had clear grey eyes and the body of a model, with a pair of perfect shaped breasts over a petite waist, curvy hips, and long slender legs. Her eyes locked with Mira's. With glowing olive skin, she wore a tightly fitted green skirt and matching silk blouse.

"*Gio, ciao, bello,*" she said in a seductively low voice. Mira waited for him to react, for him to give her the customary kiss on both of her cheeks as he did the others present. He didn't. He glanced down at her and his face became a frozen mask of non-expression. The woman extended her hand to Mira. "Hello, I'm Gabriella."

"I'm Mira, pleased to meet you."

"Yes! Mira Ellison. I know who you are. I love your work."

"Thank you."

Gabriella glanced up at Giovanni who continued to stare at her. "You have a lovely home. After all these years, I finally get to see the great Battaglia place."

The way he stared at the woman only made the awkwardness more unbearable.

"It was nice to meet you, Mira." Gabriella said and moved on.

"Who was she?"

"No one. *Andiamo.*" They walked out toward the open terrace where most were gathered. Mira glanced back to see the woman glaring after them. The polite smile had completely drained from her face. Giovanni introduced her to family members. A barrage of uncles and aunts from Palermo, distant cousins that were considered family all smiled politely and most spoke to her in Italian. She struggled to communicate so he translated. The shock and curiosity in their eyes was hard to miss. Apparently Giovanni wasn't one to parade any woman around them, let alone a black American woman. Giovanni either didn't notice or simply didn't care because he led her from one group to the next, making introductions. Mira was reminded of what he shared with her in regards to his mother and the way she was treated in Palermo while pregnant with him. Eve must have felt like she was all alone in the world.

She recovered in time to see Rocco and Zia Carlotta

stepping up into view. The old man had abandoned his overalls for jeans and a pressed plaid shirt, his curly silver hair framing his wrinkled sun bleached skin.

"*Ciao Bella.*" Rocco kissed her left and right cheeks. Mira drew back in time to avoid a kiss to the lips. The conversation was brief. Mira didn't feel the frost from Zia she had felt upstairs. She was sure the woman couldn't decide on whether she liked Mira or not. And soon Giovanni was distracted from his little game of meet and greet. Men in his family constantly approached. Several kissed his ring. She tried not to stare, but she couldn't help but see the mixture of fear and respect in several of their faces.

Rocco and Zia Carlotta left Mira to stand at Giovanni's side. Her gaze drifted across the room, and she saw Fabiana in a corner talking to Lorenzo. The swelling to Lorenzo's jaw and eye was ghastly. How he managed to smile at Fabiana and the other guests with all the bruising was beyond her.

"*Bella, prego.* Have something to eat. I'll come find you." Giovanni kissed her hand and walked off.

Alone. She glanced around and found herself again being stared at from every corner of the room. She walked toward the buffet. Fruit, pastries, and sliced meats and cheese were arranged in a colorful display. All she wanted was coffee.

"Looks great doesn't it?" A soft voice drifted through to the left of her.

Mira looked over to the woman she'd noticed earlier sipping on cappuccino. Gabriella had a thick accent but spoke English well enough.

"Yes, it does."

They remained next to each other in shared uncomfortable silence. "The place is decorated beautifully. I've never actually

been inside *Melanzana*. You know how Giovanni is about
bringing women here."

"Actually, I don't. I've stayed here for the past week, by his
request of course."

"Ah yes!" Gabriella exclaimed. "He brought you here to
design the wedding dress. I heard all about it."

Mira cut her eyes and didn't bother responding. She knew
Gabriella was fishing for something, and she had no intention
of giving it to her.

"Are you enjoying your stay in *Italia*?" she pressed. "How
long are you here? In *Italia* I mean."

"For as long as he likes." Mira smirked. "Excuse me."

"Of course."

Mira walked straight for Fabiana and Lorenzo.

"Hi!" Fabiana said.

"Lorenzo. How are you?"

He chuckled. "I've had better days."

Fabiana touched his arm. "He's much better than he looks."

"What happened?"

Lorenzo sipped his juice and placed it back on the table. "I
fell. Clumsy in this big ole place in the dark." Mira glanced to
Fabiana who pleaded with her eyes to drop it. She looked away.
Giovanni was with Catalina now. He had her in his arms
laughing. She considered Catalina's secret. Her fear that
Giovanni would kill his surrogate brother if their affair was ever
revealed seemed like a real danger.

Catalina held his hand. They walked across the lawn
toward the garden path. Two tents were erected for the family
but most crowded the terrace. He glanced once more to Mira
who sat at a table with Fabiana and Lorenzo. He had the boys

teach Lorenzo a lesson but forgot to remind them not to make it so damn obvious by pounding on his face. The Minettis were present. He could see Franco with his brothers laughing and talking. Franco wasn't allowed to speak to his bride, so they were kept separated, heavily monitored by *Signora* Clara, but Giovanni could see Catalina and Franco exchanging shy smiles and glancing to each other often. His father had chosen well. Franco would be a good husband for his sister.

"How are you, Catalina?" Giovanni asked her during the stroll.

"A little nervous." She rested her head in the crook of his arm, sliding her arm around his waist.

"I want to talk to you." Giovanni began. He stopped and turned her to face him. "You know I love you. *La mia principessa.*"

"I love you too, Giovanni. You have taken such good care of me since Mama and Papa died. I'm happy."

The love he had for her consumed him. She was his mother's daughter. Had her beauty, and spirit. She made his ache for his sweet Mama lessen each day. He could never let her go, and he spoiled her rotten to ensure her love for him remained unchanged. "Are you sure you're ready for this step?"

Catalina nodded. "I trust you, Giovanni. I understand why Papa wanted me to marry Franco. He's nice and I like him. This is what I want." She rose on her toes and kissed him sweetly on the lips.

Giovanni stared at her in amazement. His kid sister was a woman now. He saw it in her eyes and heard it in her voice. She was barely a teen when they lost their parents. Other than Zia, Catalina had no women in the family really willing to take her in and teach her tradition and their ways. Yet she bloomed into the *belladonna* that she was supposed to be, and he couldn't be happier. He had at least got one thing right, protecting and preserving her innocence, keeping her untouched from his world.

"Do you know that Mama and Papa would be so proud of you?" He touched her cheek.

"Yes, I do, and Papa would be proud of you too, Giovanni. You have taken care of us all, and I know it mustn't have been easy. Now it's time for you to take care of yourself. After I'm gone, I want you to start a family of your own. You love her, don't you?" she asked.

Giovanni looked past her to the dining area and thought of Mira. Looking back into his sister's eyes, "I believe I do."

"She's great. A little pushy, but I think she's great." Catalina chuckled.

"Enough about me. Today is your day. It's time I give you your wedding gift," he said. "I've also spoken to Franco, and he has accepted on your behalf."

Catalina grinned. "What is it?"

"My gift to you and him is your own villa here in Sorrento, plus your dowry will provide for him to expand his father's bottling business in Napoli. You won't be going to Palermo."

Catalina leapt at him, and he caught her in his arms. She hugged his neck tightly. *"Grazie amore di I esso!"*

Giovanni lowered her to the ground. "I couldn't let you go to Palermo if you wanted so desperately to stay." He kissed her on her cheeks. Yes, he indeed did this for selfish reasons. His anxiety lessened at the thought of keeping his sweet Catalina near, so he could protect her always.

"I am so happy!" she wept. "Does Lorenzo know? Did you tell him?"

"He knows."

"I must see him. I love you both so much!"

Before he could stop her she bolted for the terrace. Giovanni walked behind her. She found Lorenzo seated with the ladies and plopped into his lap. Hugging and squealing, it took a moment before she noticed how he winced, and the bruises on his face. Giovanni approached as she removed Lorenzo's sunglasses from his face. "Who did this?" Catalina shouted.

"It's nothing." Lorenzo said.

Catalina rose from his lap. She whirled on her brother with her bottom lip trembling. A hush fell over those gathered. "Did you see what they've done to him? Do you see? You punish who ever hurt him, Giovanni. You punish them good!" she said angrily.

"That's enough, Catalina." Zia marched over and took her by the hand. She shot Lorenzo and Giovanni a withering glare before dragging a weeping Catalina away.

"Drama Queen! That's what we called her as a *bambina*," Lorenzo chuckled and the men all laughed. Mira stared at Giovanni, and he made a point to not return her stare. Lorenzo rose.

Lorenzo kissed Fabiana. Without a word he walked off the terrace and Giovanni followed, as they circled the building they fell in step with each other. It was his cousin who spoke first.

"How can we get past this?"

"I don't trust you." Giovanni said. "I haven't heard one single reason from you why I should."

"I'm your blood, your brother."

"You're a fucking stain. The only reason why you're still breathing is out of respect for our fathers. Don't push me Lo, because I'm not stupid. It makes no sense that you would become Giuseppe's pawn against my wishes. He either has something on you or you're guilty of more than you confessed. I struggle with how to not cut your lying tongue from your mouth with every breath you take." Giovanni stopped. They were far enough from earshot.

"I fucked this up royally. I'm done with the lies, Gio. I'm standing here exposed. I respect you, the family, the honor we share. Enemies are circling. Angelo Calderone wants blood, and the Nigerians aren't going to sit back and be bystanders. You need to trust me again. I will earn it. But don't cut off my balls. I am the last of your blood. *La vostra famiglia*. Flavio is not! He will never love you like I do, protect you as I would. You can't shut me out. Not when we are destined for war."

Shaking his head sadly in response to Giovanni's silence he looked away, "It can't come to this."

"It has. After the wedding I want you out of my sight. Domi will work with you to see my plans through. But you and I, our brotherhood, it's done."

Lorenzo smirked. "So I report to Domi? He's finally got to be at your side."

"He's more loyal than you've ever been. I can trust Domi. He may be the only man I can trust."

"I have one request. I created this mess, and the men will not respect you if you just banish me. They will question your leadership. Let me get into the ranks with them and take out Calderone."

He nodded in agreement.

Lorenzo turned and walked away. Giovanni released a deep burdened sigh and headed in the opposite direction.

****

The breakfast went off with much celebration, and Giovanni gave a toast welcoming the Minettis into the family, assuring them that this union will make them all stronger. He saw little of his *Bella*. When he inquired he was told by Zia that she was upstairs working on the dress for the wedding. Soon the gathering of men drew him away. For the next three days he spent the morning and evenings dealing with family matters, and no time with her. When he arrived at night, he'd stand near the bed and watch her sleep in the dark. He would watch the way she exhaled her sweet breath and her chest rose and fell, to the delicate expansion of her small nostrils when she inhaled. Beauty, unmatched by any woman he'd ever dared to share his heart with.

In the mornings Flavio would be at his side reminding him of his responsibilities. He wouldn't even have a chance to say goodbye. Tonight his return had him aching to see her, talk to her. He only now understood how dependent he'd become on her.

Giovanni was disappointed to find her gone from the room they shared. For a brief moment panic settled in his gut, and he feared she'd left him and returned to her life. After all, he couldn't possibly think closing her store and moving her things upstairs would bind her to him. She could wake and walk away from him, and he'd be powerless to prevent it. To his relief, she hadn't done so. His men informed him that she worked on the dress still. He headed to the third level in search of her.

And it was true. She had turned that boarded off section of his home into a little design factory. Fabric rolls, shears, sewing machines and other instruments he couldn't name were all inside. Giovanni found her standing in front of the dress mannequin. It wore the most beautiful of gowns. He watched silently as she continued with hand stitches to the beaded bodice at the front of the dress. She had only one lamp on next to her, casting her in what looked like candle light. At her feet were cut pieces of cloth and a bag of beads she plucked from.

Tonight she'd chosen a red spaghetti strap slip dress that stopped mid-thigh, and was made out of a stretch material which flattered her figure. Gone were the wrap around dresses he loved. Still this one was just as sexy to him.

The sewing needle dropped. She bent at the waist to pick it up and the skirt rose, revealing more of her thighs, and her ass became a rounded sculpture of perfection.

"Amore mio."

Words he thought he said in his head were actually spoken aloud. Mira shot up right with a startled cry and looked behind her. "You're back?"

"I'm back."

"Three days, and I barely see you. Now you're back?"

He felt a pang of regret. "Forgive me."

She narrowed her eyes on him, and he entered with a sly smile. "Is that Catalina's wedding gown?" he asked approvingly.

Her anger melted on her soft features and the light of love he found in her eyes gleamed like amber colored jewels. In fact he could see her swell with pride as she stepped aside so he could see the dress in all its glory. His *bella* was talented, far more talented than he ever gave her credit for. The dress was stunning. "Do you like it?" Mira asked.

"Bellissima,"

Mira turned to the table next to him and picked up the veil. "I know you may not approve of the low neckline but I did make the veil long enough according to your customs to block her from view. I even cut the edges as instructed for good luck, per *Signora Clara*," she smiled.

"I appreciate it, *Bella*." He accepted the veil from her hand, moved closer to her, and placed it back over to her left on the table.

Mira tried to gauge if he was drunk, upset, or anything else to account for the reason she hadn't seen or spoken much to him in the past three days. He directed his blue eyes back to hers. "Are you okay?" she asked.

He reached and touched her neck then allowed his fingers to trace the curve as it connected to her shoulder, stopping at the thin strap of the dress holding her bosom up. He eased a finger under the strap and lowered it. Mira looked to her shoulder to see it slip off then back to his eyes. She said nothing but her heartbeat quickened from the look of wild, unbridled lust in his blue eyes. "I hated not seeing you these past few days." He admitted.

"Me too." She confessed.

He took a step toward her.

"Did you miss me?" he asked softly.

"Of course. Our time together isn't long. Before you disappeared I wanted to talk to tell you my news."

"Tell me now."

"I have to return to New York, then possibly Milan. After the wedding."

He put his finger to her lips silencing her. "That's not the news I wanted to hear. I wanted to hear that you decided on us, to be mine." Using his other hand he hooked another finger to the other strap, drawing it off her shoulder and her right breast was exposed to the nipple. Giovanni's brow arched. He assisted in peeling the fabric downward over the swell of her breasts. She didn't wear underwear. She had showered, put on the dress and come upstairs to finish her work.

"*Cara*, you are never far from my thoughts. Forgive me for disappearing, I wanted to be here. Don't leave to punish me."

"I'm not. It's business, can't you understand that?"

He lowered his face to her neck, running his tongue over her vein that delicately pulsed underneath her silky skin, and she tilted her head back welcoming him. Sliding his hand down her backside, he cupped her buttocks pushing her into him. Mira wrapped her right leg around his waist, feeling his strong muscular thigh press in on her achy core.

"I need to be inside you." His hands gripped her hips. She lowered her leg and tugged, yanking the dress down her curves, causing it to drift down to her feet. Again their eyes met. He advanced on her until she walked back and bumped up against the cool glass of the seal of the window. A slight shiver crept over her skin. Mira realized she was nude, and ever so vulnerable to him. She was angry dammit. He had disappeared for days and she missed him terribly. All she was left with was the highly emotional Catalina, and Fabiana who had become secretive and distracted. The wedding planning had been a stressful ordeal with her and Fabiana fumbling over offending one person of the Battaglia family then the other. And he barely blinked at her announcement of leaving. Did he not believe her, or just not care?

His forehead dropped on hers and his hands rubbed up and down her hips before lifting her to the windowsill, and only part of her rested on the edge. The kiss was soft and gentle. On command her thighs parted, and her hand sought the buckle to his belt. His lips caressed hers, her chin, her neck and then her nipple before drawing it into his mouth. With her back pressed to the window she could barely get his zipper down. Her actions and his became a bit desperate, and she freed him into her shaky hands, stroking his engorged length.

"Put me inside of you." He said in a gruff, almost desperate voice, but she kept stroking. Giovanni's head dropped back from pure pleasure. The tendons and muscles in his neck became profound and his jaw rigid with restraint. Again his cock felt like velvet over steel in her hands. She guided him to her core. Giovanni forced her legs up with both arms, and they hooked around at odd angles before he delivered a powerful thrust and entered her.

Mira steadied her breathing, listening as his became more ragged. He pushed his way deeper with thrusts strong and sure, while his piercing blue eyes once again focused on her before he parted her legs even wider and lowered them to admire their coupling. "Yes." She exclaimed, thrust after thrust, her head smacking the windowpane. She writhed against him. He remained fully dressed with his pants still drawn up. She clawed at his shoulders and her nails scraped down the silk threads of his shirt. Her thighs began to quiver and she could feel the tickle of his silky pubic hairs against her clit, drawing out the orgasm she wanted to hold back on. He showed her no mercy, rotating his hips and screwing her to the bitter end. He sucked at her neck so hard she winced. "Don't! Don't...leave a mark." She pleaded. She couldn't be paraded around his family with the love bites on display. It was hard enough to not take the constant stares and whispers when she entered a room personally.

Ignoring her he pushed both her thighs back until her

knees almost touched the windowpane and pounded his own needs into her. The intensity of his lovemaking had her fearing they'd burst through the glass as it rattled from his forceful demands, pinning her against it. Her cries for mercy increased and so did his grunting, and ragged breathing in her ear, before he covered her mouth with a deep kiss, his tongue lashing across hers. He went on for so long she marveled at his strength and self-control. His sweat dampened body had his shirt sticking to him and his face glistening with moisture.

Again his head dropped back, and together they both shuddered hard, teetering on the verge of an explosive climax. Just when she thought she could stand no more Mira felt the rush of his seed as he erupted inside of her, flowing and coating her womb with his love. He let go of her thighs, which she lowered gratefully. He withdrew and the separation tore at her heart. How much more of this could she stand? She eased off the window and avoided the satisfaction in his smirk. She found her dress and slipped it on immediately, ignoring the sticky drip of their mingled sex wetting her inner thighs.

"*Bella*, wait..."

Grabbing her robe, she went for the door fast. She didn't want to hear his seductive words and submit like some love starved twit, and she couldn't catch her breath to explain how consumed she was with him now. She just didn't care to hear any more reasoning from him as to why they fit. He caught her halfway in the hall and forced her to turn around and face him. "Wait a damn minute. I want to talk to you."

"No!" she knocked his hands away. He grabbed her by the elbows forcing her arms up and her body to remain still.

"I'm sorry for staying away. I know I invited you here, and we were to spend time together, but it couldn't be helped."

"Doesn't matter. I want to finish her dress, and then I'm leaving. And fucking me senseless won't change it."

He blinked, shocked by her abrupt manner, and then his eyes narrowed on her, tinged with rage. She didn't dare break his stare; he had to know he couldn't treat her like his whores. Her visit was his privilege not his right, dammit. She had a life that she'd repeatedly ignored since the day he discovered her bracelet and put it into her hands.

"Am I that bad you would speak to me like this?"

"I can't help it. I told you in Bellagio that I didn't like being ignored. If you had to go then would it have killed you to say goodbye? Instead of leaving me waiting for you night after night in the bed alone?"

"I said goodnight to you every night." He grunted.

She blinked confused. "You did not..." her voice trailed off. She thought one night she felt him in the room, felt his strong fingers brush her jaw. But when she woke she thought it was a dream. "I agreed to this arrangement without thinking it through."

"Because my every motive must be dissected." He scoffed.

"No, because of me, and my needs. I didn't agree to how empty I feel when you and I are apart. The way I feel about us is changing me, clouding my judgment. I missed you."

He let go of her arms and stepped back, his gaze softening. Unable to stand it any longer, she turned and walked away.

Lorenzo reached for his phone. Fabiana's arm dropped from him, but her sweet warm body curled up close. "What is it?"

"Your car, Boss," Carmine said in the receiver. "We got a repair truck to take it in and have it tuned. Did you request it?"

"Yea. Yea. Let them take it. Tell them to have it back after the wedding."

He dropped the phone and fell back on the pillows. He spent the past three insufferable days kept away from family business. His only salvation had been Fabiana. He turned his head and looked at her. She slept like an angel. Lorenzo drew her close to him. After the wedding, he'd leave *Melanzana*. If Giovanni didn't want him around, why stay? He had a condo in Sorrento where she and he could spend every morning and night under the covers.

The idea of it made his loins hard with lust. He rolled his beautiful Fabiana to her back and her long lashes fluttered open. She touched his face.

"Thank you *Cara*, for being here, for not turning from me when I told you... my truth."

He kissed her and her legs parted allowing him the pleasure to sink between her warm silky thighs. A single thrust drew his cock into such unbelievable warm tightness he shuddered. Everywhere she was soft, and curvy, and he buried his face in her scarlet red hair thrusting his devotion and love into her. She was his. The only good thing he had left. He would hold on tighter to her to keep his sanity.

****

Mira opened her eyes. Giovanni lay wrapped around her with the sheets tangled around his waist. He joined her in bed and though things remained tense between them they made love again. Nothing, not even her confused heart, could stop her body from responding when he touched her. And the man would not be denied.

"Still mad at me?" his hoarse voice croaked.

"I need to get up. It's morning, and today is your sister's big day."

"The day doesn't start until I say so," he said lifting and turning to his side. She looked away, and he drew her face back by her chin. "I am sorry that I wasted three days of our time together. Sorry I disappointed you. Coming home to you, it's how I want it. Don't go."

"I have to, Giovanni."

"Then promise me you'll come back?"

She glanced at him. His request wasn't about her leaving his bed, but her leaving him. Despite her determined will not to, she smiled and he smiled. "I promise."

"*Vabene*," he kissed her again. "So the dress is done? And my sister gets married today."

"She does. How do you feel about it?"

He put his arm behind his head and stared up at the ceiling. "Proud."

Mira hated the secret she carried. After three days with Catalina and no evidence of her straying toward her adpoted-brother, she was convinced the young girl had intended to marry and fulfill her role as wife to her new husband. Whatever past she shared with Dominic was done. So she kept her mouth shut.

"I have to shower. I need to be upstairs for her fitting."

He glanced over. "When do you plan to leave for New York?"

"In a few days. Fabiana's arranging it."

He rolled onto her. "I'm going to miss you." He said, and she dropped back on the pillow. Giovanni eased down and under the covers forcing her thighs to part. His face went to her center, and she gasped loudly once his tongue pierced and thrust deeply. She dropped her hand on the top of his head covered by the sheet and thrust her pelvis upward. Pleasure rolled through her body like an electric tide, and she rolled her ass, enjoying the soft licks and nibbles he put down there. Maybe she could delay it a bit longer.

****

Mira knocked twice before sticking her head in to check on Catalina. She found her asleep in her bed. "Morning," she whispered.

Catalina sat up.

"Today is your wedding day. How do you feel?"

"Excited," Catalina stretched up out of the covers.

"I need you to come upstairs with me so I can fit you for your dress."

The light of joy in Catalina's face made Mira smile as well.

"My brother here?"

"He is."

"You know he loves you."

The statement hit her hard. Just a week ago Catalina rolled her eyes every time Giovanni touched Mira's hand. Now she sat in the middle of the bed grinning at her.

"Where did you get that from?" Mira gave a nervous chuckle.

"He's told you, hasn't he? That's how our men are. When they feel it, they say it."

"Catalina..."

Throwing back the covers Catalina escaped the bed and approached her in her long cotton gown; Mira took note of the serious look on her face. "I know my brother. I saw how disappointed you were the past few days when he was gone.

Don't punish him for not being here. I can't explain it other than to say, you have to understand that he does this sometimes. It's about who he is."

"We're friends, Catalina, and I do understand."

"No. You're more than that now. He introduced you to our family." Catalina's eye stretched. "Do you understand what it took for him to do that? What it means?"

"Let's go try on the dress." Mira turned for the door, but Catalina got in front of her again. "He can be a stubborn man I know, but he really is a good person, a kind person too. Giovanni does a lot of good things. Don't you let anyone tell you different. He takes care of families, and he... he gives to the church, and he takes care of Lorenzo and me even when we disappoint him. He's a good man. He deserves... someone to take care of him. I will have my husband and home of my own soon. He'll be in this house with these men, and no one..." Her voice choked with emotion. "He'll be alone."

"This is between your brother and me. Our future is for us to decide, don't worry over it." Mira stroked her arm.

Catalina studied her for a moment. "It's none of my business, but you must know that my brother is a catch. All the girls want him. You met Gabriella didn't you? I saw her talk to you. She's his ex, the only one he kept returning to. We all thought he would eventually marry her. And maybe Giovanni did too, until he met you."

"I don't want to hear this."

"He dated her for three years and never brought her into our home. She attended family events outside of Sorrento with him, and she took me shopping in Paris. We went to New York together. He has given her gifts and..."

"Stop. It's none of my business."

"Bullshit!" Catalina snapped. "It is your business. These women will dig their nails into him and fight you hard to be at his side. You must stand firm in your feelings for him if it's what you want. Gabriella is spitting mad. My brother dismissed her in front of her family. Three years and she's done everything to win his heart, for nothing. He meets you for a few days and he brings you here to meet our family and me. He cares deeply for you. He sent a message. I think you're the only one here that doesn't know it."

Mira sighed. She threw her hands up. "What do you want me to say?"

"If you decide to be his girlfriend you do it with the kind of loyalty and devotion that changes how you love a man like Gio. Don't judge him harshly, and don't make him feel guilty for who he is. You become part of this life. Don't make him think you will be his if you don't intend to stay. Giovanni deserves to be happy, and if you don't want to be the one to do it, then let him know now."

Mira opened her mouth to speak and Catalina hugged her. "He really is happier now with you. I see it. He's a good man."

She hugged her tightly. "I believe you."

A few knocks before the door opened and Giovanni looked up to see Lorenzo enter. He paused from drying his hair, a towel around his waist. He stared at his cousin. The bruises over his face hadn't healed; in fact they'd darkened to purple and yellowish swelling around both eyes.

"What is it?"

"Welcome home."

"I'm in no mood. Leave."

"Gio, I haven't heard a word in three days. I know

something is going on. How bad is it?" Lorenzo closed the door.

"Where's Giuseppe's body?" Giovanni asked. The question stopped Lorenzo in his tracks. "Answer me."

"Bellagio, I drove it out of the Denelli place deep into the hamlets near the cliffs. I buried him and abandoned his car. No one will find the body."

Giovanni tossed the towel. "The old man doesn't believe his son is dead. He continues to order his men to search. Angelo however, called a meeting of several families and I was not invited. It's only a matter of time before he strikes. Without the body surfacing, I'm not sure who will align with him. I am certain that Angelo believes it to be you that killed Giuseppe."

"Then send me back to Bellagio. Fuck it, I can face Angelo. I can draw them away from the family."

"How selfless of you." Giovanni shook his head. "I've had to deal with the Nigerians. They've interceded with our deal with the Irish. Our guns are gone. Do you understand the ramifications of your actions now? The longer I delay the guns being delivered to Sicily the more incompetent we appear." Giovanni tossed the damp towel and glared. "You will stay the fuck out of my sight until after the wedding. I don't want or need your help."

Lorenzo wiped his hand down his jaw. "You can't always do it alone, Gio. You have to trust someone."

Giovanni gestured with a flick of his hand under his chin to fuck off. Lorenzo stormed out. Pacing he tried to calm himself. The guns gone, the Nigerians demanding a new deal. Things were falling apart. And he felt powerless to stop it.

The Wedding

Putting down the comb, she inspected herself in the mirror. She'd chosen to wear a green dress that wrapped sweetly around her curves and crossed over her ample bosom. She made it for the wedding, for him. Cut from a special silk fabric it flowed to the floor and parted with a tasteful split when she walked. Her hair had to be worn straight. She had no time to curl it after working out the thickness, so she trimmed her bangs and made sure they measured evenly across her brow and framed her face like that of an Egyptian goddess. Putting on the 2 ct. diamond earrings in each ear, she then reached for her jewelry box and removed the matching solitaire necklace on a thin platinum chain to put on her neck. Just then she heard the door open and looked up in the mirror to see who stepped inside.

Giovanni appeared wearing his black and white tux. His dark hair was groomed away from his face and his blue eyes had a clear crystal blue hue to them under long thick lashes. She smiled at his reflection in her mirror. The man in a tux was breathtaking. Together they made quite a pair.

Struggling to put her necklace on she communicated with her eyes, beckoning him to come closer.

"Let me help, *Bella*." He stepped behind her, and his fingers brushed her hands. Mira allowed it. Once done he scooped her hair in his hands and lifted her long mane to reveal her neck and back. "You know I love to see you in this dress, and this color," he said, gazing down at her backside. "Will you ride with me to the wedding?" he asked. "It's what I want."

She glanced up at him in the mirror. "I intended to." She turned and wrapped her arms around his neck. "You look devastatingly handsome too." A kiss brushed her lips from his, and she relaxed against his body. "Maybe you can come to New York with me?" she said.

Giovanni held her. "Come with you?"

"Yes. I have some business to attend to, and I can show you the city, the way you showed me Italy. I..." Mira bit on her bottom lip. "I don't know how long it will take before my return, and I'd miss you terribly while I'm gone."

"Then stay."

"Giovanni."

"You can conduct business here. Call in the people you need. Haven't I brought your dress making materials here?"

Mira chuckled. "I'm a business woman, a successful designer. My business is more than cutting fabric. Don't be so stubborn. When was the last time you took a vacation? Come with me, Giovanni. Let's discover what this is between us."

He ran his hands down her back, and she pressed in on his hard frame. "I already know what this is between us. *Amore.* I love you," he whispered.

She offered him another kiss; it was deep and plunging. Capturing her breath and pushing back from their passion she panted. "I love you too."

She felt him stiffen. He drew back and frowned down at her. Mira smirked and nodded that she felt the same.

"You sure? What about your time table?"

"When it's love, it's love."

"Yes, *Bella.* I'll visit New York. We'll work it out."

Mira felt the pressure in her chest lessen. She had to admit love this time wasn't as stifling to her as it was with Kei. The passion between them was real.

"*Andiamo.*" He took her hand and led her from the

bathroom. She barely had time to grab her faux emerald beaded clutch purse. They left in his chauffeured Mercedes limo. Sitting next to him, he kept running his hand over the soft feel of her skirt pushing the hem up so he could touch her inner thigh. She wore garter stockings, and when he discovered them, the lovely blue of his irises melted to a darker lustful color. Mira teased him with a wink and offered no resistance to his exploration, as she was used to him feeling her whenever they were alone. She listened as he spoke in Italian on the car phone installed in the back of the limo. Again she mentally vowed to learn Italian. The drive south of Sorrento wasn't long. The chapel, according to Giovanni, was over five hundred years old. Regal and beautiful, she stared up at it in wonder.

Dominic walked down the front steps of the church when they left their cars. Men were everywhere. When Mira looked at Dominic, she found a dull sadness reflected in his brown eyes. Maybe it was her head, because she knew of his love for his surrogate sister, but she couldn't shake the feeling that the day would be a difficult one for him. He gave her a curt nod and addressed Giovanni. "Everyone's inside Boss, I'll hang back to make sure we have no trouble."

"Nonsense, Domi. It's our girl. Our sister is marrying and you will be at my side to see her married." Giovanni released Mira's hand to kiss both of Dominic's cheeks and embrace him in a brotherly fashion.

"If it's okay with you, I'd rather make sure no one disturbs the service. It's equally important, no?"

Giovanni frowned. Mira cleared her throat and ran her hand down his back. "We should get inside. You need to see Catalina before she walks down the aisle."

Giovanni hesitated. "Something wrong I should know?"

"No, Gio. It's her day, and I want it to be perfect." Dominic forced a smile.

Giovanni patted his shoulder. He captured Mira's hand and led her up the steps.

"You will join me up front." Giovanni said to her as the doors opened and every face in the chapel turned to look upon them. There had to be over six to eight hundred people gathered. She froze. He pulled her hand, and she found the strength to walk inside. Catalina's words surfaced. This was a commitment he too was making by walking her down the purple, carpeted aisle in front of his people. There was no turning back.

Mira spoke without moving her mouth. "Are you sure?"

"Of you?" he glanced to her. "One hundred percent." He winked.

He led her to the front row, kissed her cheeks and then turned and headed back up the aisle. She exchanged a look with Fabiana who sat next to Lorenzo. Mira winced inwardly at the fading bruises to Lorenzo's face. The organist softly played a hymn. Mira noticed Fabiana had chosen to wear the yellow pleated sundress she'd bought on their shopping spree in Como. She specifically picked out a teal blue strapless dress she designed for her last year for her to wear to the wedding. Fabiana tossed her red hair and winked at her. Mira rolled her eyes in mock disgust and chuckled to herself. She loved her best friend so much.

The organist changed to the traditional tune and Mira's head lifted to see the priest appear from the front of the church draped in a long white robe with a gold cross stitched on either side of his lapel, holding a bible. He was followed by two other priests. The side door opened and Franco followed by his groomsmen appeared in single file formation. The wedding began without delay. She turned in her seat to watch the flower girls followed by the bridesmaids as the organist switched to a lovely melody. Mira nervously awaited the vision she'd seen this morning. Catalina was the most beautiful bride she's ever dressed. The priest instructed for all to rise, and Mira moved a little forward to get a better view.

Giovanni appeared with his sister on his arm. Catalina's veil completely shielded her face from view but, even covered, she captivated all in attendance. Mira beamed with pride at how beautiful the gown was that carved out the bride's tiny waist, with the sparsely beaded corset and belled out skirt draping off her hips. The skirt wasn't too poufy and the soft flowing material caused it to glide behind her in a long train that carried the same pattern. Mira had stitched delicate diamond cut patterns that could only be seen when the light caught it with each step she took. The dress, done in a satin silk blend from the hip down, gave her the elegant appearance of royalty.

When Giovanni delivered Catalina to the altar and put her hand in Franco's, Mira swore from her close proximity that his eyes watered. The priest read from the bible, blessing the passing of Catalina to her new husband, and Giovanni took a seat at Mira's side.

Franco lifted Catalina's veil, smiling into his bride's eyes. He held her hand leading her to the altar, kneeling in front of the nuptial bench to begin the matrimony sacrament. Mira took Giovanni's hand as the ceremony progressed, and he looked over at her, smiling warmly. In the midst of the vows being exchanged before her, she digested her role as his woman.

Chapter Fourteen

B LUE ROSES.
They were everywhere. Mira stepped off the veranda onto the grass, awestruck by the festive floral display. *Signora* Clara and her wedding crew had set up the reception in the back of the villa just beyond the pool. She'd taken painstaking measures to ensure the Battaglia grounds were made up like something out of a storybook.

The party planners erected a huge reception area made out of white, baby blue and yellow ribbons that crisscrossed each other several feet in the air connecting to the four pillared post, which outlined the dining area. The pillars themselves were adorned with ivy vines that housed the magnificent blue roses. The ribbon roof shielded the guests from the warm Italian sun, beaming over the blessed union. It was quite imaginative shading. The event was more enjoyable for outside weather. Underneath the makeshift roof were tables covered in white linen tablecloths trimmed in yellow and blue. The centerpieces on each were magnificent blue roses sprinkled with yellow flowers and baby's breath. The roses were what enchanted Mira most.

Several other guests greeted her politely and Mira smiled in response, trying to remember the introductions that Giovanni had made earlier. She wondered where her prince was. Standing amongst all this beauty, she craved his touch and soft whispers that told of the love they shared.

Twirling the stem of a rose between her fingers she looked back over her shoulder toward the upper level of the house. Her gaze located him staring at her from the second level balcony. The man named Flavio was at his side. He turned and continued whatever conversation they were having.

"There you are," Fabiana said from behind her.

"You just had to wear that dress." Mira chuckled.

"Lorenzo loves me in it." Fabiana laughed.

Mira cut her eyes to the heavens. "Whatever."

"Speaking of my handsome beau, have you seen him?"

"Not since you two left. Didn't you ride back to the house together?"

"Yes, but he said he wanted to talk to Giovanni."

Mira glanced back at the villa. "I guess they're upstairs."

"Wedding was nice." Fabiana nodded. "She looked beautiful. You did a good job."

"Thanks. I spoke to Giovanni about our leaving."

"Oh?" Fabiana looked away. "What did the great Don have to say? Did he try convincing you to give him more time?"

"He'll come to New York. He and I are going to see each other exclusively. It's real between us."

Fabiana's gaze swiveled back to her, and she frowned. "Are you saying you've decided to date him?"

Mira chuckled. "Isn't it obvious? We've been here for almost three weeks."

When Fabiana didn't smile, Mira stepped to her concerned. "What is it?"

"He's a bit controlling. You don't like to be controlled. Just want you to be sure of what you are getting into." Fabiana shrugged.

´"That's not it. What's going on with Lorenzo? Did he tell you who attacked him? Are things strained between him and Giovanni?"

Fabiana smiled at a couple of men who passed them and waited for the men to move out of ear shot. She nodded. "Yes. Giovanni did it. He had it done. Lorenzo disobeyed him, and that's his version of discipline."

"Not true." Mira said. She wanted to discuss Lorenzo with Giovanni, but he had disappeared for three days. When he returned, she was selfishly consumed with thoughts of her feelings for the man. Still she saw no evidence of Giovanni being a violent man and doubted he did anything to Lorenzo.

"It is, Mira. I'm sorry. I pushed for us to get involved with these men. Now I'm confused about what's going on with them. What it is we don't see and know."

"I'll talk to Giovanni."

Fabiana shrugged. "And what good will that do?"

"I'm not stupid. I think I can help. Let me try to talk to him again."

Fabiana sighed. "I'd rather you not. It's best we stay out of it. Agreed?"

Mira looked back up to the balcony the men had once stood upon and frowned. "Agreed."

****

"Angelo, *benvenuta*, thank you for coming. How is Don Calderone?" Giovanni walked off his balcony into the room and greeted Angelo Calderone with a kiss to both cheeks. The man did the same to Flavio. He had been told that Calderone was in attendance and expected the visit.

"The same. My uncle is sick with grief, but we have faith that we will find Giuseppe."

Giovanni clasped his hands together as if in prayer. He wore a sincere look of concern. "If there is anything I can do just ask."

"Today is not the day. Today is a day of celebration. Catalina has grown into a beautiful woman. *Bellisma!* The service was wonderful. I only wanted to extend my congratulations to you both. I brought gifts."

Angelo's men stepped forward with two offerings. The first a cigar box with Giovanni's favorite imports. The second was a thick envelope padded with money, both of which were accepted by Flavio.

"Have a seat." He gestured for Angelo to sit. Giovanni never took his eyes off Angelo. The formalities settled, he fumed inside at the disrespect the bastard had shown by calling a meeting within the *Cammora* and not including him. "Now, what is the news on Giuseppe?"

"We have not found the body. My uncle has his hopes, so does my aunt, but I know differently. My cousin is gone."

Giovanni lifted the lid of the cedar box and removed a long uncut cigar. He rolled the slender stick between his index finger and thumb. "I hear you had a meeting, recently."

Angelo nodded. "I'd already met with you twice. I wanted to reach out to the other families to make them aware of our search, seek their assistance."

"And I was not included in this discussion?" Giovanni asked, picking up his cigar cutter and slicing off both ends.

"It was not to insult you. I assure you. As I said we had met with you twice, and you informed me that you had no idea where my cousin was."

Giovanni leaned forward. Angelo Calderone knew better than to openly glare or challenge him in his home. Still the fucker had an air of arrogance about him that made Giovanni's trigger finger twitch. "You are to never go to the families in the *Cammora* without me at the table. I am deeply pained that you would do so and not extend me the invite. But I understand these are trying times for your family. In the future, you'd be wise not to make the same mistake."

"*Si*." Angelo nodded.

Lorenzo strolled down the hall in search of Fabiana. He stopped. Silvio Calderone stood outside of Giovanni's upstairs study. He thought he saw Angelo at the church, but he wasn't sure. He wiped his hand down his face and knew it best he turn and let the meeting proceed without him. However, his pride and fear wouldn't allow the sensibility. He approached Silvio. Carlo stepped into view. Lorenzo hadn't spoken or explained the messy matter of Giuseppe Calderone's disappearance to his best friend since he was exposed. Now his friend glared at him with open rage.

"I was told Giovanni wanted me to join them," he said.

"*Balle*. Bullshit," Carlo spat the word back at him.

"You calling me a liar?"

Carlo's brow arched in response.

Lorenzo's gaze cut to Silvio, who smirked in silence. To show the divide in their brotherhood wasn't something characteristically done by Battaglia men. Carlo felt the same sting of embarrassment because he dropped his head and shook it. "Your funeral." He grunted and turned, walking off. Lorenzo knew he had to make things right with Carlo, Renaldo, Nico and the others. But one crisis at a time.

Lorenzo opened the door and stepped inside. Giovanni glanced up, and Angelo's head turned. He entered with his gaze trained on Angelo. "Sorry I'm late," Lorenzo said, he dropped his gaze in Angelo's direction. "I wasn't aware we were meeting."

Angelo Calderone slowly rose from his chair. He leveled a murderous glare at Lorenzo, but he didn't speak. In fact no one spoke. Giovanni's expression didn't change, but he sensed his cousin was not pleased. So he cleared his throat and made a step toward Angelo Calderone. "*Salve.*" He extended his hand in a formal greeting. "Any word on your cousin?"

Angelo's gaze switched to Giovanni. "*Congratulazioni* to the Battaglia and Minetti families." He turned and walked out with his men following. Lorenzo fumed over the insult. When the door closed, he looked to Giovanni to explain his intrusion, but his cousin raised his hand.

"Was it something I said?" Lorenzo chuckled hollowly.

"*Non importa.* It's done." Giovanni waved off his comment. "If Angelo had his doubts before, he is certain of your guilt now."

"I only wanted to show a united front." Lorenzo reasoned.

Flavio shook his head in disgust. "So you come in here with that face? Angelo was here to explain the insult of not including Giovanni in the meeting in Genoa. You interrupted that discussion."

"Because we both know he wasn't here for that, Gio. He was here as a challenge. For the other families to see his brazen boldness at excluding you, accusing me, then coming to

Catalina's wedding. He's trashing us all along the coast. It is best for us to show them that we aren't cowering, and my presence means I'm not guilty."

"But you are guilty." Flavio walked around the desk. Giovanni observed them both in silence, the side of his face resting between his thumb and pointer finger. Lorenzo hated the old man. His calm reasoning voice was as toxic as a snake's bite. He secretly had more control over this family than he and Giovanni combined. Flavio was the problem, not him. "You put a bullet in a man you've been hustling with behind the family's back. You gave us no warning, and now we are on the verge of war."

Giovanni sighed. "That's enough. I'm tired of this game. I want you to find Domi and have him and Carlo go and collect Fish. We aren't waiting any longer for Angelo to strike, or the Nigerians to destroy what I've built with the Irish. We will gut Calderone from the inside out and take Genoa, the triangle, all of it. Lorenzo is right, Flavio. The time for hiding is done."

Mira clapped with the other guests as *Signora Clara* announced the bride and groom's first dance. Catalina was led to the dance floor on the arm of Franco. Minus her veil she looked like a princess plucked from a storybook. Franco spun her on the dance floor under the tent, and everyone applauded again.

A man's arms circled her waist. Mira knew instantly the tender embrace was from her Giovanni and relaxed in his hold. After the song ended, the couple stopped dancing but kissed so sweetly many cheered. "It's our time now, *Bella*," he said into her ear. Confused she looked at him questioningly as he took her hand. He began walking her to the dance floor. Mira's heart seized with panic. "No, we shouldn't. It's Catalina's moment."

"Nonsense," he said spinning her out in front of him and drawing her back. He held her close. Mira's arms lifted to circle his neck, and she kept her eyes focused on his. Every eye in and outside of the tent strained to see them, watch them

"People are staring." Mira said nervously.

"Let them." His hand slowly went up and down her back, and he held her closer. Mira sighed and closed her eyes, resting the side of her face against his chest. God, she could get used to this feeling.

Her hips moved erotically slow against his. They floated across the floor. Others in the family began to join them on the dance floor, and soon they were in the center of swaying couples. All of it felt right.

Giovanni lifted his face from the inside of her neck and rubbed his lips against hers. She smiled, parting them as his tongue inched inside. It twirled and pushed in deeper. Long after the song ended, they kissed. Until the explosive sounds of applauding broke the trance. Mira looked around to see that the family was clapping for them. She wiped her lipstick from his lips.

"My turn, Giovanni," Uncle Rocco said tapping Giovanni on the shoulder.

Mira's eyes grew wide. Giovanni laughed softly. "Listen, old man, you be careful where you put your hands. *Capisci*?" He let her go before she could object.

Uncle Rocco, barely five foot four, grabbed her in his arms and buried his face in between her breasts, rocking from side to side. Mira, shocked, could do nothing but hold him in return. She rocked with him as other's snapped pictures. Giovanni stood off to the side with his men. He winked at her.

Laughter erupted among the crowd when the slow tune turned to a fast paced one, and Rocco began to show Mira his moves. This woman was definitely one he could see a future with. He was certain of it now. He would have to think of a way to delay her leaving for New York until he could take her. Turning from the tent he looked up to see Dominic in the shadows, observing. Giovanni frowned with concern. Dominic approached.

"We have put in a call to Fish. I should hear from him soon."

"You okay?"

"*Si*." Dominic said, his gaze then shifting over to Catalina. Giovanni recognized the hurt and pain in his brother's eyes. He too felt bitterness over letting her go off into life without his protective influence. She was another man's wife and as such Giovanni had to see her as a woman, not the little girl that he adored.

"I understand your feelings, Domi."

"*Che*?" Dominic said.

"We're losing her." Giovanni nodded in the general direction of Catalina. "She's no longer our girl. A married woman, soon to be a mother possibly."

"She looks so beautiful today." Dominic said. "Like an angel."

Giovanni felt his chest swell with pride. "Papa would be proud of her, and Mama too. I want you to stay close to her, make sure she settles into married life. Make sure she doesn't need anything."

Dominic shook his head. "Gio, get someone else for the job."

"Why?" Giovanni looked down at him. "What is it?"

"I'm needed at your side. You've elevated my position remember?"

Giovanni let go a gust of laughter. He smacked Dominic on the back. "Of course. Put someone on it. Just take care of our girl."

Dominic's gaze shifted back to a laughing Catalina who was seated on her husband's lap. She looked up and blew them both a kiss. Dominic sighed and turned to walk away. "I'll see to it."

****

After seeing Catalina off with her new husband to their honeymoon in Greece, Mira found herself alone.

"*Ciao, Bella*," Giovanni said as his arms slipped around her waist. She relaxed into him and closed her eyes. "Take a walk with me." She turned in his arms and kissed him. They walked off down the side of the villa along a slender path through flowers and trees. The staff began taking down the festive decorations, and a few family members posed and snapped pictures with each other. The sun had set, and the large full moon hung high in the sky, lighting the path.

"These roses are everywhere. So beautiful," she said, his hand in hers as they walked down the trail.

"Did you know that seventy percent of the buds are imported from Kenya, Africa?"

Mira lifted the rose to her nose, intoxicated by its scent. "Really?"

"It's cheaper for breeders to cultivate them there. Actually they pretty much have the market cornered on the blue rose." he said walking over to her taking the delicate flower from her hand. Mira watched as he snapped the stem, flinching from the destruction of perfection, but understanding when he then placed it behind her right ear.

"My mother loved roses, but the blue rose was her favorite. Once my father discovered this he made sure they were planted everywhere she lived. Mira listened attentively while he made sure the rose fit perfectly inside of her dark locks. Once done he brought her long tresses forward over her shoulder, looking into her face adoringly.

"*L'azzurro è aumentato*. It is just like any other rose. It has petals, thorns, leaves, and a stem. It blooms and it dies like any flower would. But the rose is different, isn't it *Bella*?" he said lifting her chin with his index finger causing her to tilt her head slightly. "Because its beauty is beyond compare. Make no mistake, *Bella*, it's not your physical beauty that has me spellbound. It's your sweetness. It separates you from all the rest."

"I've never known a man like you."

"*Ti Amo*," he said and kissed her.

Chapter Fifteen

M IRA WALKED INSIDE. Rather she floated now after the day she'd had with the Battaglias. Even when alone, she found herself constantly smiling. She suffered a dull ache of desire at the thought of the night he promised her. She agreed to let him handle some business affairs and to pack a bag. Where they were headed, she didn't know. However, he made it quite clear what he intended to do once he had her alone.

A sly smile tugged the corner of her mouth.

"Signorina?" A voice said behind her. He cleared his throat in a resonant way, and she paused. A very distinguished man with stern grey eyes stepped into view. "Flavio Pricci. I work for Giovanni," he said politely, touching his silk tie and smoothing it flat to his chest. He wore a dark grey suit with a black shirt and tie. He had the most compelling grey eyes.

"Ciao Flavio. Yes. I met you a few days ago."

"Can we share a cup of cappuccino, talk?" he gestured to the open parlor that faced the back of the estate. Mira glanced inside. A staff member had prepared a tray and was setting things in order. It appeared Flavio had been waiting for her.

The challenge in his unwavering stare made it impossible to refuse.

"Sure," she said.

"*Prego...*" he nodded for her to take the lead. She felt his melting grey eyes tracking her as she passed him by. Rooms like this one were everywhere on the lower floor. Walls of windows that were pushed open to allow a constant cool breeze, and comfortable furnishings sparsely placed. Mira took a seat on a whicker sofa with large plush peach pillows and waited for him to join her. There was a remote detached feel to his manner when he did. As if this was a business meeting and not the casual conversation she expected. The young man in all white who had set up the cappuccino left without being instructed to and closed the door behind him. This too she noticed since no doors were closed on the lower level. She traveled from one room to the next uninhibited.

"Lovely ceremony today." Mira said.

Flavio stared at her for a pause then gave her a perfunctory nod. "The Battaglias are a close family, very respected. Catalina's wedding had to be special. I hear thanks to you it was."

"I don't follow?" Mira frowned.

"The dress. Quite lovely work."

Mira hadn't realized that Flavio knew she made the dress. How involved was he in the details of the family, and why did he stare at her so critically? She reached for her cup and added some sugar to ease her discomfort. "So you work for Giovanni?"

"I've been with the family for many years. His father and I were close—associates. I worked for him and now I do the same service for Giovanni."

"As? If I'm not being too forward in asking."

"Attorney, consultant, advisor."

"Oh." She sipped the coffee. The hot dark liquid seared her tongue, but she ignored it. The sting was enough to sharpen her senses. She felt the need to be alert around him.

"I'm curious about you, Mira," Flavio crossed his left leg over his right. "I've read how well you've done with your business in Milano. You are quite accomplished now that you've launched your clothes here, more so than in the States. Forgive my limited English. I don't want to sound rude."

"Go on?" Mira said curiously.

"Why are you here? Shouldn't you be attending to that business?"

"I beg your pardon?"

"The nature of your relationship with Gio? Friendship? Lovers? Exactly how long do you intend to stay?"

"That's none of your business." Mira frowned.

Flavio sighed. "Unfortunately, it is my business. Everything about Giovanni Battaglia is my business. That is who I am. If you haven't seen by now, then I suspect you have guessed he is very important to this family. I assumed his fondness with you would pass, but he's distracted. I have you to thank for this."

"How dare you? Giovanni is a grown man, and I'm his friend. He invited me here, and he and I will decide how long I stay. If he's distracted from your business, then you need to take that up with him."

"You know *what* he is. Don't you?" Flavio's smoky grey glare narrowed and she felt chilled by the malicious darkness she could see in his stare.

"What he is, is a good man, a friend..."

Flavio smirked.

Her voice faltered. Mira considered walking out on the

conversation. The air of authority Flavio exuded kept her seated. However, he would not intimidate her. First Catalina shares what it is to be a girlfriend to a Mafia boss in hope she'd stay. Now she had this man seeking to run her off. It was a wonder Giovanni had any normalcy in his life at all. "Of course you know. Or you think you know. I want to clear up the mystery for you."

"No thank you." Mira stood. "I think I'll go find Giovanni and tell him about this conversation." She walked toward the door.

"Pity your store had to close. I hear it's why you've had some of your things moved in here." Flavio reached for his coffee.

Mira stopped and looked down at him. "Yes, Giovanni was quite generous."

"Generous?" Flavio chuckled. "That's an interesting word. Don't you find it strange that the very building he wanted unobstructed access to has been closed twice without any legal documentation? On the word of some inspector who could speak no English?"

"How do you know about that?"

"It's my point, Mira. I know everything. It's you *Cara* that has been kept in the dark."

The news weighed her to the spot. Giovanni setting her up hurt, but for him to pull this off would mean that Fabiana played a part in the deception too. "You're lying," she said.

"Am I? Are you sure? Have you spoken to your attorneys, your solicitor, anyone outside of these walls since you arrived? The building meets code, it always has. You can return to it as soon as you like. I suggest, you open your eyes and realize this is not a world you belong in."

She opened the door to walk out, seething with rage.

"*Signorina Mira.*" Flavio called after her. She stopped and glanced back at him. He still sat with his back to her sipping his cappuccino. "I wouldn't confront Giovanni with what you know. After all you do know what kind of man he is."

Mira left the bastard. Her heart hammered in her chest. How could Fabiana do this? Why?

Lorenzo paced. Angry, ashamed, and bitter he ignored the murderous glare Carlo fixed on him. He had no time to deal with the rift between them. He and Carlo kept no secrets, but this thing with Calderone he had done solo. He knew his friend was hurt and confused by his actions. All of it would have to wait. Angelo Calderone had a bullet with his name on it, and he itched to pull the trigger to unleash it. How dare he come to their home on Catalina's wedding day and disrespect his family this way? How dare he? He paced more. They'd been waiting for an eternity. He was on edge.

"Where's Domi?" Lorenzo checked his watch.

Carlo twirled the toothpick in his mouth but didn't answer. Nico and the others sat around in silence. They all watched him. The door opened and more of the top *capus* in the family entered. Dominic wasn't among them. He was now underboss, so he should be leading the troops to the General. It burned Lorenzo's guts that Dominic had details Lorenzo felt he should rightfully know.

"Is it true?" Carlo asked.

Lorenzo paused. He looked up at his friend. "Is what true?"

"That all this time you were Giuseppe's cowardly *puttana!*"

"*Vaffanculo!*" Lorenzo seethed, his teeth clenched.

Carlo chuckled and a few others did as well, furthering his

humiliation. He took a step toward Carlo, and his friend rose from his lean against the wall. The dark malevolent smile spreading across Carlo's lips indicated he thirsted for the fight. Giovanni and Dominic entered the room and both paused at the rigid stance of both men. The others fell silent.

Giovanni's gaze volleyed between Carlo and Lorenzo. Both men backed away. He turned his attention to Dominic. "Where's Flavio?"

"He should be here shortly."

"Find him now. Everyone needs to hear what I have to say."

"We need to talk!" Mira took hold of Fabiana's arm. She dragged her from what appeared to be a polite conversation between Fabiana, Aurora, and a few other women in the Battaglia family. She marched toward the only door available to them, the double stone and wood carved ones that led out of the front of the estate. Battaglia family members were saying their goodbyes and loading up in their cars.

"What on earth is wrong with you? Ow! That hurts!" Fabiana backed away on the gravel circular drive with a look of confused intolerance on her face. Mira struggled with her anger. She was caught between tears and outright rage. She marched down the front steps and Fabiana backed away. The few men outside around the parked cars all stared at them.

"You lied to me didn't you? Didn't you? You've been lying to me for weeks!"

"What are you talking about?"

"Never, ever would I believe you would do something like this. Which is probably why it was so easy to feed me this bullshit."

"Would you calm down and tell me what has you so crazy

right now? What have I done?"

"Did you or did you not conspire with Giovanni and Lorenzo to convince me that the Italian Republic had my store closed?"

Fabiana's eyes stretched. "Who told you that?"

"Answer me dammit! It was all a lie. Was that man who came here an officer of the courts or just some clown in a suit? What did Giovanni give you to sell us out of our business so he could get access to those cellars? What? Did my fucking him become part of the deal too?"

"Stop." Fabiana shouted, she looked around at the others watching then stepped in close to Mira. She spoke with a lowered but exact manner that made Mira a bit wary too. "Don't say another word. We can't have this conversation out here. People are watching. Do you understand me?"

Mira summoned control, but the angry disappointment caused tears to fall. Fabiana spun and looked around at those watching. She marched to one car to yank open the door then another, but most if not all were locked. Ahead was a tow truck, on the back of it a shiny sports car that was dropped from its platform. Fabiana grabbed Mira's hand and dragged her to the car. The men looked a bit confused when Fabiana began to speak to them in an angry loud manner. They exchanged looks, unsure of her request. Fabiana snatched the keys from one and opened the door. "Get in, Mira, now."

"Where are we going?" Mira demanded.

"Get the hell in so we can talk. In private."

Mira got in the car, and Fabiana slammed the door then walked around the car and got in on the other side. The men stood outside observing. The younger one eventually signed whatever paperwork before him and walked off.

"I want to explain."

Mira dropped her head back and sighed. "I'm such an idiot. This man was playing me from day one. He told me he wanted that store, and I just fell in bed with him, believed his bullshit." She glanced over. "Why Fabiana? Why lie to me?"

"I didn't know the first time the store was closed that Giovanni Battaglia ordered it. That he tricked us when he did the favor for reopening it. I really thought they were trying to help us. I swear that to you."

Mira exhaled a pained breath. "That's right. It was a lie from the beginning."

"Things got complicated. We were given a lease that put us between two very powerful families. The Sicilian businessman I told you about, Mancini, he wasn't supposed to give us that building. Lorenzo explained it to me. It's *Cammora* territory and it's used for... for things you don't want to know. They couldn't let us stay in there and conduct business."

"Business. So you know their business now?" Mira asked.

Fabiana burst into tears. "I'm sorry. Okay? I should have told you. I felt like shit. I only did this because we were in the middle. To not do what they wanted just wasn't an option."

"Why would we care about what they want? What is it you aren't telling me?"

"Lorenzo has killed a man."

As if struck Mira drew back, the right side of her body pressed to the door, "What?"

"A man named Giuseppe Calderone. He confessed it to me. He killed a man and now he's in trouble with a very powerful Mafia family and his own. I've been trying to help him."

"How the hell could you? How deep are you in this?"

"We're in this. Trust me Giovanni Battaglia is far worse

than Lorenzo, Mira. Whatever Lorenzo has done, it comes down to those cellars and the deliveries they take in and out of them from the Amalfi coast. He's not going to tell me the dirty details but you can put it together. We can't have people that work for us in that kind of danger. I... I had to do something, that kept it contained. To remove us from it altogether."

"Then why not come to me? Why let me think this man cares about me when he was just using me? For Christ's sake, I moved my things in here. We shouldn't be here!"

Fabiana shook her head sadly. "I love Lorenzo. That's why. And you already said you've fallen for Giovanni."

"Stop it!"

"It's true! I love him. And I think he loves me. It's how they are. Secrecy and lies is who they are. When you said we should leave for New York I figured it would be best, especially since we now have to go. Lorenzo told me this morning that things here are going to get intense. So it's time to go." Fabiana nodded, wiping at her tears. "I figured I wouldn't have to tell you all of this. Let them work through their shit, and we could see them outside of this world. Maybe..."

"Stop it. You did this for Lorenzo. Plain and simple. And now that you know he's killed someone you're in danger too. Do you think that man is going to let you walk out of here with that knowledge? He didn't tell you that secret without some motives. He sure as hell isn't going to let you in and out of his life with that kind of information. You put us in the middle of this and now we're in so deep neither of us will be able to walk away." Mira put her hand to her forehead. "Want to know what scares me?"

Fabiana's teary gaze slipped to her.

"I think you knew from day one what they were into. I

think you brought us here on purpose." Mira closed her eyes. "Trapped here with them is exactly where you want us to be."

Giovanni laid it all out for everyone. Sharing with his men his failures was not an easy task. Flavio arrived half way through his announcement. Even the old man couldn't counsel him against what he was to do next. "We're closing in ranks. Collect every dime that's owed. The gambling houses in Naples are to close as well. Be prepared for anything. Angelo Calderone hasn't made the first move so..."

"We have to." Carlo nodded. "We know what this is."

"Do you?" Giovanni said. "Because every one of our business interests is to be heavily armed. The Calderones like to firebomb, and plant bombs. It's how they strike."

"Boss? *Scusi?*"

The men parted to reveal the young one who had entered. Carmine was only eighteen, and a protégé of Carlo's. He'd seen the boy around a few times. Carlo's face deepened into a red angry scowl. He appeared incensed over his arrival. Only high-ranking men in the family were to attend this meeting.

"There's trouble." Carmine said, to the men glaring at him.

"Trouble? What kind of trouble?" Giovanni asked, sitting upright from his slouch in his chair.

"The women. They're out front—fighting."

Lorenzo looked up from the chair he was seated in and his eyes met with Giovanni's. Carlo threw his hands up and began cursing, shoving the kid toward the door. The other men laughed.

"Wait!" Giovanni ordered. "Let him finish. What women?"

"Your women." Carmine said, pointing to him and Lorenzo. "They're fighting inside your Ferrari," he leveled his finger now at Lorenzo.

"My car is in with the mechanic." Lorenzo said.

"It was brought back. I signed for it." Carmine said.

Lorenzo shook his head. "No, that's not possible. I spoke to Gino and he said it would be weeks before he could look at it..."

Giovanni frowned. Lorenzo glanced to him with a confused furrow to his brow. Without a word they both bolted out of the room.

"How could you say that to me?"

"From day one you knew what Lorenzo was. Didn't you?"

"I suspected but—."

"You knew! And when he offered to dig in to our affairs you rejected it. Why did you change your mind? A wink, a kiss, what the hell made you think dealing with him wouldn't lead us here?"

"Mira, please, don't be angry with me. I made a call, a bad call..."

Mira's hand shot up to silence her. She then wiped the tears from her face. "We're leaving, now. I don't care what the hell your motives are for helping him, and betraying me. We'll deal with it in New York. I'm getting you the hell out of here before something bad happens. Now dammit!" she opened the car door and tossed angry words back at Fabiana. "I can't trust you. When we get back to the States I don't want you managing Mirabella's business affairs anymore."

"What?" Fabiana gasped.

"I know you're a partner, and we'll work it out, but if you could do this to us, it means I don't know you at all."

"I love you." Fabiana pleaded. "I made a mistake."

"Bullshit. You knew exactly what you were doing. It's time I start taking control, hell for both our sakes." Mira got out of the car and slammed the door. She began to walk away but her legs felt like she had anklets carved out of lead strapped to them. She was possibly too harsh, too quick to judge, but dammit lies weren't a part of their friendship. She glanced back hoping her friend was behind her. Fabiana remained in the car. Her head pressed to the steering wheel as she wept. Mira lost her conviction at the sight of her pain. Fabiana was in trouble. Lorenzo confessed to murdering someone, and she was helping him, how? Was she going as far as to cover it up?

Dammit. In all her anger she hadn't truly digested what her friend told her. "Fabiana!" she said about to approach the car. Loud shots erupted behind her. Confused, Mira's head turned to see Giovanni and Lorenzo running full speed out of the villa toward her. Mira froze, not sure of why they were coming after her, she panicked. *Was it because she knew about what Lorenzo had done?*

She turned and started to run toward the car away from the men in pursuit of her when a bright flash exploded in front of her face, a hot white light that blinded and rendered her deaf by its force. Her body felt as if it were on fire. In a wave of heat she was airborne for what felt like an eternity. She sailed backward then crashed hard. Darkness.

They didn't have to speak a word to each other. They knew. *They knew!* Giovanni and Lorenzo ran through the house shoving family members and staff out of the way. The men were behind them, still they couldn't run faster, and they both tried. They nearly crashed through the door together. Outside in the sunlight the cars were parked in an intricate arrangement making his head spin. Precious moments ticked by before his sweeping gaze located her. Mira was walking toward Lorenzo's car. He yelled her name. He shouted for her to get away from the car, but didn't realize he did so in Italian. Her head turned. In that brief moment of recognition, he thought he saw fear in her pretty eyes. He yelled again, with Lorenzo yelling for Fabiana. His *Bella* shocked him by running away from him. He chased after her but it was too late. The car exploded. She was thrown across the lot and landed hard on her back. The explosion knocked them all on their asses. The roof and hood of the car shot through the air, caught in a bright orange and reddish yellow fireball. Every window of every car in his drive was blown out and shards of glass rained on them. Giovanni, stunned, struggled to rise on his hands and knees. He could hear Lorenzo's groaning at his side. His head lifted, and he noticed Mira lying still on her back, just four feet in front of him.

He literally crawled to her as Lorenzo called out for Fabiana over and over. Men running with extinguishers rushed the car. Something was wrong with his hearing. It made all sounds a bit muffled at first, and then the noise level skyrocketed sending a piercing pain through his skull. One of his men shouted that the other woman was in the car. His cousin ran for the fire, and they had to tackle him to the ground. He yelled Fabiana's name over and over.

Giovanni reached Mira. Her eyes were closed, her face red and swollen, her lip bleeding and blood spilled from one of her nostrils. The sight of her sent a shock wave of guilt and grief through him. "*Bambina, Mirabella,* wake... wake..." Giovanni shook her hard. She didn't budge. He gathered her in his arms and pressed her face to his chest shouting for help.

"Now, Gio! Take her in now!" Flavio yelled at him. He

hadn't realized that Flavio had spoken to him. Apparently several were trying to take her from his arms and carry her inside. He clung to her desperately, confused. "Listen to me. There may be more bombs, get her inside! Now!"

With the help of another, he managed to rise, and then hold her steady in his arms. He carried her inside past family and others. The women inside of his home were wailing and hugging each other. Several ran over, wanting to take her from him.

"Stay the fuck back!" he yelled at them all, staggering toward the stairs. Eventually a few others swarmed him, and they helped him carry her up and into his room. He had taken a nasty fall as well. The back of his head pounded. She didn't move. She didn't speak. Her stillness was his madness. He pressed his ear to her chest and listened for her heart. He heard the faint beating and nearly wept in relief.

"The *dottore* is on his way," Flavio said.

"Fabiana? She dead?" Giovanni asked.

"Yes. Lorenzo drew his weapon outside. He nearly shot one of the boys. They have him restrained in *Villa Rosso*. The *carabineri* and *polizia di stato* will all be here soon. We have minutes."

Giovanni swayed and one of his uncles steadied him. "Who? Angelo? The Nigerians? Who?"

"Dominic's on it. Not sure."

He looked back at Mira. "She alive? Is she alive?" he shouted at his aunt who was checking her. Her heartbeat was so faint he feared it had stopped altogether with how still she remained. The old woman stepped back from the bed saying a prayer. He returned to Mira's side. He kissed her brow, her lips, but still she didn't respond. He put his head to her chest and checked for life again. She was strong, very strong. "She's going to be fine," he said to himself. "I heard her heartbeat. She's going to recover." Giovanni said in a shaky voice.

"Gio?"

"She hit her head, that's all. She's going to be fine."

"We need to talk." Flavio said sternly. "You need to be out of the villa. Now."

"Maybe I should get ice for her head...what do you think Flavio? Ice to stop the swelling? Her face isn't burned, it's just... the blast just hit her hard. Where is the blood from? Is it a head injury? Does that make you bleed from the nose? I don't see any cuts..."

He grabbed Giovanni by the shoulders. "We took a hit. Here. In *Melanzana*. You need to get to *Villa Rosso* with the men and let me handle things. Now. Before the place is filled with the *polizia* and we are unable to act. Go."

"I'm not leaving her!" he roared back, tears glistening in his eyes. "I won't!"

"I'll stay."

"Get the fuck out of my way!"

"Go, Gio. Take care of the family, and I'll stay with her until the *dottore* comes. We'll send for you."

"That fat fucker Don Calderone is to be brought to me on his knees! Oh there will be war, a war like they've never seen, and every man or woman that bears the name Calderone will spill blood over what happened here today." Giovanni stood. He shook off his shock and focused.

Flavio nodded in agreement.

"I can't leave her. She needs to see me first when she opens her eyes. I have to tell her that her friend... shit, shit, I can't leave her yet. What the fuck am I going to tell her about her friend?"

"She doesn't belong here, Gio, surely you can see that."

Giovanni looked at him. "What are you saying?"

"When she's well, she needs to return to America."

"No. They know who she is. She's safest with me."

Flavio sighed. "Giovanni she's an American. Her friend is a well-known American. Soon the press will get a hold of this. We don't have long before the world is at our door. She has to go. She doesn't understand our ways. And even greater still, you can't do the things necessary if you are consumed with holding on to her."

Giovanni looked back toward Mira. "I will protect her. She needs me now. We will get through this together."

"I've seen this before, Gio. Your father. Don't you recall the stories of his obsession with your mother, the war in the families when Evelyn's father went to Don Chicoli for revenge? How many men, men in your family, our family have lost their lives because of Tomosino's obsession? You can't make the mistake he did. She doesn't belong here."

He had to consider Flavio's warning. Things would become far worse, and life with him now would risk her own. Still he couldn't part with her. Not when her world was ripped apart. She needed him and he needed her.

Mira gasped, her chest heaving, lungs expanding as she took in a deep breath. She exhaled, coughed and sucked down air. Her head hurt so bad tears slipped from her eyes. Someone was at her side. He spoke to her but his voice was muffled, distant. He touched her, and it burned. *What had happened? What the hell happened?*

"*Mira, bambina, Mirabella!*"

She couldn't think, nothing surfaced but the pain in her head, shoulders, back and the hot feel of her skin.

"She's not responding. Where the hell is the *dottore?*" the muffled voice bellowed. It was a man's voice. She blinked and her vision remained a haze of light and shadows. Sweet merciful God was she dead, dying? The person touched her face and she winced. It felt as if a layer of her skin had been peeled away.

"*Bella...* please, look at me."

The kind blue-violet eyes of Giovanni loomed, and suddenly she felt such unbelievable relief. *It was a dream!* Just a stupid dream. He became clearer and horror settled in. His disheveled appearance jarred her. Black soot was smeared on his face, and his tuxedo shirt was marred with dirt that looked to be mixed with blood. Dread engulfed her, and her cloudy memory cleared to remind her of the bitter truth. *Fabiana and she argued. Her friend was in trouble. She cried. She needed her and she left her. Then...*

"Fabiana!" Mira screamed. "Fabiana!"

He drew her into his arms, and her face was buried into his chest. She clung to him certain that her fear was unfounded. Fabiana had gotten out of the car and was okay. Did she see her get out of the car? *Yes! Yes! She was sure she saw her. Didn't she?*

"Fabiana. Fabiana. Fabiana. Fabiana." She choked out in her sobs. "No!" she hit at him trying to break free. "No!" she struggled and bucked on the sheets until he pinned her down. Another person was at the bed. He spoke fast and hurriedly in Italian. People were all around her. She looked at Giovanni horrified. "Get away from me! You're trying to kill me! Don't let him kill me. Please! Please! Get away!"

The other man removed a needle. Giovanni shouted at him in Italian. They were going to kill her. Just as they killed Fabiana. They wanted her dead. "Let me go! Murderer! Murderer! Murderer!"

Pinned to the bed she screamed until she was breathless. Tears flowed and the sting of a needle inserted into her arm released a hot serum in her veins. Immediately the numbing daze she found herself in when she woke returned. Everything faded including the voices until there was darkness.

Giovanni looked down at her in disbelief. *She was afraid of him? She called him a murderer?*

"She's in shock. I need you to leave while I examine her." The doctor said.

"Take her to the *ospedale*, Gio." Zia said, at his side. "Take her now. She isn't well."

"No. I won't. It's not safe." Giovanni paced, combing his hand back through his hair constantly. "Not until I know for sure what... what happened here, and by who."

"Let me examine her. We can determine how bad it is. I gave her something to calm her. She'll rest."

Before the drug claimed her, her eyes lifted under heavy lids and she looked into his. For a moment there was clarity. It was soon replaced by sadness, regret, and fear. He was right. She was afraid of him. He saw it when she ran for the car, and he heard it in her voice as she shouted he was a murderer. Her long lashes fluttered under her sinking lids and shut. Giovanni leaned in and kissed her bruised, chapped lips. His tears mixed with those now glistening on her puffy red cheeks. He exhaled the deepest sigh of sadness and said a silent prayer that she found a sliver of peace in the tranquilized sleep. It took an inner strength he could barely claim to draw away from her bed. Flavio followed him out.

Lorenzo slumped forward in the chair with his head bowed. Funny, how hysteria could shift from the darkest depths of grief to full on rage. His gaze lifted, but his head didn't. He tracked Carlo with a steely glare. The boys had relieved him of his gun and knife, but if a man got close enough, any man, he'd snap the motherfucker's neck. Only Carlo dared be alone with him when he was in this state. Carlo kept pacing in front of him, ready, in case he charged him again. They fought in the room until both of them had bloody noses and knuckles. Lorenzo spat blood on the floor and mumbled curses. He wanted to fight again. Nico and Renaldo waited outside of the door ready to charge in if things between he and his best friend got worse. And they would. He'd make them all pay for caging him like some wild bull. He deserved justice. He deserved... shit! His head dropped lower, and he wept. Fabiana was dead. His beautiful girl, gone, and he'd only had her for such a short time.

I killed her. I did it. My Fabiana is gone.

The doors opened with Giovanni and Flavio stepping through. Lorenzo sat up from his lean and blinked away tears. He smeared the blood and snot from his nose and mouth with the back of his hand across his face and fixed his gaze on his cousin. Giovanni's tuxedo shirt was covered in sweat, soot, and traces of blood. Blood. He fixated on the blood, then looked down to the back of his hand and stared at the red blood. Red like Fabiana's hair. Did his woman's body disintegrate in the explosion? Had she suffered? Were pieces of her blown apart before she knew what happened?

Dominic arrived. His voice broke the tense silence that had fallen over the men. It drew Lorenzo from the trance he'd fallen into. "Flavio, the *carabineri* wants to meet. I told them Giovanni required medical attention from the *dottore* and could not be interviewed. They are currently interviewing our men and the few family members I selected. Rocco is among them, and Uncle Vito."

"I'll take care of it. Don't join us." Flavio ordered.

Giovanni went to the shelves of wine bottles in the room. He grabbed one and removed the cork with his teeth. He then paced with the bottle in his hand, never taking a sip. Flavio nodded to Dominic who watched him go and closed the door behind him. Lorenzo closed his eyes and tried to see Fabiana, remember her. She was so vivid in his mind he half expected her to walk into the room. He felt dead inside.

"*Porca puttana!* A bomb? They planted a bomb in my fucking home!" Giovanni grimaced.

"I spoke to Carmine. The delivery of the car was by one of Marcello's men, they've been known to do work for Gino at times. It was a hit within the *Cammora*, the Marcellos are on the side of Angelo Calderone. The Nigerians couldn't gain this kind of alliance so soon. It has to be Angelo, and from the looks of it he planned the bombing to happen after his visit today."

Lorenzo wiped his hand down his face and accepted the news he already believed. "How did she die?" his voice croaked.

"The bomb was for you." Dominic continued. "The women were outside arguing. No one is sure why but Fabiana approached Carmine for the keys and insisted he give her access to your car. She said you okayed it."

Lorenzo shook his head that he hadn't.

Dominic nodded. "The argument continued in the car. At

some point Mira left the car, but Fabiana remained. One of the boys says he heard the engine turn over right before the explosion. She had to have ignited the bomb when she started the car."

A thunderous crash exploded in the room. Lorenzo glanced over to see the bottle Giovanni had carried was now smashed to smithereens after colliding with the crimson stained wall. His cousin was on edge too. But no one knew the depths of his pain. His Fabiana was dead and it was as if he'd set a match to her himself. Giovanni ran his hand through his hair that now hung over his brow into his face. He then looked at his cousin and processed the shared hell they found themselves trapped in.

Lorenzo rose slowly.

Giovanni's vision narrowed and only Lorenzo remained in his sight. "This is the price you pay for betraying our brotherhood, for allowing snakes into our garden."

"I accept it. I only ask that you grant me one thing. Revenge. I want to do Angelo Calderone myself."

Dominic threw up his hands and stepped between them. "Wait. We have to first meet with the families. We still have friends in the *Cammora*."

"No! No fucking meetings! Did you not see what happened to her?" Lorenzo shouted at Dominic. He returned his gaze to Giovanni. "There isn't enough of her left to bury. I would gladly die for what has been done to her, but I want justice, revenge!" he choked out.

Giovanni nodded. "Go! Dig up Giuseppe's stinking corpse and deliver the rot to his mother's doorstep. Get that bitch Fish is fond of and send him a message as well."

"There is time to fix this, Gio, to find a way to resolve it peacefully." Dominic said. "Hear Flavio's plan first, a meeting with the families for justice. Let the collective decide, and we will know who our allies are."

"Do as I said. I will make calls to our friends to get you all the manpower you need. I don't need a fucking meeting to know who our friends are. We'll have war, but not the one Angelo thinks. And we'll deal with the Nigerians too."

Nico and Carlo grunted their agreement. They walked out with Lorenzo.

"Lorenzo is wrong. We don't need vengeance when we're so close to legitimizing this family. I know I speak out of turn and Flavio is your *consigliere* but I think..."

"However I run this fucking family I decide who lives or dies! Not the fucking Calderones! I decide what is just and unjust! Not you or Flavio! None of you are to question me! Lorenzo has paid a price for his sins; he lost his woman today. My *Bella* lost her best friend. They will have vengeance. Angelo is going to die slow for daring to come into my fucking home and challenge me!" Giovanni grabbed a chair and threw it at the wall. "I want them dead. I want everything breathing with the name Calderone dead!"

Dominic turned and walked out.

Giovanni struggled to capture a breath. He staggered over to his desk and sat down on it so consumed with rage his chest felt like a pretzel knot. After a knock on the door, he collected his composure and Dominic escorted the doctor in.

"How is she?"

"Resting."

"How is she?"

"Nothing internal. She has some bruising from the

explosion. Her skin will be raw, but she'll heal. I'm leaving this." The doctor passed over some pills. "She is to take one every eight hours, and no more than three a day. They can be addictive. She's in shock."

"*Grazie.*"

Dominic nodded to Giovanni and walked the doctor out. Giovanni stared at the pill bottle in his hand. After minutes of guilt and grief, he gave in to his desperation to see her. He left his outside villa and entered the house from the back once more to not be seen. As the doctor stated, she rested under blankets. His aunts were by her bed. One read from the bible to her.

"Leave," he said.

The women rose and one by one they came to him offering kisses of encouragement before granting his wish and leaving him with her. Giovanni closed and locked the door. He stepped out of his loafers and walked over to the bed. Easing under the covers with her gently he drew her into his arms and held her against his chest. Her screams and terror overwhelmed him with guilt. He held her tighter than he should and her limp response tore at his gut, burned away his pride. He felt himself on the verge of a meltdown. He came close, too close, to losing this woman. If he had any doubts before they were now gone, she belonged in his heart.

The tears didn't come, but the self-loathing and doubt did. He needed to make this right, restore order, win her trust and love and keep it. How the hell could he do it all in succession?

****

Two hours later

Mira opened her eyes. She now laid on her side with Giovanni's arm draped across her middle and his warm body nearly covering her from behind. She felt so small and helpless in his hold. To move would wake him and she didn't want that. She didn't want to face him or hear his apologies. She didn't want to listen to him explain how he would make this up to her. What she wanted was her friend.

Unable to cry anymore she remained still looking toward the wall. She could hear Fabiana's pleas for forgiveness and the bitter refusal she gave her. If she had listened, forgiven, then Fabiana would have left the car too and they would have walked out of Italy together. Her stomach cramped from the unyielding churn of her grief. She should have never gotten involved with a violent man like him. Now, no matter how she felt for him, they would always have Fabiana's death between them.

The cramping became worse. It wasn't grief. It was whatever poison they gave her to make her submit. She shifted in his arms, and he sat upright.

"*Bella?*"

"Don't call me that," her voice croaked hoarsely.

"Are you in pain? Do you need anything?"

She pressed her quivering lips together and squeezed her eyes shut to block the sound of his voice from her head and heart.

"*Cara*, my beautiful *Cara*. Please. Talk to me."

Opening her eyes she turned. Giovanni only loosened his hold enough for her to turn and look into his face. "Let me go. I want to... to go."

"No." He dropped his forehead to hers.

Mira wept and he kissed her tears.

"What do you want from me, Giovanni? You've taken my heart!"

"Don't push me away."

"I can't be here, anymore!" She moaned.

"You can if you trust me."

"She's dead. Do you understand that I lost the only family I have today? She's my best friend, my only friend, she's dead!"

"I understand."

"Then help me. Let me go back to America! I won't tell anybody what I know. I swear it."

He lifted and stared down at her with a hard, inquisitive look that made her stomach muscles quiver.

"What is it you think you know, *Bella*? You called me a murderer. Why?"

She shoved at him and rolled away from him. She cried into her pillow. When he touched her back, she shivered and his hand drew away.

He hated the sounds of her tears, and no matter how desperate he felt he couldn't comfort her. Giovanni sat up. "I'm not leaving you, Mira, and you're not leaving me."

"Go away!" she shouted. He pulled her back over, pinning her to him so she couldn't run from him. "Cry *Bella*, scream and shout. You should be angry and I promise you the people who hurt Fabiana will pay for what they robbed you of." He kissed her eyelids until they closed.

Mira turned her face away. "Pay? What the hell does that mean! You're going to murder somebody too!"

"Too? Murder? That is the second time you call me a

murderer. I did not want the death of your friend!"

"Don't pretend you aren't a murderer! Lorenzo is a murderer! I know all about it. It's why Fabiana died isn't it? Because of murder!"

Giovanni couldn't capture a breath to speak. "What was it you and Fabiana discussed? Why were you arguing?"

"Let me go!"

"*Bella,* answer me. What do you think you know?"

"That you don't love me, you only wanted to use me to get to whatever you needed from my building. That Lorenzo murdered a man named Giuseppe and asked Fabiana to help him cover it up. She was scared. It was the only way she agreed to do what he wanted, what you wanted. You manipulated us both and now my friend is DEAD! Murderer!"

He let her go. She turned away from him again crying hard into her pillow. Stunned he couldn't bring himself to comfort her. He rose from the bed and walked out.

****

"You did well." Flavio said to Dominic breaking his train of thoughts.

"Giovanni did not want this meeting. He won't be happy."

"A face to face with *Don di Petro* was necessary. Giovanni is currently distracted by that woman."

"We have to worry about the press now. How we tell the story of this American woman's death. We've bought some time with talk of peace."

"It was just talk." Dominic scoffed. "Right now Lorenzo and Carlo are on their way to Bellagio to dig up Giuseppe Calderone."

Flavio smirked. "Let them. There will be no war. We can

say Lorenzo acted outside of the family, which he has, many times before. When the Calderones come for his head, they will have it."

Dominic frowned, "Giovanni would never allow it. Neither would I. He's our brother!"

"He's a fuck up. *Imbroglione!* He will destroy this family. It is up to us to make sure he does not."

"I won't betray Gio and Lorenzo."

Flavio sighed in the back of the limo. "That's not what I'm saying. If we bring Giovanni peace and the triangle on a silver platter he will see that war is too costly. Lorenzo's fate is his own. He acts outside of the family then he must survive the same way. It's how it's done. He took an oath and pissed on it when he went behind Giovanni's back to deal in business with Giuseppe Calderone."

"Being *consigliere* doesn't make you boss, Flavio. Giovanni is the boss of this family, and I would think you should remember that."

Flavio gave a half smile and continued to look straight ahead as they rocked in the back of the limo. "I don't want to be boss. My job is tougher than his. And yes it's unfortunate that the Fabiana woman died. It will be messy to handle with the authorities. That is the price we pay for the life we choose." Flavio said hollowly. "You would be wise to remember everything you've seen today. *Love* is a luxury that men like ourselves can't afford. It makes you weak."

"Bullshit, how are we to have sons if we don't have women."

Flavio chuckled. "By all means take a bride. I love pussy too. Just never love her more than you love the family. Even Lo understands this. Do you think he gives a shit that the red-haired woman is dead, or is he angrier over the insult? Giovanni, is too much like his father, his downfall will be the love of a woman. Tomosino fell for a red-haired Irish woman that had no place in our world. And his son?" Flavio scoffed in disgust. "That woman should have never been brought here."

Dominic fully understood the reasoning Flavio used and it was one of the reasons why he let Catalina go. She was in his heart, a part of his soul, but their love was forbidden. Blood or not she was his surrogate sister, and the lines they crossed would stain his soul. He could go forward without another love. Falling for Catalina had made him weak. Had cost her her innocence and robbed her new husband the right to be her first lover. His shame burned deep. Men like them were not to be in love.

"The Nigerians. Giovanni thinks we're arranging the meeting. We are. We have. I've set it up for a small inn near Mt. Vesuvius. You will accompany him."

"Where will you be?" Dominic asked.

Flavio didn't answer. Dominic didn't question him further.
****

Mira listened to him shower. He had returned only ten minutes after she hurled the must hurtful accusations at him. And the worst of it was he denied nothing. She glanced over to the food he had brought up. A plate stacked with leftovers from the wedding, including cakes and pies. She cut her gaze away. Her heart ached. It was a physical pain that left her weak and disoriented. When he walked out of the shower, he seemed surprised to see her sitting up.

He had changed clothes. Was he leaving? Good. Go. She didn't need him. Still her heart raced at warp speed over the thought of being left alone.

"I won't be gone long," he said as if reading her thoughts. "One meeting and I'll be here, with you."

She eased the covers aside, and stood with her hands clenched into fists. "Go. Go and never come back!"

A slow smile lifted the corner of his mouth. "You're feeling better. Giving me orders."

She charged at him, flew across the room. He watched her and caught her arms by the wrists. She struggled to break loose, but he held her with little effort, staring down at her. Finally she gave up the struggle and she was able to snatch her wrists free. She glared. Standing on her own two feet she swayed a bit but the nausea passed.

"Lie down. Eat. Gather your strength, and then we will talk."

She opened her mouth to insult him again, but the soft look of love and concern stalled her thoughts. Defeated, she heaved a sigh. Her gaze again switched to the tray of food. Her stomach clenched with hunger, and her mouth watered. He started to button his shirt, but he didn't take his eyes off her. Even when she looked away, she felt the heat in his stare. He had no intentions of letting her go, and it dawned on her she had nothing to go to. Her condo in New York was one she shared with Fabiana. To return there alone would be devastating. And Italy had not yet become home. Odd as it sounded this room, his bed, all of it felt like home. Her gaze lifted and she took a step back, but his touch to the side of her face stopped her retreat.

"You are feeling better. Aren't you? Shall we talk now?"

She nodded.

"I love you," he said. She shook her head in disbelief, but the words didn't come. He smiled and kissed her gently on the lips. "I never lied to you about my feelings."

"Why... why did you use us? Bring us here?"

He sighed. "I was weak. I didn't want to let you go. I should have in Bellagio, but I couldn't."

"I was weak too. I knew what you were, what you did. Fabiana and I both knew. I shouldn't have trusted this thing with us. I just... I couldn't help it."

"We are the same. Weak. Lovers. Friends?" He nodded.

She went over to him stiffly and his arms opened naturally to welcome her. She held to him. Despite it all, she loved him, needed him. His embrace felt as if she was cradled in his arms. It covered her with warmth and security. She would believe the lies if she could just hold on to this feeling. Finally, since the nightmare began, she felt as if she could breathe. They didn't speak. There were no words. She just needed to feel that what they shared wasn't going to evaporate, too.

He stroked her back.

She rubbed the side of her face against his chest.

He kissed the top of her head and held her.

"Please forgive me, *Bella*. Can you try?"

She nodded that she would. Her head went back, and she managed to look him in the eye.

He kissed her brow. "Flavio will be here to see after you. I promise not to be long. I swear it. And then I will take you from here."

"She's dead... don't leave me. I can't... I can't be alone right now."

He lifted her in his arms, and she held to his neck. He walked away from the bed to the large sofa chair and lowered into it awkwardly while holding her. Mira curled up on his lap. She buried her face in his neck and inhaled the strong woodsy cologne on his skin and felt safe in his strong arms. She'd never been so afraid of herself and someone else in her life. When she was with him, she was weak. She should blame him, try to escape him, but now all she wanted was for him to remain with her. "I don't know if I can ever leave this room, without you, I can't take it. Life without her, I can't. I'm not strong enough."

He didn't answer. They sat in silence for a long comfortable time. He just held her and protected her. Soon the drugs in her system made the lethargy return. Her head felt heavy. She felt as if she was weightless and knew he was returning her to bed.

"Don't.... go. No more. Don't do it."

"Rest. I'm not what you think I am. I promise to come back."

"Don't!" she grabbed his arm and clawed at him trying to hook her hand around his neck to bring him down in bed with her. "Don't! They'll kill you too. That's what they want right? To kill us all? Right? It's how it works."

"*Bella...*"

"Dammit! Dammit! Dammit!" she beat her fist against his chest. He pinned her down to the bed. She screamed out of frustration. He had no choice but to come into bed with her. To bring her into his arms and hold her. She relaxed and settled into his embrace. Tears streamed but the panic in her chest lessened.

"Stay," she said as she began to drift.

"I'm here. I'm not leaving you."

The last of her strength slipped and she eased back into sleep.

****

Mira woke from a touch to her shoulder. "Giovanni?"

Confused she blinked twice to see the face clearly. Flavio stood over her bed. His face was stern, almost a scowl. His grey eyes were polarizing. Surprised, she scooted away drawing the sheet up close to her.

"*Signorina,* you will need to get dressed. Now."

"Why are you in here? Get out."

"I have unfortunate news."

"Is it Giovanni?" She sat upright. "Is he hurt?"

"He sent me. You have to leave. You aren't safe here."

"What? He said he wouldn't leave me. Where is he?"

"Gone. You must get dressed while you still can. Take what you can, and we will send your things. There is a plane waiting for you in Napoli."

"You're a damn liar!! He wouldn't break up with me through you! Not after my friend died today, not after... everything. He wouldn't!" she shouted at him.

Flavio yanked the coverlet off her, and she swung and hit him in his face with her fist. The rage in his eyes made her quickly scoot away, almost scramble. She got out on the other side of the bed ready to defend herself if it came to it.

He sneered at her. "*Puttana*! He doesn't care for you or that tramp who died today. You put on clothes and be ready to leave now or I'll drag you out of here as you are."

"NO! Giovanni!" Mira ran for the door. Flavio had to have anticipated her actions because he caught her and dragged her back from it. The door opened and a young man looked in, shocked. Flavio shouted something to him in Italian, and the young man closed the door. He then grabbed her by the throat and slammed her against the shut door. Mira blinked from the force of his actions and the dull ache that cut through her skull.

"Listen to me. Run, scream, make this difficult in any way and I will shut you up. Permanently!"

Mira shook her head sadly at him. Flavio let her go, and she gasped for air, moving quickly out his reach, her hand to her throat. He yanked open the door and stormed out of the room. Putting her hands to her face, she cried once more.

****

The caravan of cars that moved along the country road began to slow down as all the vehicles one by one extinguished their lights. Giovanni clenched and unclenched his fist staring out into the night. His heart hammered in his chest, his throat felt dry as sandpaper, and his eyes watered from the constant strain of not blinking. "Where are the Nigerians?" he asked.

"They will be here." Dominic ended the call. "We just need to wait."

"And *Don di Petro's* men?" Giovanni's gaze swept the forested trees. The single road that drove up to the inn was free of cars. If the Don had sent his men they would be on foot, in the dark, and ready with his men.

"They're out there." He ended the phone call he was on and set the receiver back in the phone box situated in the middle of a leather console between the men. "Carlo confirms that Giuseppe's rotting corpse was delivered to the Don's wife."

"*Bene.*" Still Giovanni couldn't relax. He needed to get back to his *Bella*, to be there when she woke again. He remembered her holding him, how she pleaded for him not to go. Right now she was confused, the *dottore* said it was shock. Giovanni knew it was far worse. He suffered the same grief after watching his father gunned down in front of him. That kind of pain changes a person. He would do everything in his power to take the pain and fear from his *Bella's* heart.

"Gio, there's something you should know."

"What is it?" he mumbled, and continued to stare out of the window.

"While you were tending to your woman, Flavio and I paid *Don di Petro* a visit on your behalf."

Giovanni's gaze swung to Dominic. "I said there would be no meeting. I made a call to the Don."

"And we paid a visit to ensure that he would adhere to your request. In exchange we vowed there would be no war between the *Cammora* and *Ndgrangheta.*"

Dominic now commanded Giovanni's undivided attention. He specifically gave an order. Why would his *consigliere* and under boss both defy it so openly? "Are you saying you went against my wishes?"

Dominic nodded. "Flavio is convinced that peace is the best way and that you are distracted. He also believes it's because of your woman, the American."

"Well you both are wrong. And I will deal with Flavio when I return."

"He's going to sacrifice Lorenzo. I think he's going to counsel you to cut him loose. With him in Genoa now dumping Giuseppe's body, I'm worried it might be a trap."

Giovanni cut his eyes back to the window. He'd deal with Flavio, Lorenzo, all of it later. One fuck up at a time. Six cars arrived in the night. The bastards who dared interfere with his product from the Irish were filing in one after another. Several got out of their cars. A cold dark wave of satisfaction moved over Giovanni. He leaned forward and squinted, counting the men present. The one named Enu emerged last. Dominic made sure to point him out to Giovanni. Even under the silver glow of the moon, he could see they were armed.

The doors to the inn opened and three men from Giovanni's family walked out. They spoke to the Nigerians who didn't understand the greeting. And then it happened. Men from every direction of the forest stepped out firing, as did the men on the front steps of the inn. Bullet spray and cannon blasts from all the guns firing at once reminded him of a fireworks display. It only took three minutes for the Nigerians to lie dead in the streets. He relaxed in his seat and Dominic told the driver to take them down out of the valley to the inn.

"I want to see Flavio, now."

****

Mira struggled to process her grief, anger, and heartbreak over a single thought. She had her purse and passport but not much else. Each time she tried to put clothes in a bag she broke down in tears. Finally giving up she went out of the room with a guard on her heels heading to Fabiana's room. Opening the door she immediately smelled her perfume. Mira covered her mouth as the image of Fabiana standing in front of her wearing that damn yellow dress she hated, twirling around tauntingly, came into view then faded.

Laughter surfaced as she recalled Fabiana teasing her about the dress. For years she put her best friend in her best designs, and the day of her death she wore that monstrosity. The humor drained from Mira's lips. She glanced around the room at Fabiana's things. Seeing her cosmetic bag open on top of the vanity, she smiled weakly. Going over she stuck her hand inside, moving around the multiple lipsticks and glosses. She was reminded of how Fabiana fussed over her makeup and hair whenever they had a show. "You always kept us together," she mumbled.

Flavio stepped into the room behind her. She could feel his presence. "The car is ready for you."

Mira looked over at him, "I want her things sent to me, and her body, if there is a body," she said weakly.

"Of course, I'll contact you shortly after you land to arrange it. The press has made calls. They are trying to reach you for a comment." He stood under the door glaring at her. "We will discuss how you will share with the world this unfortunate accident."

Mira picked up Fabiana's purse, stepping away from the vanity. Dressed now in jeans and a t-shirt with a bruised face and heart, she nodded in agreement with Flavio's demands. She cared nothing about her appearance and only wanted to get away from this place and the heartache she felt over Giovanni using his attack dog on her. For abandoning her.

Fish had backed his Vespa up a hill under the dense cover of trees outside of the Battaglia villa. Even the patrols were not able to see him from this distance. He scanned the front of the estate with night binoculars. The American woman that they learned was staying at the compound was escorted into a car. Smiling he lowered the binoculars. Angelo anticipated that Giovanni would send the other bitch to America after the botched attempt to kill Lorenzo blew up the redhead. It was Fish's mission to follow and take her out. This he did willingly. They made a big mistake taking Maria. Neither he nor Angelo could agree on much, but Maria's life and safety was one of the few.

He'd blow up the fucking universe to have her back.

Fish started his Vespa. He bristled at the low rumble the bike made. Hopefully no one was close enough to hear. He put up his binoculars and removed his gun just in case. He wanted to kill the Battaglia bitch Catalina and her new husband. Angelo was against it. Taking out Lorenzo Battaglia was a gem Fish had to agree was far better. Now the women presented an even greater opportunity. Apparently they were well known in America. The deaths of them both would bring plenty unwanted media attention to the Battaglias and cripple the family's prestige in the Republic. Breaking them from within would then make the families in the *Cammora* loyal to Calderone. Yes. This was a better plan.

****

Giovanni stepped out of the car. The air was tinged with sulfur and the bitter smell of blood. The men had shredded the Nigerians and most of them were unrecognizable bloody heaps. However Enu, the leader, lie on his back very much alive. He wheezed with a chest full of holes. How the fucker remained alive was a mystery. Giovanni glanced up at Dominic and his underboss nodded. He removed his piece and fired directly into the man's skull ending the man once and for all.

****

Mira fastened her seatbelt and reclined back in her airplane seat. Flavio had been specific. Fabiana died in a terrible fireworks accident behind the walls of Melanzana. The explosion came after the celebratory party for seeing Catalina off to her honeymoon. A ridiculous story she was sure she could never adhere to, but nonetheless she agreed. In fact the

Italian media had already reported Flavio's version of events and the press in the United States were running with it.

This was all she was left with. The sweet promises she and Giovanni had made to each other had evaporated. Three weeks and her life was in shambles. The plane began to taxi down the runway, and she closed her eyes. Maybe when this was all over he'd come back to her. Maybe he'd leave this madness behind and come for her. Bursting into tears she shook her head sadly. The truth was there were no maybes. This was the end.

Chapter Seventeen

G IOVANNI HURRIED UP THE STEPS of *Melanzana*. He'd check on Mira first then summon Flavio to *Villa Rosso*.

"Gio." Flavio called out to him as he raced up the stairs to his bedroom, to her. He paused and looked down. Flavio stood at the base of the stairwell, staring up. "She's not there."

"Who?"

"The woman, Mira, she's gone."

"Gone? What does this mean, gone? How can she be gone?" He stalked back down the steps.

"After you left, she made a call to her American friends. She threatened the family, you, with exposing the truth about Lorenzo and Fabiana. She insisted we take her to the airport, put her on a plane. I had little time to react. She left me no choice."

"I told you she was not to leave here!" He collared Flavio. "You gave her my jet?" He shook Flavio hard. His men grabbed at his arms but his rage would not be restrained. "Are you lying to me old man? She's barely five-foot five and a hundred and twenty pounds. How could she be a threat? Who gave her a fucking phone?"

"I'm not lying son. Call the plane if she will speak to you. I swear it."

Giovanni's nostrils flared. He battled with indecision. He shoved Flavio and looked to Dominic who stood off silently watching. Something didn't feel right. She could barely stand without weeping. Now she was a gladiator, fighting to get home. It made no sense. "Call the pilot, have him turn the fucking plane around! Now!"

"Wait!" Flavio said holding his throat. "This might not be a bad thing. Think of it. She goes home, and she is safe. We have sent our men after Catalina and Franco to make sure they are safe. You still have Angelo and the Calderones to deal with. They've bombed *Melanzana* once. They could return, do worse. At least this way you keep her safe."

"I hear that I don't know how to do anything anymore without your counsel?"

Flavio frowned.

"You making deals behind my back. Bartering peace? Sacrificing my blood to save this family without my consent?" Giovanni shouted.

"Angelo Calderone is actually more of a threat than we conceived. He has friends in the *Cammora*. We need to stay strong with our alliances. Show that we are the ones wronged; make sure if blood is to be shed it's out of necessity not blind vengeance. That's the sign of a strong leader."

"You didn't answer my question."

Flavio glanced back to Dominic then to him. "I only made sure that the night went off without an issue. Are the Nigerians dead?"

Giovanni wiped his hand down his face. "Fuck all of this.

Get the plane back now." He turned and stormed out to the back of the villa. He'd go outside and deal with the rest of this mess from *Villa Rosso*, after he got a call to his *Bella* to convince her to return to him.

Mira requested to use the in-flight phone on the jet. She knew Giovanni had one. When she dialed the numbers her fingers trembled so bad she had to keep breathing deep breaths to still her nerves. The phone rang and Kei answered immediately.

"Hello?"

"Kei?" she said, her voice weak, small.

"Mira? Mira what the fuck is going on? It's on the news. They say Fabiana is dead, and no one knows details. Are you alright? Where the hell are you now?"

"She's dead, Kei," Mira wept. "She was... it was an accident."

"What kind of accident? Where are you?"

"On my way home. I didn't know who else to call."

"Calm down, babe. I'll be there when you land. You can tell me about it. We'll figure it out."

Mira wept. "She's dead. Fabiana's gone."

"Can you tell me what happened? How did this happen?"

Mira thought of Flavio's warning. "An accident."

"Damn. Damn it. I'm sorry babe. So very sorry. We'll figure it out. Just hold on."

"I'm trying."

****

Giovanni frowned. The phone on the plane was busy. Mira had to be on it. Who could she be talking to? He put his face in his hands consumed with bitter resentment that she would leave him and go home. It was indeed his fault, but still he had hoped that she had some faith in him.

"Can I come in?" Flavio asked.

He reclined in his chair. "Did you reach the pilot?"

"No. I couldn't get through."

"Me either. I tried to call the plane three fucking times, and the line is busy."

"I wanted to speak to you about Calderone. We need to be sure of our next move."

There was little he cared to discuss on it. The day had completely drained him physically and emotionally. "What we need is sleep. I can't keep going like this." He rose exhausted. "Maybe she's right, and she needs to be free of this madness. Have you made sure Catalina is safe?"

Flavio nodded. Giovanni thought he saw relief in the old man's face. He understood. The more irrational he became, the harder it would be to stay focused and keep from making big mistakes. "Get her home number. She should be landing in..." he drew back his sleeve. "Six hours. I will take a shower and get some sleep. Make sure Lorenzo and the men are all here by morning."

"We will handle it."

****

It was after nine at night when she landed. Exhausted, Mira went through customs and the airport in a daze. If Kei hadn't seen her, she would have walked right past him. It felt so good to be with someone familiar, someone she could trust. Kei held her until she felt semi-normal and coherent. Thankfully he didn't question her. She had little strength to filter all that she'd been through. Lying about Fabiana's death to him was hard; maintaining the lie when she desperately needed someone to talk to would be impossible.

And Giovanni? Her thoughts were never far from him. Yes, he had manipulated her, but he had also changed her. Kei's driver waited outside of the terminal, and once in the car she rested in his embrace. "I'm tired." She mumbled.

"We will go to my place in Brooklyn."

"No. I still have my condo in Manhattan. Take me there. Please."

"Sweetheart the press is all over this. You don't want to go there."

Mira closed her eyes and sighed. "Okay."

****

Giovanni woke and immediately reached for the phone. Dominic had located an American number he believed to be for an answering service of Mira's. Flavio had left for the evening, promising to return in the morning. Though he was furious with the old man for having a meeting behind his back and allowing Mira to escape, he respected Flavio and his advice. He refused to believe either was done maliciously.

He listened to the rings and an automated voice instructing him to leave a message. "*Bella...* it's me," Giovanni sighed weakly. "I know you're angry *Cara*, and I... I know it's my fault. I shouldn't have left you alone. You needed me and I wasn't here. I understand. I can't be without you, *Bella*. I need... I don't want to be cut off from you. Things are... difficult. I will fix it. I will come for you. Forgive me. *Ti amo.* Call me..." He left his number and ended the call.

Dropping back on his pillow, he stared up at the ceiling and thought of her. The last time she smiled for him. He remembered the smell of her skin, her passion, the feel of her body, the soft laugh she'd give him no matter how serious he became. Flashes of memories with her spanned more happiness than he'd ever experienced with a woman. And their time was short. It was decided. As soon as it could be arranged he was going after her. He'd win her back. He would propose. It could be a long engagement, but he would do it and prove to her that he wanted a future with her. It couldn't change what she lost, but hopefully it would heal them. Maybe.

After a rapping on his door, it opened. Dominic stuck his head inside. Giovanni squinted at him. He threw his legs over the side of the bed and dropped his face in his hands. He needed to get up and out of bed. It was time. "Lorenzo and Carlo back?" Giovanni asked.

"Si. They are in *Villa Rosso* waiting for you."

"Time? What time is it?"

"Eleven."

Giovanni couldn't believe the time. He had slept well past what he intended.

"Can I have a word? There's something you should know."

Giovanni sighed. His head pounded from the back to the front of his skull. All he wanted was a shot of espresso and a good cigar to get his body under control. Not morning news of more bullshit. "Can it wait? I need a minute."

"It's about your woman."

Giovanni's face lifted from his palms. He leveled his eyes on Dominic. "Mira? What about her?"

"After Flavio left last night I met with our men." Dominic

walked to the center of the room. "The version of events he shared with you isn't the truth according to them."

He rose. "Go on."

"There was an argument. Her screams could be heard on the lower level. Carmine hurried to her room to see about her and discovered Flavio there. She didn't demand to go. She was forced to leave. Flavio told him to stay out of it."

Giovanni listened silently.

"He then dragged her from the villa in tears. She was barely allowed to take her things. Carmine tells me she asked to speak to you repeatedly."

Giovanni walked over to his closet. He threw the doors open. Her dresses hung on the hangers and her suitcases were pushed to the back of the closet. He went to the drawers and saw her undergarments in place. There had been no packing. If he hadn't been so full of guilt and loneliness for her he would have noticed these things last night. Sucking down deep breaths he now understood what the old man had done. "FLAVIO!!!" he yelled.

****

"I'm sorry you couldn't return to your condo," Kei said setting a fragrant cup of black tea in front of her. She glanced up at him. Kei was still strikingly handsome, even in his Princeton t-shirt and long shorts he looked like a dream. Tall, athletic, he had long blue-black hair that he wore combed back from his face and bound in a leather band at his nape. His deep olive skin and magnetic dark eyes made his features appear to be more Native American than Chinese. And when he wore a suit, his quiet, yet serious nature commanded such an air of authority most women, gay or straight, stopped to look his way.

Suddenly she saw the similarities between Kei and Giovanni. Both men were powerful, respected, complicated, and controlling. Both men overwhelmed her with their desires and needed to possess her. And with both men she felt lost yet protected in ways that frightened her. Why did she constantly gravitate to these kinds of men?

His touch was different than Giovanni's. He cupped the side of her face with a bit of hesitation. Mira understood. Their parting words had been strong. He accused her of not knowing true love. She accused him of only wanting to control the woman he loved. Now she was back with him, and again she was falling into the routine of being his.

"Does it hurt? Your face." He asked.

"No. Not anymore. I must look a sight." She lowered her gaze. Kei lifted her chin with his finger hooked beneath. Her gaze was forced to lift and meet his.

"You've never looked more beautiful to me, Mira. I've missed you." He leaned forward and kissed her forehead, then lowered his face and tried to kiss her lips. She turned away from the kiss, and instead he pressed his lips to her cheek tenderly.

"The reporters are everywhere. Even at my office. You're safe here." Kei drew back the chair and sat down. "I need your permission to handle your answering service. To get my assistant involved to screen your calls and take care of them. They are leaving messages at all of your offices. Your staff is overwhelmed."

"Fabiana handled the press. She would know what to do." Mira said hollowly, staring down at her tea.

Kei stroked her hand. "Let me put my people on it. We'll deal with it. Make sure the story sticks."

Blinking out of her stupor, she looked up at Kei curiously. "Sticks?"

"I know Fabiana didn't die in a fireworks accident. At least not the one you told me. It was a bomb. Wasn't it? At the Battaglia's?"

"How did you..."

"You and Fabiana have been seen in Bellagio with the Battaglias." He put the STAR magazine on the table. She glanced down to a picture of her at the *villa Melzi*, an image of them walking hand in hand with her skirt hem ruined by the water she'd fallen into. She blinked in disbelief.

"Sweetheart, you're an even bigger celebrity now after your show in Milan. You have the biggest fashion runway show of your career and then disappear. Of course they were looking for you. How far did things go with this man?"

"I don't want to talk about Giovanni with you." She picked up her tea and sipped it.

"I made some calls when you were gone, to learn more about the Battaglias. I have friends in Italy too, Mira."

"Let it go," she sighed.

"He's a criminal. A powerfully dangerous man. What were you and Fabiana thinking?"

"Stop it!" she shouted.

Kei sat back with a scowl on his face. She never raised her voice to him in anger. He never raised his voice in anger to her. It was not the nature of their relationship. Arguing with him was always a discussion. No matter how passionately they felt about something, they found a way to talk to each other. Right now she wanted to throw her tea in his face. She wanted to scream and kick until all the pain in her chest lessened.

"You should have never gotten involved with them."

"Don't you think I know that?" she asked calmly. "My best friend is dead. I saw her die in a car explosion." She looked up to Kei. "It got out of hand, out of control. I don't know who or what to blame anymore. Fabiana's dead, and I feel that way inside."

Kei nodded. "You aren't dead, and I intend to make sure it stays that way."

"He wouldn't hurt me." Mira looked away. "In a few days, he and I will talk and..."

"No." Kei said firmly. "The man is in the middle of a very nasty Mafia war according to my contacts."

"Your contacts? Since when do you have contacts?"

"Mira, I've always had them."

She stared at him and believed him. She'd seen Kei's friends and the ones he never introduced by name. She just chose to ignore it, as she had with Giovanni.

"Your associations with Giovanni Battaglia have to end, for your own safety."

He loved her. That part had been real. She believed it. But he cut her lose, and at first she thought it was for him, now she was beginning to believe he did it for her.

Kei took her hand and helped her rise. He wrapped his arms around her. "We're in this together, from now on."

****

Fish hated many things but America topped the list. It was a noisy confusing place. People were always in a hurry. The women looked like men, and the men looked like women. A fucking wasteland of over indulgence. He sat behind the wheel of his rental car with a map spread across the steering wheel.

He was told to park here, under the bridge and wait. He'd waited for over an hour. Could he have been wrong about the location? Fish crumbled the map and grimaced. It was all bullshit! He needed to get in and out of this country fast. He had no time to deal with the Americans to make his business happen.

A passenger van drove up. Two men jumped out of the back, one in a black and white sweat suit with a thick neck and fat jaws walked toward him. Was this the cousin of Angelo Calderone? The man opened the door and got in.

"We have everything," he said in Italian not bothering with introductions. Fish glanced to the van and watched the men start to unload the products he needed to create the explosives.

"The bitch you want has a condo in Manhattan. Reporters are all over it right now, might be tricky so we got you this."

The man had a bag with him, a shopping bag. He showed Fish some kind of uniform. "You'll go in as a maintenance worker to do the job. My boys are going to work on getting you a badge for the building. From there you can come and go without issue."

Fish removed a padded envelope from the glove compartment and passed it to the man. He then got out of the car and popped the truck. He didn't need any help. He'd set the explosive and be home to Maria before they could find all of her body.

****

Mira stepped out of the bathroom and turned off the light. She was surprised that Kei kept some of her clothes there. She had a t-shirt and pajama shorts in his drawer. Did he think she was coming back to him? When she padded out into the loft she saw him standing near one of his windows sipping his tea. He turned and looked back at her. "Better?"

"I need my things."

"Call Angelique. I have an idea." Kei set his cup down.

"What kind of idea?" Mira walked towards Kei, and he threw his hand up to tell her not to. She glanced to the window and stepped back. A news van had found them. He was certain they wouldn't look here. "Go upstairs. Let me handle the reporter. Call Angelique. Okay?"

She nodded and went for the stairs. Kei watched her. He winked. She smiled and climbed the stairs, hurrying to his room to avoid being seen.

****

Only Dominic joined him. He wasn't ready to see the men. Word had been sent that Flavio had to meet with some of their friends in the Republic to address their concerns. The delay in Flavio's return made Giovanni's rage hot and fiery in his chest. He drank to keep a cool head.

Dominic rose and opened a cabinet. He then picked up a remote and turned on the television. Giovanni barely responded until he heard an American broadcaster. He glanced to the screen. The runway show was on. Mira's fashion show. The scene switched to Mira and Fabiana being interviewed, then to Fabiana alone speaking to the press. A running tab beneath announced her death in a fireworks accident along the Amalfi coast.

"This is Flavio's work?" Giovanni asked.

"He's cleaning it up." Dominic confirmed.

"Cleaning up." Giovanni scoffed. "He thinks he's Don. I've given him too much power and he's turned on me."

"I believe he did this for you."

Giovanni cut his gaze to Dominic. "Is that what you believe?"

"Flavio has always done what is needed for the greater good. Giovanni, can you honestly say that you have a clear head with all that has happened? I'm loyal to you, all of us are, but we need you here, in this fight with us. I don't agree with Flavio's methods, but I understand why he went to the extreme. For Battaglia. For what we are poised to lose if we don't contain that." Dominic pointed to the television screen.

"You want a leader?" Giovanni gave a bitter chuckle. "I'll give you one."

****

Over the years everyone, including Kei, joked that Angelique could be her twin. When his assistant wore her hair down and sunglasses, they were strong lookalikes. The plan Kei hatched had to work. He wanted Angelique seen by the press in Manhattan. They agreed that she would return to her condo and collect Mira's things and then have them brought to his office where he'd have his assistant bring them to his private airport. They would leave for Switzerland. She could escape the reporters and recover. It was a solid plan. Why did she still feel hopeless?

Mira turned the channel, flipping from one to another. Kei entered the room. He dropped on the sofa next to her, close to her. She didn't want to give him the wrong idea. Though she needed him, being with him again felt like a betrayal. As crazy as it sounded, her heart remained very loyal to Giovanni.

"Turn to the news."

"No." She continued to channel surf.

"Mira."

"NO."

He put his hand on hers. "We need to know what they are saying. You need to hear it. To face it. We aren't running; we're regrouping. Soon you are going to have to face these reporters. I suggest you start getting stronger about it now."

She sighed. Turning the channel to CNN, she raised the volume. They sat in silence as the market report was read. Afterwards it was switched to an anchor. The newscaster cut in on his report.

I'm being told Mira Ellison owner of Mirabella's franchise, and friend and business partner to the late Fabiana Antonia Girelli, has just arrived at her Manhattan condo. We will take you now to the scene. Mira and Kei sat forward. The camera zoomed in on Angelique. Flashing bulbs and rowdy members of the press obstructed Angelique's attempt to enter her building. A microphone was shoved in Angelique's face, and her head almost lifted to reveal more of her face. Thankfully, it didn't. Angelique wore dark shades and a silk scarf that covered her head and wrapped around her neck. She walked with her head down pushing past the crowds by the help of one of Mira's staff members Eduardo. He and Angelique bounded up the steps, refusing the reporters a single comment. They went inside with the doorman holding the door. *This is David Young reporting live for CNN. Mira Ellison is here. We have seen so little from the fashion starlet since reports of her return from Italy. Here is what we know. Mirabella's fashion premiere was a success in Milan this year, having received rave reviews from international and domestic press. Since the launch of her new line she's been spotted throughout Italy with businessman Giovanni Battaglia. Our sources tell us that she and Fabiana Girelli were together the day of the incident at the Battaglia wedding in...*

A loud blast exploded and the person holding the camera must have been knocked back. Mira frowned and Kei sat up. There was complete chaos of running feet on the screen. The camera was then lifted from the place it fell to show car windows blown out and people from the press screaming and rising from the ground.

"What is it?" Mira asked, her heart racing. Kei put a hand to her knee and squeezed it.

David are you there? What's going on? The CNN newscaster Sylvester Blake asked. *I'm here Sylvester,* David appeared before the camera, a bit winded. The blares of car alarms nearly drowned out his voice. People ran behind him. *There has been an explosion. I repeat an explosion on the twentieth or so floor.* The camera panned upward and flames shot out of the entire floor. Then another explosion happened, and the cameraman must have ducked. Mira shook her head, repeatedly. It couldn't happen again. It couldn't!

"No! NO! It's not Angelique. No!"

"Stay here. Let me find out what happened.

Mira stared at the screen in disbelief. *It couldn't be Angelique. It couldn't be.*

****

"Are we sure about this, Gio?" Lorenzo asked first. It was the question every man in the room wanted to ask. "We're talking about killing Don Calderone, Angelo, the entire top line of their family..."

"We're talking about more than that. We're talking about being true to who we are. We show the Calderones, sympathizers, the entire world that to strike against me and my family will bring death. Each of you will do it alone, and clean. In and out. And I want it done starting now."

Dominic rose to answer the phone ringing in Giovanni's office. He glanced back to the door. It could be his *Bella* returning his call. He itched to run after the phone himself.

"I want Fish." Nico said. "That runt needs to die by my hands."

Giovanni didn't care who did what on his hit list. Just that it was done. They hadn't been able to locate the woman Maria, Fish's woman, but he knew that justice would require her life as well. Again he felt nothing.

"Giovanni!" Dominic yelled form the other room. The men all sat up. Giovanni was on his feet marching toward the door. Dominic ended the call when he entered.

"What is it?" Dominic pointed to the television screen. Giovanni stood in front of it trying to understand the chaos. He turned up the volume and listened.

We have confirmed it. Mira Ellison is dead! I repeat Mira Ellison owner and founder of Mirabella's is dead. Today a bomb was planted in her penthouse apartment. The news flashed to a scene of Mira struggling with the press to get through the crowds to the door. A young man with spiky hair helped her. Giovanni could barely see her face, but it looked like her. *She arrived today at six this evening and entered the building behind me, only five minutes after her arrival an explosion claimed her young life. This on the eve of her best friend, Fabiana Antonia*

Girelli's death.

Lorenzo walked in, and Giovanni stumbled back from the television. If not for the chair, he would have landed on his ass. A cold knot formed in the pit of his stomach. Everything, including the television became vague and shadowy. Dead. She couldn't be dead. *Mirabella wasn't dead!*

****

Mira held to the inside of the door. Kei was driving through the streets of Brooklyn like a madman. And she was so close to a complete meltdown she struggled to breathe. Someone was out to kill her. In fact, right now, the world thought they had succeeded. "This will never end, will it Kei?"

"Don't worry. My pilot is ready. We're leaving."

"They'll keep coming after me. Whoever they are... I don't even know who wants me dead. Oh God!"

"I think I have an idea," Kei seethed.

"Giovanni? No. He was trying to protect me," she said.

"By sending you here, with no one? Right after your best friend was killed."

She squeezed her eyes shut. Kei reached and squeezed her knee. "I'll get you out of here sweetheart. You know I will."

She closed her eyes. He extended his hand. She placed hers in his palm. He was the only one she could trust. And she intended to. For the past few years she had let everyone take care of things for her. This time she would have to do what she'd done since the day she left Virginia. Find the strength to take care of herself.

****

"It's a lie! A fucking lie! She isn't dead." A faint thread of hysteria was in the back of his voice. Lorenzo and the others stood silent. Giovanni paced with his hands to the side of his head. "No. It's not Mira. I would know if it was Mira. I'd fucking feel it!"

"What is it? What's happened?" Flavio asked entering the room with a slight hesitation and surprise in his hawk like grey eyes.

Giovanni paused. He turned stiffly, almost stumbling, and gave the man he trusted above all else a blue-eyed glare. The events of the next minutes came to him in flashes. Such as him grabbing Flavio and throwing him to the ground, followed by a flash of him pounding his fist into the old man's face viciously. Each blow bringing forth a release of more hatred and rage than he ever knew lived within him. Something broke beneath his fist, possibly the old man's jaw or chin. Blood sprayed from Flavio's mouth as he tried feebly to ward off the attack with his arms. Another flash hit Giovanni in strobe like frequency. This time he felt constrained. He was lifted and carried out of the room by three of his strongest men as he yelled until his voice disappeared in hoarse croaks. And the flashes kept coming. Chaos. Shouting voices. The destruction of everything in his sight when he was forced into a room, happened in slow motion, as if his madness was winding down to nothing. And soon he realized it had. He had nothing. She was gone.

Later

Lorenzo wiped his hand down his face, taking in a slow breath. He felt so bone weary he dropped a hand to the wall to keep standing. Behind him he heard footfalls and glanced back. "What the fuck happened? Why did Gio attack Flavio like a lunatic?"

"Is he in there?"

"Yeah. I got three of the boys on him. He's fucking lost it."

"Mira Ellison is dead. Flavio may have had a part in it. The old man is in a bad way. I'm trying to contain it. The *dottore* is with Flavio now. I need Gio's approval to take him to the *ospedale*."

"Shit! Are we sure she's dead?" Lorenzo dropped his head back on the wall. Now both of the girls were gone. And no matter how you sliced it, this was on him. His cousin had never come apart this far. Ever. Not even after the shooting of Papa Tomosino and the killing of the Russians Lorenzo pinned the hit on. "What are we going to do?"

"What we have to." Dominic stepped past him and threw open the door.

Giovanni stared at the television. He was brought to a guest room. It was a room the boys frequented to play cards and watch television. The Italian press was now reporting on Mira's death. The screen then flashed again to her fashion event. Mira's lovely face came up. She was being interviewed, and Fabiana was at her side translating.

"*Oh yes. I love your country, absolutely love it! Italy is a dream. This is my dream come true. That's why I moved here. It's the beauty of Italy that I find inspiring the most. Oh and the men are nice too!*" The reporter laughed, as did Mira. Giovanni felt the corner of his mouth twitch into a smile. *My fashion line for the fall was to encompass the spirit of Italia, and I hope I did that with this showing,*" she beamed happily. Her bangs covered her brow and her hair was wound curly around her face. She wore a green blouse. She looked very much like the woman he met.

Not the one who could barely stand when he left her. His angel.

On the screen Fabiana leaned in and whispered something in her ear. Mira nodded and said her goodbyes. The image froze with a screenshot of her smile. The dates 1964 to 1989 were beneath her. *Mira Ellison the founder and head fashion designer of Mirabella's died today at the age of 25. She was killed in a bombing outside of her penthouse in New York City. She will truly be missed by her peers and friends throughout the fashion world."*

Giovanni, with a shaky hand turned the television off.

"Gio, we need to talk." Dominic said.

Giovanni kept his back to his men. He wiped his hand down his face and cleared it of tears. He cleared his throat, though it was physically painful to speak. Every fiber in his bones, tendons, muscles hurt. "Go. Go and follow my orders. But you have a new one. Flavio Pricci is dead to me. He is no longer *consigliere*. Bury him tonight." Giovanni lifted his gaze. "You will be the one to put the bullet in him Domi. You will be the one sitting in his chair."

"Are you sure? I came to tell you Flavio needs medical attention..."

Giovanni shot Dominic a glare. Nothing else was said on the matter.

"Gio, I can stay." Lorenzo offered.

Giovanni dropped in a chair. "Go."

Left alone, he sat in silence. The shock and disbelief had numbed all of his senses. He couldn't see well. His hearing was off, and he smelled and tasted nothing. He purely existed. He hadn't risked his heart on a woman ever. And if he dared do so, he was prepared for rejection. This, however, was something he couldn't live with. Her blood was on his hands. And he swore silently to get her justice.

Giovanni sat up, and then forced his legs to hold him as he stood. A light wave of dizziness gripped him but he barely swayed. He walked to the French doors in the room and drew them open. Out on the balcony he let the bright sunrays sober him, and his gaze lowered. Flavio was being helped out of the *Villa Rosso* by two of his men. The old man's arms were draped over the shoulders of the men who assisted him on both sides. They handled him with care. Out of respect for his position and authority, they afforded him the dignity that even Giovanni would have forgone.

Flavio's head lifted as they drew closer. He looked up at Giovanni. For a moment the exchange between them softened Giovanni's heart. The man was the closest he'd had to a father since his own father's death. The moment passed. Then he and Flavio knew there would be no reprieve.

Giovanni turned and went back inside slamming the doors to the balcony shut behind him.

Epilogue

Eight months later

IN THE MIDDLE OF OCTOBER a blanket of snow coated the roads, fields, hills and her five-bedroom cottage. Mira had found it to be a winter paradise at times, but that feeling was fleeting. Tonight the chill of an approaching winter seeped in through the windowsills and under the doors. She rubbed heat into her hands and rose from her favorite chair. In a thick, wool lined maternity robe and furry moccasin boots that reached just above her ankles, she opened the door to the patio at the back of her cottage and stepped out into the twenty degree weather. She didn't mind the cold. She loved the protective cover it gave her. It was after eleven and her little *bambina* was up standing at salute in her belly. She couldn't sleep and during nights like this she didn't try. Hugging herself, she smiled and looked out at the faint dark outline of the mountains.

The baby kicked. Mira put her hand under her belly where the tenderness could still be felt. "You will go to sleep tonight, honey," she said.

Last month she found out she was having a girl. For reasons she didn't understand she felt the divinity in this blessing. Her baby, their baby, was created out of love. Six months ago she didn't believe it, but now she did. She'd had a lot of time for reflection. She learned a lot about her heart, and herself. This baby was his gift to her, the life that came out of so much pain. Now she had peace.

"Mira what are you doing out there in the cold?"

Her head turned. Kei stood inside shivering. He wore a deep scowl of impatience.

"Sweetheart? You'll make yourself sick."

"Go back to bed."

"Join me." Kei teased. Mira shook her head laughing. She turned and locked eyes with him. The man became sexier on nights like this. Not since Giovanni had she let any man between her legs, and Kei tried often. The swell of her breasts and hips kept him groaning when they passed each other close in her kitchen. She considered it more than once, but still she couldn't go there. Even if she wanted to purge Giovanni from her heart, he was constantly between them. His child kept her chained to him.

"I don't think so. We're friends, remember?"

Kei crossed his arms over his tightly muscled chest. His dark black hair was parted at the center and blew lightly from his strongly handsome face. He only wore a white t-shirt and silk pajama pants. Sex with Kei was always a spiritual experience. He worshipped a woman's body and taught her things she never knew possible. With Giovanni it had been different, more of a ravishment. His love overwhelmed and overpowered her. Now with her hormones raging she wondered what lucky woman was in Giovanni's arms now.

"I'm glad to see you up and walking around." Kei said. "You feeling stronger?"

"I am. I think it's the herbal massages you give my feet."
She winked.

"I can give you more than that."

Mira rolled her eyes. "I know. You keep telling me."

Since she was in her last trimester of her pregnancy, he insisted on staying with her. The doctor said she was to stay off her feet because her blood pressure kept elevating. That was easier said than done. Living in isolation could be so draining. It was necessary. At first a trip to Switzerland seemed like the perfect place to refocus, start again. But Kei's plan took on another life. Angelique's body was identified as Mira at the scene. Kei used influence Mira didn't know he had to make sure the reporters believed it. They actually had a funeral for her. Celebrities, dignitaries, people from all walks of life came to pay their respects. She wept through the service. Her funeral was the last time she saw Giovanni.

To her surprise he appeared among the mourners. Giovanni Battaglia had flown in to New York. If the press hadn't made such a big deal over it, she might not have ever known. She watched him linger near a closed casket with dark shades. His face showed no expression, but she knew his pain, love, regret would swirl deep in his blue-violet eyes. The sight of him and his men moving out of the church, disappearing into a waiting car nearly broke her. She desperately wanted to call him and share the truth. She couldn't.

The State Attorney General's office and the F.B.I. had erased her identity. They grilled her over what she knew of the Battaglias, and she told them very little. They even asked her about the Calderone war. Apparently several members were gunned down, including the elder Calderone, and his nephew Angelo was in hiding. She knew nothing, only the love he had shown her in their brief affair.

Kei said she would have probably returned to him if she hadn't discovered she was pregnant. Mira was inclined to believe him.

"You are so stubborn." He disappeared inside and returned with a heavy coat that he draped around her shoulders.

"It feels great out here," she smiled.

He stepped to her side and looked up at the moon.

"You sure you have to stay? Maybe you should go back."

"I'm staying until the baby is born."

"I can warm you some milk. Is the little one up at it again?"

Mira took his hand and pressed it to her tummy. "Feel."

Kei's eyes stretched. He looked up at her stunned. "She's a fighter."

"Like her father." Mira chuckled. When she looked back at Kei, she saw his frown. He had made his feelings clear months ago. Mira declined his offer of marriage and his request that she let him into her bed. Her baby was all she needed, not a man. And she surely wouldn't do that to Kei when she knew he wanted a wife, a future she would never have.

"C'mon, let's go back in."

He captured her hand. Mira stopped. He brought her palm to his mouth and pressed a kiss there. "I'm still very much in love with you, Mira."

"I know, Kei, but..."

"No buts. We have all the time in the world. I'm here for you and the baby. You know that."

"Yes." She pulled on his hand and then returned inside.

"Then you should consider my proposal." He came inside and closed the door. Mira lowered slowly into her chair. "Let me give the child a father."

"My baby has a father." Mira reminded him.

"That man can never exist to the baby. You know this. He's dangerous, and he thinks you're dead. What would he do if he knew you were here keeping a baby from him?"

She had nightmares over what Giovanni would think of this betrayal. To him it would be the ultimate destruction of their trust to deny him his child. "Doesn't matter. I won't replace him in her life."

Kei sighed. "You know me Mira. I won't give up. I won't." he turned and walked away.

Mira heard the door close down the hall. She pushed up from the chair and wheezed. Walking through her cottage she went to the bonus room that she kept locked whenever Kei visited. He never questioned her about it. This was her room. She removed the key from the inside of her robe and opened it. Once inside she locked the door and turned on the light. All over the room were sketches and drawings she'd done of Fabiana. Her best friend remained her muse and she designed clothes with her sketchpad with her lovely face and figure in mind. There were other drawings. Each depicted her time in Italy. She had drawn Bellagio, and the lake view from outside of her bedroom window, the vineyard in Chianti, the wedding dress she made for Catalina. She'd even sketched the faces of Rocco and his wife. Her entire story could be told in pictures.

There remained however one sketch she never uncovered, one she only visited on the rare nights her loneliness couldn't be replaced with TV or a good book. She flipped the sheet back and uncovered the portrait.

"There he is sweetness," she said. She softly touched the canvas, tracing the tips of her two fingers over the sharp outlines of his face. Her baby kicked again and she chuckled, "I know, I know, Momma wishes it too. He made his choice, and we made ours." She rubbed her belly. It was still painful to look upon Giovanni, but she did so anyway to remind her of the love they shared. No man would be a father to their child but him. Never.

"*Ti Amo.*" She whispered putting her fingers to her lips then pressing them against the picture, "*Ti Amo.*"
****

Giovanni sat in the leather recliner staring into the flames dancing around in the large fireplace. A lot had happened in six months. Vengeance came at a bloody price. Without Flavio's counsel he slipped deeper into his grief, and madness. The first casualties were Angelo Calderone's twin sisters. They were both married and in their early twenties living in Napoli. Executed. The shock of the killings forced Don Calderone out of hiding. He was gunned down in Genoa at the funeral. Killing the *capus* in the Calderone family had become a sport for his boys. They ran them down between Turin, Venice, Firenze to the back streets of Roma. And if they showed any allegiance to Calderone they were dead.

He took a drag from his cigar. A dark smile curled his lips as he recalled one man begging him for forgiveness. There was no mercy for his *Bella*. There would be no mercy for them.

Angelo remained on the run. He had hopes to rectify that soon, but even Lorenzo and Carlo kept coming up empty in their pursuit. For now he took possession of everything Calderone owned, family property they'd had for centuries, businesses both legitimate and otherwise. Since he stomped out the Nigerians, the Irish were dealing with them again, and the men in the *Cammora* bowed when he entered a room.

It was enough.

Yet he wanted more.

He'd adjusted to being feared, hated.

Giovanni let a curl of smoke escape his mouth and drew it in to his nostrils before exhaling again. He had gone to America for his *Bella*. Dominic thought it unwise. The *Polizia di Stato*, Interpol, and the U.S. F.B.I. wanted him for questioning. He obliged the insult just to attend her funeral and he was granted the opportunity to say goodbye. But his heart refused to let go. Seven months had dragged on, and he missed her as if she had just left him yesterday. The women in his bed only made him bitter and resentful.

Things were different now.

He was different now.

Dominic had accepted the role of *consigliere*. It was unheard of to have someone so young and inexperienced in such a coveted position. But Dominic had paid the price. He knew ordering him to put the bullet in his mentor had taken a toll on Domi. He could see it in his face, and the weeks that followed with Dominic drinking more and more. Lorenzo was his left hand once more. As underboss, his cousin more than redeemed himself. Whatever jealousy made him turn to Giuseppe before was gone. They were inseparable by the shared pain of losing Fabiana and Mira. Dominic and Lorenzo both proved to him that they knew when to lead and when to follow. A trait the old man Flavio never quite understood. They followed his orders to the letter, and he rewarded them. The blood he shed set back all efforts to legitimize the family. He didn't give a fuck. He cared about nothing. The gambling houses were open, the whores were back in business—and business was good.

Giovanni reclined further in his chair glaring at the

dancing embers of the fire. His retreat had worried his aunt so much that she and Rocco had left Chianti and moved in. And still that wasn't enough. Catalina had convinced her new husband to move in as well. He let none of them get close. He preferred the emptiness. He wasn't a man that deserved anything better.

Some nights when the booze didn't get the best of him he could sense her presence. Hear her voice. And on some nights he could feel her warmth under the covers of the bed. He had found the ability to dream without nightmares of his father's murder. In his dreams she was his *donna*, pregnant with his child, loving him unconditionally. Giovanni liked those dreams most of all.

The door opened.

"Gio? Are you in here?" Catalina's soft voice echoed behind him. She would have to step further in the room to see him seated before the fireplace.

"I said I was not to be disturbed." He answered dryly.

"You missed dinner."

"*Lascilo*," he mumbled.

"You really have to stop this, Gio," she placed a tray on the small table he used to set his bottle of wine or whiskey on that he drank from often. "I want you to start attending dinner. Zia and I have discussed it. You can't go on like this."

Giovanni took another drag from his cigar and ignored his sister.

Catalina folded her arms and sighed, "Franco wants to help. He's asked Domi to let him."

"Domi knows that Franco is to have nothing to do with my business."

"Gio, he's my husband, and he wants to help."

"*Esca!*" he shouted.

Catalina threw up her hands in defeat and marched out. Giovanni extinguished the fiery end of his cigar in the plate of pasta she had prepared for him. He reached for the bottle of whiskey and managed to stand. Drinking from the bottle, he walked past his bed to the open balcony. It was a bit chilly in the evening, but he preferred the cold. He stood under the largest moon he'd seen in a while. He smiled. Somehow he felt her in that moon. "I'm not done with them yet, *Bella*. They'll all pay *Cara*. All of them."

He turned and walked back in to his room to settle for the night.